YOUNG POWER

By Andrea Blythe Liebman

ONE

"An Americano, please."

Liv stared down at her phone, simultaneously scolding herself for not having the courage to look up at the barista. She came here every day and didn't even know his name. But asking would be awkward now, after her fourteenth time coming to the same coffee shop, ordering the same drink, and continuing to avoid eye contact for the reason she still did not want to think about.

"That's $2.50, Olivia."

Liv's face immediately shot up.

"How do you know my name?" She spat, terrified that he somehow read her mind, then blushed, realizing her tone to be a little too accusatory for a simple coffee shop interaction.

The unnamed-barista simply chuckled in amusement, "I asked you earlier... for your drink?"

Smiling, he turned her soon-to-be Americano cup around and showed Liv's name scribbled on the cup: Olivia.

"Figured you come in here every day, might as well remember it."

"Good point."

Liv relaxed, running her hand through her thick blonde hair, trying to appear casual as she gazed across the room, hoping to seem like she was looking for someone.

But of course, she was brought back to reality when only blank faces resided in front of her. She didn't know anyone here. She had been at college for over two weeks and hadn't made a single friend. Liv had come to this coffee shop every day and never connected with one other soul who was a regular. Not that she ever really tried, anyway.

"Here's your Americano, Olivia."

Liv turned around, coming back to her present. As soon as she made eye contact with the barista, she looked down at her feet immediately, in reflex.

Grabbing her coffee quickly and mumbling, "thanks," Liv bolted to her favorite table in the coffee shop, thankful that her cozy spot by the window was open and thinking that if she ever had an opportunity to find out the barista's name, to prove she cared just a little, that was it, and the moment had passed.

Liv hadn't always been this way: shy, insecure, anti-social. In fact, she had *never* been this way. She used to be lively, bright, interactive–but, after high school graduation, it was just as if a part of herself left with spring, leaving her to dry out in summer and freeze in the fall.

How long does it take to act a certain way before it becomes a description of who you are, a definitive part of yourself?

Liv shuddered, not letting her mind go there.

She placed her bag down against the tiny cedar table and sat in the cozy, velvet chair against the wall, opening her Italian textbook to review past-tense verb conjugations for an upcoming test.

After memorizing every conjugation form and unique verb case, Liv checked her watch: 10:30AM. *Damn*, she thought to herself–she still had another hour until her next class.

While trying to troubleshoot how to keep her mind occupied, Liv glanced outside to find the sky filling with much darker clouds than the morning. Liv shrugged, probably another rainy day. It had been cloudy every day since she arrived, and rained on most.

Coming from California, Liv had been warned about the Pacific Northwest, but even she underestimated just how gloomy a campus could be in October. She kept promising herself the lack of sunshine was definitely a contributing factor to her change in demeanor, but she knew it was a lie.

Liv turned from the window, looking around the coffee shop. She always loved spending her free time here; it was calming, peaceful–almost like her new version of home. The mix of gray walls, wooden industrial tables and various-placed succulents brought her mind to a peaceful state.

She noticed a young man across the coffee shop, reading a book by himself and enjoying his own moment of solitude–Liv smiled at the sight.

A group of laughter caught her attention, so Liv cautiously glanced over to the table on her left, noticing all the seats filled with endearing friends catching up and telling stories. At another table, Liv found a guy sitting by himself, but then, another man walked over and waved for his attention, politely asking if the chair across was taken, and then sat down to study.

Liv looked across her table to the empty seat, a little saddened that nobody had ever tried to sit next to her.

Not that Liv was a parasite or anything–she did catch guys looking at her most days and tried not to notice jealous girls constantly giving her envious looks on the others.

When she wasn't wearing all black, blasting her newest playlist to tune out the world and had her head hovered inside a book, Liv was actually quite attractive. She was athletic, 5'8 with long sun-kissed blonde waves and bright blue eyes.

But Liv wasn't exactly looking to make new friends here, so figured she probably gave off a 'zero fucks given' aura. And that was *her* decision, not theirs.

With her confidence slightly restored, but not entirely, Liv figured she could work on next week's math assignment, so went to grab her textbook, sighing.

So what if she was a week ahead in all of her classes?

Liv muttered to herself, "Including the non-required reading assignments."

At this rate, she'd graduate next year and could be done with this hellhole.

With that, Liv paused. Forcing herself to look around the room again at all the smiles, carefree laughs and interactions with her fellow students, Liv noticed a girl and a boy in the corner, holding hands and quietly sneaking in a small kiss–which sent an aching pang through her chest. Liv looked down at her book, angry that she let her mind wander so far this morning and see the exact things she was trying to avoid.

She felt a tear trickle down her cheek; it softly hit her textbook.

Tomorrow was her birthday. She would be turning eighteen and already felt like her life was a wreck. She wasn't even a legal adult and "adulting" was hitting her in the head and laughing at the bumps created. How did she get to this point? Any other college freshman would be giddy at the thought of a new school, a new life and new opportunities, but all she had done was live in a ghostly shell of who she used to be.

But how could she change it? So far, Liv had been drowning herself in her studies, or binge-reading countless fiction novels when she ran out of homework–but that wasn't really living, was it?

There had to be more to this life, there just had to be.

Liv nodded her head in agreement. She needed to start living her life again–and not run from the past, any more.

She looked back to the handholding couple, first in disgust at their perfect romance, then in disgust at herself for wishing unhappiness to everyone she encountered, even to strangers in this world. Maybe she just needed to start looking around again and really begin to notice things, instead of always existing inside of a book–make herself live again, be present and feel, even if it hurt.

Liv turned her head back toward the window, at first just glancing outside, but then realized the rainstorm had begun, strong pellets of water angrily hitting the concrete outside.

Well, at least it matches my mood.

Liv rolled her eyes and lazily switched her people watching back indoors.

Suddenly, across the room, a set of the most intense light grey eyes pierced toward Liv, instantly grabbing her attention, but by the time she could focus in on the source, the owner had already ducked his head back into his book.

Calming down from the shock, Liv relaxed, reminding herself it was nothing new. She chuckled at her sudden cockiness, but remembered her unique tan exterior–thanks to being a swimmer and beach volleyball maven (and indulging in these sports a bit more than usual this summer); Liv was a rarity in the land of no sun, and very much used to getting creepier stares.

She gazed at the guy whom she had previously dubbed 'solitude reader' in her mind, but now she was curious. He was concentrating too hard on his book, alas he look up and get caught staring again. He had light chocolate skin and walnut-tinted hair shaved close to his head, and wore a trench coat the color of the lighter clouds outside. A color, Liv imagined, that matched his beautiful eyes, perfectly.

As Liv blatantly continued to study the solitude reader, a hand tapped her shoulder, causing her to look up, a bit off guard. A new stranger motioned to sit at her table, causing Liv unconsciously to remove her headphones and smile. He looked pretty cute, in a geeky, unintimidating sort of way.

The stranger started taking off his backpack and then caught a second glance at Liv–giving her a thoughtful look before making an apparent decision.

"I think you're in my Astronomy 101 class?"

Liv looked across the table at him, noticing his eyes were a bright auburn color and seemed very inviting.

"Possibly." Liv shrugged, "Tuesdays and Thursdays at 10AM?"

She couldn't help but detect how calm she already felt around this guy. Liv didn't want to stare away from his beautiful eyes, but tried very hard to remain coy.

"In Columbia 150?"

"I'm very impressed you were able to recognize me out of 200 students." Liv couldn't refrain from teasing, ending her accusation with a smile. "Usually everyone is a blur."

The guy leaned back in his chair, combing his hand through his jet-black hair, seemingly also trying to play it cool.

"Well, you're tall and always reading a book, so it's easy to notice-you make it appear as if a book is floating in the air."

Liv was a little taken aback, not sure how to respond. She sat back and folded her arms in her chair, letting silence join their conversation, and looked at him speculatively.

"Okay," the guy rolled his eyes dramatically, causing Liv to grin again. "It also helps that you're quite stunning. But, typically in the rules of meeting people you're not supposed to disclose that observation so soon."

"Well, I prefer honesty." Liv smiled, "And thank you." She held out her hand to shake his, "I'm Liv."

"I'm Finn." He smiled, laughing as he shook her hand, "Nice to meet you."

Finn and Liv worked in silence, but Liv couldn't help but notice him as she tried to concentrate on her math assignment. Did she look like she was concentrating too hard? Was she hovering over her book too much? And her legs! They hadn't moved for 20 minutes (she did not want to run the risk at accidentally kicking him), so they remained frozen, even though her left foot was starting to fall asleep. Every time he moved, she responded with a subtle gesture-their school supplies and upper bodies a chemical reaction, dancing through the balance of order on the table.

After what seemed like forever and yet only ½ of a math problem for Liv (notably, she would have been done with the entire assignment if the circumstances had been different), Finn stood up.

Liv simultaneously looked up, then froze-not sure if she was supposed to say goodbye and internally prayed that she didn't look like a sad puppy being abandoned.

"It was great meeting you, Liv–I'll see you in our next class." Finn raised his eyebrows in goodbye and walked away.

Liv took a deep breath as if she had been holding her breath the entire time. Had she been?

Before she could answer, Finn was back.

"Hey, can I get your number? I mean, purely for educational purposes. It would be nice knowing someone in the class-"

"Sure."

Liv couldn't believe how quickly she responded, or how on edge she was acting in his presence. There was definitely something unique happening, but it wasn't like Liv was attracted to this guy–why was she acting so weird? Not wanting to admit a socially awkward development, Liv looked away and again caught her solitude reader's eyes glanced at them. They did match his trench coat perfectly.

Finn handed her his phone, which she quickly shot herself a text–*Liv from Astronomy.*

"Here you go."

She handed back the phone, unsure what to do next.

"Thanks, I'll see ya next week, or *honestly speaking*," Finn said mockingly, "I may just ask you for homework answers." He laughed, his eyes devious in anticipation for Liv's response.

"Oh. I see how it is," Liv jokingly rolled her eyes in return. "See ya, Finn," but when she finished with her dramatics, he was gone.

Shocked, and uncertain as to why, she immediately looked across the room to find her solitude reader.

But he was gone, too.

Liv didn't recall seeing the solitude reader exit the coffee shop, so looked to the door and then consequently wondered to herself why she cared so much.

… Maybe she really did need to start living her life again, or just *get one* in general.

Pushing it aside in her conscious, Liv saw her roommate entering the coffee shop–the roommate whom Liv had tried about negative five percent to be friends with since starting school.

Instinctively, Liv bowed her head over her math book, justifying that Peyton had been busy with Sorority Recruitment and that was why they hadn't gotten to know each other.

But then she recalled her eighteenth birthday pact she had made just before Finn sat down, and Finn wasn't so bad. In fact, the whole interaction helped distract her from *him*.

Liv shook her head, getting that thought out of her head immediately, and without a second thought, hollered at Peyton, waving for her to come over.

Oh well. It was time to try and live.

Peyton looked shocked to see Liv acknowledging her presence, let alone proactively starting an interaction. She turned around, making sure there wasn't another Peyton magically behind her that Liv may have actually intended to call over.

As Peyton walked over, her hazel eyes glanced at Liv apprehensively. Liv noticed Peyton wearing an Alpha Beta Mu sorority shirt proudly, and mentally noted to congratulate Peyton for her bid, eventually. But Liv had other plans for this specific conversation, knowing she would need to get to the punch before changing her mind.

"Hi Liv," Peyton's silky voice was soothing and inviting, but the complete opposite of her current stance, standing by Liv's table, refusing to sit down across from her. "Er–how are you?"

"Good. Thanks for asking." Liv paused, hesitantly looking outside, then back at Peyton. "What are you doing tonight?" She finally spit out.

"Oh! It's bid night–I got into Beta Mu," Peyton pointed at her Greek shirt (as if Liv wouldn't have noticed), "So we're celebrating with our new sisters, tonight."

"Fun." Liv resented herself for how dry she sounded, so smiled immediately after and tried to show encouragement, "I mean, bummer for me, I was hoping you would want to… go out tonight, but… bid night will be so much fun!"

Liv couldn't believe her very un-smooth ending, embarrassed. Maybe this is why she didn't hang out with Peyton.

Accepting the interaction couldn't get worse, Liv continued, "What I mean is, tomorrow is my birthday. Any interest in celebrating with me?"

"Oh, my gosh! Your birthday!?"

Peyton slid into the chair across from Liv, her short auburn lob bouncing as she landed.

"I would LOVE to celebrate tomorrow! Don't you worry about a thing, I'll plan it all."

Lowering her voice, Peyton began chattering non-stop. "My big just got me a fake ID, but I have another sister who looks JUST like you," and then continued, almost as if she was talking through the plans just to herself, and not Liv, "I'll totally ask if you can use it and we can celebrate like we're supposed to! I know that Sarah has…."

Liv was a bit overwhelmed by the 180-degree interaction between Peyton and herself. But of course Peyton was sweet enough to want to celebrate and plan the whole shindig, even though it actually was not her responsibility at all.

Since moving into their dorms, Peyton had asked Liv to go out with her every night. At first, she was super excited at the idea of Liv being her roommate, explaining she was the only sister of four brothers, but slowly Liv could tell it was just becoming a common courtesy.

The past week Peyton only invited her anywhere with a look of pity, the wishful hope Liv would actually be the roommate that Peyton had always wanted, diminishing–but no matter what, or how many times Liv turned her down, Peyton never rudely left her out.

Liv was more so just thinking dinner and a movie for her birthday, but before she could even try to interrupt Peyton's planning with herself, her roommate had jumped up, clapping her hands in excitement. "Okay, so we'll just plan to pre-game around 9pm tomorrow–can't wait!" And with a quick hug, Peyton had bolted out of the coffee shop, not even realizing she, in fact, had never ordered a coffee.

The rain had cleared up. As Liv left her Italian classroom, she knew it was her chance to sprint back to the dorm, hoping to avoid getting her favorite black leather jacket wet–she definitely wanted to wear it tomorrow night and didn't want it to be entirely soaked.

As Liv power-walked through campus, trying to think about what she should wear to celebrate her birthday, she couldn't help but notice the beautiful fall colors penetrating the campus, saturated in color from the gray, stormy backdrop. The School of Business glowed through the green and yellow leaves sprinkled throughout the lawn.

"Guess there is a reason why students choose to go to this school," Liv mockingly joked to herself, trying not to notice that she didn't actually mean that jab this time around. As she looked around, the architecture and trees truly made Oregon a picturesque campus.

Liv just hadn't noticed it before–she was either avoiding a downpour of rain between classes or was book-walking (head glued to her newest literary-binge as her eyes tried to keep her mind at ease). This was the first time Liv could remember not having a book open while she walked.

Try to live.

Absorbing the scenery, she heard a flock of blackbirds passing over her head, and when she looked up, saw they were in the shape of an "O."

Liv smiled. O for Olivia–it must be a good sign. It had to be.

Out of the corner of her eye, Liv saw a bus passing and after an unconscious glimpse, quickly turned her head back to look, eyes and mind alert, searching for what she could have sworn she just saw–Hayden, sitting on the bus.

Him.

But as she stared at the empty seat, there was no remnant of a soul having sat there. The bus continued on, driving out of sight.

Stunned, Liv shook her head, angry with herself for letting her mind get to that point of ease. Right when she thought she could go five seconds without thinking about him, she let her brain create an illusion of his existence.

But he's not here.

When Liv realized she was still staring where the bus had driven by, she headed over to the nearest bench and sat down, still in a slight daze. Shocked.

Pulling out her phone, Liv stared at the blank screen, curiosity getting the best of her. She began searching for his profile on social media and then paused, feeling devious.

It was no longer her place to understand or know what he was doing anymore–*that* was clearly obvious, even if nothing else was.

With a sigh, Liv put her phone back in her bag, trying not to notice the pain building in her chest, the heaviness returning.

Luckily, Liv noticed a dark cloud heading her way, which meant it was again time for her to sprint for cover, but literally sprint, and immediately.

Running through campus, dashing past trees and students, everything around her became a wet blur, her eyes streaming water, almost in unison with the downpour from the sky.

As soon as she arrived to her dorm building and ran up the entrance steps, the rain powered on and to a new extreme. Liv turned around and looked out, staring at the splashing bullets, noticing each pounding drop hitting the concrete and breathed deeply, feeling hollow inside.

TWO

Buzz. Buzz.

Buzz. Buzz. Buzz.

Lying on her bed, Liv opened her eyes from her afternoon nap, squinting at her cell phone screen lighting up and buzzing for attention from her desk.

Rolling up sluggishly, she grabbed her phone, seeing text messages from her mother multiply by the second.

HI SWEETIE! DID U GET MY PACKAGE?
SHOULD HAVE ARRIVED IN THE MAIL THIS AM
ACCORDING TO UPS
I'VE EMAILED THE TRACKING NUMBER JUST IN CASE
IT SAYS ARRIVED AND SIGNED FOR
I CALLED THIS AM TO CONFIRM BUT JUST WANT TO
MAKE SURE
...

Liv saw the '...' icon, indicating her mother was still on a roll. So in efforts to stop the madness, Liv quickly responded:

Hi Mom. Got the package! Thanks much – LOVE YOU! XX

She still saw the '...' icon, so immediately added:

Have fun plans tonight and tomorrow to celebrate–can't wait!

Guiltily pushing send and tossing her phone across the bed, Liv realized that lying was becoming too easy.

Well, at least this time her white lie was *partially* true.

Looking around at her empty dormitory with boredom, Liv's eyes wandered over to Peyton's cluttered wall, decorated with posters, photos and brightly colored cliché motivational quotes that she clearly printed from Pinterest–'Stay focused and extra sparkly' (light pink), 'Choose kindness and laugh often' (mint green), and Liv's favorite, 'She loved life and it loved her right back' (light purple).

Liv's side of the room was a little less cheery. Her wall was bare–she hadn't felt like decorating since arriving to college–and the only color on her side of the dorm, if you didn't count her grey laptop and books, was a dark purple velvet plush pillow. Her mom insisted she have it so her roommate wouldn't think she was a freak, but it turns out you can own a purple pillow and still have no friends.

After consequently staring at her velvet pillow for longer than any normal teenager would, Liv instinctively leaned over to her desk and grabbed the next book to entertain her for the night.

10 hours later, Liv shut the book, feeling even more empty and lonely than before.

The book was about 'soul mates' and true love enduring a curse over millennia, and while now in reflection of the story, Liv couldn't help think about what she once had, or what she thought she had.

Out of habit, Liv went over to her window, immediately looking up at the stars for guidance.

But of course, it was raining and cloudy. It was always raining and cloudy here.

Figures.

It was an irrational idea, but growing up, Liv always found peace in staring up at the stars–allowing her mind to ease and make whatever decision was initially troubling her.

As a young girl, she heard of ancient sailors using Polaris, the North Star, to help navigate the seas at night. Ever since, Liv had adapted the concept, "look to the North Star for direction," literally. It was a silly notion now, but a part of her remained to believe that she could find her way through the darkness as long as she took the time to observe the stars.

Buzz. Buzz.

Liv turned to her phone, perking up when she saw a text from Lacey. It was exactly midnight and her best friend didn't miss a beat.

HAPPY BIRTHDAY LIV!!!

Smiling, she picked up her phone and sent a quick, "*Thanks pretty lady!*" in return.

As soon as she put down the phone, there was a knock at her door.

Apprehensive to what, *or who*, would be there, Liv tiptoed quietly to her door and cautiously looked through the peephole, but after craning her gaze for as wide as the perspective allowed, she saw no one.

Liv slowly opened the door and peeked through the slivered gap, her heart racing. Still seeing nobody in their hallway, she looked down and discovered a beautiful bouquet of white anemones–her favorite flower, decorated with peonies, white cherry blossom, eucalyptus, baby's breath, and white hyacinth.

Liv eagerly jumped around the flowers and into the hallway, running toward the common room, pausing only momentarily upon arrival to the elevator to try to hear anything–but all she heard was silence.

She raced back to her room, darting to the window that overlooked one of the building entrances, hoping to see a trace of some evidence for the unexpected delivery, but no activity could be seen.

Well, except for an innocent intoxicated girl zigzagging her way up the stairs barefoot, heels in hand.

Liv sat on her bed, leaning against the bare wall, and slowly peered her gaze toward the doorway. Biting her lip, Liv continued to stare at the floral bouquet that still remained in the hallway.

But no, it couldn't be…

She stood up and determinedly walked over to her perfect gift, picking it up and robotically bringing it back into her room, where she placed it on her desk and watched it for another astonished moment. She saw a card in the bouquet, which made her relax, but simultaneously tense because she could actually find out whom it was from.

But alas, opening the card, she was to remain stumped, only seeing a generic printed message: HAPPY BIRTHDAY.

Don't be desperate. It couldn't be him. Other people know your favorite flower.

"Like Mom!" Liv enthusiastically yelled out, "Of course!" and began dialing.

After one very long ring, her mom picked up the phone.

"What's wrong?!"

"Oh! Sorry, Mom. Nothing's wrong. I just wanted to call and say thank you for the beautiful flowers."

"… Flowers?" Liv's mother yawned, slowly dozing back to sleep now knowing crisis had been averted.

"My birthday bouquet?" Liv tensed up again, pleading that her mom was only trying to be funny, "The flowers you sent were just delivered."

"I'm sorry sweetie, I'm only responsible for that box delivered yesterday… have you opened it yet?"

"Oh, no… I was going to open it today." Liv gulped.

"I promise there's a wrapped birthday gift inside that I think you'll love."

"Thanks Mom. Sorry for calling so late, I lost track of time."

Liv could feel the smile growing on her mom's face, ironically as her face was on the verge of crumbling into tears.

"Never a problem. I understand how college goes. Thank you for calling, and honey?"

"Yes?" Liv still hoped that this was a terrible prank.

"Happy Birthday. I'll call you later today after I've had some coffee."

"Thanks, Mom. Bye."

Liv hung up the phone, shrugging, eyebrows creased as she angrily stared down the flowers. She leaned forward to smell them, and became even more frustrated when they were a perfect balance of a creamy and fresh scent.

Who else? There had to be someone else. *Don't get desperate Liv.*

Lacey? No, she definitely didn't know Liv's favorite flower was a white anemone, but maybe it was just a great selection choice by her friend?

Liv grabbed her phone again and scowled at the flowers once more before texting Lacey.

Do you know what my favorite flowers are?

Liv continued to glare at the flowers, as if having a staring contest with them and refusing to lose.

Buzz. Buzz.

Liv looked down at her phone.

No. Why?

Hesitant to share her birthday surprise with Lacey, she realized she couldn't really explain the random midnight question without telling the truth.

I just got an anonymous bouquet at my door.

('...' icon from Lacey)

It must be one of your secret admirers!
THE GUY AT THE COFFEE SHOP?!

Liv realized she was getting way too good at 'plussing' up her college experience. Although feeling guilty while responding, she sent a quick *"possibly! J"* and then threw her phone across the bed, and returned to her floral stare down.

Only one person knew her favorite flowers. Only one person ever got her this bouquet arrangement. Hayden.

Hayden, her best guy friend (of 4 years) and more recently boyfriend (of 3 years), and more, more recently, ex-boyfriend (of 3 months).

Hayden, the guy she had planned to go to Oregon with–where she would study science and he would study business.

That was the plan they had made, together.

Until the last week of school, at graduation, when Hayden told Liv he wanted to break up with her, because in actuality, he was going to school across the country and 'didn't want to do a long distance relationship.'

And after they said their goodbyes, it was like Hayden no longer existed on the planet.

Liv felt stupid for texting him when something reminded her of him at first, but after seven years of having a person, 'your person,' you just get in the habit of texting or calling without thought. But after a month of no response–she quickly felt like an idiot anytime she accidentally pushed send. Another silent month passed, and she clearly understood–picture taken. She was out of his life, and he was out of hers.

But then the birthday bouquet happened.

She wanted to thank him for the flowers, but knew that would just lead to another night full of desperate anticipation for a response that would never come.

For now, believing that they were from him and pretending that he still cared was better than nothing–that could be Liv's birthday gift to herself.

And that night, Liv dreamed of Hayden.

They were flying through the stars, together, toward Polaris.

THREE

Liv awoke to Peyton shutting the door, tiptoeing her way to the bed and unsuccessfully trying not to wake her roommate.

Refusing to open her eyes and embrace the day, Liv just mumbled, "Good morning."

Peyton froze, a kid caught sneaking under the Christmas tree to see what Santa brought.

"I brought coffee?" She extended a treaty of truce, holding out the hot cup. "Americano? You like those, right?"

Liv sat up, never one to refuse coffee.

"Thanks. How was bid night?"

"Oh my gosh, so much fun. I crashed at the sorority because we were out so late," Peyton snuggled into her bed across the room, leaning against her colorful wall to face Liv. "But, more importantly–happy birthday!"

"Thanks!" Liv said genuinely (for once) and smiled. Peyton's constant cheer and kindness was beginning to grow on her.

Liv took a sip of her coffee, which was delicious. "Oh, this is the best way to start my birthday."

"I don't know," Peyton pointed to Liv's birthday bouquet. "Those flowers definitely weren't there last night. Who sent them?"

Liv shrugged, "I have no idea."

"A secret admirer? Well, I figured you would have one by now. I mean, look at you." Peyton was so nice that even her jealous remark came off as a sincere compliment. With a big smile, she added, "Maybe he'll reveal himself tonight."

And with that, Peyton lay in her bed and closed her eyes for some much-needed sleep.

Liv put her Americano next to the floral bouquet (to Liv's dismay, it smelled just as amazing in the morning), and grabbed her mom's gift.

It was a small box, beautifully gift wrapped in silver and tied with a light blue ribbon, the same color as Liv's eyes.

She set the box aside and opened the birthday card first, even though she knew it was from her mom.

The card was a bit unusual; the front was a black-and-white photo of a brunette woman and blonde man walking on a beach with their backs to the camera. Intrigued, Liv opened the card to see her mom's recognizable calligraphy writing.

Liv,

I know I don't talk about your father often, but he gave me this, and it's time that you have it.

He would have been so proud of the intelligent, kind, and strong young woman you have grown to be (as I am). You are truly beautiful inside and out, and never forget that.

He passed away before we took a photo together, but the one on the cover looks just as I remember him, so I thought you could use it to keep his memory alive.

Happy eighteenth birthday my darling young lady. Your future is bright–just follow the stars.

Love,
Mom

Liv felt a tear trickle down her cheek. She flipped the card back over to the front so she could study the man. Although Liv resembled her mom in facial structure, she was told she had her father's light features–bright eyes and sun-kissed hair–quite the opposite to her mom's mahogany mane and mocha eyes.

The man was tall, built but lanky. Liv always assumed she got her height and body structure from her dad. She hovered over her mom by half a foot and was never blessed with her mother's voluptuous genes.

Liv blushed internally, realizing she was trying too hard to study a photo that wasn't even of her Dad.

Her mom never talked much about him, because really, she didn't know a lot about Liv's father–he passed away unexpectedly and before Liv was even known to be in existence–but her mom did try to tell Liv all she could.

But after about a month of inquiring at a young age, Liv had already memorized all the details her mom shared and grew tired of hearing the same repetitive, simple responses–or the dreaded and unfulfilling one, "I don't know," in return to her various questions. So, for the past decade they had just stopped talking about him.

What Liv did know was that her parents met at the beach while on vacation during the winter. Her father and mother fell in love instantly, and spent an entire day together, one of her mother's best days–aside from the day that Liv was born and every day after that, of course (Liv always rolled her eyes at that sentiment).

After one amazing week together, vacation was over and so her parents departed their separate ways; her father, Liam, promising to visit her mother, with address and phone number in hand. But, her dad didn't call. He never came.

A couple months later, her mother found out she was pregnant.

Once learning of her condition, Liv's mom returned to Southern California and tried to find out how to contact Liam, his family or any connection for that matter, but fell short–she didn't even know his last name–and anyone who would have recognized or remembered him had already left or returned to their own homes months before.

Finally, after pleading for some form of an answer, one final attempt to figure out what happened, Liv's mom encountered one soul who remembered Liam–a friend who said he had played Volleyball with Liam once that winter.

A blessing in disguise–because what Liv's mom learned next broke her to pieces.

Liam had been attacked and murdered the night after they departed. He was found the morning after on the beach, almost as if he had been washed up from the sea.

Sadly frowning at the young woman's despair, the friend added that the news reported Liam did not have any known relatives.

And for Liv's mom–that was the end of it all.

Liv looked at the unique box, remembering what her mom once told her about a necklace her father had given her on their last night together, saying that she held all of his power, and Liam would always be at her mercy, because without her, he would be nothing.

Liv quickly opened the box, intrigued. She always thought it was such a romantic sentiment, but at the present, felt uncomfortable being the new owner of such a symbol.

But, upon opening the box, Liv gasped.

She had always assumed the necklace in question was a gold chain that her mom always wore, but what the box contained was pure silver, with a stunning white Druzy baguette stone.

She pulled it out, amazed by how brightly it sparkled with just the faintest glow of sunshine entering the room–but every slivered ray of light hit the crystal, making it glow.

Liv put the necklace on immediately, and when the stone hit her skin in unison with the fastener locking, it was as if she was filled, more complete. Stronger.

She finally felt like she had a piece of her dad with her, and it fit perfectly. Permanently.

After changing into her destroyed ink denim, grey cotton tee, leather jacket and black combat boots, Liv quietly grabbed her Americano (Peyton was still sleeping), which caused another whiff of the intoxicating birthday bouquet, so Liv scowled as she tiptoed out of the dorm.

Upon exiting the building, Liv covered her eyes immediately, blinded by the unexpected brightness. It was sunny–it was her birthday, and it was actually sunny!

Liv eagerly dropped her backpack (and more carefully her precious Americano) to surface her sunglasses and put them on.

As she enjoyed a leisurely walk to her first class, she spotted the solitude reader from yesterday's coffee shop session leaning against a nearby oak tree. Although he seemed to be chatting with a tall, modelesque blonde girl, he was definitely watching Liv as she walked by.

Taking advantage of her dark-lensed sunglasses, Liv kept her head forward with her eyes peeled sharply to her left in his direction.

He kept her gaze at first–he really *did* have the most beautiful eyes, and instinctively they reminded her of Hayden's, whose eyes were always a brilliant arctic blue–but when she began approaching him and his friend, the solitude reader casually turned his focus back to the girl, smiling–an act that seemed too natural, almost strategic.

After passing the couple, Liv sped up her pace to get to class quickly. When she arrived to the quad, busy with students rushing between classes to their next destination, Liv still felt like she was being watched, so she cautiously turned back to see the solitude reader.

He was no longer there, but instead, the girl he had been conversing with was standing firm, staring at Liv through the crowd, her jaw clenched.

Liv darted left toward her Chemistry class and into the large auditorium, Columbia 150. Although she was surrounded by hundreds of students, and technically safe, she still felt very intimidated by the blonde girl's presence and encounter outside. Liv felt intruded upon–she didn't even *know* her, and Liv had been minding her business and literally keeping to herself in every way possible since arriving at school. Liv shuddered; it was as if she could still feel the girl's death stare on her, even indoors.

A pair of waving hands caught her attention; Finn was standing and gestured for her to come over. Happy to recognize a friendly face for once, and welcoming a distraction from what she just witnessed, Liv smiled and waved back, walking toward his direction to sit down.

She normally sat in the front of the class, but aside from Peyton, Finn was really her only other prospect for a friend, so she figured it was worth trying to make an effort for once. Plus, they apparently had this class together, in addition to Astronomy.

"We meet again." Finn smiled.

"Lucky you, more homework answers." Liv smirked, as she sat next to him and pulled out her notebook.

The professor walked out to begin class, and right as the bell rang, Liv noticed the solitude reader slide into a seat below. More so, she noticed his eyes first, trying not to acknowledge that meant they were in her direction in the first place.

However, Liv could admit she was looking forward to an entire hour where he would be at her mercy. She must have never noticed him before because she always sat in the first row, but now that she was in the back, Liv could try to figure out what his deal was for the next uninterrupted 80 minutes.

He was sitting rigidly in his seat, arms folded neatly on his desk, sporting his light grey trench and resembling a stone statue, not even opening a binder to take notes.

He seemed tense and conflicted, but truly a beautiful specimen. Liv felt a gravitational pull toward him, even when she tried to concentrate on her professor–she couldn't help but keep him in her peripheral at all times.

Similar to how she felt anytime she was near Hayden. Liv shook the idea out of her head immediately. The solitude reader and she hadn't even talked yet! Liv was truly becoming a crazy person.

"If you stare any harder, you'll burn holes through his back." Finn nudged Liv playfully, "Maybe what we have will be more about you needing my notes?"

Liv smiled, thankful to have met Finn. She could feel his presence, too–even when distracted by the solitude reader. Finn just seemed simpler, more approachable, comfortable and frankly, not as dangerous for her concern.

For the remainder of class, Liv focused on taking notes, even if the words were going through one ear and out the other. The only thoughts that stayed implanted in her head were the solitude reader's eyes and Finn's arm lightly touching hers.

Before the professor could conclude the lecture by saying, "thanks everyone, enjoy your weekend," the solitude reader was out of his chair and had already exited the building.

How bizarre, Liv thought to herself, borderline deciding if she should chase after him.

Finn was going on about a class project due next week.

"What?" Liv interjected, hearing the deadline.

"Were you even in class today?" Finn laughed. "I swear a girl who looked just like you sat next to me, but clearly that mustn't have been you?"

"Sorry," Liv frowned, then perked up, raising her eyebrows, "Any chance you want to be my partner for the project?"

The rest of Liv's birthday was relatively uneventful, but after napping, frantically deciding what to wear all afternoon and taking too long to blow dry her hair with an accompanying smoky eye, Liv and Peyton had pregamed for an hour and were now approaching Taylor's, the college campus bar.

With each step, Liv's heart beat a little faster, the complete opposite to Peyton's strong steps, perfect posture and the look of such determination. You would think she owned the bar or ran legislature for legal drinking. Liv had never been to a bar before (obviously, she wasn't even of age to drink), but tried to adapt Peyton's beaming confidence, remembering her roommate's tips: just act like you belong, keep eye contact and don't sweat–with enough make up and boobs they'll think you're twenty-five!

The two girls got in line and began waiting.

"Oh! I almost forgot!" Peyton dug through her purse, pulling out a driver's license and handing it to Liv, "Happy Birthday–here's your gift!"

Liv took a look at her new identity and had to admit, the resemblance was uncanny.

"Just remember you're a Sagittarius, born in Carmichael, CA–that's near Sacramento–zip code is 95608 and you're twenty-two years old."

"Got it." Liv automatically replied.

But truthfully, Liv hadn't gotten it yet.

She spent the next five minutes imprinting the card to her memory. Aimee Sanders. Blue Eyes. 5'6. Liv secretly wished she hadn't worn her black stilettos, she was easily close to 6 feet at the moment, and also lamented the extra shot of Fireball she took before leaving their dormitory. Liv was definitely feeling the whiskey now, and combined with her great heels decision, the effort of keeping her balance to appear like less of a lightweight and more in control was becoming more challenging by the second.

They turned the corner and could see the bouncer. Peyton nudged Liv to put her ID away, so Liv obliged.

Slowly approaching the entrance, Liv wondered if her outfit was okay enough. She wore black skinny jeans and a silk, olive green strappy top with a high squared-neckline. She initially thought it paired perfectly with her favorite biker jacket and caged-silhouette sandal heels, but now, she felt like her outfit was too obvious–trying too hard.

"Let's go home." She gulped, terrified of the bouncer.

"No!" Peyton laughed, then lowered her voice so nobody could hear, "It's your birthday. We're dancing and celebrating tonight. You'll be fine. Promise."

Easy for Peyton to think, she radiated confidence. She had a beautiful sheer beige long sleeve bohemian crop top, with the most beautiful navy embroidery and gold beading. Peyton's hair also encompassed the perfect beach wave, with her sun kissed brown perfectly falling into a no-effort shoulder-length bob. Paired with her light denim skinny jeans and gorgeous suede booties, she was the essence of cool. Liv hadn't noticed how stunning she really was until this particular moment.

Soon, they were in front of the bouncer, presenting their ID's. Peyton got in without a hitch, but when Liv handed over her fake, it was as if time paused. The bouncer studied the ID card, and then examined Liv, eye for eye, chin for chin, nose to nose. (She was thankful he was short and stocky, so he would never guess she was 6 feet tall at the moment.)

Finally, he gave her back the ID and nodded for her to go in.

Don't appear relieved.

Liv darted in after Peyton.

Peyton promised celebration and dancing, and that they did. Peyton had told every guy it was Liv's birthday, resulting in an unlimited supply of free vodka sodas throughout the night. Liv was feeling great and alive for the first time in months.

She flirted, she giggled, and she made new friends she'd never remember the next day, but most of all: Liv was actually having fun.

"We HAVE to come back here." Liv ran over to Peyton, giving her a hug as they jumped to the music. "You're also, like, stunning Peyton." Liv lightly brushed her hands through Peyton's hair, with positive envy. "I never noticed, but you look so beautiful tonight. And your outfit is EVERYTHING."

"Thanks, Pretty lady! Next to you, I'm surprised anyone has noticed me at all!" Peyton raised her class to cheers Liv. "Happy Birthday Roomie! Love you!"

Liv continued dancing to the contagious beat, but suddenly a pair of light grey eyes caught her attention. The solitude reader looked away immediately and started to walk away, but Liv would not let him get away this time.

With the help of liquid courage, Liv ran over to him, grabbing his arm so he had to turn back around and face her.

"Why do you keep following me?" Liv demanded, looking him straight in the eye.

The solitude reader flashed a monstrous look, filled with rage, causing her to second-guess her idiotic maneuver, but the moment passed and he calmed down, a second later looking composed again.

"It's a small campus." The solitude reader sniped back.

"So you don't deny it?" Liv refused to look away–she was not backing down.

"Look, we probably have a similar schedule." The solitude reader grabbed Liv's hand, releasing it from his arm, "It's bound to happen. There are over eighteen thousand students here, you know?"

He was challenging her, encouraging her to admit her fault in observation. But for some reason, Liv couldn't accept a coincidence and she didn't know why. She just hoped it wasn't in hindsight for wanting it to be true, for purpose of another distraction.

Her brain finally caught up to her impulse decision, realizing embarrassingly that she just verbally attacked a guy she thought was attractive, and she had to admit–he looked good in his light blue shirt. What was she doing?

"I'm so sorry." Liv took a step back, shaking her head, along with her thoughts. "You're right. I'm totally being rude."

He wasn't giving her any slack; he just stood there, still.

Liv continued, "I've just been a little on edge lately. Can we start over? I'm Liv."

As she extended her hand to shake his, a guy bumped into her from behind, spilling his drink and inadvertently hers all over her silk top.

After assessing the damage, Liv looked up, but the solitude reader was gone.

But he was just here!

Liv ran outside, trying to catch up with him before he left. As she looked around, frantically, she couldn't find him anywhere. Not enjoying the sudden rainfall that had started, Liv turned dejectedly back onto the patio stairs, but the bouncer stopped her–there was no re-admittance after exiting the bar so she'd have to stand back in line.

Liv looked behind him, the line seemed longer than when they were standing in it an hour ago and there was no way she was going to wait in the rain again.

Angrily, she pulled out her phone and texted Peyton.

GOT BEER SPILLED ON ME L. I'M GONNA CALL IT A NIGHT–SEE YOU TOMORROW?

Liv stomped away back toward her dorm, hearing the clouds thundering in the distance. *Typical.* Grudgingly, she stormed back between trees for cover, really wishing that she had researched Northwest weather before moving to this cursed place.

FOUR

Liv had been waiting all week for her Friday Chemistry class, knowing that the solitude reader would be there and anticipating what she could ask him. Would she extend a courtesy wave to start over, ask him to sit down and become her friend? Or would she wait for him to arrive and sit next to him right before class?

And why was it so challenging to figure out a way for them simply to have a regular conversation?

Liv wasn't sure, but the only thing she knew was that she needed to figure this guy out.

Upon entering the large auditorium, however; another pair of gold eyes welcomed her into the class and she immediately spotted Finn–his gaze sparkling at her as he eagerly flagged her over to sit.

Liv kept her gaze near the sets of entrance doors, mouth clenching tighter as she saw the clock hands ticking closer to 11AM–where was he? She walked over to Finn, sitting down disappointedly.

"Hey, you're tall." Finn stated blankly, turning toward her.

Liv couldn't help but smile. "Great observation," she teased, still looking at the door.

"Did you ever play volleyball by chance?" Finn seemed a bit nervous, on edge, almost like he had never talked to a girl before, let alone sit next to Liv for the past week in their classes.

"By chance, I did. What's up?" Liv kept her eyes glued to the doors but tilted her head toward Finn to show encouragement.

"Well, I joined an intramural volleyball team–would you want to play?"

Liv paused, and the professor entered, motioning to start class. It was past 11AM and the solitude reader was nowhere to be found.

"Hey, leaving a potential team mate stranded here which is very unsportsmanlike, maybe we shouldn't have you join after all..." Finn nudged Liv, demanding a response.

Liv was weary. She hadn't played volleyball since moving to Oregon, but she did love the sport and it was one of her best coping mechanisms this summer. Her mom had actually told her she was worried Liv was playing *too* much volleyball, and should reduce her time on the beach–giving her the whole 'experience other things' parental spiel.

It could be a good way to meet new friends, and in celebration of her eighteenth birthday promise, Liv figured this could be the easiest way to experience more, while still distracting herself accordingly.

"Sure. Count me in. When are the games?"

"Mondays, our first one is at 7pm."

"Cool–I'll be there."

With that, the professor hushed the class to start his lecture. Liv luckily was much more focused than last week's class, but she couldn't help panning the room just to make sure she hadn't missed the solitude reader. She felt like he was close, but definitely did not have that tension she experienced during the previous week.

When the class was dismissed early, Finn and Liv were the first ones out of the building. The one advantage, Liv learned, of sitting near the back exit. She didn't have to deal with the masses rushing to get to their next destination (and yet somehow moving slower than anyone with a mission would ever reasonably accept otherwise).

Finn was telling Liv about the other team members when she exited the building and spotted the solitude reader sitting across the pathway on a bench.

"Finn, I've gotta go. I'll see you Monday." Liv quickly muttered, darting in the solitude reader's direction.

"Great! I'll text you the schedule for this season!" Finn yelled after her, but Liv was already gone.

Determined with curiosity, Liv ran up to the solitude reader before he could react and leave.

"Hey, how come you weren't in class today?" Liv asked.

The solitude reader quickly stood up, with the same instant look of shock and malice, before forcing composure, but Liv could tell he was still on edge.

"Oh, I was running late–but didn't want to interrupt the lecture, so figured I'd just talk to Professor Laine after class, I actually better go catch him–"

He moved to leave, but Liv grabbed his arm, yanking him back and forcing him to stay.

The solitude reader looked at her in shock and froze. His eyes were piercing with rage.

Liv took a step back, looking down. "Sorry, again. Not sure why I keep doing that, or why you keep leaving so suddenly actually." She looked back at him accusingly, but then immediately ceased upon encountering his foreboding glare. "Look, I just wanted to offer you my notes–I can make a copy of them and bring them next week… so, you can have for the midterm." She couldn't believe she was actually stuttering, but his gaze was so intense.

"Thanks." He replied with a terse voice–the solitude reader obviously wanted nothing to do with Liv. He immediately turned around and left.

Once relieved from the interaction, Liv began to calm and think again. Why did he keep running away? She was so confused by this character. How could he already hate Liv when he didn't even know her?

I guess he did need to catch Professor Laine….

But he didn't have to be rude about it.

Liv wanted to follow him so perhaps they could actually have a conversation after he spoke with their professor, or maybe have time to just casually grab a coffee?

Filled with adrenaline, Liv darted back into the classroom, only to find both Professor Laine and the solitude reader already gone.

She ran across the classroom to the other exit, in case they were heading toward the professor's office or something. She couldn't figure out why she was so curious, she had never acted like this toward anyone before, but she just seemed drawn to him, naturally.

His eyes (when they weren't enraged) had reminded her of Hayden's. Liv didn't want to admit it, but in fact, so much of the solitude reader's demeanor reminded her of Hayden, she was beginning to question if her infatuation was only because it felt like a remote link to her ex-boyfriend. And with that thought she shuddered, wondering that maybe she should just leave him alone.

It was probably for the best, anyway.

She exited the classroom to return to her dorm, when she spotted another herd of black birds passing through the sky, right over her head in an arrow-like form, pointing and heading toward a large oak tree.

Liv followed them, unsure why she was so curious.

When she altered her direction eventually to go around the oak tree, she spotted the solitude reader talking with the blonde girl who had stared her down the week prior, so Liv darted back for cover behind the large tree stump.

The girl looked nervous, and Liv was desperate to know why.

She quietly tiptoed over to a closer Pine tree, carefully keeping herself out of sight so she could try to get near enough and hear what the two were talking about.

"You need to be more careful, Rei. She can't keep seeing you, she'll get suspicious," the blonde girl hissed.

He immediately sniped back, "Do you think I've been trying to be seen?"

Liv carefully rotated herself around the Pine tree so she could hear better and desperately concentrated on lip reading to make out their words, already noting the solitude reader's name was Rei.

Rei lowered his voice, "I know what the repercussions are. And you know that I want nothing to do with her!"

"She saw you sitting in her class, you could have made that one harder." The blonde girl spat back maliciously.

Liv jumped back behind the oak tree with her heart racing.

They were talking about *her.*

"I was told she would sit in the front row." Rei clenched his jaw, tension rising in his voice.

"So, maybe you shouldn't rely so heavily on your sources and rely more on yourself," the girl sneered back. Liv already could tell she did not like this woman.

Rei's voice was thunderous, "He's the reason why I'm here in the first place!"

The blonde hushed Rei immediately and started looking around, clearly paranoid of being overheard.

Rei took a breath, trying to pacify his anger with reasoning. "Besides, Ollie has become more perceptive in the past week or so. I've noticed. She's looking around more and discerning things, like she has some sort of newly found intuition."

Liv froze, in complete shock.

They had called her by her nickname.

They knew her nickname.

Nobody at this campus knew her nickname.

Liv almost lost track of what she was doing, but refocused when the blonde girl started taunting Rei.

"So what? She's not head deep in a book or concentrating on her phone like the first two weeks of school? Is that too much for you to handle, now?" The blonde asked in a degrading, baby tone.

Rei kept his composure, but Liv could sense he was still tense. "Whatever she's doing is none of our business."

"Well, whatever she is doing, you've gotten lazy. You're just supposed to stay invisible and make sure she stays out of trouble."

Liv heard the two walk their separate ways, but she couldn't move. She didn't care if she was seen any more.

Only one person had ever called her Ollie–and Hayden had made it more than clear that he did not care whether she was dead or alive.

The question was: then why did these two strangers care so much?

By the time Liv returned to her dorm, after walking around campus for the better part of the afternoon in a daze, Peyton was already in full-throttle going out mode.

"Where were you?" Peyton asked. Part of her hair was halfway caught in her mouth, another section mid-twirl in her curling iron.

"Oh, just walking around." Liv sat on her bed, still in a bit of a trance.

Peyton just stared at her, her eyebrows raised, demanding more.

"I lost track of time." Liv lied.

"Well, you're coming out tonight? Right?" Peyton stared at Liv, willing for her to give in. "We had so much fun last weekend!"

"I don't know, I'm a little tired, honestly…" Liv leaned back on her bed, just needing a book or some form of distraction; she wasn't really in the mood to socialize.

"No! You can't be! You've BARELY used your ID! You have to admit, you were having a blast until that lame guy spilled his beer on you, and that never happens… okay, it usually happens, but for you and on your birthday it was just terrible luck."

Liv stared at Peyton, trying to craft an excuse to get out of this social nightmare.

"Here! Drink this. It's like coffee for adults." Peyton handed Liv a silver flask.

Liv eyed the flask, and then Peyton, admiring her room-mate's pertinence.

"Okay." She conceded to Peyton's wishes, grabbing the flask and taking a swig.

"Oh god, is this tequila?" Liv's mouth cringed.

"Coffee for adults. Here–lime." Peyton handed over a slice to relinquish the after taste.

"Thanks." Liv sucked onto the lime, puckering her mouth, "That would have been helpful before I took the shot."

"Au contraire, if I had given you the lime, would you really have taken a gulp?" Peyton smirked, relishing in her victory as she ran back to the mirror to continue curling her hair.

"What are you going to wear tonight?" Peyton asked Liv, casually.

Her roommate was too good at this. Kink out all the details now and leave enough time to troubleshoot so Liv truly could not get out of it later.

"Um, I haven't really thought about it. I have a cute black tank top I could wear. Could I borrow your black waxed denim?"

If she's taking me down, I'm taking her down with me.

But her request didn't even faze Peyton.

"Um, you can of course borrow my jeans. But black? You always wear black. Go through my closet while you're at it and grab something with color for once."

"I don't always wear black!" Liv shrieked defensively, but then looked down at her outfit, and realized she was indeed wearing all black, aside from a light grey chunky cardigan she only had put on because she was cold.

"Grey, black, white–they're all shades of the same hue." Peyton nodded to her closet. "Go. Choose. Brighten your perspective."

Liv dramatically pulled herself out of bed, heading toward Peyton's rainbow of prints, patterns and clothes. Looking through her top section, Liv found some contenders.

"You know, I do own color. I just choose not to wear it." She combed through a couple more shirts, finding a gorgeous seafoam green chiffon tank with Aztec gold beading. She could pair it with a black lace bralette (and secretly prayed Peyton would let her swing it). The bralette would be perfect for the low cut in the back.

"Is this okay, fashion police?"

Peyton turned around, nodding. "Good choice. I won't comment on the fact that if not black, your go-to color seems to only be olive green or navy. But, baby steps, of course." She smiled and then demanded, "Now, start your make up—we all know how long that took last week."

Liv rolled her eyes, laughing, but happy to feel that between the tequila and her new friend Peyton, she was beginning to feel lighter, like she could maybe handle this new life.

Liv and Peyton arrived at the bar and seamlessly got in (with a much less stressed but equally drunk Liv). They headed directly to the dance floor after getting complimentary drinks from the first set of guys who started talking to them.

"It's because of your top, Liv. Hot. Damn." Peyton laughed, holding her drink up to Liv. "Cheers to a smoky eye, open back and plunging neckline."

Liv laughed, holding out her drink and clinked it with Peyton's. She had to admit; she felt fierce in her outfit tonight, almost stronger than when she typically wore her black leather jacket—what she considered to be her usual armor. She loved how the lacy bralette peaked out of her top in the perfect places and complimented her dark-almost-leatheresque skinny pants by adding a soft balance to her overall very edgy look. She also loved how the light green top accentuated her eyes, making them more sea green than their typical sky blue. She felt good, confident, almost like the Liv she lost in the spring.

"Alas, Serena would get nowhere without her Blair. Cheers to you, my relentlessly devious, floral hippy minx." Liv smiled, holding out her drink again. "And seriously, thanks for literally dragging me out tonight."

"Why thank you and anytime." Peyton laughed, adding a twirl to show off her stylish navy, peach and red floral dress and spun her auburn wedges on the dance floor, effectively showing off her toned legs. Her sleeves hung off her shoulders, midway onto her arms, and her hair perfectly curled for a sun-kissed bohemian wave.

After finishing her spin, Peyton puckered her ruby red lips and smiled.

"Now, let's dance."

The girls had fun switching between chatting with fraternity guys and dancing with them, but unlike Peyton, who seemed to fall in love with each new guy they met, none of the potential beaus seemed very special to Liv.

Liv was talking to the sixth new guy on the dance floor, and just as usual he was way more into her than she him, and Liv felt nothing. She made up some excuse about seeing a friend to get away, but then noticed Peyton still in a dancing trance with her newest conquer, so decided to walk around and see what the whole bar was about.

She secretly wondered if she would see Rei tonight because she found him here the previous weekend. She also realized she felt a little weird about learning his name from eavesdropping earlier today. Then again, two could play this game. While he was trying to stay incognito from her, maybe Liv could try to stay hidden from him, too. The only problem was, she just needed to find him first.

After walking a loop around the bar, Liv found Peyton once again making out, but with a new guy. Not wanting to interrupt, Liv turned away. She looked around for any friendly face but, of course, recognized no one, not even the various guys she had danced with throughout the night.

Well, this is what happens when you only have one friend.

Soon, Liv started realizing how drunk she was and just how sloppy everyone looked in the bar. What was she doing? Liv felt empty, lost. This wasn't who Liv was: dressed in a skimpy top and tight jeans.

She needed to get away from this scene. She needed air.

Liv ran outside to the patio and took a deep breath, looking up at the stars, almost on the verge of tears.

There had to be something out there bigger for her, bigger than this. Drinking alcohol and going out dancing was just another coping mechanism, another distraction.

Liv knew she was capable of so much more than the life she was living. She just knew it.

The possibility of a purpose, or a fate–she couldn't let herself believe that her life would be like this for the next 4 years. It may be normal for most college students, but for her–it was too simple, unchallenging. It couldn't just be studying, drinking, meeting new guys each night, getting free drinks and then the cycle, continued. Her life was too normal, where was the magic?

Liv shivered, wishing she brought her leather jacket, and automatically looked up to the stars for guidance. She hadn't searched in the sky for weeks, and immediately regretted it when she spotted her constellation, Ollie, visible between two emerging clouds. It was as if it had magnetized to her, pulling her attention, forcing its presence to be acknowledged.

She wondered if he could see it, too.

Liv and Hayden were on a camping trip with some friends to celebrate the start of their senior year. It happened to be the weekend before Liv's birthday. And on the first night, Hayden brought her out to the dock for an early, intimate celebration with just the two of them.

Holding a cupcake topped with a lit candle in front of Liv, Hayden donned the biggest grin on his face, with pride emanating from successfully pulling off his secret plan.

"Happy Birthday, Ollie–make a wish!"

Liv took a deep breath; eyes sparkling as she joyfully blew out her birthday candle.

"Do you want to know what I wished for?" Liv grabbed the cupcake from Hayden's hand, dipping her finger in the frosting to taste: buttercream, her favorite.

"Um, that's not how it's supposed to work, if I recall correctly. Cupcake good?"

"Delicious." Liv took a full bite this time, amazed at how moist and light the chocolate cake also tasted. "This is seriously the best dessert I've ever had," Liv applauded with her mouth still full.

Hayden laughed at the sight. "I'll be keeping that attractive moment in my memory forever. You're lucky you're cute."

Although teasing Liv, the love radiating from Hayden's eyes soothed her confidence instantly.

As Liv grinned and enjoyed her cupcake, Hayden continued with his plans for the night. Pulling out a wool blanket to sit on and another one that he immediately wrapped around Liv, he dug through his bag for various essentials.

"Champagne, so we can toast to your 17th birthday and our best year yet to come, together." He filled up two flutes and handed her one; they clinked their glasses together and whispered, "Cheers," both with sparkling eyes matching that of the drink they sipped.

"Tea, because I know you'll never drink more than one flute, and of course to keep you warm." He handed her a canteen. Liv took it, graciously.

"Häagen-Dazs pint of Chocolate Peanut Butter ice cream, because what sort of boyfriend would I be forgetting his girlfriend's favorite dessert for her birthday celebration?" He handed her the pint with one spoon and added, "Figured we could share that."

"Bold assumption, Hayden." Liv joked, "You're lucky I like you."

"And finally," Hayden made a grand gesture, showing her a beautifully wrapped gold box, decorated with an anemone, "Your birthday gift."

He set it in her hands, and then sat down next her, bringing the blanket around his shoulders and wrapping Liv inside his arms.

His mouth came close to her ears, his warm breath tickling her neck as he breathed. "Because I love you and always will." He finished with a gentle kiss on her cheek.

Liv didn't want to move, she wanted this exact moment to last forever, or at least be imprinted in her memory for eternity. To remember the touch of his soft skin, warmth of his minty breath, the smell of him–a vibrant mix of sensual basil verveina, cedar and leather notes–how it felt to be held tight in his strong arms, and snuggled in the warm, thick blanket. This moment, to be locked in her archive of perfect memories, was one she'd never forget.

"I know your birthday is next week, but you do realize I gave you the gift so you can open it tonight…" Hayden whispered.

Liv smiled, she could tell Hayden was excited to show her his present. She could sense his eagerness, even though he was trying to remain playful and calm.

"Okay, I'll open it–the wrapping is just so beautiful, Hayden."

She turned around so she could see his face and witness his beautiful sparkling crystal blue eyes radiating with joy. She wanted to watch him watch her open his gift, Liv could tell it meant a lot to Hayden.

"Really, thank you for all of this, everything you did–it's too much. But, I appreciate it, and I appreciate you for making me feel so special."

"This? Nothing compared to everything you do for me, every day." Hayden leaned in for a kiss on Liv's lips and she obliged, willingly. He pulled away, too soon; Liv wanted more–she could never get enough of him–and instinctively moved forward, gravitating toward his soft lips again.

Hayden kissed her, responding to her need, but then gently pulled her away.

"Liv, I want you to know something." Hayden looked determined, but gave away no emotion or hint as to what.

"Sure Hayden, what's up?" Liv asked, curiously.

He looked at the gold box in Liv's hand, and then held his hand over it, "First, open."

Liv smiled, anticipation building as she eagerly unwrapped the gift.

Upon opening the box, she found a beige piece of paper. She unfolded the paper, finding a map of the constellations, with an outlined constellation in silver, titled, "OLLIE."

"Did you get me my own constellation?" Liv looked up to Hayden, completely speechless, affection radiating through her heart at the thoughtful gesture. "I love it!" Liv cried, throwing herself into Hayden's arms, relishing in her body against his strong chest.

She could feel Hayden's smile growing larger against her cheek.

Once they separated from their passionate embrace, Hayden pointed up to the sky, showing her where the constellation Ollie existed. The night sky glittered, all the stars welcoming their new set of organized beauty.

Then Hayden turned Liv back toward him,

"This gift, I just," Hayden swallowed, looking back into Liv's eyes for strength. And with shining determination explained, "I want you to know that as long as you look to the stars for guidance, instead of looking for Polaris like you usually do," he softly smiled to himself, "find this constellation." He furrowed his brows, looking down and willing himself to go on, "And just know that I can see it too, and that I'll be there for you, no matter what, for whatever you need."

Liv lifted Hayden's head to meet her eyes, searching in his for an explanation.

"But we won't ever be apart." She stated bluntly.

Although she was asking Hayden to expand upon his reasoning for this gift, she refused to make that phrase a question; it was a fact and she would never put it up for debate.

Hayden shrugged, "We don't know who's going to get into what college, or if you'll get your scholarship, or where we'll be a year from now. I just want what's best for you." His face saddened at this last statement, but grabbed Liv's cheek affectionately and forced a smile.

"All that I'm saying is, if our life doesn't go as planned, and we end up going to different schools or if we have to spend time apart, this can be our connector–our own little piece of eternity."

Liv felt a tear falling down her cheek and immediately wiped it off her face as she stared at the patio floor and took a deep breath.

When she looked up, she couldn't believe her eyes.

It was Hayden.

He was standing outside another bar across the street, with Rei's blonde-haired-bitch.

Hayden's eyes caught Liv's for a moment that felt infinite, but passed too quickly.

Liv felt a pain go through her chest, as if her heart was literally being torn from her body and breaking into pieces.

Hayden's gaze immediately filled with sadness, as if he felt her pain, too—as they saw each other for the first time since graduation, now two completely different souls from the last time they were together, now two strangers in each other's lives.

The blonde girl noticed Hayden's trance and turned to see what caught his attention, noticing Liv across the way. She smirked at Liv, and then smiled back at Hayden, putting her arm around him and leading him inside.

Liv dropped to the ground, head in her hands, undaunted by the rain that began pouring over her.

FIVE

"**Liv, you have** to leave this room. It's super depresso in here."

Peyton marched over to the window, opening the blinds and shrugging at the result, a terrible rainstorm was taking place outside.

"Not that it's super happy outside either, I guess." Peyton turned around toward Liv, frowning, "Gloom-galore out there, too."

In response, Liv turned over in bed and buried her head under the pillow, groaning.

Unluckily for Liv, Peyton was not one to give up on a lost cause, so she sat down on Liv's bed, completely content with the challenge of conducting an interesting conversation with just herself.

"Did you know? It's apparently like the worst fall term Oregon has had in forever? My sorority sisters keep complaining that they've never had this disgusting weather before during Fall Term, not until November at least!" Peyton peeked over at Liv, a little disappointed with the little progress she had made. Usually by now, she had face time, or at the very least, a slight smirk from her roommate.

"I heard there's actually a room in the health center that we can go get UV rays? Like, we can actually get Vitamin D with a fake sunlight simulation. Maybe we should go check it out?"

Silence. Liv was clearly not in the mood to talk. Peyton decided a different strategy would need to be implemented stat: Bad Cop.

Peyton yanked out Liv's pillow, followed by her bed comforter. Liv jumped up, confused to how such a tiny girl could have so much strength.

"What are you doing?!" Liv shrieked.

"Liv." Peyton pointed her pointer finger and middle finger together, like a gun–that meant business. "You can't just go all 'Silencio' on me or else I'm going to have to 'Imperious Curse' you to get you to talk. AND, I'll keep making Harry Potter references until you want to 'Aveda Kadavra' yourself…"

Liv smiled, she couldn't help it.

"I mean, until this very moment, I was under the impression you already wanted to 'Aveda Kadavra' yourself…" Peyton shrugged, sitting on Liv's bed. "What happened?"

Liv didn't even know where to start. She didn't want to share the Rei part, because although he technically *was* stalking her, she couldn't really prove it and didn't want to seem crazy to her only friend here.

"I saw my ex-boyfriend last night. And what's even more fucked up is that he told me he was going to school across the country, which is why we needed to break up. Long-distance my ass." Liv shook her head disappointingly, but also felt relieved to finally be talking to somebody about everything she had been suffocating herself with since the summer.

"He told you he was moving across the country, but he's here? Crazy." Peyton put her arm around Liv, "I'm sorry friend. Boys are the worst."

After a long hug, Peyton jumped up and ran to her desk, "I almost forgot! You know what is the best?"

Liv chuckled and mockingly asked, "What? What is *the best*?"

"Americanos! Voila!" She ran over to Liv, presenting a warm cup of coffee.

"Oh my gosh, thank you." Liv took the Holy Grail, internally appreciating her brown nosing roommate who always offered coffee at the most ideal times. As she watched Peyton open her lid to blow on the steaming beverage, Liv noticed Peyton's hair was blonder.

"Did you get your hair done? It looks lighter."

Cheerfully, Peyton responded, "Well, someone's gotta brighten the mood around here somehow!" Then she raised her coffee cup to an invisible toast before taking a sip.

Most of Liv's weekend was spent lying in bed, drowning in her misery, only with spurts of lightness whenever Peyton clawed her way back into Liv's soul.

She did try to make it to one of her classes, but after exiting her dorm, felt like she was being watched–whether by Rei, the blonde bitch or Hayden–and realized she still hadn't processed how she felt about everything she had learned over the weekend. Nor did she feel comfortable from those experiences, so immediately turned around and ran back into her bed.

Buzz. Buzz

It was now evening, and Liv had just finished her newest book, a mass murder mystery. She lethargically reached over to her phone and saw a text from Finn.

MISSED YOU IN CLASS TODAY–ARE YOU COMING TONIGHT?

Crap. Her volleyball game was tonight.

Initially, Liv ignored the text, not wanting to go, and instead, hibernate forever. But then she looked over at her desk and found that her supply of books had been depleted from having read three over the weekend.

She looked back at her phone, biting her lip.

It could be fun, and she would be distracted during the game–plus, Peyton wouldn't be back until later tonight–she had some weekly meeting with her sorority, Alpha Beta Mu.

After pulling herself out of bed and changing into her volleyball gear, Liv did feel better, almost excited to play. If anything, she could just imagine Hayden's head as the volleyball when she spiked it.

She jogged over to the campus gym, looked up at the sky and saw dark clouds hovering overhead, foreshadowing a terrible thunderstorm to come.

She ran into the Student Rec Center and immediately spotted Finn. Liv jogged over and slapped his back, ready to play.

"Sorry, I'm a little late." She apologized.

Finn looked happily surprised, "No! I'm just glad you could make it." He turned to the team, "You guys, our pro is here!"

Everyone waved with friendly smiles as Finn introduced Liv to the team.

"This is Jax—he's in my bio class, and Tarryn—she knows Jax from their dorm, and this is Jaycie..."

Jaycie was wearing an Alpha Beta Mu tank, so Liv jumped in.

"Jaycie? You're in Alpha Beta Mu?"

Jaycie nodded, encouragingly.

"Oh! My roommate is in Alpha Beta Mu, too—do you know Peyton?" Liv asked excitedly.

Jaycie tilted her head, eyes looking up in recollection. "I don't think so, is she a freshman?"

Liv nodded her head, "Yeah, Peyton Stone? She's a brunette with sun-kissed highlights and shoulder length hair."

Jaycie shook her head. "No, sadly not ringing a bell—but either way, don't tell her I'm here, okay?" Jaycie playfully nudged Liv, laughing. "Low key—I sort of told my chapter I had class tonight to get out of our weekly meetings."

"Your secret is safe with me." Liv smiled, glad to see this new person trusted her enough with a secret. Maybe this volleyball thing would be a good idea.

During the game, Liv was killing it—she forgot how much she loved playing the sport, and how good it made her feel. She started her serving rotation with two aces, and by the end of the game, was being purposely passed to so she could spike the ball, although she tried to gently pass it to other team members every other turn so they could participate, too.

After the game, Finn ran up to Liv, putting a hand on her shoulder. "You, my friend, were the best recruit I could have made for this team."

Liv smiled, but felt very uncomfortable with his hand touching her.

"Thanks for including me, this was exactly what I needed."

Liv strategically stepped away, picking up her water bottle to seem less obvious.

"Where's your dorm? I'll walk you home." Finn inquired.

"Oh? No, it's okay–it's just right across the way, I'll be fine."

"No, it's dark outside, and it's on the way back to mine, anyway." Finn insisted.

"Okay. That works." Liv shrugged.

After exiting the building, Liv had to admit she appreciated having Finn's company. After nightfall, the campus emptied of activities, classes and students, and developed an overall very creepy feel. The tall trees that border the pathways made room for a lot of shadows, creating a lot of unknown space, which put Liv a little on edge.

It wasn't as if Rei scared her–if anything, it felt like the reverse. But, for some reason the conversation she overheard terrified her–that she might be in danger and not even know it.

Finn was making small talk; Liv hadn't really been listening, but upon approaching her dorm, Finn followed her up the stairs to the entrance door.

Liv paused, confused. She wasn't sure if he expected an invitation to come inside, or if he was pursuing some form of a southern gentleman act.

Awkward and unsure what to do, Liv simply stated, "Well, this is my dorm building. Thanks for dropping me off on your way home."

"You're not going to invite me up? I'd love to see your room." Clearly, Finn wasn't getting the picture–he had stepped in closer to Liv, a little too close for her preference.

"I totally would, but…" Liv panicked, trying to come up with an excuse to let him down gently, "my roommate has a huge exam tomorrow. So, I don't think she'd appreciate the unexpected social scene. Sorry."

"That's too bad. Well, I guess this is good night." Finn put his arm on the wall, cornering Liv against it and unexpectedly going in for a kiss.

Liv ducked under his arm, barely dodging his lips, with her eyes wide open from shock.

But Finn wasn't catching on to her social cues. He grabbed her arm, forcing her toward him.

"Finn, I don't think this is a good idea–"

"What? Isn't this what you want?" Finn grabbed her shoulders with his arms, shaking her, "You have to admit there's something between us. I've wanted to do this for so long…" He went in for another kiss.

"STOP!" Liv screamed, hearing thunder overhead, "Get away from me!" She pushed Finn with all of her strength, nearly throwing him across the lawn. Simultaneously, a lightening bolt hit a nearby tree, causing it to go up in flames.

Liv's jaw dropped as she stared at Finn in disbelief at how far she pushed him. She immediately looked down at her hands, terrified.

Praying Finn would be okay, Liv darted toward the entrance, frantically trying to get her keys out of her backpack–but her hands were shaking. She quickly turned back toward Finn and saw he was getting up. She looked up to the stars, trying to calm herself down, and immediately spotted her constellation in the sky, Ollie.

She couldn't help but get angry. If only Hayden was here, and didn't abandon her at this hellhole of a school, then none of this would be happening.

Feeling calmer, just enraged–Liv went into her backpack and hastily started looked for her keys again.

Soon, Liv could hear Finn running back toward her.

"Stop! Wait!"

She finally found her dorm key, rapidly entered it into the hole and started to turn the lock when Finn swatted her hand away from the door and grabbed her arm, pulling her alongside him.

"You're coming with me." He sneered, carrying her away from the residence hall.

Liv started to cry, yelling for help between deep breaths of panic. But as she looked around, Liv realized campus was completely dead. Finn continued to drag her across the lawn against her will.

Nobody would be able to hear her.

Liv started accepting her fate, thinking this must be it–this was how she'll die, and it would be tonight.

Looking at the ground, Liv accepted defeat, and watched a small tear drop from her eye and splash onto the concrete.

Suddenly, her arm jerked and Finn let go. She watched as a big blonde mass grabbed Finn from behind and into a headlock, forcing him to the ground.

Hayden.

Hayden kneed Finn in the back, causing him to surrender as his entire body fell to the ground. Hayden jumped on top of Finn and with one mighty punch, knocked him into unconsciousness.

After confirming no retaliation from their new enemy, Hayden immediately ran over to Liv.

"Are you all right? Oh my god, Ollie." Hayden was frantically looking Liv up and down, to make sure she was okay.

"Don't call me that." Liv automatically responded.

Liv wasn't thinking straight, she felt dizzy.

Hayden bowed his head, guiltily. "Of course. Anything you want."

They stood together for a moment, in silence.

Finally, Hayden suggested, "Lets get you back to your dormitory."

When Liv didn't register the idea of moving, Hayden squirmed. He hesitantly put his hand on her back and gently guided Liv to her building.

Although Liv couldn't process her surroundings, she could somehow absorb everything Hayden was doing. It was like he was connected to her. Her mind was blank, but she could feel that he was on edge, and automatically understood that he was anxiously looking around to ensure they were alone and not being followed or visited by any more unwelcomed guests.

Once they got back to her resident's hall entrance, Hayden picked up Liv's backpack and keys, handing them over to her, but keeping space between them.

It was like a 180 from her time with Finn five minutes earlier. Hayden was keeping his distance, but all Liv wanted him to do was get closer. He wasn't insinuating any interest in taking Liv up to her dorm, but all she wanted was for him to come. Liv hated herself for still wanting him, but even more so for not knowing how to be around him anymore.

"Well, thanks, for–um, being there." It took all the strength and courage Liv could fathom to look up at him, painfully making eye contact as she opened the door.

She was a little surprised to see the same sadness reflected in Hayden's gaze.

"Of course," he replied with a shrug. "I'll always be there for you."

"No." Liv tried to remain calm, but was infuriated with his response. "No. Not always. Not anymore."

She stepped toward her dorm building but decided she couldn't leave without finally getting closure to her unanswered questions.

"Why are you here, Hayden?"

Hayden opened his mouth, starting to explain, but then paused.

Shaking his head, he sadly chuckled to himself, "If I could even try to explain, I would."

Annoyed at his ambiguous response, Liv pushed for some explanation. She concentrated on just stating the facts and refused to let herself cry.

"You lied to. And told me you were going to school across the country." Her voice wavered, so Liv took a deep breath, determined to continue, "Was that because you just needed an excuse to break up?"

Hayden stared at the ground, clenching his jaw.

Infuriated, Liv pressed on. "Couldn't you have just said 'I don't love you anymore?' Don't I deserve more of an explanation?"

Her soul was open, vulnerable; Liv was putting everything out there, again, but Hayden's silence was enough of an answer for her, and she didn't need him to say it aloud, she did not want him to. Liv had spent the last four months accepting his silence, already believing that it was over, but had just refused to accept it.

But, now she knew.

Feeling herself on the verge of tears, Liv looked away. "Don't answer that–it doesn't matter anymore."

She headed toward the doorway when Hayden grabbed her suddenly, turning Liv back into him, and lifted her head so she was forced to look into his eyes.

"That's not true." Hayden searched anxiously in her eyes, almost as if trying to communicate something through his gaze. Hayden clearly wanted to say something, but held back. He let go of her, knowing she would stay.

Bowing his head guiltily, he admitted, "I did lie." He looked up at Liv, pleading forgiveness. "But because I had to, not because I wanted to…" He caught himself, stopping in mid-sentence.

Liv wanted to see if he would continue, but instead Hayden just took a deep breath and looked at her. "Just, be careful, Oll–" he stopped himself, starting over again. "This campus isn't safe for you, I don't want you to get hurt."

Furious, Liv blurted out, crying, "Why do you even *care*!? And why do you have your friends following me around!?"

Hayden just looked at her, imploring her to understand. "I can't tell you. I'm sorry."

Liv was beyond self-control at this moment. She had four months of anger pent up that had just been waiting to explode, and now that she was finally facing her desired target, it had all shot to the surface, a blood battle that would not allow any survivors.

"We're not together anymore. You're not allowed to *care* anymore! I'm not *yours* anymore so stop having your friends follow me around!" She realized she was shouting, tears streaming from her eyes, but she didn't care. She had wanted to scream since she got to this goddamn school and even more so after she saw Hayden with that blonde bitch.

But then, witnessing the genuinely hurt expression on Hayden's face, radiating masochistic pain, she felt bad about her outburst. He still felt like hers, and she still cared for him too much, so she didn't like seeing him suffer. Liv was sure Hayden felt the same about her, even if he didn't love her anymore.

Liv heard more thunder and lightning–but noticed the rain was combating the tree's fire, slowly diminishing the flame that resulted from the earlier strike. Nonetheless, it did not look friendly outside, insinuating a very powerful storm to come through.

She took a deep breath, wanting so badly to run into Hayden's arms for comfort, but Liv knew she couldn't anymore–there was no point in seeking comfort in the person who was causing the pain you were looking to heal.

Looking down at her sneakers and shifting her weight between each foot, Liv was slowly becoming more exhausted from the night's events.

Quietly, almost just to herself, Liv muttered, "I just wish you would have spared me the pain of coming to this school, where the whole foundation of this place reminds me of you. And now that I know you're here," she paused, grasping for every bit of strength that she could bolster, continued, "just, try to pretend that I'm not, okay? And I'll do the same. Like you wanted."

Hayden eyes saddened, "I don't want to pretend you don't exist, Ollie. You're the best thing I have in this life."

He went to hold her hand, but Liv flinched. She was still a little upset about Finn–*god, what the hell would she do in their next class together?*

Finally registering what Hayden had said before he tried to touch her, all Liv could say back was a correction.

"Had." She stated blankly, without emotion.

She looked up at Hayden, with everything she could give him–love, happiness, support, kindness, and added softly, "But do you want it again?"

He immediately went toward her, swiftly pulling her into his arms like she was his lifeline.

"God Ollie, I want to." He hugged her harder, "I want you so badly."

Then, too soon, he released her and pushed her away. Hayden angrily turned his head away from Liv, adding with confirmation, "But we can't."

Liv froze. The soul that had just encompassed her body suddenly turned into ice. She turned her back to him, and immediately responded, "Okay."

She couldn't believe what she just did–that she had just accepted it and pulled herself further away so willingly, feeling numb but oddly at peace with her reality.

Liv felt tired from all that happened tonight. She was just hoping to have this one last resolved moment with Hayden to remember.

"Well, I better go." She went to open her the door, but then recalled one last favor she needed to ask Hayden to feel safer. "Can you have Rei or any of your other friends stop following me around?"

Hayden looked stunned, but avoided the question, only responding with another question. "How do you know Rei's name?"

Liv wasn't getting anywhere with Hayden tonight. Giving up, she finally opened her building door and without looking back, responded, "I suppose the same way he knows my name is Ollie."

She let the door close behind her, trying with all of her power to keep walking forward and away from Hayden, as the tears poured from her eyes.

And with that finality of their situation, Liv accepted that tonight–she needed to succumb to the darkness.

SIX

Liv finally fell asleep, dreaming of her and Hayden together—nothing in particular, just the two of them, sitting by a fire near campus. It was nice, the peace of just being together. Comforted in his warm arms, Liv sighed happily as Hayden kissed the top of her head in her make believe land.

A burst of lightning penetrated in front of them, forcing Liv to open her eyes and gasp back to reality.

Peyton had opened the blinds in their room, emerging sunlight directly onto Liv's face.

"Rise and shine, sleepyhead!" Peyton smirked, running over and handing her a coffee.

Liv squinted her eyes, taking the cup, but secretly hated, and wondered, when her roommate had become such a morning person. She rolled herself up in her bed, mildly groaning—her body was seemingly limp with excruciating soreness, and her head pounded from the rush in movement.

"Who put glitter in your step this morning?" Liv mumbled sarcastically as Peyton gave her a disapproving glare. Liv then noticed Peyton's hair was again significantly lighter than the prior week.

"Another highlight sesh? Looks good. Thanks for the coffee." Liv added, pacifying her roommate—she figured she should stay in Peyton's good graces and not let her decaffeinated monster deteriorate the only friendship she had left on campus.

Taking her first sip, Liv relaxed, the warm beverage immediately soothing her headache.

"Did I already thank you for the coffee? But really, thanks–this is a lifesaver."

"What happened to you?" Peyton sat on her bed, concernedly studying Liv from across the room.

Liv took a deep breath, rolling her eyes at the thought of explaining the previous night. "Honestly? You wouldn't even believe me if I told you."

Peyton stood up and walked over to Liv's bed, sitting down cross-legged with her coffee in hand, the other kindly placed on Liv's knee.

"Well try anyway, sister–I ain't got all day." Peyton smiled, eyes sparkling as they warmingly invited Liv to start her story.

Liv took a deep breath. Peyton had done nothing but be unconditionally kind, bring Liv coffee every morning to welcome the day and serve as her personal alarm clock, and truly seemed to care about her well-being. It was time to bring her roommate fully up to speed.

"Well, Finn tried to put a move on me last night, after our volleyball game."

Peyton seemed wary, as if she could already tell Liv was not into him. "He did? What happened?"

"Well, I tried to let him down easily, but then… things got aggressive." Liv gulped, unaware at how tense she had gotten remembering all the details.

"Are you okay?" Peyton eyes genuinely looked concerned, as if expecting the worst.

"Oh, yeah–I'm fine. Just a little bruised," Liv automatically hugged herself, as if trying now to protect the body she couldn't the night before.

"I am so sorry."

"Well, it would have been worst, but then Hayden showed up."

"Hayden showed up?!" Peyton's eyes went wide–it was as if she was more emotionally tied to this story than Liv. "What did he do!?"

"Nothing." Liv said hurtfully, remembering how they left each other last night. She looked up at Peyton, realizing her friend was about to burst with anticipation, so quickly added, "I mean, he got rid of Finn, but then we talked and…"

Liv sniffled, realizing just how much she needed somebody to talk to. She had been keeping this entire ordeal to herself for so long, she just needed to say it aloud.

"I can't help feel like an idiot." Liv took a deep breath and wiped her tears, looking back up at Peyton, "I mean, I saw him with another girl last weekend! I don't even know what I was thinking–I just thought that maybe there was a sliver of a chance that he still wanted me. Now, I've had my hard knocking dose of reality."

Peyton immediately interjected, understanding they were about to go into a dark territory. "Boys are weird. They never want to settle in college–he's probably just playing his rounds but obviously still cares about you. C'mon! You, my friend, are SUCH a catch!… AND, you play volleyball!" Peyton paused and chuckled before noticing Liv looked even more hurt at the mockery, so took a deep breath to explain. "Sorry, I just realized I don't actually know that much about you, come to think of it. Are you even good at volleyball?"

Liv quietly smiled, taking another sip of her coffee, "Quite good, actually."

At least she was starting to feel better–Liv honestly didn't know what she would have done without her unique roommate.

Peyton grinned, genuinely happy she could make Liv feel better. "Well, I suppose I need to come to your next game then and see for myself."

Peyton decided to go to Liv's astronomy class with her, expecting to see Finn and didn't want Liv to be alone for the first encounter. At first, Liv insisted it wouldn't be a big deal, that she could handle it, but as Liv approached the astronomy lecture hall, she began to appreciate Peyton's pressing support, feeling a little weak at the thought of facing Finn again.

But, when they sat down for the beginning of class, Finn was nowhere in sight.

"Serves him right." Peyton scowled, opening her notebook.

"You're actually going to take notes?" Liv raised her eyebrow, surprised at her roommate's dedication to a class that she wasn't enrolled in.

"Hey, I'm here, right? Might as well learn something." Peyton shrugged, with a hint of a smile on her face.

The following week, Peyton loyally remained at Liv's side, persistent that she go nowhere alone. After the first day, Liv was grateful, but after a couple more days without solitude, she realized it was hindering her attention span to search for Rei on campus.

Liv hadn't seen him all week, and although she didn't exactly want a reminder of Hayden per se, she couldn't help to hope she'd run into him because he was the only connector with her ex-boyfriend left, and maybe now that he knew Hayden's attendance was no longer a secret, he'd be willing to talk to her for an actual conversation.

And yes, she knew she was acting desperate, but she figured she'd throw herself a bone and let it pass for the time being–she could judge herself next week after she had recovered from the past week's crazy rollercoaster that she had been on.

By Friday, her hopes had diminished completely of seeing Rei when he was again a no-show in the lecture they had together. Liv figured he must have dropped the class, only because he was so adamant about making up his missed class the previous week. Finn also didn't attend either, which relieved Liv and gave her hope that she could return to a normal college experience, whatever that might be for her.

As the professor wrapped up the last class on Friday, Liv could feel Peyton's excitement, dreading what she already knew Peyton would propose for the night.

"I think tonight calls for dancing." Peyton looked over at Liv, smiling.

"I think tonight calls for wine and a murder mystery." Liv retaliated, although after almost experiencing a murder mystery of her own with Finn, the idea sounded less appealing.

"And by wine and a murder mystery, I'm sure you mean Fireball and a bar. Plus, it's Halloween Weekend!" Peyton stopped in front of Liv, raising her clenched hands up in front of her, jokingly pleading. "Please, please, please, please?" Then Peyton added sternly, "We need this. You know we need this."

Liv laughed, "Halloween isn't until Tuesday and since when do I dictate your social life? Don't you have sorority sisters who would be eager for a night out?"

Peyton shrugged, waving their hand off unimpressed as she muttered, "They prefer house parties."

That reminded Liv of the girl at Volleyball, "I actually ran into a sorority sister of yours–she plays on my volleyball team. Jaycie…? Does that ring a bell?"

Peyton looked caught off-guard, for once, not responding immediately.

"What did she say?" Peyton asked apprehensively.

"Nothing really." Liv shrugged, "She didn't recognize your name but mentioned your pledge class is pretty large."

"Yeah–her name doesn't ring a bell either… I'll introduce myself at our next meeting."

"Oh, crap." Liv remembered her promise to Jaycie. "Don't tell her I told you about volleyball. She didn't want you guys to know she ditches your Monday meetings."

Peyton looked a little relieved, "Your secret is totally safe with me. Now, what are *we* going to wear when *we* go out tonight? Costumes to fit in, or normal clothes to stand out?"

Oxymoron aside, Peyton was back to her normal self, determined and persistent with getting her way.

Liv and Peyton were at their favorite spot on the dance floor, and Liv hated admitting that Peyton was right (per usual). She just needed to blow off steam, dance mindlessly and ultimately have a great time tonight.

Peyton knew how and when to fight her battles, so tonight Liv got away with wearing all black–a crop top blouse, high wasted destroyed pair of jeans and her favorite booties–donning no color aside from a bright red lip, and she felt great.

Peyton on the other hand, went with a 90s goth look, wearing a dark burgundy velvet top, a wine lip color and a black leather skirt, topped off with fierce combat boot and a black choker.

Liv was about to head over to the bar to order another drink, when she spotted the blonde bitch she saw Hayden with the week before, talking to a guy. Liv initially froze, wanting to leave right away, but also needed to study this woman and understand her appeal to Hayden, so spied on her while the blonde bitch flirted at the bar.

She looked harmless enough, but Liv had to admit the girl just naturally put out a bitchy vibe. She was tall, with a permanent smirk and dark, judgmental eyes. And Liv could tell, even just from how she was interacting with her friend, or potential date–whoever the poor guy was–she was bad blood. Liv rolled her eyes, turning herself away, but couldn't help but look back, still curious.

The blonde girl was wearing a very low cut top, the slit in front almost going down to where her shirt tucked into her pant, but strategically had an "x" of string connecting both sides to her chest, keeping the entire blouse from falling apart. Liv hated herself for thinking the long-sleeved shirt looked chic, but observed it looked expensive and felt better with the justification that anyone with brains would *never* wear a pricey top to a college bar. At that, the blonde bitch ran her hands through her hair, almost purposely showing off her beautiful gold bangles, letting them appear and sparkle on her wrist.

With one last internal gag, Liv figured it was time to go. She walked away (proudly) looking for Peyton, but realized that telling her roommate why she was leaving would be embarrassing enough, and Peyton would never actually let her go on that note. So instead, Liv darted for the exit, shooting a quick text as she left the bar.

HEY! I'M HEADING BACK–HAVE FUN! SEE YOU
LATER. J

As Liv walked through campus, she began feeling on edge, seeing only darkness aside from the dimly lit lampposts–a very similar scene that reminded her of Monday night.

She shook it off, justifying that she was drunk, so was just being paranoid and that it must be the alcohol thinking. But Liv still clenched onto her phone a little tighter for reassurance.

Liv heard a gush of tree branches being thwarted by movement, immediately witnessing black birds flying overhead toward her dorm.

And when she glanced ahead again, she saw Rei.

He was just standing in the middle of the pathway, almost as if waiting for her.

Liv felt like she should be terrified, creeped out, or scared at the idea of him and her alone on campus together, but truthfully, at the sight of him, she felt relief.

"You missed astronomy class again," Liv muttered as she walked toward him, waiting for him to make an excuse and run away.

But instead, Rei just smiled, like there was an inside joke he was enjoying to himself. "Yeah, I'm not sure astronomy is really my thing."

As Liv passed Rei without stopping, he chased after her, shocked.

"Hey, where are you heading?" He jogged after her. "You really shouldn't be walking alone at this hour."

Liv kept walking, continuing her path back home. She was actually surprised he was voluntarily following her for once.

"Did Hayden send you to serve as my babysitter for the night?" She asked accusingly, picking up her pace.

"If he did, I wouldn't tell you," Rei responded curtly. He also sped up, finally catching up to Liv and walking by her side.

"*Hmph.*" Liv rolled her eyes.

They walked in silence for a while, making Liv wonder if Rei had ever conducted a civil conversation with a girl before.

Well, at least he was walking with her, instead of running away. Baby steps.

"So, how do you like Oregon?" Tipsy, Liv decided to extend a branch, "Or, are you from here?"

Rei kept looking around–not really paying attention to Liv, but mindlessly responded, "Not from here and don't really care for Oregon. Let's go."

Rei picked up the pace, forcing Liv into an awkward power walk-jog combo. Four steps power walk, four steps jog, six steps power walk, four steps jog and so on...

She couldn't help glance at Rei during the power walk portion of her steps, wondering how a guy so gorgeous could be so peculiar and socially awkward. Sporting an olive green satin bomber jacket and denim jeans, he wasn't even dressed in costume! But then again, technically neither was she.

"Why did you come here then? If you don't mind me asking." Liv wanted to get to know Rei, at least figure him out and learn his story. She also tried to ignore her pleading desire to understand how he knew Hayden, too.

Rei slowed down, looking at Liv with a confused look.

Liv continued, cautiously, "I mean, you're not from Oregon, nor are you particularly a fan of the state, so why are you here?"

"Oh," Rei picked up his pace again, adding, "Duty–I suppose."

He looked at Liv, studying her curiously. Rei then shook his head, releasing whatever thought was in his mind and gently touched her back, pushing her forward to keep up his pace.

When they arrived at an intersection with her residence hall in sight, Rei paused, and to Liv's disappointment, looked relieved.

"You're close enough to your dorm–you should be safe now."

Taking advantage of their stop while she could, Liv dug through her purse for her building key, but when she looked back up to thank him, Rei was gone.

Talk about a spooky Halloween tale.

It was as if her kneepads were calling to her.

Lying on her bed, Liv had been staring at them for the better part of an hour, debating whether she should go to her volleyball game tonight.

Before the whole Finn thing happened, Liv actually had a great time–the first time she had enjoyed herself (without alcohol) in college. But on the other hand, Finn might be there.

And Peyton had already promised to skip her weekly sorority meeting to come in support, but Liv still wasn't sure if she was ready to face Finn–it was easier pretending he didn't exist.

Liv knew she couldn't run away from Finn forever–and it might be better to encounter him with witnesses and Peyton by her side. Eventually she was sure she would see him again–for example, there were only so many coffee shops on campus (and really, only one good one worth visiting).

Liv continued staring at her kneepads, considering all the what-ifs and worst-case scenarios when Peyton entered the room.

"Um, what are you doing?"

Peyton came over and lowered herself to desk level.

"What are we watching?" Peyton asked, staring at the kneepads in unison with Liv.

Liv looked at Peyton, then back at the kneepads.

Peyton stood up. "I hate to burst your bubble, but even if you stare hard enough, I don't think you'll be able to get them to move or evaporate. Not my fault, just law of physics, sorry."

Liv rolled her eyes, sitting herself up.

"I was just second-guessing going tonight and was hoping my kneepads could give me a sign."

"And?" Peyton inquired.

"Apparently kneepads don't do that sort of thing, either." Liv turned to Peyton, who was brushing her hair at her desk. "Should I go? Or quit the team?"

Peyton stopped brushing, "Do you want to be a scared hermit for the rest of your life? Or do you actually want to enjoy yourself?"

She had a good point. Liv grabbed her kneepads.

"Okay, let's go. Now. Before I change my mind." Liv ran out of the dorm, determined, with Peyton immediately at her toes.

They walked over to the Student Recreation Center, and Liv took a deep breath as they opened the door into the volleyball court. She immediately saw Jaycie, who gave her a friendly wave.

"That's your sorority sister," Liv nodded to Jaycie, waving back. "Want me to introduce you?"

"Nah, no need." Peyton shrugged, "It's one thing to tell me she skips our meeting for this game, but you actually inviting me to come visit as a witness, I don't think it'll fly well. Best we stay unintroduced for the time-being."

Peyton pointed to the bleachers, "I'll just be over there. Cheering loudly for my girl." And with a clap yelled, "Go team!" as she straightened her arms into a perfect cheerleader 'V'.

"Oh god." Liv rolled her eyes laughing and then ran over to Jaycie to get ready for the game.

Liv didn't spot Finn anywhere in sight as the team walked onto the court for the start of the game. She was still on edge, but as soon as the first player served the ball, her mind turned to only focus on the game.

This time, she relished in spiking the ball, imagining it was Hayden's head or Finn's face, which proved to be an immediately cathartic therapy outlet. Liv was on fire–she served three aces and four point-winning spikes just in her first rotation, but when she went in for her second round of serves, she heard a faint, "Ollie!" almost as if she could hear a conversation in the bleachers. She shook her head, assuming she imagined the noise, so compelled herself to concentrate on the game. She aced another serve, the ball landing right between two guys (who were too busy checking out their female teammates asses than the ball to react quickly enough).

Her team ran up to her, cheering her on, but then Liv heard another faint, "Go Ollie!" to her right, so she turned her head to the sound and looked up into the bleachers to find Hayden cheering and sitting next to Rei in the top row.

Liv was furious, so made it her goal to end the game as quickly as possible and get the hell out of there. Instead of alternating point-winning hits with assists for her team to participate like the week before, every ball opportunity that came near Liv resulted in a point won for her team. The second set passed quickly with the opposing team only scoring two points.

As soon as she scored the final point to win the game, Liv quickly said goodbyes to her teammates and abruptly ran outside, avoiding eye contact with the bleachers or anyone in that direction.

"Hey! Wait up!"

Liv stopped, completely forgetting that Peyton was there. She turned around to apologize, but froze when she saw Hayden and Rei right behind her roommate.

Hayden walked up to Liv, smiling as he congratulated her on a great game.

Liv just stared at Peyton, ignoring Hayden, and mentally tried to communicate to her roommate that she wanted to leave, now.

Hayden looked at Peyton and then back at Liv, eyes sparkling with humor.

Holding out his hand in front of Peyton, he introduced himself, "I'm Hayden. Who are you?"

Peyton rolled her eyes, giving Liv a secret pang of happiness.

"Peyton. I'm Liv's roommate. Nice to meet you." She extended her hand and shook Hayden's, giggling, and consequently giving Liv a pang of jealousy.

Of course Peyton would find Hayden charming and gorgeous–he was. But Liv was hoping Peyton would at least hold on to her attitude for a little bit longer.

Liv turned to Hayden accusingly. "What are you doing here?"

Hayden turned to back Liv. "I learned you joined a volleyball team, and I've never missed a game. So, here I am." He said it like it was an obvious explanation.

"You came to my game last week?" Liv asked, hopeful and shocked at the same time.

Nonchalantly, Hayden replied, "Of course I did." Then, with more appraisals continued energetically, "But, tonight your serve was on another level! What was it? Seven aces?!"

He playfully bumped Liv's side with his fist, but it was too friendly for Liv.

Angrily, Liv sniped back, "That was because I imagined the ball as your head." Then turning to Peyton and blatantly ignoring Hayden's reaction, said, "Let's go."

Peyton and Liv were midway to their dorm when Liv noticed black birds circling over them. They were sweeping in closer, and then Liv noticed black shadows within the mix.

Unexpectedly, Peyton ran in front of her, arms out–as if trying to protect Liv.

"Ollie! Stand back!" Peyton yelled, pushing Liv back into a tree with force.

Liv was shocked that Peyton had just called her Ollie, but before she could process it, a black blur crashed into her, propelling her against another tree.

Recovering from the collision, Liv looked up, seeing lightning across the lawn, but soon became dizzier, lost her balance and collapsed into the ground.

Liv saw flashes of light, bringing herself back to consciousness. Finally opening her eyes, Liv tried to work out what was happening in front of her. When her eyes finally focused, she screamed. Finn was standing in front of her.

"Well, well, look who it is." Finn maliciously smiled, "Arlo! She's over here!" He grabbed her arm and pulled her up. Liv could make out Peyton across the lawn, being held by another guy in dark clothes, struggling to escape.

"PEYTON!" Liv screamed, trying to loosen Finn's grasp so she could save her friend.

"I'M OKAY!" Peyton squeaked, trying to sound assuring. But, then the guy, Arlo, kicked her in the stomach to shut her up.

"Liv, Liv, Liv–what on earth shall we do with you?" Finn laughed. He put his hand to her cheek, a mocking smile plastered across his face. "All I wanted was to conduct a test. One that you succeeded in, yet failed so miserably. One where I was left with nothing, but also everything I ever needed. And, if only you had kissed me, you may have been in such a different place than you are now."

Finn tightened his grip on Liv, bringing her arm up to his throat. He kissed her hand and then pulled her to him. "Now, let's finished what we started."

As soon as he went to kiss her, she heard a faint, "OLLIE NO!" but before Finn's lips could touch hers, Liv felt a huge impact–causing her to fly back and abruptly hit the ground.

Mind cloudy from the impact, Liv hazily looked up to see a tall blonde guy, amidst fireworks, fighting her enemy, before she closed her eyes and lost consciousness.

SEVEN

Liv rolled over in bed, immediately cringing as her body retaliated with soreness and shot bursts of pain throughout, so she fell limp. Then, after assessing and accepting the huge headache she currently had, Liv softly felt around, realizing she had too much space surrounding her body than her dormitory bed would ever allow.

Liv opened one eye, shocked that even that small movement ached. She looked around to find herself laying in a serenely decorated room, beautiful and perfect to her taste. But she was right; it was definitely not her dorm.

Liv slowly turned her head to the left, careful not to strain her neck, and saw a bouquet of White Anemones on top of a simple cedar bed stand, accompanied by two aspirin, a glass of water and note that said, "Take me."

Determined to pacify the pain, Liv slowly pulled herself to an upright position, extending her left arm for the aspirin and glass.

After painfully swallowing the aspirin (and discovering her throat was sore, too), she looked around the room, trying to figure out where she was.

The entire room was cream and white, with light cedar furniture and soft gold accents. To her right, the most stunning antique armoire Liv had ever seen, and directly across her bed, a beautiful white brick fireplace, adorned with candles and bordered by a cozy sitting area. On the couch, Liv spotted her dark purple velvet pillow from the dorms, which perfectly matched a bouquet of Prairie Gentian and Lavender, placed opposite the fireplace.

When she turned toward the window to her left, letting her eyes adjust to the brightness, she found a desk and was surprised to see the office chair occupied by Hayden, whose head was resting on his arms, asleep.

Taking advantage of the peaceful moment, Liv studied him, watching for any sign of who he was now. His skin was smooth as caramel, gold hair perfectly waved–she always loved his hair–and his lips a soft light pink, forming the perfect kissable pout. Liv had never overlooked how handsome Hayden was, but in that moment, she realized she had forgotten just how *beautiful* he was, too. She studied his muscular arms and chiseled abs–easily visible through the white shirt he wore.

Liv sighed, because to *her*, Hayden was perfect.

She tried to set down her water glass quietly, but Hayden woke up in response to the subtle clinking sound.

Rushing over to Liv's bed and sitting down, Hayden asked, "How are you feeling?"

Liv automatically touched her head, wishing she had ice for the part of her brain that ached from processing the words. Luckily, her hand felt cold enough, so she let it sit there for a moment.

"I've been better." Liv slowly relaxed herself against her headboard. "Where am I? Is Peyton okay?"

"Peyton's fine. And Puerdios University." Hayden responded, shrugging, "Also known as where I go to college."

That caught Liv's attention. Now alert and fighting her headache, Liv focused, needing an explanation.

"Wait, you go here? Where even is Puerdios? I've never heard of it."

Hayden sighed, "It's hard to explain."

Liv eyed him, demanding that he continue; but between the silence, the two heard a subtle cough from outside.

Hayden looked over to the door, eyebrows furrowing. Then he relaxed, turning back to Liv. "I don't have time to tell you everything right now. I'm not even supposed to be here, but," he gently lifted his hand to move some hair out of Liv's eyes, "I just had to make sure you were okay, Ollie."

Hayden's touch felt so good, all Liv wanted him to do was stay and comfort her in his arms.

Another cough interrupted the moment.

"That's Rei, I've got to go." Hayden stood up.

"Rei is here too?!" Liv shrieked, looking at the door.

Hayden turned back to Liv and whispered, "I'll be back. Rei will be outside if you need anything, but you have nothing to worry about. Just rest."

Hayden walked toward the door, nonchalantly adding, "Oh, and your stuff is here, too." He pointed to the boudoir, "You didn't have much aside from clothes in your dorm, but it's all there."

Liv slightly started to panic as Hayden continued toward the door. "Wait! Hayden–how long am I supposed to *stay here?*"

Hayden didn't turn fully toward Liv, but only looked half way back and instead stared at the ground, "Only temporarily." His voice was quiet and sad, but affirmative.

He walked out and shut the door before Liv could ask any more questions.

She instinctively ran after Hayden, but halted as soon as a piercing bolt of pain struck her skull. Upon recovering from the shock, Liv determinedly ran to the door, opening it until she heard Hayden talking to Rei.

"She's resting. Don't let her out of your sight, or let her leave this room until I come back."

"Of course." Rei confirmed.

Liv's heart began pounding, anger boiling through her chest. She refused to be somebody's prisoner–it was the 21st century! And besides that, there was no way she'd be *Hayden's* prisoner.

He hadn't talked to her in four months, and then suddenly Hayden appeared and could start controlling her life? He had no right!

Liv ran to her bed, grabbing a pillow and throwing it across the room.

The exertion caused her head to throb again, so Liv threw herself angrily head first into her remaining pillow and screamed.

Rei ran into the room immediately, frantically looking around while asking, "Are you okay?!"

Liv rolled over on her bed, facing him, slightly embarrassed. "Uh, considering the circumstances, I guess so."

He looked under her bed, explaining, "I heard thunder and lightning, and I thought I heard you scream?"

Liv turned a brighter shade of red, as she looked outside the window at the rainstorm, refusing to make eye contact with Rei as she answered, "You did."

Rei was awkwardly fidgeting, looking below her desk, around the couch and various nooks and crannies throughout the room. "I thought he would be here…" Rei mumbled to himself, dumbfounded.

"He? Who's he?" Liv asked inquisitively.

Rei stood up straight, stiff as a board, frozen.

"I've said too much. And clearly you're fine. I'm going back out there. So you can stay in here, alone. Ok? Okay." Rei ran out and shut the door.

Liv laid back down, still confused, but much more calm. All of the commotion she had just experienced began to affect her, and she started feeling drowsy.

Closing her eyes, Liv slowly fell asleep, dreaming of Hayden.

Liv woke up in the middle of the night. Noticing that she didn't have covers on, but still felt warm, Liv realized there was a body next to hers. But, instead of panicking, Liv felt comforted.

She turned over to see Hayden sleeping beside her, radiating light.

The moon made his hair look brighter, his skin radiating a warm glow.

He smiled as he opened his eyes, and whispered "Hi," sending chills through Liv's entire body.

Even his eyes were bluer, clearer in the light, and his perfectly fitted shirt added to his entire desirability.

"Hi."

Liv smiled back, shyly. Why did Hayden always have this effect on her?

"How are you feeling?"

"Better."

Liv yearned to reach out to Hayden, to grab his hand or touch him in some way. But she held herself back.

Hayden felt the same connection, holding his breath, and then sat up playfully. "So, I'm sure you have some questions for me. Now is probably the best time for you to ask them."

Still recovering from their intimate moment and from the shock of him being so close, Liv couldn't even grasp where to begin. She had so many questions she had wanted to ask him all summer, and even more questions to ask him from recent events. But, Liv figured she should start with a simple question, possibly the easiest one, first.

"So, you go here, Puerdios University."

Hayden nodded.

"How far away is it from Oregon?"

Hayden grinned, "Pretty far, but it's not easily found by… mortals." His jaw tensed at that word.

Mortals?

"Okay, so I'm far away from where I'm supposed to be." Liv gulped, taking a deep breath. Trying to distract herself, she quickly added, "What are you studying here?"

Hayden relaxed, "Political Science, I suppose you would call it."

Deep down, this small talk was killing Liv. It seemed too formal, and yet so familiar at the same time.

"Why am I here, Hayden?" She finally blurted out.

Hayden shifted in the bed. "Well, you weren't safe at your campus. Finn proved that, twice, despite our security measures. So, we brought you here."

The mention of Finn brought back all of those memories from the night before to Liv's conscious.

Liv slowly got up, trying to distract herself by pacing across the room and fighting her sore body's retaliation to the undesired movements.

"How do you know Finn? And *why* is he out to get me?" Liv made her way over to the window, looking out.

The sight she found was breathtaking. Her room overlooked a beautiful courtyard, surrounded by a medieval castle structure, stunningly lit with silver and gold candles, emitting a warm glow throughout each window. The whole effect gave the view an iridescent, twinkling sight. So serene, it instantly calmed Liv.

After her momentary distraction, she turned back to Hayden, ready for an explanation.

"Well, that's where it gets complicated to explain." Hayden got up and walked over to Liv, grabbing her hand and turning her toward him, asking cautiously, "Do you trust me?"

"Of course I do," Liv confirmed, and then added, "However, the topic of liking you is up for debate." Liv cracked a weak smile, but Hayden remained serious.

He took a deep breath, pausing and looking for truth, for some form of assurance in Liv's eyes. After a deciding nod, he let go and turned away. "The thing is, Liv–in my world, there are Pure Gods and Dark Gods."

Hayden peeked over his shoulder to gauge Liv's reaction.

Liv, in return, was trying to determine if she was in shock–wondering if her brain mentally had compounded from whatever the hell happened the night before, whether she had misheard him, or if he was playing a very bizarre joke on her.

But Liv agreed internally that she felt fine, her ears hadn't let her down before, and the expression on Hayden's face did not look that of a jokester.

"I'm sorry, did you say *Gods*?"

Hayden nodded, studying her, assessing her reaction.

"Like Poseidon and Hades?"

Hayden chuckled, "Not exactly, or anymore at least. Our lineage does trace back to many of the Greek Gods, but the myths you know don't really give our ancestor's justice."

Liv looked around her room, not sure what to think. It looked so normal. She turned back to Hayden; he was glowing in the moonlight, similar to the iridescent castle.

"Are you a God?" Liv swallowed, trying to process the idea.

Hayden could see her struggle with the idea, and looked down, ashamed, before he quietly said, "Yes."

"And you didn't think once to tell me?! We were only best friends for seven years!" Liv threw her hands in the air, frustrated with another lie.

Hayden looked back up, guilt written all over his face. "I couldn't. It's forbidden."

When Liv said nothing, Hayden ran over and gently turned her toward him. "Plus, it didn't matter then."

"It didn't matter then? Well, it bloody matters now!" Liv was riled up—she wanted to punch something.

"Liv," Hayden tried to pacify the situation, choosing his next words carefully. "Gods don't get their powers until they're eighteen. So really, I would have been lying if I said I was a God, then."

"Is that why you could go to school with 'mortals?'" Liv asked, mockingly emphasizing the word 'mortals' with finger quotes.

"Yes, but, only some Gods are able to live among mortals, temporarily. It's a part of our education—"

"Oh, okay. Education. Of course!" Liv was being dramatic, but she didn't care. "Well, was Finn a part of that program?" Saying his name now seemed all the more terrifying; her body was beginning to shake.

Hayden opened his mouth, looking wounded, as if stabbed. "Finn? Oh God no, Ollie." Hayden ran over to Liv and wrapped her in his warm, muscular arms. "This is all my fault. I'm so sorry."

Liv almost lost her train of thought; it felt so comforting to be held by Hayden. Secure. Safe.

"Why is he trying to hurt me?" Liv finally let her vulnerability seep through, taking a deep breath, which resulted in continuous sniffles, the effects of the past week finally catching up to her.

Hayden sighed, giving her an assuring squeeze, and then loosened his hold a bit.

"Like I said, not all Gods are good."

He let her go and stepped back.

Liv felt cold, yearning for him to come back and fill the space he had created between them.

Hayden sat on the bed, patting a spot next to him and encouraging Liv to sit down. When Liv remained standing, he sighed and continued.

"It's mostly politics. Some Gods believe in certain things–how things should be run, structured–and others think differently. Finn falls in the category opposite of myself, my family. We call them the Dark Gods–they aren't necessarily always bad, they just have different viewpoints."

Liv started to feel queasy, so she opted to sit on the bed after all, but kept a distance between Hayden and her.

Hayden continued, "To my knowledge, one Dark God–an extremist, I guess–has been trying to infiltrate the system, attract supporters to ultimately gain control and power over the Gods. To overthrow the Pure Gods." Hayden paused, cautiously looking at Liv before proceeding.

"We suspect he wants to use you as leverage for negotiation, or worse, a decoy to start a war."

Liv's jaw dropped.

"Me?" She questioned, perplexed at the enormity of everything and so confused by her involvement in any of it. "But why do I have any value to him, to anyone, in all of this?"

Hayden instinctively drew toward her, putting his forehead to hers. Liv wanted him to say because he loved her, because he needed her, because she was the most important thing in the world to him. She felt it; she knew it already, but needed him to say it.

But when Hayden opened his mouth, he paused, and then moved away. His eyebrows furrowed together again, the look he always gave when he was debating too much in his head, and stayed where he was, just staring at her–his face becoming a blank slate before he answered.

"No idea."

Two words. That's all it took for Liv's insides to completely crumble, again–and yet, the process was equally as painful as the first time, if not more.

Liv sat on her bed, unsure of what to say.

Hayden started for the door, knowing it was time to leave.

Do not let him see you cry. Liv thought to herself, willing herself to hold it all in.

Before opening the door, Hayden turned back to Liv, "I told you more than you are ever supposed to know, but before I leave–do you have any more questions?"

Liv just stared. As if this was all a dream and it was the last time she would ever see Hayden again. She stared into his beautiful, piercing blue eyes, noticing again the way his blonde hair so perfectly waved to the side, how his shirt sculpted his toned torso and accentuated his strong arms–was his being a God the reason why he was so irresistible to her?

But that was the least of Liv's worries, now.

She bit her lip. "You mentioned Poseidon–God of the Sea, and Hades–God of the Underworld, that they actually existed. If that's the case, what God are you of? Er–I mean, what's your responsibility?"

Hayden looked at Liv, first her wounded but memorizing eyes, then sadly down to her entire body, nostalgically thinking of the wonderful times they had before he changed, before everything had changed. He bowed his head down, defeated, knowing that they could never be anymore.

"It doesn't matter."

Then he turned around and left.

Liv couldn't wrap her head around everything. She continued staring at the door, almost in a daze, trying to process it all. When she finally lay down, she felt a tear trickle down her cheek, and soon, her crying resembled the rain outside: pouring and relentless.

EIGHT

Liv wasn't sure when she finally fell asleep, but a knock on her door in the morning startled her awake to a sunlit room.

"Rise and shine, sleepyhead!"

The voice sounded familiar enough to force Liv out of her bed and sluggishly walk over to open the door.

Peyton pushed the door wide open after the handle had barely turned, startling Liv as she gracefully stormed through the room.

"Well, this is certainly an upgrade from our dorm room now, isn't it?" She smirked.

Peyton spun around to get a better view of the room. She was holding two coffees.

Liv was shocked, surprised and so grateful to see her friend. "You're here?"

"Not exactly. I don't go to Puerdios anymore… I graduated a while ago." Peyton shrugged, guilt radiating from her conscious.

"Wait, you're a God, too?!" Liv couldn't have been more blindsided, realizing everyone she had befriended weren't even students at her actual college. She turned away, unable to comprehend how her world had just completely turned into complete bullshit.

"Yes, but–"

Peyton suddenly remembered she brought coffee, strategically holding out a cup in front of Liv, attempting to pacify her.

"Before you get mad at me, I'm here with a peace offering." She extended the coffee further, with a hopeful smile.

At this point, Peyton was still Liv's only friend in this strange place, and that proved even more valuable now. Liv turned, glaring at Peyton while she contemplated accepting her apology, then figured it would be better not to dismiss her.

"Forgiven." Liv confirmed, grabbing the coffee immediately. "On one stipulation: please don't lie again. Everyone has been lying to me. And we're friends. Right?"

Peyton grinned. "Of course. From now on, no lies. But..." She lifted her hands up in surrender. "In full transparency, I may not always be able to tell you the full truth; however, with our newly found oath of friendship, I can just simply tell you that I am not allowed to tell you. Does that work?"

Liv was a little confused at the end, her head still aching from the attack on campus, but Peyton seemed genuine, so she gave in, shaking her head with a simple, "That works."

Almost instantaneously, both girls ran together to give one another a big hug. Liv had to admit; it was nice knowing just one person in this new world with whom she felt comfortable.

Once they left the embrace, Liv was able to fully appreciate Peyton's outfit, a complete 180 from her sorority girl campus look. In a white long sleeve mini dress beautifully embroidered in gold with sequins and bead detailing, she looked like a baroque masterpiece. Her hazel grey eyes sparkled and highlighted hair shone in the light, perfectly matching her chic gold embossed booties.

Liv looked at her silky silver slip dress, feeling very underdressed and exposed. She walked over to the boudoir, finding all of her clothes neatly folded and organized into different compartments.

Grabbing a chunky cream knit turtleneck, Liv put it on and asked, "So, why are you here exactly?"

"Security. I'm a God of the Warfare and Protection pillar–also known as the Security Pillar, but today," Peyton shot up her pointer finger in the air, proudly, "I'm here to make sure you're okay."

Liv nodded, tipping her coffee cup in Peyton's direction and grinning, as she jokingly said, "Now caffeinated, I think you're doing quite well with your job."

Peyton rolled her eyes. "I mean, I assumed you would be." She walked toward Liv excitedly, "But, more importantly, I'm here to give you a mini-orientation for your classes."

"My classes?" Liv didn't think she could become any more stunned, but she stood corrected. "How on earth would a school for the Gods have any curriculum even close to what's needed for my college degree?"

"You'd be surprised, actually." Peyton handed over a piece of paper. Liv looked at the typed schedule, impressed by the normalcy of subjects she was enrolled with.

ASTRONOMY
1 / 3 270* SR
NORTH TOWER

ENVIRONMENTAL SCIENCE
1 / 3 330* SR
HERBOLOGY WING 9A

HUMANITIES
1 / 3 60* SS
EAST AUDITORIUM

CHEMISTRY
2 / 4 270* SR
SOUTH TOWER BELOW LEVEL

LATIN
2 / 4 330*
ELITE MUSEO HALL

METEOROLOGY
2 / 4 60* SS
NORTH TOWER BELOW LEVEL

STUDY HALL
1 / 2 / 3 / 4 120* SS
GALLERIA LIBRARY

After further inspection and not understanding how her schedule translated, Liv felt more intimidated by her current situation and exactly what challenges may lay ahead.

Confused, Liv finally gave up trying to decipher the paper and asked, "Peyton, what does this numerical gibberish mean?"

"Oh!" Peyton ran over and snatched the schedule from her. "I cannot believe I forgot!" She scribbled on the paper. "I thought I was being so clever by not using roman numerals, I didn't even think! Also, where do you want your books? I'll write in the dates and times while they organize."

"Er—my desk works?" Liv searched around, trying to figure out where the books were in her room.

Peyton, head already bowed over the schedule and fervently writing, simply snapped her left finger and continued translating.

Suddenly, Liv's door opened, with a stack of books levitating through her room. Liv was in even more awe when the tower of large, old books hovered over her desk, and landed lightly on top, not making a sound.

"Did you just do that?" Liv asked, eyes wide.

Peyton smiled and shrugged. "That wasn't really anything, to be honest. Here," she handed over the schedule, her notes written neatly on the side, "It's quite simple actually. We just prefer numbers to words for scheduling, that's all."

Liv looked at Peyton, eyebrows raised.

"Our ancestors implemented it, so it stuck." Peyton sighed.

Leaning over, Peyton pointed to what she meant, explaining, "Monday is 1, and Tuesday is 2 and so on. We refer to time with the degree of the shadow cast when you point your finger north—SR just means sunrise and SS is sunset. So, at noon it's 0 degrees or 360 degrees–whatever you prefer. It's sort of like the debate 'of the glass being half empty or half full,' I guess."

Peyton looked outside the window, assessing the sun location. "You should be okay with those estimations for a while, but I'll work on getting you a digital clock to help with the moon and sun rotations–they're constantly changing, and nighttime might prove difficult with all of the clouds in the sky."

Liv looked back to her schedule, a little dumbfounded, but very appreciative of Peyton's translated notes.

ASTRONOMY
1 / 3 270* SR – Monday/Wednesday 9AM
NORTH TOWER

ENVIRONMENTAL SCIENCE
1 / 3 330* SR – Monday/Wednesday 11AM
HERBOLOGY WING 9A

HUMANITIES
1 / 3 60* SS – Monday/Wednesday 2PM
EAST AUDITORIUM

CHEMISTRY
2 / 4 270* SR – Tuesday / Thursday 9AM
SOUTH TOWER BELOW LEVEL

LATIN
2 / 4 330* SR – Tuesday / Thursday 11AM
ELITE MUSEO HALL

METEOROLOGY
2 / 4 60* SS – Tuesday / Thursday 2PM
NORTH TOWER BELOW LEVEL

STUDY HALL
1 / 2 / 3 / 4 120* SS – Monday–Thursday 4PM
GALLERIA LIBRARY

"I also added a map on the back, tada!" Peyton turned the paper over, amusingly showing off her helpful drawing. "That way you should be able to maneuver around without my assistance. But, of course anyone on campus can help you if you need it."

"You aren't going to stay?" Liv pleaded, instantly turning red at how desperate she sounded.

Luckily, Peyton just laughed.

"I'm sorry, do you want me to walk you to your first class like a child?" She smirked. "No, afraid I have to investigate some celestial oddities by Jupiter and report my findings to the Security Elite before the moon rises, so I have to leave soon, actually."

Liv lifted her eyebrows, not even beginning to try and process what she just heard. Peyton just laughed again.

"You'll get used to the lingo, eventually."

Liv felt like she had butterflies creeping up her throat.

Peyton walked over and put both hands on her old roommate's shoulders. "You'll be fine. Promise." After looking at the window once more, she turned back to Liv, "I have to go. You have about an hour until class."

Peyton turned toward the door.

"I'll be back! Don't have too much fun without me!"

And with that, Peyton was gone.

Liv sat on her bed, staring at her books. When she got a chill from a cool breeze, her fireplace automatically turned on, like her room knew she was cold. It was definitely going to take some time getting used to this place.

She walked back over to her armoire and opened it–contemplating what to wear for her first day of classes. *What did Gods typically wear?*

Liv eventually decided either way, she wanted to feel tough and strong, even if internally she was feeling anything but that. She pulled on her favorite black sweater, dark grey hoodie and favorite leather jacket.

Black is good. She put on her ink destroyed denim jeans and leather combat boots. Black was her preferred armor of color. She smiled, thinking of Peyton gasping at her choice of clothes.

She had never liked wearing much black before, but with the need for new clothes–not only because of the beyond freezing weather Oregon's winter provided (what she had used as leverage to convince her mom for a shopping spree), but every other item in her closet and colors she saw in stores always ended up reminding her of Hayden (what she didn't tell her mom). Black was the only color she could wear and still exist. So, black became her something new, her no tolerance for emotional bullshit, and her support in fighting the endless battle of simply getting on, even if it was accomplished without feeling.

Looking in the mirror, she was thankful her blonde hair was cooperating. She brushed it quickly and added a smoky eye. Once done debating if she should change into a completely different outfit or re-do her make up entirely, Liv decided that she at least looked like she was not scared to be surrounded by powerful Gods.

Liv went to grab her books for the day, noticing the top of the pile included a notebook with pen and sticky note from Peyton that said, "*No laptops allowed at Puerdios–sorry!*"

Shrugging at the rule, Liv noticed all her books were titled in some unfamiliar language.

Astronomia I
Liber I
Latin I
Simulium Scientia I
Studia Humanitatis I
Meteororum I

Slightly panicking, she opened the first book and noticed the actual text was legible. Never having been more thankful to see English, she closed her books and tried process of elimination.

"Astronomia has to be astronomy," Liv picked up the book and set it aside with her notebook. Looking back at her next class, she read "Environmental Science..." then glanced at her book titles, puzzled. She picked up *Simulium Scientia* and opened it, flipping through the pages to find plants, weather and ecosystems in general, and decided it was a good bet. But then she saw *Liber I* and cringed–could that be Environmental Science?

As the old textbook was quite heavy to begin with, Liv picked it up and added it to her pile grudgingly, and muttered to herself, "So much for orientation, Peyton." She dropped the book, resulting in an agreeing, "THUMP!"

After grabbing *Studia Humanitas I*, Liv put her map on the top of her book stack, took a determined breath and left her room in pursuit of her first class.

Walking through Puerdios campus was a stunning sight all around. Every turn around the hallway presented another massive marble stone staircase, high arches and pillars with gorgeously painted depictions of Gods on the ceilings. Each new corridor and room was lit by exquisite chandeliers, an elegant mix of candlelight ones and crystal ones each emitting soft glows.

Liv couldn't look around enough without feeling that she was missing so many beautiful details. It was like she was walking through Michael Angelo's very own custom-designed 21st century castle. And yet, all the visible beauty remained warm and inviting–portraying a welcoming space, pure and not intimidating, to Liv's delight.

As if to match the beauty of the school, the students that Liv passed were all elegantly dressed, either wearing couture-worthy gowns or dashing suits; the result making Liv question her choice of outfit today, feeling quite underdressed in her urban-inspired tough streetwear look.

Since she was still trying to locate where she was on Peyton's scribbled map, in general, Liv figured that finding her first class was definitely more important than trying to master a new outfit now, accepting that whatever attempt she made would fail to even compete with the high-end fashion world she was witnessing all around.

After studying her map a little more, Liv guessed if she walked up one more staircase and turned down the corridor, she would either be at the entrance of the North Tower, or completely and utterly lost in this iridescent castle. She turned left to begin her trek up the stairs when she suddenly thumped into a statue and fell onto her back from the collision.

"Are you all right?"

Liv had both eyes closed, so opened one of them, too embarrassed to look up at her witness completely. He bent over, extending his hand to help her up, but all Liv could see was his piercing caramel eyes and a dazzling smile.

Grabbing his hand, Liv muttered, "Thanks," as the handsome stranger helped her up.

The man handed Liv her books, but just how *quickly* he was able to do it must have been a Godly power, Liv thought to herself.

She took her books, realizing she hadn't let go of his hand yet, and immediately released her grip.

"I'm so sorry about that–today is my first day and I was just trying to find my first class and…" Liv looked at her statue of a human, with his beautiful camel coat, perfectly fitted light charcoal silk wool suit and grey knitted tie adorned by gorgeous brogue shoes. She held back her desire to cry. Liv clearly did not fit in here, at all.

The handsome stranger just continued to smile.

"I'm Kai." He held out his hand again.

Liv looked at him again, smiling weakly as she took his hand to shake, "Liv."

After composing herself, Liv realized she hadn't even asked about his state. "I'm terribly rude. Are YOU okay? I'm so sorry for bumping into you like that."

Kai chuckled, "I'll be fine, although…" He mockingly rubbed his arm, "You may have broken it, or it's definitely going to be permanently bruised." He jokingly stretched out his arm, testing its limits with a grin on his face. Then, in all seriousness, but still a sparkle of amusement in his eyes, he stated, "Liv, you are a force to be reckoned with."

Liv blushed.

Kai paused, looking up the staircase, hesitantly, then back at Liv. "So, you said you were trying to find your first class?"

Liv held up her scribbled map. "Er, yeah. Any chance you know where the North Tower is?"

"I do–that's exactly where I was heading myself. Here," He grabbed her stack of books as if they were the weight of feathers, and shared another infectious smile. "Follow me."

Liv wanted to point out that he was originally going in the opposite direction when they collided, but remained silent as they walked up the stairs because in all honesty, she desperately needed his directional guidance more than an explanation. As they walked, Liv couldn't help notice how nice Kai smelled, a mix of cinnamon and vanilla.

"Over there, you'll see the Statue of Zeus at Olympia," Kai pointed to an ivory sculpture with intricate gold plating, ornamented with ebony, ivory, gold and precious stones. "It was made in 435 BC by Phidias. It's considered one of the 'Seven Wonders of the Ancient World,' because it was supposedly lost and destroyed in the 5th century in the human world–but alas, you see the original here." He deviously smirked, as if Liv should have understood the irony.

"And over there," Kai pointed across the hall, "Is Pegasus. The winged horse only shows loyalty by presenting himself to Gods who have earned it, but hasn't been seen since Heracles' fall."

"How interesting." Liv mentally noted to Google Heracles when she got back to her room.

Kai continued, "The statue was originally made by Aristodemo Costoli for the House of Medici in the 19th century, but shortly after we acquired it from the Boboli Gardens in Florence–a replica stands in its place there, now."

"There seems to be a theme with art thievery here," Liv joked, but secretly wondered if every piece of art she had ever seen was actually a fraud in her world, and that all major works were here, in what seemed to be the most extraordinary curation of original collectable art she had ever encountered.

"The school was built during the Roman Empire, so we've just had the unique opportunity to be very selective about what pieces we've wanted to acquire for the past couple millennia."

Liv purposely turned her face away from Kai, eyes wide in shock at the thought of that numerical note. *Two thousand years.*

"But, we do have a standard rule to only acquire pieces that depict our ancestors, it's our history, after all. We're not out to get the Mona Lisa or anything like that."

By the time Kai had explained a couple more pieces of art, truly impressing Liv with the amassed culture that lived in her temporary university, they arrived at the North Tower.

The time with Kai seemed to pass by too quickly; Liv was actually a little disappointed when he said his goodbye outside her classroom door.

"I'm sure we'll see each other again," Kai smiled, and then walked away.

Once he was gone, Liv glanced over to another guy walking by, trying to look friendly in case he was a classmate, but instead, the man ignored her, quickly looking away and picking up his pace as he passed.

Liv furrowed her brows, realizing all the other males she had passed had been interacting with her like she was the virus of hell, aside from Hayden and Kai (and those relationships weren't exactly in steady shape, either). Thinking back to her conversation with Kai, she smiled, appreciating the normal conversation they just had, even more.

NINE

Knowing how late she was, and how close it was to 9AM–she corrected herself: 270 degrees–when Liv entered the classroom, it surprised her to see only one student sitting down, studiously taking notes and not looking up.

A little confused, Liv walked over to the girl and asked, "Sorry, I thought... is this Astronomy?"

The student didn't look up. Liv looked back to the professor's desk, as if expecting a teacher to magically appear.

Liv turned back to the student. She had a short, pixie bob with a glossy midnight hue, as if stars were actually twinkling on her head–but overall a very edgy style. Liv looked at her own 'hard core' outfit, and just from this girl's head, knew she couldn't even compete with the level of coolness everyone seemed to emit naturally at this unfamiliar school.

Disappointed, Liv headed to another desk, but then stopped, refusing to let her be intimated by these people.

Liv walked back up to the girl and waved in front of her face, "Hello? Is this Astronomy?"

The girl jumped back from her book, looking shocked and terrified at the same time. She had the most beautiful light blue eyes, Liv was a little taken aback–noting she needed to get used to these incredible features the Gods commonly presented.

"Sorry!" The girl looked around the class, noticing it was just the two of them. "You were talking to me?" She asked curiously, but still apprehensive.

"Yeah. I mean, is there anyone else I could be talking to?" Liv started to grin a bit, surprised by this girl's unexpected behavior, but also a little endeared to find that not every God was in the caliber of Peyton, Kai or… Hayden.

Liv cringed in pain at the thought of her ex, but the girl immediately prevented Liv from going down that dark hole by interjecting.

"SO sorry. I usually keep to myself, that's all. Yes, this is Astronomy– it's only been me in the class, so I guess you're new?" She was trying to remain calm, but Liv could tell this girl was anxiously excited to be talking to someone.

"Yup, I'm Liv. Nice to meet you."

"I'm Piper, nice to meet you, too."

"Can I sit here?" Live pointed to the desk next to Piper.

"Of course!" Piper's eyes widened as she nodded her head toward the empty seat.

Once Liv had sat down and pulled out her notebook, she leaned toward Piper, "So, where is our Professor?"

"Oh! Professor Deligne? We have a couple minutes. She is like, freakishly into living by the constellations or whatever, so she literally only walks in when the sun and moon actually align to the nearest nano degree. I'm more of an estimator, so always just arrive five minutes early to be safe. She'll probably be here in the next–"

Professor Deligne opened the door, causing Piper to close her mouth, squeal, and sit up straighter than humanly possible.

Liv tried to mimic Piper's posture, but fell short. For a moment, Piper actually seemed relaxed, normal. But she was back to her shaky demeanor as Professor Deligne wrote on the chalkboard.

JUPITER

"And no, we are NOT talking about Zeus today." Professor Deligne chuckled to herself. Piper obnoxiously giggled, forcing Liv to look over, flabbergasted.

"Well, of course you may not understand, Miss...?" Professor Deligne trailed off as she enthusiastically turned to Liv.

Liv snapped her head back. "Olivia Monaco, but you can call me Liv."

"Of course, Miss *Olivia*." She emphasized the Olivia part. "Jupiter was the Roman equivalent to our ancestor–the God of Sky and Thunder, the King of the Greek Pantheon, and more commonly known as Zeus."

Professor Deligne circled back in front of the class. "Of course, the planet Jupiter is the largest in the solar system and fittingly, was named after Zeus' Roman name. Now, please turn to page 67 and tell me–what is Jupiter mostly composed of?"

Piper's hand shot up in the air; Liv looked around, trying to determine if both Piper and Professor Deligne saw more students in the classroom than she could.

"Yes, Miss Piper." Professor Deligne nodded, prompting Piper to answer.

Piper took a deep breath, "Jupiter is primarily composed of hydrogen, with a quarter of its mass being helium."

"And, how does it compare to the other planets in the solar system?"

Piper first looked over to Liv, giving her a chance to answer. When Liv shrugged, Piper's hand shot up into the air again.

"Yes, Miss Piper?" Unfazed, Professor Deligne continued to act as if they were in a massive lecture hall.

"Well, Jupiter is the fifth planet from the Sun, and like the other gas giant planets, it lacks a well-defined solid surface. So, along with the Sun, the gravitational influence of Jupiter has helped shape the Solar System."

Professor Deligne smiled, "Very good. How so?"

Piper looked a little panicked, but took another deep breath to continue, speaking as if she had memorized the response strictly from their textbook.

"The orbits of most of the system's planets lie closer to Jupiter's orbital plane than the Sun's equatorial one." Piper looked over to Liv as she added, "Mercury is the only planet that is closer to the Sun's equator in orbital tilt," then back to Professor Deligne. "The Kirkwood gaps in the asteroid belt are mostly caused by Jupiter, and the planet may have been responsible for the Late Heavy Bombardment of the inner Solar System's history."

Piper paused, but when Professor Deligne did not comment, she continued. "Along with its moons, Jupiter's gravitational field controls numerous asteroids that have settled into the regions of the Lagrangian points preceding and following Jupiter in its orbit around the Sun. These are known as the Trojan asteroids and are divided into Greek and Trojan 'camps' to commemorate the Iliad."

With a nod from Professor Deligne, who then turned back to her board, Piper exhaled in relief.

During the remainder of class, Liv couldn't help but peek over at Piper every now and then. She seemed so overly engaged with Professor Deligne's every word, and raised her hand for every question. Liv wondered if this was how the class was oddly structured even before there was another person to actually call on.

Piper was also in a striking ball gown–a pale blue strapless bodice chiffon dress, with a beautiful light pink, navy and silver abstract print. It was as if every color complemented and enhanced her already outstanding features. The light blue matched her eyes, perfectly. The navy accented her eyeliner. The pink brought out her light skin, rosy cheeks and peach-toned lips. The silver added the perfect shimmering effect for her already radiant complexion.

Finally, Professor Deligne cleared her throat, noticing Liv's infatuation with Piper.

"Please turn to page 84 to answer all the questions on Jupiter and expand on its properties. Due at the end of the class. You two may work together if you choose." And with that, Professor Deligne sat down at her desk and started reading a book.

Piper scooted toward Liv. "Sorry I answered so many questions. I'm not used to having someone else here, I guess. I'll try to hold back more next time."

Liv flipped through her textbook, and upon reviewing the questions she was expected to answer, was very happy to have encyclopedia Piper at her side.

Piper looked over the questions, too. "They look simple enough. The first one is easy. Jupiter has been called the Solar System's vacuum cleaner because of its immense gravity well and location near the inner Solar System. It receives the most frequent comet impacts of the Solar System's planets. Funnily enough," she looked up with a big smile, "It was thought that the planet served to partially shield the inner system from cometary bombardment; however, recent computer simulations suggest that Jupiter does not cause a net decrease in the number of comets that pass through the inner Solar System, because its gravity perturbs their orbits inward roughly as often as it ejects them."

Piper paused, waiting for Liv to respond.

Liv was just trying to process what language her classmate was speaking.

Piper turned red, mouth open and realizing what context she had just claimed as a joke. "I'm sorry, that wasn't funny at all," she realized and stated aloud to herself, in a panic.

Liv felt bad, so quickly offered, "I don't think I get it?"

Piper looked up shyly, admitting, "I forget that normal deities don't typically discuss planet research in normal conversation. Er–at least, that's what my cousin says." She shrugged her shoulders, looking back down at the paper.

At her unexpected innocence, Liv burst out laughing.

"How on earth do you know all of this information by memory!?" She chuckled, as she pointed to the textbook. "I love astronomy, but this course is a whole new level. *Describe how the temperature and pressure inside Jupiter changes toward the core? How does the mass change? What's the Great Red Spot?"*

Piper still stared at her textbook, timidly. "The latter questions are definitely a lot easier to answer. The temperature and pressure inside Jupiter increase steadily toward the core, due to the Kelvin-Helmholtz mechanism. At the 'surface' pressure level of 10 bars, it's about 67 degrees Celsius, but at the phase transition region..." Piper paused to check-in on Liv, but saw a blank face so continued explaining. "The phase transition region is where the hydrogen is heated beyond its critical point and becomes metallic–pressure is about 200 GPa and it's about 9,700 degrees Celsius."

Liv thought they were done with that portion, but alas, Piper continued. "The temperature at the core boundary is estimated to be 35,700 degrees Celsius and interior pressure is about 3,000 to 4,500 GPa."

Liv stared at Piper, mouth open, but impressed as she scribbled down notes the best she could. "Thank you for knowing this information. You're like a God."

Piper just exhaled, relieved to have found a friend.

Now was Liv's turn to be awkward at her expression. "Literally, a God. Sorry, I still have to get used to all of this."

After finishing the thesis her professor and classmate considered an in-class assignment, Liv turned pleadingly to Piper for the remaining questions.

Finally, they addressed the Great Red Spot and Liv finally felt like she was getting the hang of the class as Piper shared her briefest explanation yet.

"The Great Red Spot is the best-known feature of Jupiter–it's a persistent anticyclonic storm that is actually larger than Earth and located 22 degrees south of the equator. It's known to have been in existence since at 1831, but possibly 1665."

The girls finally turned their papers in to Professor Deligne, collected their books and exited.

"Is there always this much homework between classes?" Liv had just been assigned a term's worth of homework compared to what she was used to at Oregon.

"Yeah, there's a handful. That's why they schedule study hall daily so you can work on it during that time. Professor Deligne's course is definitely more vigorous, but I'm happy to help wherever I can... What other classes do you have?" Piper looked over hopefully, but still asked shyly, not wanting to push any boundaries.

Liv handed her schedule over, "Are you in any more of my classes?"

"Yes!" This time Piper didn't try to mask her excitement. "We have Environmental Science together next–and Humanities after! Chemistry and Meteorology tomorrow, too–are you in the Elements Pillar?" She turned her head curiously at Liv, "I don't recall ever seeing you before."

"Oh, no. I'm only here temporarily," Liv shifted her weight, unsure how Piper would take the news. "I, er... I am not actually a God."

Piper just looked confused, but luckily not judgmental, so Liv continued, "I'm studying to become a meteorologist, so I suppose that's why I was placed in these classes. I know it's weird–but for some reason, I've always had an interest in weather."

"Not weird to me." Piper cut in, "And honestly, I don't really care where you're from." She smiled, and then shrugged, "I'm in the Elements Pillar, but I'm far from Elite. Trust me, I'm with you–I barely constitute as a God, too."

Liv was about to interject and explain that she was 100% NOT a God, but Piper kept rambling as she started toward their next class.

"My dad does reporting for the Elements Pillar and my mom does the same for the Candor Pillar–but mostly research. Their occupations are pretty low on the pillar hierarchy, hence why I'm enrolled in majority borderline mortal classes."

Liv was a little baffled. "Wait, what?"

Piper looked at Liv, equally confused and stopped. "What?"

Liv smiled, "I mean–why are you enrolled in these classes? Just because of your parents or is this what you actually want to study?"

Piper stared at Liv speculatively, a little hesitant to continue the conversation. She still had a wall up and was trying to figure her new classmate out. "Sure, the classes are fine–but it's not like I have enough powers to learn anything else."

Liv couldn't wrap her head around this medieval apprentice-like structure.

"So, because your parents conduct research and report for these pillars, you automatically take classes to prepare yourself to take over their role? Even if you don't like what your parents do, or want to?"

Piper simply nodded. "Of course, but you already knew that, right?"

She looked over at Liv, eyes widening as it dawned on her that Liv was truly mystified by this notion.

"Oh, you really aren't from around here." Trepidation grew on Piper's face as she looked at Liv's outfit, her eyes getting wider. Finally, Piper leaned in closer to whisper, "Who are you?"

"I said I'm not from around here. I know nothing about the societal norms or culture of this school. Or the simple day-to-day structure of Gods, in general." Liv put her hands up in surrender, "I'm just a regular mortal."

Piper's eyes grew even wider, larger than Liv thought possible. "You're mortal!?"

She started circling Liv in the middle of the outdoor campus square, like she was a science experiment. "I mean, I gathered you were different because of your whole look, but you have features like a Pure God…" Piper was looking at Liv's blue eyes so close their noses were almost touching. Without thinking, Piper then grabbed Liv's hair to study more, resulting in Liv swatting her hand away.

"What do you mean by my outfit? And looking like a Pure God?"

"Oh," Piper giggled, accepting Liv was indeed harmless, "We're really starting from scratch here, aren't we?" She leaned over to Liv, "Come on, explaining everything will take much longer than we have. Let's get to class and I'll work on clueing you in as much as I can."

They found their way to the Herbology Wing of the Greenhouse quickly enough and sat down together in a miniature outdoor auditorium, resembling the semi-circle structure of Greek Theatres. That, Liv remembered from history class, she recalled proudly to herself.

Piper was panicking again, "Oh no, she's coming." Piper immediately lowered her head down inside her Herbology book and started frantically flipping through the pages, failing at her attempt to look invisible as Liv just stared blankly at her quirky friend.

Liv looked over and saw the same blonde model she saw with Hayden that night at the bars. Her nemesis was in an all silver tank dress, with gold feathers beautifully hanging near the bottom and a matching headband decorated with gold-plated feathers in her hair. Liv dreaded the confrontation she knew was about to occur, as the girl walked up the stairs, looking up at them with a smirk on her face.

"Well, Piper, I see you finally made a friend?" She smiled with malice at Liv.

Stay calm, have courage and be kind.

Liv didn't even address she had been brainwashed by Peyton's mortal-dorm room.

"I'm Liv. Nice to meet you." Liv gulped, keeping her head held high. She refused to let this creature, God or not, intimidate her.

"Pleasure." The girl said spitefully, turning her head back to Piper, who clearly was the weaker link. "Makes sense. The two outcasts have found each other. How pathetic."

She turned back to Liv and looked her up and down. "And next time you come to class, *Liv*," she emphasized her name in a mocking tone, "Think about not wearing the Dark God's wardrobe of choice, no matter how lame of styling you execute." She smirked at both of them, causing Piper's book to magically close at her bidding, and walked back toward her seat.

Liv was burning with rage. She stood up, unintentionally, and before she could think, blurted out, "At least I'm not dark on the inside, like you clearly are."

The girl paused. She turned around, slowly, making direct eye contact with Liv.

"Somebody who tries to fight back. Oh, this will be fun." She replied calmly, giving another wicked smile and joining her friends in laugher as she returned to her seat.

"I can't believe you spoke back. Oh my gosh, I'm doomed." Piper grabbed her book and hit her head with it.

"Stop it." Liv muttered, pulling the book away from a dreadful-looking Piper, but thankful for the lighter mood Piper unintentionally provided, "Who is that?"

Piper rolled her eyes. "That is Cleo. She basically thinks she's the shit. Which, she kind of is, so I guess it's more just like she knows she's the shit."

Liv raised her eyebrow, requesting more information, so Piper continued. "Her parents were both born Elite, which is rare for the Gods–her mom is the Arts Pillar Elite and her Grandmother was the God of the Elements, but she passed away a year go, so her older brother succeeded her and is now the Element Elite. Cleo will most likely succeed her mother, too and continue the legacy as an Elite."

Liv studied Cleo from behind; intrigued by her story, but also hating that she had so much natural power.

"Plus, she's also been paired up with the Prince of Gods since like, before they were even born. Some prophecy predicted it or something. So, she's also future royalty on top of being an Elite. So basically, a triple threat, and all those menu items unfortunately serve up bitchitude."

"Prophecy?" Liv was dumbfounded, "You guys actually believe in that shit?"

Piper sighed, not admitting she believed and instead just went on with the story. "The black birds relayed the message. According to their history, a prophecy was made at Delphi to the King: That only when the heir to his throne and a daughter born of Elite status fall in love, can the Pure Gods' hierarchy defeat the Dark ones and bring peace to the Deity world."

Liv looked back at Cleo, she couldn't help but stare. Yes, she was beautiful, but she was clearly ugly on the inside. Still, Liv couldn't help but feel mesmerized by her glowing skin and skinny modelesque physique.

"And Cleo is the only daughter born into Elite status?" Liv already knew the answer, but needed to ask for confirmation.

Piper frowned, "Sadly, yes. So our fate also resides in hers. Masochistic, right?" Piper rolled her eyes, forcing Liv to laugh; but Liv still continued to glance at Cleo from afar.

Finally, Professor Claredon appeared on stage of the amphitheater, looking a little frazzled. "Is everyone all right?!"

With confused looks from his students, he boldly yelled out, "Tectumque!" and dramatically pointed to the sky. A spark emerged from his finger, expanded into a solid ceiling, and grew around the auditorium.

Liv's jaw dropped, as she watched the roof and walls grow out of thin air, transforming the outdoor area into a completely covered theatre.

Once his power completed, Professor Claredon looked appeased, took off his glasses and started cleaning them as he explained, "Tremendous thunderstorm passed just outside, nasty bugger, with earthquake momentum when they roared. But anyway, it's passed now so just a safety precaution. Please turn to page 57–today we'll be discussing ecosystems in the rain forest, and how to preserve them properly."

The walls then transformed into the illusion that they were sitting in the rainforest. Liv looked to Piper, scared that she was losing her mind.

Piper waved her hand nonchalantly. "The amphitheater is an enclosed building, Professor Claredon just uses his transfiguration powers to change it to an outdoor scenery, or to whatever ecosystem we're studying for the day." Piper looked around speculatively, and then concluded, "I could see how it would seem trippy if you didn't know otherwise."

TEN

"So, how does lunch work here?"

Liv couldn't remember the last time she ate, and panicked when she realized that aside from coffee this morning, she hadn't eaten since before her volleyball game Monday night… what had that been, a day and a half ago?

"Well, there is a thing called food. And we put it in our mouths."

Piper began acting it out, causing Liv to burst out in laughter when her new friend began 'fake chewing.'

"I'm familiar with that concept. Thanks." Liv rolled her eyes, "I meant, where do you get it? Is there a cafeteria or kitchen of some sort?"

Piper cut in, smiling. "Of course. The Dining Ballroom is where all meals are served. Deities don't actually need to eat of course, but it's still considered to be a nice pastime here. We do that whole sit around with friends, enjoy some delicious bites, relax–it's the *whole* spiel. Is that considered silly where you're from?"

"No, we do it too." Liv confirmed, but she was still trying to wrap her head around the simple fact drop that Gods didn't actually need food to survive.

Did Hayden just pretend to have a favorite ice cream flavor to appease Liv's favorite date night activity of going to an old-fashioned parlor every Monday? Every time he planned a dinner date, was that really just for her and because of her kind's romantic customs? Every day she learned more about who Hayden really was, and it made her feel like she never really knew him at all.

They walked across the courtyard and up to the grandiose mansion with a beautiful circular marble staircase and tall water fountain in front. Liv was beginning to understand why everyone wore couture everywhere, she felt incredibly underdressed simply by the stunning architecture of the campus. Even the greenhouse in the Herbology Wing had gold floral details and beautiful, crystal clear glass paneling throughout the building that reflected the mountain view.

They walked down a long archway lit with floating candles. Passing more stunning dresses and suits filled with glares at Liv's current outfit finally gave her the courage to ask Piper for help in securing a more appropriate wardrobe.

Liv squirmed during the entire request–she was never one to conform to the crowd. Liv loved her style, but also couldn't help but absolutely admire how elegant everyone else looked around her in comparison. Plus, she justified to herself–if she was supposedly in danger–she should probably try to minimize attracting attention.

"Of course!" Piper clapped her hands, excitedly. "My aunt is a seamstress in the Design sector of the Art Pillar. I can easily get you some dresses by the end of the week." Piper did a loop around Liv, eyeing her up and down. "You look about my size, so in the meantime, I'll let you borrow some of my clothes."

"You are seriously my Fairy God Mother. Thank you!" Liv hugged Piper graciously.

Piper stayed stiff as a board, arms glued to her sides, taken aback by the affectionate action.

"What's a Fairy God Mother?" Piper asked cautiously, as Liv released her grasp.

"Oh, you have *a lot* to learn about my people, too." Liv joked, but immediately became side tracked as they entered the cafeteria.

It was the most peculiar, yet beautiful sight she had ever seen.

Four large long tables filled up the room inside, accompanied by a beautiful balcony overlooking the hills, with the sun gleaming and brightening the stone structures in various degrees.

But half of the room was split with tables filled with dark colors, and the other half, metallics.

Leaning towards her friend, Liv asked, "Piper, what's with the whole spectrum split down the middle of the room?"

Piper looked over, unfazed. "Oh, that's because Dark Gods and Pure Gods don't intermingle with each other."

"Okay, so where do you usually sit?"

"Er, that depends," Piper hesitated, "Typically I avoid this scene entirely."

"But where do you fit in?"

"Oh, that's an easy answer. I don't."

Piper's ambiguous response astonished Liv; she needed to understand more. "You don't? But by the looks of the room, I have a feeling that's not really a choice?"

Piper looked very uncomfortable, so Liv felt awkward addressing her status as an outcast.

"I mean, technically I associate myself with the Pure Gods, but they don't associate themselves with me. It's because my hair is an anomaly–it stays dark, no matter what I do."

"And you don't like the Dark Gods enough to hang out with them instead?"

"Not exactly. I don't mind some of them. But they don't trust me enough because of my eyes. I have the eyes of a Pure God." Looking over to the Dark Gods, Piper shivered, then waved Liv in her direction, "Come on–let's find a table out on the patio." And before Liv could ask another question, Piper was walking toward the outdoor space.

Liv jogged over to catch up with Piper, were all Gods naturally this fast?

"I'm sorry to pry, but how does that work? You mentioned your hair and eyes, but isn't that just your genetics?"

Piper took a breath, not excited to continue the conversation.

"Yes, and no. Our appearances change over time, depending on loyalties and beliefs. There is a legend about how past King's subjects betrayed him and unsuccessfully tried to take over the throne. So, the King implemented a rule to the Gods that they had to show their true colors, so that one can always understand the intentions of their peers. So basically, Pure Gods have lighter features and wear metallic–and Dark Gods have darker features, wear darker colors and materials like leather and fur. The features aren't a choice, but the clothing is more so a way to strengthen your loyalty stance."

"And the Gods just follow the rule? Interesting." Liv couldn't believe this entire world existed–with their histories, politics, social stipulations and powerful, beautiful peers–without her, or any mortal's knowledge.

"Well, that's the power of the ruling Gods. The God of the Gods' bloodline has a unique, special power over every God who is allegiant to the throne. Every Elite has the strongest power in their pillar, but the Royal Family of the Gods has the strongest powers of all the deities and Elites. They can will any God to do their bidding, so long as the God is loyal."

"So much for democracy." Liv bluntly stated, rolling her eyes.

The girls approached an empty table in the corner of the balcony. Liv dropped all of her textbooks in a chair, relieved to get rid of that weight. She sat down, appreciating the sunshine, and looked around the whole balcony to absorb the beautiful scene. But, amidst enjoying all the commotion of watching her fellow students socialize during their lunch break, a much too familiar blonde head shone in the sunlight, consequently catching Liv's attention.

Hayden was laughing with Rei, Cleo and a couple others who Liv supposed to be Cleo's minions on the opposite side of the balcony. He was in a beautiful light crème suit, with a gold tie and crisp white shirt, adorned with a metallic silk green bomber jacket. Liv pouted, he looked so sexy, and he was wearing her favorite sunglasses, making her long for him even more.

"Liv? Liiivv!" Piper looked over to where she was staring and laughed.

"Let's make it two." Piper folded her menu and handed it to the waiter.

"Two?" Liv had unlocked her trance.

"I ordered you a Panini–hope you like hot sandwiches. Although, don't think it will be as hot as Hayden…"

"Be quiet. I'm not interested in him." Liv blushed, awkwardly choosing to start looking at her menu again, ignoring the fact that Piper had already ordered for them. Her internal justification was that she *should* know what other lunch options were available at this location, so next time she'd be better prepared.

"Hey, it's okay if you are." Piper looked over at him, longingly. "Every girl here is, and he is most definitely swoon-worthy."

"Well, why don't you date Hayden, then?" Liv snapped, accidentally.

As if he heard his name, Hayden looked over to their table, his arm around Cleo. When he spotted Liv, he got up, making Liv panic as she watched him head over in their direction out of the corner of her eye.

Liv pulled herself together and apologized to Piper, whispering, "I'm sorry, I didn't mean to snap. Hayden and I just have a history, which I will tell you about later because-he's-heading-over-here-right-now." Liv sped through the last phrase.

"What?" Piper started turning but Hayden was already there.

He lifted his sunglasses, exposing his piercing baby blue eyes directly at Liv.

"Hi." He said, smiling.

"Hi." Liv said, trying not to make eye contact with Piper, whose mouth hung open.

"Can I sit down?" He hesitantly asked.

"Um, I don't…" Liv stuttered trying to come up with a reason against it.

"Yeah, sure. Go ahead." Piper quickly interjected, beating her to the punch.

Liv kicked her underneath the table.

"Ouch!" Piper growled at Liv.

Liv noticed Hayden give a small chuckle, but was holding back his humor. He turned to Piper. "I don't think we've met. I'm Hayden. Thanks so much for showing Ollie around today."

"Liv." Liv irritatedly corrected.

"Not a problem. Anytime." Piper swooned.

"This is Piper." Liv stated, kicking Piper again as she continued to stare lustfully at Hayden. That got her out of her trance.

"Ouch times two!" Piper hissed.

This time, Hayden couldn't hold it in. "I see you're putting your soccer leg to good use." He nudged his leg against Liv's, laughing. A bolt of electricity shot up her leg, giving Liv chills.

Unaware of the effect Hayden was having on the two girls, and oblivious to Liv's tension from their touch, he leaned back and concernedly asked Liv, "How's your day going so far?"

"Great." Liv nodded, "I, um, have a lot of classes with Piper."

"That's perfect." He smiled at Piper, genuinely.

Liv noticed Cleo behind Hayden with her arms crossed; she was giving a death stare in their direction. Cleo's whole existence made Liv want to strangle her.

"Your *friends* seem like they want you to return to them." Liv nodded in Cleo's direction, angrily.

Hayden turned, saw Cleo and turned back around, waving her off. "They'll manage."

Piper's panicked look grew stronger when she noticed Cleo.

Liv was done and couldn't take this whole small talk encounter any more.

Hayden leaned back in his chair, eyeing Liv, "So, you decided to go the all black route for your first day of school? Edgy, Ollie. I like it."

Liv was about to cry, which made her even more livid. She wouldn't let Hayden get to her, not anymore.

Ignoring his comment, she furiously replied, "I would actually prefer you go back over there because the longer you talk to us, the more your *girlfriend* Cleo will get jealous, which means the more likely and frequently she will try to make our lives a living hell. You certainly chose your friends well." Liv noted sarcastically, "And the last time I checked, you have yours," she waved over at Cleo and Rei as she smirked, then turned back to Hayden, glaring, "And I have mine."

Hayden opened his mouth, looking hurt and simultaneously shocked.

Liv waved him along, ignoring his response. "And I would prefer if my friend," she pointed to Piper, who looked like she was about to faint, "Made it to her classes today with no more harassment."

"That's fine." Hayden lifted his hands up, in surrender. Getting up, he quietly added, "Glad to hear you're doing okay, Ollie," and walked away.

Once Hayden was gone, Piper came back to life.

"Hold. The. Phone. Ollie?" Piper asked, eyes wide. "Like, Hayden's Ollie? Holy smoke. Holy Zeus. Why didn't you tell me!?"

"First. I'm not *Hayden's Ollie*." Liv relaxed, but now that he was gone, she felt like a piece of her was missing. She shyly looked toward Hayden, who was already laughing and punching Rei jokingly. "At least, not anymore," she mumbled as she sadly looked down at her Panini's arrival.

Gaining composure, Liv looked back up at Piper, who was clearly not giving her a break.

"And?" Piper insisted.

"And what? It's over."

"Well, obviously." Piper shrugged. "Everyone knows he's with Cleo, now. But you still could have told me. You're like a living legend here." She kindly nudged her leg against Liv's, "Hey, I'm your friend, right? That's what you said earlier? So, as your friend, you're allowed to tell me these things, okay?" Piper smiled, as she grabbed her sandwich. "But first, we eat."

After enjoying their delicious lunch, Liv and Piper headed to their next class, Humanities.

"So, what is this class about?" Liv asked Piper, speculatively.

"History and study of the mortal race, of course. You've never studied history?"

"Well, yeah, but in my world we just call it 'History Class' typically. But, I guess it makes sense that you need to learn about, er, us."

"And history is inclined to repeat itself." Piper added.

Soon, the Humanities teacher, Professor Montagnes, walked into the large auditorium, "Hush, hush, everyone–now take your seats."

The bustle of students started to calm down when Hayden swiftly sat in the seat next to Liv.

"Hi," he said cheerfully and mischievously smiled. "Guess we have this class together."

Liv rolled her eyes and got up to leave when Professor Montagnes caught her in mid-stand.

"Um, please take your seat now, Miss...?"

Liv froze. "Olivia Monaco, sir."

"Oh! Of course!" Professor Montagnes smiled, "Welcome to Humanities, Miss Olivia. Yes, please take your seat. Where you are is fine."

Liv, who had turned bright red, slithered back into her seat.

"Today, we'll be talking about the Five Races of Humankind. Please turn your books to page 120."

Liv, Hayden and Piper simultaneously flipped their textbooks to the designated lesson.

"As you all know, our ancestors have classified the human race into five categories. The first age was The Golden Race. These beings knew toil nor old age, life consisted of feasting; death came like sleep. It was a jolly time for mortals; one might say the perfect existence. This time, of course, took place under the sovereign of glorious Kronos–and most say one way of imagining this 'time before Zeus,' was a lovely idyll."

Liv was quickly scribbling all the notes she could on the Golden Race, secretly thinking what a wonderful time to have lived.

"The Race of Silver," Professor Montagnes shuttered, "An inferior and rather immature breed, who lived in blasphemy only until Zeus angrily put an end to the madness. Which leads us to the Race of Bronze. Supposedly, Zeus created these mortals out of ash-trees. They were a warrior race that devoted itself to the work of Ares–the war god, of course."

Liv was a little offended at the concept of so easily exterminating the human race and resetting them to the God's desires, but continued scribbling.

She also noticed Hayden's touch against her left arm, sending warmth throughout her entire side, and an occasional chill when his jacket brushed her arm just right.

"However, to Zeus' dismay, the Men of Bronze exterminated themselves through their relentless fighting," Professor Montagnes shook his head, sadly, "A terrible and unexpected fate for the God's to witness."

Then, as if to dramatize the lecture, his spirits lifted as he pointed his finger up, "But then came the Heroes Race, mighty mortals who fought courageously, but tragically died at Thebes and Troy. In many ways they resembled the Bronze race, but they won much glory and some were to have been rewarded with a post-mortem existence in the Isles of the Blessed, somewhere at the edge of the world beside Okeanos."

Liv shuddered at the thought of all those men dying, but then questioned sadly, have times even changed now? Between all of the loyalties and contrasting beliefs, it felt as if her world was always in a constant battle. Was there any difference in humankind adapting, or was history a whirling wheel, always destined to repeat itself? Would it continue in every world, no matter how different?

"Which leads us to The Race of Iron," Professor Montagnes introduced gloomily. "This is the human world as it lives today. Toil and misery exist, and it is expected to get only worse. We suspect that in the future, there will be a lack of respect, impiety and every sort of villainy. So, class, as Gods, we are responsible for helping the humans fight this war against themselves. We are responsible for guiding them out of this terrible race and into one that is more peaceful, prosperous and kind once again."

Liv turned to Piper, trying to hide her apprehension and refusing to acknowledge Hayden's comforting touch on her left arm through this worrisome news.

Professor Montagnes continued, to Liv's relief. "Now, you'll be working on a semester long project. I'll be assigning groups–now hush, hush," Professor Montagnes tried to calm the groaning Gods.

"Oh, okay, how about a compromise, then?" Professor Montagnes offered, trying to pacify his dreary class, "I'm sure you're sitting by your friends. So let's do this–I'll assign groups based on those around you?" At the sound of the class calming–aside from Liv, who was now riled up– Professor Montages confirmed his plan, by looking to the first group of students in front of him, claiming them as a group.

Liv was secretly angry with Piper and her valedictorian ways, as Professor Montagnes looked directly at Piper, Hayden, and her in the second row.

"You three–Hayden, Piper and Olivia–group two. Should prove to be an interesting team."

Liv could feel Hayden smile in triumph and simultaneously hated that she could remember and identify his moves without even seeing them.

ELEVEN

After a busy first day of class, Liv passed out as soon as she got back to her loft Monday evening; however, throughout the night, she tossed and turned thinking about everything that had been revealed in the past couple of days.

As the sunlight lit up her room, Liv gave in to her consciousness, opening her eyes to the soft dim with a need to clear her head. She hopped over to the armoire, checking to see if her workout clothes had been included in her closet rampage.

As if twinkling at Liv, her black running shoes smiled on a lower shelf. She immediately grabbed them, along with her favorite black sports bra, grey tank top and oversized running hoodie. And after swiftly pulling her long hair up into a ponytail and snatching her headphones, Liv was out the door.

Liv began jogging throughout the castle and continued to be in awe and admiration of the beauty surrounding her–was it like everything touched by God's automatically dazzled?

She thought of Hayden, who always had a gravitational pull with her, a compelling influence that attracted her to him; his presence never failing to mesmerize her, enchant her. Was all of that just because he was a God? Or was that simply unconditional true love?

Could it be both?

Liv tried to assess what the hell was going on in her new life and this new world. She wanted to figure out how she felt about everything, even without fully understanding it.

This is what she knew: Her ex-boyfriend, his family and his friends were all extremely powerful. The Pure Gods were in some sort of danger, and still unsure as to why, she consequently was, too. This world, as she knew it, involved aggregated studies, intense personalities and breathtaking beauty all around – but it wasn't her world, it was only temporary. Hayden wasn't hers, nor would he ever be; him being in her life would not be forever, and she needed to prepare herself for their inevitable separation.

She had entered the pavilion by this time, falling into a strong pace; she forgot how much she enjoyed physical exertion and felt livened as she crossed the courtyard and exited toward the forest. There had to be some form of path she could makeshift into a running route.

Soon, she was picking up her pace as her favorite running songs played on her mix. The crisp air and sunlight glow through the leaves made her feel alive and in control of her life for the first time in weeks–a sliver of short-lived happiness, no matter how temporary it might be. By the time her best cardio song was playing, Liv was sprinting–with small intervals of her favorite allegro dance moves.

Liv was nowhere near a professional dancer, but had studied ballet and contemporary dance growing up. In the rarest of circumstances when she was running, she couldn't resist getting in the extra muscle work by adding her favorite leaps, turns and pirouettes, occasionally executing a Grand Jete or Passe when the rhythm would allow.

She probably looked ungraceful, youthful and without a care in the world, but she appreciated the calmness surrounding her in the forest–nobody would be able to control her out here.

For the grand finale, she put in all her energy, gaining momentum with each push off her leg, lunging herself into a 'C' jump, and when she landed, she smiled, pausing to take in her charming scenery and panting as she caught her breath.

"Nice legwork."

Liv jolted upright, whirling toward the mysterious voice.

Kai was casually leaning against a tree, smirking at his prey, caught red-handed in the wilderness.

"You know, you probably shouldn't be out in the forest, alone–especially this far away from the castle," he added smugly.

Although already flushed from her workout, Liv could feel her cheek temperature rise. She was tired of hearing what she could and could not do, what was or was not safe–she was eighteen! The year of independence–the year she was supposed to grow and mature as an individual. She balled her hands into fists, putting all of her energy into the pressure of her fingers against her palm and tried to remain calm.

"I was just going on a quick jog. Us, *mortals*, enjoy physical activity in the morning, sometimes." She hissed through her teeth. Liv could feel the sun beating through the trees, consequently heating her entire body up.

Kai put his hands up in surrender, "Hey, I'm not saying it's wrong. Heck, if it's an excuse to hang out with you more, I'm happy to join for future morning runs. *Our kind* also appreciate an outdoor morning with nature every once in a while."

Liv paused, registering what Kai had just subtly said about wanting to hang out with her more, and tried to disregard the butterflies she felt in her stomach. She willed herself to stay strong internally, but she had to admit, he *was* very handsome.

"Who said you could keep up?" Liv retorted, eyeing Kai's unfit running attire: a khaki trench, chunky silver sweater, charcoal slacks and leather dress shoes.

"Oh, challenge accepted." Kai snapped his fingers, resulting in an outfit change to Liv's amazement. She needed to get used to this idea of magic at their fingertips, she figured she must look ridiculous every time her face showed shocked amazement at these creatures' capabilities.

Now, Kai stood before her looking an entirely different being, wearing white running shoes, silver basketball shorts and a fitted white hoodie. He seemed almost approachable now, not an intimidating power source anymore, but just a regular guy.

"Sure, that was just my warm up, anyhow." Liv mockingly grinned as she started to run away.

Kai turned out to be a great running partner. Liv's competitive spirit drove through, relentlessly disallowing her from slowing down or refusing to admit physical defeat. She wished she could show off a bit to impress Kai, but kept that thought cornered in her mind because she felt as if she were cheating on Hayden. So instead, she buried it and avoided addressing it for the time being.

They were rounding back toward the castle when Liv supposed they had clocked in at least 7 miles, not including the mile she had completed without him. She was secretly proud that she kept up with Kai, although grudgingly, he looked like he could easily run another 7 miles. Liv? Not so much.

To Liv's internal delight, Kai slowed down as they approached her pavilion.

Liv tried to pacify her breathing as she teased, "Tired already?"

"You got me." Kai laughed, without having broken a sweat. Liv on the other hand, was drenched.

"Actually," Kai took a breath, looking nervous for the first time since Liv could recall, "I wanted to ask you something."

"Ask away." Liv began stretching, awkwardly unsure what to do, but not wanting to depart from the attractive man before her.

"Do you have any plans tomorrow night?" Kai inquired, hopefully.

"Hmm, let me see..." Liv playfully put her finger to her chin, looking up at the sky. She enjoyed watching Kai sweat a little, even if it didn't result from their jog. "Considering I have one other friend beside you, and I'm not allowed to go 100 feet away from my room unaccompanied, looks like I'm quite available tomorrow night. What did you have in mind?"

"Oh sorry? I didn't mean you and I should do something together, I was just being nice..." Kai looked at Liv, beautifully innocent.

At first, Liv was horrified. Then she caught a mischievous spark in his devious eyes, and jokingly punched his arm, "You little jerk!"

Kai laughed. "Too easy. You're cute when you're embarrassed."

Blushing, Liv demanded, "Okay, get on with it. The moment's passed."

"There's a symposium tomorrow–it's a ball in honor of the King. Would you want to go with me as my date?"

"Wow, I… I would love to go." The words surprised Liv as they left her mouth.

Kai beamed.

Her mind, temporarily pacified by Kai's glowing state, finally caught up with her, and began to think through the details, resulting in panic. "But a ball, and a king, in one description sounds pretty fancy. I'm not sure I qualify for that type of spectacle."

"Don't worry about that. I'll pick you up at 225 degrees… and now I'm going to leave before you can change your mind." With a quick smile, Kai turned and left.

Liv giggled internally, rolling her eyes as she headed back to her room to get ready for class.

When she got her loft, she noticed the door was slightly ajar. She cautiously opened it and sighed with relief when she spotted Piper on the bed with a pile of large white boxes.

"There you are!" Piper exclaimed, throwing her hands in the air and running to meet Liv at the door. "I brought you some clothing options for school. Where have you been?!"

"Out on a run." Liv stated blankly, eyes preoccupied by the large quantity of boxes piled on her bed. "Piper, how many dresses did you *bring?*"

"Oh, twenty or so–and some jackets, shoes and jewelry. Take a look!"

Liv was stunned, she eyed Piper cautiously and then opened the first box.

Inside was a beautiful gold trench coat with soft gold feathers from the waist down.

"Piper, this is beautiful. I cannot accept this!" Liv gaped at the intricate detailing; she had never owned anything so exquisite in her life.

"Nonsense. My aunt was so excited to craft this–she's just happy it will get to be worn."

Liv eyed Piper suspiciously. "What do you mean?"

Piper froze. "I've said too much. Just take the clothes and don't ask questions."

Liv laughed, rolling her eyes. "Okay, sketch."

"Sketch?" Piper inquired.

"You answer my question and I'll explain." Liv negotiated.

"Okay, okay. But don't tell anyone." Piper was serious, making Liv a little on edge. "My aunt is like the lowest tier in the Art Pillar. She essentially just cuts the fabrics for her higher colleagues–she's not allowed to design, so she does this in her spare time, under the table."

"She's not allowed to design? But this coat is amazing!"

"Exactly. She's so talented, but if anyone knew she designed the coat, she'd be sent to the Underworld. So, if anyone asks, just don't mention her, or my name."

"Deal." Liv was positive nobody would care what she wore, so wasn't too concerned. She went for the next box, finding a heavy bronze long sheer sleeved dress, with a bronzed short skirt with metal pleats and matching plackets on the wrists. "Wow, are you sure these pieces aren't supposed to be on display in an art museum?" She continued to admire the fabrication on the dress.

Piper looked outside, antsy with the time. "Okay, at this rate we'll never make it to breakfast. Just choose something and let's head out." She replied, anxiously.

Easy for Piper to say, she was wearing a crop top shirt with a matching pencil skirt, embellished with pastel beading and silver pumps. She already looked incredible.

Liv opted for a white silk chiffon crewneck tee and a full silk organza crème skirt; it seemed the most casual option out of the stunning gowns. After quickly hopping in the shower, she carefully stepped into the skirt and pulled the shirt over her head, loosely tucking it in. As she braided her hair into a messy French braid, she called out to Piper in the other room.

"Hey Piper, what do you wear to a symposium?"

"A symposium? Depends–who invited you?" Piper appeared in Liv's bathroom, curious, eyeing Liv's choice of clothes and finally nodded her head in approval. "PS–that looks great on you! You're a natural."

Piper moved closer, eyeing Liv's birthday necklace, "Unique necklace, too–it's beautiful." She went to touch it, but Liv jumped back, unaware of how unconsciously protective she was of her one prized possession from her Dad.

"Well," Liv tied her hair, trying to brush off her unexpected movement, and then grabbed her favorite red lipstick to apply on her lips. "I sort of have a date."

"A date?" Piper raised an eyebrow, surprised, eyeing Liv a little speculatively with concern, "With whom?"

Liv, surprised by Piper's response, replied defensively, "I was invited to go to the symposium tomorrow night in honor of the King?"

"Oh. Did Hayden invite you?" Piper seemed to relax, but still a little on edge.

"Um, no." The thought of not going with Hayden stung Liv internally. Quietly, Liv explained. "Just a friend. But what should I wear?"

Piper paused, thinking as she eyed the boxes on her bed. "If it's in honor of the King, it needs to be top-notch." She headed toward the bed filled with gowns, "I'm not sure I brought anything that could work for that."

Suddenly, she turned back to Liv, eyeing Liv up and down and then focusing on her red lips when an idea sparked.

"I have *just* the gown for you."

Liv and Piper headed to breakfast in the great hall. Liv felt much more confident in her stunning outfit and killer heels as she passed her peers in the corridor. She actually felt powerful and strong, which was saying something, considering everyone who surrounded her.

As Liv entered the great hall, she immediately felt Hayden's stare from across the room. Why was it she could *feel* his presence whenever he was near? She pretended to ignore him as she and Piper passed, walking out to the patio to enjoy their meal.

As soon as they sat down, Liv exhaled.

Piper looked at Liv. "What's up with you? You look like you just fought in a battle."

Liv looked down sadly, "Does it ever get any easier?" She cautiously looked over to Hayden, whose back was now facing her. "The hurt, the longing–the loss of someone you once loved?"

Piper shrugged, "Sorry girl, I'm not the person to give out love advice, I have negative zero experience in that category." She nudged Liv encouragingly, "But hey, you have your date tomorrow night–that has to help a little bit, right?"

Liv smiled, thinking about Kai. "You're right. It does."

"Who are you going with, this 'friend' of yours, anyway?" Piper questioned, emphasizing the word *friend*.

"Oh, just a guy I met yesterday and ran into this morning. Kai? Do you know of him?"

"Kai?" Piper's mouth dropped. "Oh, I know of him. He asked *you*?" Her entire face was frozen, stunned at the idea.

"Okay, you can try to tone down your surprise a little bit. Hurting my ego over here." Liv chuckled, thankful for her avocado toast arriving at the table for something to occupy herself with until Piper recovered from her shock.

"Do you know what God Kai is?" Piper asked rhetorically. "Of course you don't." She rolled her eyes. "Liv, he's an Elite. *The* Elite of the Elements."

Piper grew even more aggravated when Liv clearly wasn't registering the enormity of the concept Elite. To Liv, it was just a title, which made little sense to her in the first place.

"Okay, that clearly didn't hit a nerve for the excitement I was going for." Piper continued, "So another angle that I think you'll appreciate, or just relate to at the very least is that Kai is also related to our arch nemesis, Cleo. He's her brother."

"What?" Liv eyes went wide, automatically looking over to Cleo as if she could hear them. Cleo was preoccupied vying for Hayden's attention, laughing forcefully in his direction.

Piper smiled, finally attaining the reaction she originally expected from Liv in the first place and shook her head in agreement. After a moment, she relaxed, cautiously proceeding.

"Look, not to burst your bubble or anything, but I thought it *was* weird for a God to ask you on a date in the first place. No offense, but you're a mortal and our code is not to interact with your kind–I only bit my tongue because you were so excited." Piper looked over at Cleo angrily, then back at Liv–forcing eye contact. "Obviously you're an exception because, well, you're here, and I'm an exception to the rule because well, I'm an outcast and nobody cares about me... But for an Elite to be asking you to the King's symposium, especially one related to Hades reincarnation as a Goddess herself, just–I guess what I'm saying is–be careful."

Liv wanted to be angry with Piper, but the look of genuine concern that her friend radiated during the struggle of giving her the reasonable warning, Liv accepted that in general, it was a *peculiar* situation. Piper was just the messenger of the less than joyful news.

"Warning taken and appreciated." Liv nodded, furrowing her brows as she looked back over at Cleo, and angrily took a bite of her avocado toast.

TWELVE

"Liv, you are going to LOVE me!" Piper shrieked, swinging Liv's door open and holding a tall, oversized box that was twice as wide as her frame.

Piper excitingly placed it on Liv's bed, squealing, "Open it!"

Liv had just hopped out of the shower, so quickly threw on her favorite baggy jeans, a white tank and a chunky oversized cardigan as she raced over to the bed, thrilled to see her friend posing next to a beautiful silver matte box.

"My aunt worked all night on it, so I hope you like it. Otherwise, well you're potentially screwed, but let's not think about it just yet." Piper rambled, and then pushed Liv toward the box, animatedly yelling, "Come on!"

Liv smiled, heart beating as she eagerly, but carefully, lifted the box top.

She unfolded the shimmering tissue paper; unsure how the dress could even top the presentation it was delivered in.

But alas, Liv gasped in awe of the absolutely stunning gown that sparkled in its container.

"Piper, it's perfect." And that was all Liv could get out, she was speechless at its beauty.

The silver gown, hand embellished with crystals and gems, caught every light, dazzling everywhere. It was like a pure cut diamond glimmering in the sunlight. Her hand traced the larger stones, embroidering the plunging low-cut neckline that would perfectly shape her chest and waist; it continued through seamlessly to make her straps. She lifted the dress up, looking at the intricate web of beads that crossed behind, revealing an open back silhouette. Looking closer at the detailing, she noticed the dress itself was silky satin beige with so many silver gems and stones and tiny gold accent beading that it only appeared to be a delicate crystal chandelier, floating in air.

Piper clapped. "I knew you would like it!"

She bent over, pulling out a smaller box and opened the top to reveal silver heels, adorned with intricate gold plated wings.

"And it matches your necklace," Piper nodded to Liv's baguette stone. "So just add these shoes with that stunning red lip you rocked yesterday, and Kai will be so infatuated with you he won't even remember if he's supposed to be executing some evil plan or not…. which, of course, is our evil plan," she added with a wink.

"Seriously Piper, I cannot thank you enough." Liv said earnestly, wondering how she would ever repay her friend back for her kindness.

"Don't even start. Here," Piper grabbed Liv's hands, "We need to start your glam pronto. It's almost 210 degrees and Kai will be here in like 25."

That time concept still made no sense to Liv, but she obliged as Piper quickly started filing her nails.

Piper looked outside the window, assessing the sunset, and then gazed anxiously back at Liv and her hands. Her eyes said it all, the work that needed to be done was far too much for the limited time they had.

"Do you trust me?" Piper asked, inquisitively.

"So far, you've done nothing but absolutely everything for me–and with perfection, so of course."

"Okay." Piper took a deep breath and then concentrated on Liv's fingertips as she mumbled, "Pingo."

Liv's nails went from horribly unmanicured to exquisitely painted with a sheer nude color, adorned by a thin silver stripe across the middle.

Piper nodded her head, happy with her work, and then admitted to Liv, shyly, "I've never tried that power before."

"Well, maybe you're more powerful than you give yourself credit for." Liv replied, in awe at how beautiful her hands looked.

By the time Piper finished playing makeover with her dress up doll, Liv barely recognized herself as she looked at the stunning reflection in the mirror.

It was as if she had a luminescent glow about her, her skin radiating off the shimmering crystals and gems on her dress and necklace. Piper had given Liv a subtle smoky eye, mostly natural shades of brown with a hint of silver sparkle on the interior lid, which perfectly balanced her pop of red lip color.

Her eyes sparkled back at her reflection; Liv could almost see every speckle of blue and silver glistening underneath her long, full eyelashes.

Liv put her hand through her wavy illuminated hair, naturally texturized with just a hint of curl. It fell naturally back to place with a light bounce.

Looking at the back of her dress, Liv had to admit–it fit like a glove, hugging her actually existent curves (for once) in all the right places. The low-cut front curved her chest, exposing only a classy hint of her chest. The gown magically bodiced together at Liv's smallest part of her waist, and hung low enough in the back to still give definition to her behind. Nothing felt too tight, and all fell naturally–no bumps or creases visible anywhere.

Liv never considered herself to be a vision of any sort, but tonight, she felt like a force.

"Wow. Stunning." Piper grinned. "If Kai didn't know better, I would think you to be an Elite. He won't be messing with you tonight, no sir." She nodded proudly at her work.

Liv blushed. "Thank you Piper." She took a step forward, forgetting the only downfall of her wardrobe for a split second, how heavy the dress was on her body.

"Piper, is there any spell for you to, uh, make this dress lighter?"

"Oh my gosh! Of course." Piper ran over immediately. "That would be the diamonds."

"The diamonds!?" Liv's eyed popped out of her head.

"Hush, I need to concentrate." Piper closed her eyes. "Minuo Gravitas"

In an instant, the dress felt featherlike. Liv twirled.

"Okay. Kai should be here at any degree. My work here is done, so I'm going to head out." Piper hugged Liv, "Please be careful."

Piper headed toward the door when she turned, remembering something. "One more thing, hold out your hand."

Liv obliged, and Piper snapped her fingers, "Adducere vinum in calicem."

A glass of white wine magically appeared in Liv's palm.

"Enjoy. And don't spill." And with a wink, Piper left, closing the door behind her.

Liv had just finished her glass of wine when Kai knocked on her bedroom door.

When she opened it, Liv took a deep breath, trying to remain calm at the handsome man standing in front of her. Kai wore a satin burgundy brocade suit, with black velvet loafers that matched his black button-down shirt and solid red tie.

"Wow, Liv–you look stunning." Kai smiled in return, awed at his date for the night.

"Thank you," Liv blushed. "You clean up pretty nicely yourself."

With a dazzling smile, he led the way outside of Liv's room toward the corridor. "Come on, I have our transportation arranged downstairs."

They walked out to the pavilion, where Liv saw an embellished gold carriage with four majestic white horses.

"After you," Kai opened the carriage door, leading Liv inside.

"Feels like a Cinderella sort of night," Liv observed, mesmerized at the interior. "Are the horses going to turn into mice at midnight–er–360 degrees?"

"Cinderella? What kind of night is that?" Kai asked, sincerely confused.

Liv looked at Kai, amused. "Nothing, just magical." Then she remembered the horses, "Do Gods really use horses and carriages as transportation? Seems a little outdated, don't you think?"

Kai tilted his head, "How so?"

Liv shrugged, "I would suspect by now you would have conquered apparition, or at the very least flying, us mortals figured that out decades ago."

"Oh, we'll be flying to our destination, all right." Kai confirmed, snapping his fingers and revealing two glasses of Champagne, in which he handed one to Liv.

"Cheers." He grinned.

"Salut." Liv smiled back, feeling the carriage lightly lift from the ground and begin its journey through the starry sky.

They landed a short time after, on the grounds of an exquisite estate. The castle twinkled with candlelight as Liv captured her first glimpse of the Royal Palace. When the carriage stopped, the door automatically opened and Kai hopped out, extending his arm for Liv to leverage on her descent. As she stepped out of the carriage, she automatically looked up, instantly recognizing her constellation sparkling in the sky, striking and demanding attention.

It seemed that even when she was distracting herself from the past, her history would continue to crawl itself back into her present, no matter what far off land or world she was living in. She ignored the ache in her heart for Hayden as she focused her attention back to Kai, smiling shyly at him as she absorbed the enormity of greatness surrounding her, trying not to be dissolute by the magnitude of the night.

They walked up the grandiose staircase, arm in arm–Liv thankful for the strength and support of her date, as her insides were trembling with each step.

The entrance of the castle reminded her very much of the Palace at Versailles, chandeliers hanging by the dozen with beautiful baroque paintings and sculptures adorning the walls and rococo furniture perfectly placed throughout. Liv was too occupied looking up and around at the spectacle ambiance than at the other Gods who were all staring at her, the unknown beauty.

Liv walked through the doors and entered the great hall, all to find another immense staircase she would need to walk down to arrive onto the event floor.

When she stood at the very top, an unknown announcer called out, "Miss Olivia Monaco, accompanied tonight by Kai, Elite of the Elements Pillar."

Liv looked around, trying to figure out who knew her name and why they insisted on making her inscrutable presence notable. She was finally beginning to understand Piper's infatuation with the idea of an Elite taking interest in Liv, a mere mortal. All the heads in the ballroom turned to Liv's direction, in shock, judgment and awe: all Liv wanted to do was duck out and run away, finally understanding her place in the God hierarchy.

"They're amazed by your beauty." Kai whispered next to Liv, smiling. "Hold my arm, and we'll enter the jungle together." He joked, "Just beware of the lions. They tend to bite."

Liv chuckled, feeling again at ease. It was intense just how much the Gods' presence had such a penetrating influence over her.

"I meant to ask you–how does an Elite find himself at Puerdios University?" Liv asked shyly as they glided down the stairs.

Kai smiled, smoothly explaining, "I had a meeting with the Dean–to ensure curriculum for the Elements was up to par with our Pillar's expectations; however, after helping you locate your classroom, our meeting was cut short, so we rescheduled for the next day."

"Oh, of course."

Liv felt mildly embarrassed for being so speculative with Kai, secretly cursing Piper for putting that caution in her mind.

"To my luck, I ran into you, literally, so alas, it all worked out." He smiled, reassuringly. Then put his hand on her back, gently. "I'll go grab us drinks–are you okay to stay here by yourself for a second?"

A little scared, but not wanting to show her insecurity, Liv just gulped, shaking off her fright.

"Of course–I'll be fine," she added with a reassuring smile.

"I'll be back." Kai grabbed Liv's shoulders, lightly squeezing them in reassurance.

Liv looked around, trying to spot any friendly face, and came scarce. She did find beautiful gowns and suits, which served as the most fun kind of people watching–almost as if she was at her own personal couture runway show. Ladies were adorned with feathers, sequins, lace and leathers, all shaped into unique designs. The guys wore suits of various silks and patterns, mostly accented with metallic accessories of some sort.

Suddenly, Peyton's face peaked out of the crowd, running over toward Liv and embracing her with the warmest hug.

"Why hello gorgeous! I had no idea you would be here!" Peyton marveled at Liv's look, "I barely recognized you in this get-up." She eyed Liv's lips, admiring the pop of color her roommate finally decided to don.

"Me? Look at you. Fashionable as always." Liv smiled, impressed by Peyton's navy long sleeved cutout gown, adorned with sparkly gold beads and subtle sparkly star embellishments.

"So, although I can't express how happy I am to run into someone I actually like at one of these things for once, I must ask, what brings you here?" Peyton inquired, looking around for a sign of Liv's connection to the soiree.

"Kai invited me. How about you? I didn't realize you were so close to the King?" Liv speculated.

"Kai?" Peyton looked concerned, but brushed it off immediately. "I'm here with Rei."

"*Rei*?" Liv clarified, making sure she heard her ex-roommate correctly. "Like, the-refuses-to-talk-to-girls, socially awkward Rei?"

Peyton laughed, "He's not socially awkward. Maybe around you," she joked, "but that's because of Hayden. Rei and I sort of have a history."

"A history?" Liv was stunned, "And why did you refrain from telling me this?"

"Well first, it's none of your business." Peyton smirked, "And second, it wouldn't have been appropriate when you didn't know who we really were, and third–this resurfacing is sort of a exploration that recently came back to life. So there wasn't really news to tell, until tonight."

Peyton still looked curiously around the room, as if she was trying to spot someone before proceeding. She nodded her head to an older man, dressed in a beautiful light blue floral printed silk suit, who looked a lot like Rei.

"That's Rei's father, Silas. He's the Elite of our Security and Warfare Pillar." Looking back at Liv, Peyton added, "That's why Rei could help Hayden out with supervising you at Oregon and get away with it."

"And you?" Liv asked Peyton, intrigued.

Peyton immediately stopped, contemplating whether to go on, and ultimately decided to bring Liv closer when she whispered. "I used to be a Dark God."

She saw the immediate terror form in Liv's eyes, so Peyton quickly grabbed her friend's arm, allowing herself time for an explanation before Liv departed for safety. "I more so believe that it's okay to interact with humans–I was *never* an extremist, but recently, the Dark Gods motives had gotten, let's just say much darker and more polar, so in brief summary–a lot worse–so my loyalty changed back to the Pure Gods."

Liv relaxed, now understanding why Peyton may have been more willing to befriend her than other Gods tasked to the challenge of supervising a mortal.

"Rei and I first broke up because of our opposing beliefs after my declaration to the Dark Gods, but truly, I never stopped caring for him. So, when Rei and Hayden asked for my help, I figured it couldn't hurt to prove my loyalty and try to be in their good graces–hoping first they would forgive me for my... lack of judgment... and ultimately, possibly, put in a good word to their family if my position came back into question."

Liv looked at Peyton's hair, now almost as blonde as her own. "That's why–your hair, I thought you were getting non-stop highlights."

Peyton smiled, glad that Liv understood. "Exactly, it's hard to prove your allegiance when your physicality still aligns with the Dark Gods, but now they know my intentions are Pure."

But soon their conversation was interrupted as Kai approached, handing Liv a flute.

"Peyton." Kai greeted, bluntly.

"Kai." Peyton hissed in return.

Liv was a little confused by the unfriendly encounter, but figured maybe Peyton had more romantic histories unknown to Liv, and so decided to ignore the tension.

"Thanks for the champagne." Liv nodded appreciatively.

Kai's face relaxed as he smiled at Liv, "Of course. I have some people I'd like to introduce you to. If you don't mind, Peyton." He glared back at Liv's friend.

Peyton appeased, not breaking eye contact with her seemingly personal arch nemesis. "Not at all, Kai. See you later, Liv." And walked away.

"Sorry about that." Kai turned to Liv, pulling her away from the scene. "Peyton and I have an unpleasant history."

"I gathered." Liv agreed awkwardly, taking a sip from her flute.

Kai walked around introducing Liv to various colleagues, friends and acquaintances, always being kind to include her in as much conversation as possible, which deemed rather difficult whenever he talked business or encountered an old family friend, but Liv nonetheless appreciated the effort. Kai was charming, easily making every girl swoon. Liv wanted to see a future with him, but couldn't help wonder about Hayden throughout the night. What were his Friday nights like in this world?

Liv spotted Rei at one point nearby, talking with his Dad and wearing a dark navy velvet double button blazer and edgy gold pants. Liv assumed he had paired his suit to coordinate with Peyton's dress.

She tried to wave him over to chat, but Rei blatantly ignored her and continued his deep conversation with his father. But when they parted, Rei looked back over at Liv, and finally waved back, spastically so no one would see, before turning away suddenly in the opposite direction.

Liv laughed to herself, wondering if she and Rei would ever get past their awkward encounters, but enjoying them for the time being.

Finally, a trumpet song played, announcing an important arrival to the symposium. All the guests' heads turned to the entrance, excited for the King's arrival.

"We should head up to the front with the other Elites–we always greet the royal family first." Kai explained, gently pushing Liv towards the grand staircase.

Liv began feeling butterflies in her stomach as she followed Kai–she wanted to blame it on the champagne she had been sipping all night, but figured it was really the anticipation of seeing the royal family of the God's for the first time.

"Silas, how great to see you." Kai greeted Rei's father as he took his place next to him on the end of the Elite line.

"And to you," Silas nodded, sternly turning to Liv for the introduction. "And who is this divine creature you brought tonight?" He asked, sincerely smiling at Liv.

Liv held out her hand for him to take, in response. "Liv, sir. A pleasure to meet you."

"The pleasure is all mine." Silas nodded approvingly to Liv, then turned back towards the stairs as the trumpeting ceased.

"Miss Jocelyn, Princess of the Gods." The announcer's voice vibrated through the room.

A dazzling blonde woman, adorned in a long-sleeved olive green silk gown, embellished with gold jacquard and accompanied by a sleek matching cape, walked down the stairs gracefully, nodding in joy to acknowledge and greet her peers. Her hair was loosely pulled back into a low bun, but she looked none-the-less regal.

Jocelyn greeted each Elite, variously hugging, cheek kissing or delicately holding out her hand for appraisal, depending on the soul. Her eyes sparkled at the small talk and laughed joyfully at any attempted jokes. All in all, Liv assessed Jocelyn seemed quite approachable for a royal God, and felt she looked oddly familiar, as if she knew her already.

Soon, the announcer roared again. "Miss Cleo, Family Elite of the Arts Pillar and Elements Pillar, accompanied tonight by Hayden, Prince of the Gods."

Liv's head immediately turned toward the staircase entrance, jaw dropped in shock and heart pounding louder as she processed what she had just heard.

There was Hayden, holding the arm of Cleo, who looked smug and entitled as ever, as they descended the staircase. Hayden appeared distracted, concernedly looking around the room, as if searching for someone in attendance. Liv felt a pang stab her chest, as she breathed heavily, trying to calm down her racing heart.

Hayden looked handsome, sporting a perfectly fitted charcoal three-piece silk suit, topped off with a stunningly metallic velvet blazer that matched his tie, and consequently made his eyes radiate silver in unison.

He finally spotted Liv, and they locked eyes, almost for too long and what seemed like only an instant. Hayden's eyes first widened with excitement of finding her, but then saddened, almost as if trying to communicate an apology for the unexpected surprise.

Cleo nudged Hayden, demanding back his attention as she continued lavishly waving to people she didn't know and dawning a transparently fake smile. She was wearing a striped dress, Liv grudgingly observed, noting that Cleo tried too hard to match Hayden's suit and obnoxiously used the same silk and velvet pattern as his. But really, it just made Liv want to throw up.

Luckily, Jocelyn had approached Kai and extended a warm and inviting welcome to Liv, distracting her and genuinely making Liv feel like the most important person in the room.

"It's so lovely to meet you, Liv. Are you enjoying yourself tonight?" Jocelyn's eyes sparkled, and Liv noticed they were identical to Hayden's. She secretly shamed herself for not having put the name and resemblance together, before Hayden was announced.

"The pleasure is all mine." Liv smiled back; so happy to have finally placed a face to all the hilarious, heartwarming and very-brotherly stories

Hayden had shared with her over the years. "And, tonight has been an absolute dream! This palace is stunning, and…"

Liv wanted to say so many more things to this person she knew so well, and share how excited she was to finally meet Joss, Hayden's sister, but then remembered that to Jocelyn, Liv was a stranger.

So instead, Liv held back by adding a simple, neutral sentiment. Jokingly lifting her flute as it bubbled, she stated, "Plus, the Champagne is a delight."

Jocelyn laughed back endearingly, music to Liv's ears. "Well, truly, the honor was mine to meet you, please enjoy yourself tonight." And with a delightful nod, Jocelyn was then hugging the next lady aside to Liv.

With being so infatuated by Hayden's sister, Liv didn't even notice Cleo and Hayden were now approaching Kai, as well. Luckily, the trumpet went off again, causing everyone to pause and return their gaze to the entrance for the final introduction.

"Daphne, Queen of the Gods is accompanied tonight by her husband, whom we celebrate tonight, Rowan, King of the Gods."

A burst of clapping emerged from the ball as everyone cheered the King and Queen's entrance. Liv was thrown a little off guard by Hayden's mother, who was wearing a bold cut out black and gold geometric silk structured mermaid dress with a dramatic pillowed train. She was very elegant and poised as she walked statue-like down the stairs, and although smiling, her joy did not reach her eyes, which stood cold as she looked out ahead of her peers. She was still a stunning sight to see, but Liv noticed a sadness to her beauty that she was trying to mask during the celebration.

Opposite of Daphne, King Rowan glowed in a gold suit, exuberating the warmth she had felt from Jocelyn and knew of Hayden. The king waved, stoically and strong–he was a force to be reckoned with, but still radiated kindness and sincerity for those who came to celebrate with him tonight.

Liv could see where Hayden got his handsome looks, as she studied the pair–Hayden was the spitting image of his dad–and both his father and mother looked youthful, barely ten years older than Hayden, almost as if they were older siblings rather than parental figures to him and Jocelyn.

When Cleo and Hayden moved over to Kai and Liv, Cleo yelled out a very loud, and very disingenuous, "Hello *OLLIE*! It's SO great to see you!"

Jocelyn, who was still chatting to Liv's right, turned her head immediately at the mention of Ollie.

"Ollie?" She looked to Liv, questioning softly, "You're Ollie?"

"Liv." Liv snarled through her teeth as she fisted her hands at her sides, giving Cleo a death stare for calling her that.

"Oh? I'm so sorry Ollie, I didn't mean to call you that. Oh, look at me again." Cleo fake laughed as she touched her chest, "I just did it again." She smirked.

Liv was boiling inside, she did not understand why or how this bitch had such an effect on her. She wanted to turn in disbelief to Hayden, but refused to succumb to the need for an explanation–she had no right to care about his obviously ridiculous choice in wanting to spend time with Cleo.

Hayden chose Cleo, and Liv had now chosen Kai.

"*Liv*," Jocelyn interjected, eyeing Hayden warily. "I would love to show you around. We have some exquisite art and it would be a delight to chat with you more." She gently put her arms around Liv, graciously excusing herself from her current conversation and consequently, Liv's.

Once away from Hayden and his stupid girlfriend, Liv breathed, realizing how she had just acted in front of Hayden, Kai, Cleo and Jocelyn.

"I am so sorry." Liv apologized, eyes wide in horror as Jocelyn continued to direct her through the crowd.

"Oh? That? Water under the bridge, seriously." Jocelyn stopped, smiling encouragingly at Liv and showing no offense or judgment. "Cleo is a unique personality, I daresay." She looked over at Cleo, disgust penetrating through her outer mask of peace.

Jocelyn turned back to Liv, genuine happiness returning and sparkling through her eyes. "Honestly, I'm just, so happy to meet you, finally!" Jocelyn gasped, throwing her arms around Liv and pulling her into a very informal hug.

"Oh, me too! I was so happy to meet you earlier, Jocelyn." Liv smiled, relieved and feeling the warmth radiating back into her body.

"Please, call me Joss." Jocelyn waved her hand to insist, "Hayden has told me so much about you. I just–didn't realize how, or expect you to be, so breathtakingly beautiful." She smiled, adding, "On the inside and out."

Jocelyn already felt like the sister Liv never had, but had always wanted. Liv always envisioned the moment she could finally meet Hayden's sibling, the one he spoke so proudly and highly of, and how she had always known they would just *click*. Now that all of it was coming to fruition exactly as Liv had dreamt, that Jocelyn was just as warm and kind as she had always believed her to be, Liv sadly realized her dream would never truly be a reality–that they would never really become sisters.

With all the craziness that Liv had been thrown into during the past week, and having one thing happen how her brain had actually thought it would, Liv was overwhelmed. She didn't realize just how overly in need she was of something expectingly *normal* to transpire.

Suddenly a rush of emotions came over her, and already feeling at ease with Jocelyn, but saddened at the loss of her imaginary relationship, Liv unexpectedly went back to hug Jocelyn again, trying to hold back her tears.

"Thank you. It's just so nice to meet you, too. You're exactly how I had envisioned you to be, and yet even better than I could have ever imagined."

They separated from their embrace, smiling at each other, unaware they were being approached by King Rowan and Queen Daphne–Hayden and Jocelyn's parents.

"Joss, who is this stunning lady you are chatting with?" Daphne shyly eyed Liv and then turned to Jocelyn for a response.

"Mom, this is Ollie." Joss squealed, then coughed, "I mean, Liv. This is Liv." She looked at Liv, with a mischievous grin at her mishap.

"Liv, what a joy." Daphne smiled, genuinely looking happier than her descent down the entrance stairs.

"Nice to meet you, Liv." Rowan blankly stated, distracted by Silas approaching. When he turned back to Liv, it looked as if he had seen a ghost.

"You do look familiar, have we met before?" Rowan studied Liv, trying to place her face.

Dreadfully, Liv started to explain her history with Hayden, but luckily Silas approached before she could answer.

"Sir, sorry to interrupt," Silas looked apologetically at the ladies, and lowered his voice as he spoke close to the King. "There was unexpected, thunderous activity that surrounded the palace. It's gone now, but suspicious."

The King looked at Liv, unsure he wanted her to overhear their conversation. Liv casually glanced around the room, as if not paying attention.

Finally, King Rowan sternly asked, "And it's completely gone?"

Silas confirmed, "Not a trace that it ever happened."

King Rowan took a deep breath, relieved, patting Silas on the shoulder. "Thank you Silas. But please!" The king jokingly begged, "Then have a cocktail! You're my guest, not my security tonight. We have enough completely capable guards surrounding the palace."

After Silas departed, The King nodded, excusing himself from the ladies and followed his Elite Guard to the bar, obviously to discuss further.

Daphne took a deep breath in. "How is it we can no longer enjoy one simple symposium without some security breach?"

"Mother, he's just doing his job." Jocelyn rolled her eyes.

"Well, that alone is an excuse for a glass of wine if I ever encountered one." Daphne smiled, excusing herself from the two girls. "Liv, what an absolute pleasure. Hayden has told us so many wonderful things about you. Please do enjoy yourself tonight." And with a genuine arm squeeze, Queen Daphne left.

"You know, Hayden really talks quite highly of you." Jocelyn continued. "If you ever wanted to run for President, or CEO, or whatever, he would be your best campaign advisor."

Liv grinned. Coming from Joss, that was truly a compliment. She even let the whole 'running for CEO' concept slide in appreciation of the kind sentiment.

"Joss, there you are!" A handsome young man approached the two girls; arms open for an embrace as he forced Jocelyn into a stiff hug. He was wearing a flamboyant floral printed silk suit, with a light blue bowtie.

"Liv, this is Demetrius–he's the God of the Solar System."

"Enchante." Demetrius forcefully grabbed Liv's hand, allowing him to kiss it.

"Nice to meet you, too." Liv stated, eyeing Joss in question.

"Joss, you must dance with me." Demetrius insisted, grandly extending his hand for Joss to take.

"Oh, Demetrius, I'm sorry but I... um," Joss was eagerly looking around for an inspiring excuse to dodge his dancing proposition.

"Promised to show me that sculpture I have been dying to see," Liv interjected. "I have been trying to chase this gem all night Demetrius, and I'm sorry, but I refuse to let her get away for a dance now."

Demetrius looked at Liv and then back to Joss, who simply shrugged.

"Maybe the next dance?" Joss offered.

"You bet, sugar lips." And on that note, Demetrius left, unfazed by Joss' escape.

Liv turned to Joss, shockingly surprised and dying for an explanation.

"And who would that be, *sugar lips?*" She mockingly inquired.

"Oh, Demetrius. He's a sweetheart really, but he's all talk – no action." Jocelyn shrugged again. "He's technically an Elite, but doesn't even want to acknowledge that responsibility. We dated for a while, but nothing serious. And unfortunately I don't think anything serious *would* ever come of it, so why bother?"

Joss actually looked saddened at the thought, so Liv bumped encouragingly into her. "I'm sorry. But hey, at least you know he's there if you ever want to have fun?"

"True." Joss agreed, sighing as she longingly looked at Demetrius, across the room. "But is it really fun if the fun lasts forever?"

"Liv, there you are!" Kai exclaimed from behind, "I've been looking for you all night." He turned to Joss, "Hello again, Joss–would you mind if I stole my date for a dance?"

Joss looked at Liv for permission before responding. Liv nodded, appreciating her concern.

"Not at all–she's all yours." Joss smiled, leaving them.

"I'm sorry about my sister Cleo–she can be a lot to handle some-times, and frankly, a pain in the ass most times."

Liv felt immediately better after Kai's confession. So she chose the higher road of pacifying the situation, instead of igniting it even more by offering peace. "No, I overreacted. Being called Ollie just triggers some nerves, that's all." Liv waved it off, not wanting to get into the details of her hatred toward Cleo.

"Well, I know you can jump, dance and run–but, can you waltz?" Kai asked, challenging Liv by extending his hand to lead Liv onto the dance floor.

"I've never had the opportunity to learn, but I'm a quick study."

Liv smiled, taking Kai's hand and forced herself to ignore Hayden across the room, who was staring at them as they entered onto the dance floor together.

"Just follow my steps." Kai whispered, taking his left foot forward, then diagonally, followed by the right. Liv had to applaud Kai, who led with the correct foot.

"Are you left-handed?" Liv asked, as they glided through the dance floor.

"How did you know?" Kai inquired, impressed by her observation.

"Well, to start–you've been handing me drinks with your left hand all night, and you naturally led with your left foot, but typically my dance partners always wanted to lead with their right."

"Well, left is correct for the waltz, but also correct for my dominant side, too. You're very intuitive, Liv." Kai smiled as they continued the beau-tiful dance, occasionally adding a turn or lift.

Liv noticed Cleo pull Hayden onto the dance floor. She tried to focus on Kai's sexy confidence, but unaware of herself anymore, all of Liv's atten-tion directed toward Hayden. If Kai wasn't such a great waltzing leader, she would had easily tripped and fell in a heartbeat.

Hayden looked at Liv, making direct eye contact with her as he put his hands into place on Cleo's tiny body and joined the dance. Cleo was beaming, but had no idea her dance partner's attention was focused entirely on somebody else.

Liv continued in awe, trying her hardest to avoid dizziness as Kai spun her. She automatically focused on keeping her eyes in lock with Hayden's for as long as she could, almost as if she was practicing 'spotting' while doing her chaînés floor work in ballet class. Hayden, being her target, was feeding her back with equally mesmerizing stares.

He moved so gracefully with Cleo; Liv had no inclination that Hayden was such a beautiful dancer—but that was the theme of this entire disaster. Hayden was a mystery to Liv, one she would never solve.

As the dance concluded, Liv beamed at Kai, thanking him for the lovely dance. She was just about to exit the dance floor when Hayden approached them.

"Kai, would you mind if I borrowed your date for a dance?" Hayden calmly requested, not taking his eyes off of Liv. "Your sister requested you join her at the bar."

Without waiting for Kai's response, Hayden held out his hand. Liv grabbed it without a second thought, as she naturally magnetized toward him, unaware of everyone's eyes on them, but only noticing Hayden's intense glare, full of desire and need.

"I didn't realize you were such the expert in ballroom dancing." Liv accused, as she placed her hand delicately on his shoulder. She bit her lip, fighting the urge to kiss him. Liv hadn't been this close to Hayden—touching him—in months, and it was overwhelmingly intoxicating.

"Our high school prom didn't exactly present the best opportunity to showcase my hidden talents." Hayden smoothly replied, as he swiftly twirled Liv, bringing her closer to his torso.

Liv breathed heavily at the unexpected closeness, she could feel his breath on her neck. Liv looked up into Hayden's eyes, as her lips gravitated toward his, an instinct his naturally reciprocated, as he whispered, "Liv, you look so beautiful tonight."

But before their lips could touch, suddenly Liv was twirling again and gliding in every direction by Hayden.

For Liv and Hayden, it was only the two of them, nobody else was there–they were in their own private world, one that they had both missed dearly since their time spent apart.

And at that moment, Hayden didn't care that every guest in the room was gaping at him, as he willingly danced with the mortal girl–the Prince of Pure Gods, openly and publicly sticking it to the code.

"Having fun with Kai tonight?" Hayden playfully smirked, dipping Liv in the direction of Kai at the bar, whose gaze was determinedly and frustratingly focused on the two twirling together.

Liv quickly looked in her date's direction before Hayden continued their waltz around the floor–a silver blur to all who watched.

"He's just a friend." Liv lied.

"Seemed like more than a friend a second ago." Hayden retorted.

This forced Liv to raise her eyebrow, appalled. She stopped dancing.

"Oh, and you? What about Cleo? Are you two just going to live happily ever after together? AND do you want to talk about the fact you're the Prince of the fucking Gods? Or did that not cross your mind of something you should have shared with me in all of this?"

Then it all clicked.

"Oh, my god." Liv covered her mouth, remembering Cleo's prophecy.

Cleo was destined to be with the Prince of the Gods. Cleo was destined to be with Hayden.

Now very much aware of everyone staring at Hayden and her on the dance floor, Liv slowly backed away from her dance partner, cautiously looking around, trying to distract herself from crying. It was no longer them–Ollie and Hayden–together. Hayden had moved on and Liv was an outcast here, a mortal. She had no right to be at this castle, interacting with this world–she didn't belong here in more ways than she could fathom. And at the moment, looking at her dress, she felt foolish–did she really think she could play 'dress up' by throwing on a dazzling gown and adding a red lip to magically fit in with these powerful entities?

With all of her exponential mistakes calculating together and blowing up in her mind, Liv quickly turned and ran out of the great ballroom, trying to find an escape. But when she approached the entrance, she realized she had no idea how to summon or drive the carriage that brought her here.

She was stuck until Kai or Peyton found her.

But at the moment, she didn't want to be found. She didn't want to exist.

Liv turned back into the castle, quickly dodging to the right of the grand ballroom and found another corridor to take, leading her far away from the party.

After attempting to open a couple doors, she finally found one that was unlocked. Breathing a sigh of relief, she entered, unsure where the door would lead.

The room she found herself in looked like the starry sky with twinkling lights that softly glowed throughout the room. If there was ever a space for solitude, this was it. The cozy room seemed so far distanced from the enormous symposium taking place only a hallway away.

Liv found a bench and sat down, staring out into the night sky, taking a deep breath to try to calm herself down.

She looked around the room, noticing the beautiful mosaic design with tiles and stones, and then thought sarcastically: just another room too grandiose for Liv's presence. Darkly mocking herself, Liv decided that the air was probably sacred in here–too pure for a mere *mortal* to inhale.

"Breath less than, mortal." Liv solved, mumbling to herself.

"Please don't do that." A velvety voice echoed in the darkness.

Liv spun, alert and slightly panicked at whom was spying on her.

"It's me." Hayden stepped out, the twinkling lights now reflecting on his skin. "I was going to say 'don't worry,' but given the circumstance, I'm sure that I'm the last person you want to see. So, feel free to worry or get mad, I guess." He said solemnly, shrugging.

"Why are you here, Hayden?" Liv asked, monotone. She didn't have the energy to raise her voice or fight any more.

"I wanted to make sure you were okay. Things sort of exploded on the dance floor." Hayden sat down, cautiously looking at Liv. "You know, I knew you would be here tonight." Hayden softly smiled, looking up at the sky, then back at Liv. "You must have looked at your constellation."

"Are you connected to it, somehow?" Liv asked, intrigued, but hating herself for being so.

"You're connected to it, too. Whenever you see the stars, it triggers your emotion and location and shares it with me through a feeling, it's sort of hard to explain. That was my initial attempt of trying to make sure you were okay once we had to go our separate ways." Hayden gulped, and then added with a gloomy chuckle, "Clearly, it didn't work as well as I had hoped..."

Liv smiled, reminiscing on all that had transpired in the past week, but then paused, sadly remembering all that had also been discovered tonight.

"Hayden, why didn't you tell me? About your family, and you being royal, and everything that comes with it?"

"That I'm a prince?" Hayden frowned and then looked down at his hands, taking a deep breath before beginning. "You fell in love with me when I was just a regular person, whose biggest accomplishment was being on the football team." He mockingly laughed at the sentiment of his known feat. "You had no idea I was born into this fate, or what immense power I would inherit."

Hayden looked back at Liv, his eyes showing the first grain of joy since their outburst earlier. "I could just be myself around you, no title, always comfortable, and knowingly accepted for who I was – I never had to think about questioning your intentions." He looked back down, ashamed. "I missed that feeling, I guess. Just being Hayden, a guy. Not Hayden, a very powerful God, born into royalty, the fate of the deities residing in his reign. I guess I just wanted to relish that reunion, a sliver of my past brought back to life for a little longer. So, I didn't tell you. And, I'm sorry for that."

"Nobody tells me anything here," Liv sighed.

Hayden grabbed her hand, pleading, "I want to be honest with you, Ollie–I really do. You *have* to understand that. But we have a code and I have to abide by it. And, consequently, it leaves you in the dark more than I would ever wish you to be."

"What *can* you tell me then?" Liv pressed. "Am I not allowed any answers? Am I meant to just be *stuck* here, not allowed to do anything, but wonder and stay confused about *everything*?"

Liv looked at Hayden, painfully as he remained silent–he was so handsome, even when he was frustrated, and she wanted all of him, so badly. But she had to remember he was no longer hers to have anymore.

Exasperated, Hayden stood up, raising his arms and putting a distance between them. "All of this–the confusion, the pain, forcing you to come here, and having to see you every day, but not being able to touch you, or talk to you… Ollie, it's tearing me apart."

Liv looked up at Hayden, witnessing the immense grief he had been enduring the past months, finally surface. His jaw clenched, but his expression broke its façade, finally showing her just how much he had been in agony, too–just like Liv had been experiencing since their painful separation.

"When I turned eighteen, and came into power, I had to break up with you because of this world, our stupid code." Hayden kicked a nearby stone bench, and to Liv's amazement caused the entire structure to break instead of his foot. "Pure Gods aren't supposed to be with humans, not to mention be *in love* with them. And I couldn't tell you *why* because I didn't have a reason to end things with you beside that, but I wasn't allowed to tell you that I was a God." Hayden was clenching his jaw with his arms in fists–he truly was angry at the situation he had fallen into during the summer.

"So, I told you I was going to a different school, which I was–Puerdios." He shrugged. "I never lied to you, Ollie. I never want to lie to you."

His entire story was pouring out, Hayden couldn't keep it in any longer; the floodgates had been opened.

"First, I had to give up my entire life, and then I had to completely ignore you. Otherwise you could become a target to the Dark God, a way to get to me. So, security warned me that if I showed any sign of still caring for you, the Dark Gods would try to capture you as a way to get to me, or my family. I just wanted you to stay safe, Ollie. So you could live your best life, even if it had to be without me. But they still figured it out, and they still attacked you, even despite all of my agonizing security precautions. And until I figure out a way to make peace with their cult or solve this split in views..." Hayden's fists gripped tighter as he looked back at Liv with concern. "That's why you've been in danger Ollie, and you're still in immense danger. The Dark Gods know I still love you–I never stopped, and I can't bear it anymore."

Liv's eyes widened as she heard Hayden say the words she had so desperately wanted to hear. *He still loved her.* Liv finally understood that the pain and hurt she had felt these past months had been matched equally by Hayden, but she had the gift of not knowing, not being in control of their grief apart. She wanted to jump into his arms at that very moment, tell him she still loved him too, but she paused, remembering that their situation was still, at most, only temporary.

It wasn't worth the risk of re-opening all those emotions, putting Hayden in danger, herself in *more danger*, when ultimately they would be forced to the same fate, to be torn apart again, because Hayden's ultimate destiny rested with another soul.

Cleo.

"Say something, Liv." Hayden pleaded.

"I don't know anymore, Hayden." Liv shrugged, apologetically. "Before all of this happened, I would have opened my heart and given you my all, happily. But it's all dangerous, and only provisional, as you've said, so I understand now. And I agree, I… don't think it's worth the risk."

Hayden went over to Liv, sitting next to her and pulling her into a strong embrace.

Liv wanted to stay there in his arms, forever, but ignored all of her desires, her comfort, and forced the inevitable to be said.

"You have to let me move on, Hayden." Liv said quietly, bowing her head in acceptance; a tear softly comforting her cheek.

"I can't." Hayden choked, grabbing Liv's hands and kissing them. "It's all been for you, Ollie."

"The prophecy—we're fighting fate." Liv stated, sadly in acceptance. "You might be powerful, Hayden, but I'm not—and even together, neither of us are a match for that."

As Liv stood up, it felt like a knife had stabbed her in the chest, and with each consequential step away from Hayden, the blade wedged itself deeper and deeper, until she was torn to pieces and could no longer breath.

Hayden slowly looked up at Liv, face raw with tenderness. He sighed, once again allowing practicality to triumph his selfish desires. "I guess you're right. It wouldn't be safe for you if we were together. But," he added weakly, "at least you know the truth now."

He stood up, defeated and in a daze. "I'll grab Peyton—she can take you home. I don't trust Kai, and you should be careful around him, too."

Liv wanted to joke about Hayden being the jealous ex-boyfriend, but from his facial expression and tone, she knew that his warning was not to be taken lightly.

Before he left the room, Hayden turned to Liv, stating blankly in retrospect, "I guess all of this came at a good time anyway—I'll be gone for a while. I have... some things to tend to." Hayden paused, debating how much he should share in lieu of their recent honesty, ultimately deciding that ambiguity would be best for Liv's safety. "That will give you the time and space you need to... move on."

And with an accepting nod, Hayden turned and left.

THIRTEEN

As **Hayden had** promised, he was nowhere to be seen the following week, and although Liv appreciated the space to clear her thoughts, she remained on edge wondering where he was, or what he was doing the entire time. Liv may not have known the specifics, but a part of her knew it was dangerous, and at times she felt as if she could sense something was wrong with Hayden. She shook it off, beginning to think she was becoming mad. But as each day passed, and Hayden and his cocky smile refrained from entering the Great Hall or Class throughout the week, she grew more concerned.

What was he up to? What was he trying to achieve?

Did she make the right choice at the symposium?

Piper was the best distraction Liv could have asked for during Hayden's absence – she was like the humanized version of Liv's textbooks and fictionalized novels, barely leaving Liv alone to her thoughts, aside from sleeping.

Piper had never asked for specifics about the Symposium Ball–just the basics–and automatically understood that yes, something *big* happened and *no*, Liv did not want to talk about it. Easily inferred from her friend's short replies and vague descriptions of the event, Piper did not press on about the party details after the first day of asking.

Instead, Piper helped Liv catch up on her studies, homework and projects, all while sharing relevant histories of the gods and juicy insights to her classmates during their breaks. *Did you know Cleo's minion, Elsa, once blew up the Galleria Library? She was angry that Cleo didn't approve of her outfit and couldn't control her power! And Rei, before dating Peyton, used to be a huge player? Once, I heard he hooked up with Elsa AND Adelaide during the same campus symposium!*

Liv couldn't help but enjoy the gossip; it was better than any of the plot lines in her favorite books, plus it helped give personalities to all the strange classmates surrounding her.

And, to Liv's amusement, Piper even gifted her a volleyball, offering to play with her in the courtyard, although Piper declared that she didn't fully understand the point of repeatedly hitting a ball over a net.

However, even with Piper's distractions, Liv still felt like there was a void in her day to day with Hayden now gone. She knew she was supposed to be moving on from Hayden, but she couldn't help but believe something was missing in her life, that something wasn't right.

She wasn't *trying* to worry about Hayden, but Liv *did* want to make sure he wasn't worrying about *her*–or at least, that's what she told herself each night before she went to bed and looked up at her constellation in the sky–but really, she just wanted to feel connected to him, somehow. The first night Liv actually felt disappointed when he didn't annoyingly appear uninvited after glancing up into the starry night sky.

So, by Friday, Liv almost fell out of her seat when she saw Hayden enter the Great Hall for breakfast. Piper, mid-bite into her avocado toast, pivoted around to see what caused the commotion. Upon seeing Hayden, Piper calmly shrugged, trying not to make as big of a deal as Liv accidentally had with her reaction, stating blankly, "Oh. Hayden's back."

Liv shifted out of her seat, trying to watch Hayden as he limped over to Rei's table. He was obviously injured, something bad *had* happened to him. Hayden smiled softly at Rei, grimacing as he sat down, clearly in pain as he grabbed his shoulder.

"Liv, stretch any further and you're gonna fall out of your chair." Piper muttered mockingly. Liv didn't notice.

"Piper, Hayden looks hurt. Can Gods even get wounded?"

"We're immortal, not invincible." Piper confirmed. "It just takes a lot more power to do damage, but luckily, nothing's permanent. That's all."

"He looks tired, too." Liv observed, concernedly.

"Probably because he's been running through your mind all week." Piper retorted, snorting at her joke.

Liv scowled at Piper, "Not funny."

Piper blushed, hiding her shame by taking another bite of her toast. But Liv's eyes were already back on Hayden, unconcerned with her friend's guilt.

"He's getting up." Liv immediately got up in response.

"Thanks for the play-by-play?" Piper mumbled to herself, grinning.

"I need to talk to him." Liv decided, grabbing her gold-feathered trench as she sprinted off toward Hayden, proving to be much more difficult in stilettos than her combat boots.

"I guess I'll grab your books then!" Piper hollered to Liv's back, "We can work on our project later – see ya!"

Liv was oblivious to her friend; she couldn't keep her eyes off Hayden. Walking toward him was the most relieving feeling she had experienced all week, almost as if she had been fighting a magnetic pull by being away from him, and now finally giving in to the gravitational need, a sense of ease overwhelmed her body with each step in his direction.

"Hayden! Wait!" Liv yelled.

Hayden paused, turning toward Liv immediately, but stood still as she approached him.

"What happened to you?" Liv inquired, worriedly eyeing Hayden up and down. His hand was clenched around his torso now, clearly in pain just from the act of standing. "Where have you been?"

"It's none of your concern." He scowled, grimacing as he turned away.

Liv chased after him, she would *make* it her concern. All of her worrying during the week had been exactly correct. She had *felt* something was wrong, and needed to know why.

"Are you okay!?" Liv called after him.

"I'll be fine." Hayden sneered over his shoulder, but didn't stop his pace.

Liv halted, taking the hint. Hayden wanted nothing to do with her.

How dare he? Liv thought angrily to herself, blood boiling in her chest as she clenched her fists. *How could he act so distant?* She had been wondering where he was and worrying about him all week, and he couldn't give her the time of day to just *explain* what he had been doing to get himself so bloody punched and wounded?

Liv was about to continue to chase him down and give him a piece of her mind, when she remembered that *she* turned him down last weekend, not the other way around.

She couldn't expect anything from Hayden anymore, not now.

Liv sadly watched Hayden's body slowly vanish down in the hallway. It was weird. Liv felt weird. She had thought she knew Hayden so well, but each day, was beginning to understand that she might have never known him at all.

After tossing and turning all night, witnessing numerous nightmares all of which Hayden got attacked by creatures imagined by Liv's darkest of thoughts–Liv welcomed the sunlight as it lit up her room, serving as the perfect alarm clock (not that she needed it), and jumped out of her bed.

Liv looked outside, excited to see only a partly cloudy sky–a torrential thunderstorm throughout the night had served as another reason for Liv's less than restful sleep–but as the storm had now passed, Liv was relieved she could go on a much-needed run.

She changed into her running clothes and noticed a new metallic charcoal silver and lightening yellow outfit had majestically entered her armoire. Grinning to herself, while also wondering how Piper's aunt knew how to make workout clothes, she figured she might as well try it out.

Originally planning to embark on her favorite running loop, Liv eyed the forest mischievously as she passed by it. She knew she shouldn't venture so far from the castle, but her typical loop wasn't very long and since she didn't have class today, Liv had so much more time to invest in a longer workout. So, with a rebellious grin, Liv turned back, jogging toward the forest entrance, feeling a sense of freedom encompass her with each additional step onto the muddy soil.

Liv had been running for a bit when she started hearing distant noises. Making sure it wasn't a part of her playlist, Liv paused her music, staying still and quiet as she heard more voices nearby. Her heart was beating fast, and not just from her run, but from the adrenaline pulsing through her veins as she carefully tiptoed toward the intense shouts. Liv knew she should stay away, she was no match for whatever thing or creature she may encounter, but at the same time, figured it would be better to understand what was out there, to assess precisely how fast she should back to the castle for safety.

Finally, the yells were audible. Ducking behind a tree, Liv slowly popped her head out, to see what all the commotion was. Her eyes widened as she covered her mouth to make sure she didn't gasp.

Cleo was hanging in the air, wrists seemingly bounded by invisible shackles suspended in the sky. Below her, Hayden, Rei and Peyton stood in front, cautiously assessing their next action for escape as a group of Dark Gods, looking furious and ready to fight, encircled them.

Hayden, as if hearing Liv's breaths, immediately turned in her direction, looking shocked at her sudden appearance in the forest. He focused in on something behind her and then turned casually away as to not appear suspicious. But soon, his gaze was back with such an intense force on his face, it was if he was trying to communicate something mentally in her direction.

"You should not be here, Liv." Piper appeared suddenly behind Liv, sending a jolt of shock through Liv's body as Piper grabbed her arm to leave. "We need to go. NOW."

Liv was so surprised by Piper's appearance, and the sight of her with wings, that Liv easily gave in to Piper pulling her closer and hugging her as they levitated above the ground.

Piper began flying Liv away to safety, when they abruptly paused mid-air.

"Well, well. It seems the guest of honor finally arrived." A voice echoed in the forest.

Suddenly, Liv was being suspended through the air, as if invisible ropes had her limbs, pulling her away from her friend. The more Liv struggled, the tighter the ropes became.

Soon, Liv was in the air, parallel to Cleo, overlooking the group of Dark Gods and cringing in pain as she witnessed Piper joining Hayden, Rei and Peyton inside the circle.

"Now, the fun really starts."

Liv saw a man emerge from the Dark Gods' pack, positioning himself between Hayden and Liv. He looked darker than any of the Dark Gods Liv had previously met; his eyes were black, and he wore an all black leather ensemble with an oversized black mink wrap.

"Maybe now, you should consider my proposal seriously. Adding your precious Ollie to the equation seems to be helping." The man sneered at Hayden, a devilish smile appearing on his face.

"Hayden DON'T!" Liv yelled instinctively, "Don't do it!"

Liv wasn't exactly sure what was going on, but she did know she never wanted to be the reason Hayden appeased to any darkness, no matter what it would cost her.

"Shut up, little mortal." The man flicked his hand and the invisible ropes pulled tighter on Liv, and Cleo too–she angrily responded by growling with her teeth clenched.

"Leave them alone, Arlo!" Hayden ran forward toward the Dark God, but was stopped to Liv's horror, by Finn.

Finn looked so different from the young boy in her Astronomy Class. Now he was adorned with red leather and a black coat, strongly holding Hayden back.

"Ah, looks like I got little prince boy's attention, now. Don't I?" Arlo smirked.

Fighting Finn's resistance, Hayden growled, "Don't hurt them."

Arlo laughed, evil radiating from his mind as he pointed his finger in the air. "How about a little game to speed things up, shall we? You hand over your throne. Or, I kill them both."

"Don't you dare." Hayden's voice stood firm as he stared down Arlo with absolute hatred.

Cleo started fighting her restraints, eyes wide and yelling from the resulting pain.

"Well, they clearly aren't helping me get what I want. So, why not?" With a malicious grin, Arlo turned, lifting his hands up.

Hayden had released himself from Finn's grasp and as a red fog emerged out of Arlo's hands toward the girls, Hayden rocketed in front of Liv, holding his arms and legs around her as a fortress, protecting her as he blocked her from the blast of impact and took the blow himself.

Hayden fell to the ground, unconscious.

Liv screamed.

Arlo smirked, nodding to Finn to run over to Hayden.

Finn cut Hayden's wrist quickly with a knife and placed a cloth immediately on top of the opening to absorb the blood. As soon as he returned with the red-soaked fabric, Arlo glanced up, looking content with his accomplishments, and looked to his troops with a nod, giving them permission to attack with free reign, before vanishing suddenly.

Mayhem broke out between the gods. Rei and Peyton started blasting curses at the Dark Gods in offense, while Piper stood in front of Hayden, powering defensive spells directed at him, protecting him from more harm. But soon, terrified at Rei and Peyton's very vengeful and powerful wrath, the Dark Gods began flying away to find refuge.

Finn was the last Dark God to accept defeat, as he took flight and vanished into the sky.

Once all was safe, Peyton immediately flew over to Liv and held her hand over the bindings, releasing them. Liv fell into Peyton's arms, and Peyton carefully brought Liv back to the ground. Simultaneously, Rei did the same for Cleo, who looked like she was in shock.

With one glance from Rei, Peyton nodded her head and handed Liv to Piper.

"Take her to her room. NOW." Peyton commanded.

Piper immediately obliged as she pulled Liv away, but Liv fought back in desperate need to get to Hayden, trying to resist as she shrieked, "Where are they taking him!?"

"Hospital Wing." Piper replied, but Liv was no match for Piper, who kept pulling her away, dangerously looking around. Panicked, Piper mumbled to herself, "This isn't good. No, this isn't good at all."

Liv kept fighting. "I need to be with him, Piper. I love him. I've been so stupid. I, I…" Liv started crying, the enormity of the situation coming into realization. If only she had listened to him, had taken the opportunity to clear everything up with him. Tell him how he still really made her feel, always.

Piper turned to Liv, eyes wider and angrier than ever. "Don't say that ever again. Do you not realize the magnitude of what just transpired? Oh Zeus, and I was there. I might have to be a witness. Oh no, this is *not* good."

Liv couldn't handle it anymore. She stood firm, not letting Piper pull her anymore. Piper looked stunned, confused at Liv's stubborn strength.

"Of course I understand the *magnitude* of what just happened!" Liv stated, mockingly emphasizing the word Piper had used. "Arlo, the Darkest of all Gods, was just here. On campus and in the flesh. But you know what? Hayden just…" Liv choked, unable to say the word out loud, not yet. "I need to go back to him."

"Wait!"

Piper caught up to her.

"What!?" Liv screamed, tears flooding her eyes.

"Listen to me, Liv. Hayden will be FINE." Piper confirmed.

Liv took a breath. "He's not dead?"

Piper relaxed, now in hold of Liv's attention, again. "No. I mean–he definitely took a blow, one that would have definitely killed you, but he was quick enough to shield it. The real issue is that he chose you, over protecting Cleo–his own kin. That is forbidden."

Liv was confused. "Forbidden?"

"Look," Piper paused, trying to find the right words. "I like you. You're like, literally my only friend. But if word gets out about what happened this morning, I will not be able to help you. Hayden just left his future, fated betrothed to die, the one with whom he is destined to defeat the Dark Gods." Piper grabbed Liv's shoulder, looking her straight in the eye. "My advice is to stay away from Hayden, for his well-being and yours."

As they walked back to her room, Liv felt guilty, but relieved.

Hayden was still alive. She was his, and he was hers–Hayden chose *her*–and they both still loved each other. That's all that mattered, even if every force was trying to tear them apart.

Piper stayed with Liv in her room for the time being, in silence. She lit a fire and sat on the couch across from Liv. Both girls grabbed a book and consumed themselves with reading as they tried to distract their minds from what had just happened in the forest.

Finally, there was a knock on Liv's door.

Liv jumped up immediately, simultaneous with Piper, both welcoming a new distraction. Peyton walked in with Rei, but although Peyton went to join the girls on the couch and magically snapped a glass of wine to drink, Rei remained by the door.

"How is Hayden?" Liv immediately asked.

Peyton sighed, taking a sip of her wine. "He's good. Conscious, but in pain. Tough hit to take, especially when he was already injured from the previous week."

"How injured is he, now?" Liv prompted.

"Well, he re-broke his shoulder, but it's mending–so, he should be okay in a couple days, pending the recovery of his bruised ribs. He got a concussion, but that's healing too, and fortunately we were able to remove an internal curse that made his intestines burn to ashes."

Liv gulped, trying to process the last portion of medical analysis.

Peyton looked around and back at Rei, rolling her eyes at his distance. Then, she leaned forward, adding in a lower voice, "If anyone asks, only you were captured. Cleo wasn't there."

Liv was stunned. *How could Cleo pretend she hadn't been captured and held hostage by Arlo?*

"Is Cleo really going to go along with that? Why would she help us?" Liv shuddered at the idea of Cleo's reaction to her supposedly beloved throwing her to the Dark Gods to die. She could not have been taking that lightly at the moment.

"She's not willingly helping us. She, er–has no choice."

Liv looked at Peyton bewildered, and with her eyebrow raised, demanded an explanation.

"Can you never just accept what we tell you without needing all the details?" Peyton rolled her eyes, exasperated by Liv's continued determination for information. "Hayden commanded that Cleo forget everything about tonight."

"And that's it? He commands and she just, does?" Liv stated, baffled.

Rei finally interjected, angrily. "It's not as simple as that. We had to keep her unconscious and hidden until Hayden woke up. Yeah, he can will her to obey, but we almost got caught, shy of a dozen times in the process! Do you even know what the penalty is for keeping an Elite hostage!?"

"Rei, calm down." Peyton gracefully hopped over to the couch in his direction, putting a hand on his shoulder, in efforts to pacify him. "This isn't Liv's fault. Today, more than ever, justifies exactly why Hayden brought her here. She wouldn't have had a sliver of a chance to survive in the unprotected world, even with our help."

Rei wasn't appeased by that sentiment, retorting with a snarl. "She's putting us ALL in danger. And these are already dangerous times!"

Soothingly, Peyton cautiously continued, "She's here because of Hayden. And Hayden is our friend."

Rei walked away, throwing his hands in the air. "All the more why she shouldn't be here!" Accusingly, he pointed at Peyton. "You saw what happened tonight. That *cannot* happen again."

And with another puff of anger, Rei exited Liv's room. Peyton shrugged at Liv to apologize and then left in pursuit.

As the sun began to set, Liv looked up from her book at Piper, who was still trying to keep herself busy in Liv's room, but obviously running out of things to read or do.

"You can leave, Piper. It's okay–I won't try to break out or doing anything irrational."

Piper looked back at Liv, unconvinced. "How do I know that, for sure?"

Although appreciative of Piper's company, Liv needed to be alone, unwatched for a while, to figure out her thoughts and properly reflect on everything that happened. Deviously, Liv figured that for once, she could try to use her friend's power to her advantage for solitude. "Cast something on the door, I don't know, an alarm or something if I try to leave the room before dawn?"

Luckily, Piper looked convinced at that idea, but shook her head. "Even if I tried, I wouldn't be able to execute that power correctly, anyway. Besides, I trust you. So, I could have lied and told you I did it, but as friends, I think honesty is key." She got up and headed toward the door. "Promise you won't do anything stupid?"

"Scout's honor." Liv nodded, saluting her friend.

"Okay." Piper sighed, "I assume that means, yes?"

Liv chuckled, "Yes." Then noticing her friend's hesitation, added with a wave, "Now go! Don't worry about me–you clearly are in need of memorizing a new encyclopedia or writing a thesis on the exploration of the unknown Solar System, your brain is clearly not stimulated enough here in my humble abode."

Piper rolled her eyes. "Okay, good night. I'll be back tomorrow."

And with her friend's exit, followed by closing of her door, Liv was finally alone.

FOURTEEN

Liv stayed true to her promise, simply reading until the ignited flame of her fireplace died out. Then sluggishly, and obediently, she rolled into bed, letting her mind wander as she dozed off into a peaceful sleep.

In the middle of the night, she heard a soft knock on her door, and sat up alert, hearing her door screech as it slowly opened. Liv peeked around the corner from her bed, seeing Hayden in the doorway, looking like he had been through hell and back.

Liv ran to his side, gingerly wrapping her arm around his torso for support, feeling terrible when he grimaced in pain at the effort. She helped him to her bed, quietly whispering, "What are you doing here?"

"I just needed to, make sure you were okay." Hayden winced as he softly sat on the bed, working toward a more relieving, horizontal position.

"Me!? You're the one that's hobbling like a weak old cripple!" Liv chuckled at the thought.

"Wow, hit a poor man while he's down." Hayden held his side as he carefully swung his legs onto the bed, sighing relief as he leaned against the bed's backboard in success.

"Sorry." Liv bit her lip, ashamed. "You're going to be okay, though–right?"

"Yeah, I'll heal fast, and be as good as new in a couple days."

Hayden closed his eyes as he eased into a more comfortable position. Then, he softly snapped his fingers, lighting all the candles in her room at once. Liv tried to ignore the slight wince that accompanied the small, yet incredible gesture.

"Okay." Liv couldn't help smile as she saw his beautiful body on her bed. His light grey cashmere sweater perfectly showed off his flat stomach and chiseled muscles through the thin material. She carefully sat herself next to him, "Because, I'm sort of really enjoying this moment where you seem like a normal guy again, and not some all-mighty immortal super powerful God of royalty." She threw a pillow in front of her face, trying to hide the smile emerging.

"God, I'm sorry. I'm terrible!" She couldn't help but laugh, but dropped the pillow in pure amusement when she heard Hayden's velvet chuckle.

"I'd injure myself a million times more, just to keep seeing that smile of yours." Hayden retorted, blissfully.

Liv rolled her eyes at the corniness, but suddenly, began to feel shy. She grabbed a throw pillow nearby, focusing her attention on trailing the beads with her finger so she could avoid eye contact and get out what she needed to say-what she had been thinking about ever since they departed after the King's ball, and even more so after this morning's situation.

"Hayden, I wanted to thank you." Liv gulped. "For, what you did this morning-to protect *me*. I understand how dangerous and risky it was to do what you did. And really, thank you for trying to protect me through all of this. I know I don't understand half of everything you're dealing with right now, but I know that me being here makes it all the more complicated and difficult-so, long overdue, but thank you. For everything."

She finally looked up, hopeful, and relieved to see Hayden's eyes kind, longing and twinkling back with happiness.

He grabbed her hand, assuringly stating, "You being here, makes everything I'm dealing with *worth it.*"

Instead of pulling her arm away, Liv left it there, enjoying the feeling of their touch, no matter how dangerous it was. It warmed her entire body and awakened her soul. Their connection, it was unique. Liv knew it, and

Hayden did, too. They couldn't ignore their gravitational pull any longer. Hayden sat up, instinctively leaning forward and pressing his forehead to hers, finally fulfilling a desire he had been fighting for months.

"Never think you are the problem, Ollie. You are the complete opposite. I've tried to imagine a world without you in it and it's a dark one. You are my light, and without you, I am nothing. A shadow of the person I am supposed to be. Don't ever forget that."

Hearing those words were exactly what Liv needed to hear to justify her thoughts, feelings and internal debates she had been having ever since he left her in June. His thoughts toward her matched exactly what she had been feeling in a world where she wasn't apart of his life, and yet she had still longed for him, unconditionally and never understanding why. And for the past five months, she had felt cold, empty. But now with him by her side, radiating heat, warming her body and filling her with so much joy, she knew now, there was nothing more to debate.

Liv needed him, completely and insatiably, if she were ever going to have the strength to survive in her world, or his. Instinctively, and yet with no control, she moved her body closer to his, matching his leaning mouth until their lips finally touched and an explosion of fireworks blasted inside her soul. Eager, Liv needed more, more of him, all of him. She gently pushed him down, aligning her torso with his as she wrapped her legs around him, pressing against him, allowing herself to be consumed by him, slowly moving up and down on top of him, touching all parts, letting him fill her, letting them become one, as it always should have been.

Soon, they were lying next to each other, when Liv noticed a huge green and black bruise expanding across Hayden's torso, and remembered that he was injured.

"How are you you feeling? Did I hurt you?" She softly whispered.

Hayden laughed. "Ollie, trust me, you could never physically hurt me. Even if you tried."

Looking at Hayden's stone structure, Liv agreed. Hayden gently wrapped his arm around her, bringing her head to lie on his muscular chest.

"This is the best I've felt all day, and definitely the happiest I've been in a really long time. You are my perfect medicine." Hayden murmured, nuzzling his nose into Liv's daisy-smelling hair.

Feeling safe and secure in his strong arms, and warm from his body, Liv couldn't disagree. She didn't want the night to end.

She snuggled deeper into his neck, smiling, but felt Hayden wince in pain, so she froze, still shy, but nevertheless content and relaxed.

"Can you tell me how you got injured, er–the first time? Is this going to be a typical thing, seeing you bruised and banged up?" Liv asked.

Hayden sighed, "Ideally no, but these are dangerous times, so realistically, I can't guarantee anything."

Liv looked up at Hayden, horrified, begging him to continue.

Hayden succumbed to her pressing gaze. "I was with my Dad–we went to…" Hayden paused, hesitating, then deeply breathed in, giving into the truth being shared, "to spy on the Dark Gods. We visited their base to see what type of army they have been building and try to figure out what they are up to."

"And?" Liv urged, compelling him to explain, "Did they find you?"

"Not exactly."

There was a small pause, but long enough for Liv to feel her frustration growing.

"Hayden. You can trust me. I won't tell anyone. And you definitely cannot leave me on a cliffhanger like that."

Hayden smiled, slightly amused, but Liv could tell his mind was elsewhere.

"Hayden, look at me." Liv pleaded, turning his face to her, so she could look into his eyes. "You don't have to tell me if you don't want to. I understand this is all new and me being here is different…"

Hayden took her chin and lifted it to his lips. A deep, passionate kiss, filled with urgency.

When Hayden lifted his head from Liv, who was recovering from a romantic daze, he sighed, looking worriedly into her eyes.

"I just keep questioning why I brought you into all of this. It's a dangerous time to be a God, let alone a mortal. If anything happened to you here…" Hayden shook the dark thought from his head and sighed again, looking at her with uncertainty. Brushing it off, he shook his head. "I'm not sure if I'm stupid, selfish, or actually protecting you."

"Maybe a combination of all three?" Liv nudged, teasing. "But, if it's any consolation, I'm glad I'm here, with you." Then, prompting him to continue, added, "Even if you are a terrible story teller…"

"Okay, so you be the storyteller then." Hayden smirked, jokingly. Liv hated how charming he was, especially when he was trying to get his way.

Liv exasperated, adding a dramatic head nod, "Come out with it already!"

"Okay, okay." Hayden caved, "So, along with checking in on the Dark God Army base, we were also planning to stop by other entities, to see where their allegiance resided, in case it ends in war. We first met with the Centaur clan– "

"Centaurs actually exist?!" Liv interrupted.

"I'm sorry, but who's telling the story again?" Hayden teased. Then he quietly added, "And yes, they do."

Liv shook her smiling head, blushing as Hayden continued.

"So, the Centaurs still have allegiance to the Pure Gods, but unfortunately we found out the Cyclops have gone Dark." Hayden bowed his head, "They were heading into the Dark base and heard us from afar. I wasn't paying attention and unfortunately spoke too loud." He looked abashed, embarrassed as he struggled to continue, "A Cyclops grabbed me, and started hitting me against anything he could find, his grip too firm for me to escape." Hayden shuddered, "If it wasn't for my father, well… who knows what condition or where I would be right now."

Frustrated with himself, Hayden admitted, "I was so stupid. How am I supposed to be responsible for all of the Pure Gods when I can't even be responsible with myself?"

Liv sat up, alarmed at the sudden turn of emotion. "Hayden, it was a mistake. You can't be perfect all the time, you're only–well, I guess *not human,*" Liv blushed at her error. "But what I mean is you CAN learn from it, become better in the process, move forward and grow stronger."

Hayden still had his hand covering his eyes. Liv pulled it down and held it as she sat up to look him in the eye.

"Look, you are doing your best–and that's all any of us can ask for and expect from you. You're constantly putting everyone else before yourself; you obviously love your subjects and clearly take this responsibility very seriously, unconditionally seriously–and that's all your people want from you–your absolute care." Liv bit her lip, hoping to communicate just how amazing she thought this man was in front of her. Even after what they had been through, Hayden could still do no wrong in her eyes. "Maybe you just need to learn how to find that balance and prioritize yourself first, sometimes."

Hayden sat up, putting his hand on her cheek, cupping her head and bringing it toward his. Upon their lips locking, Liv fell gently on top of Hayden as they landed in her soft pillows–still kissing.

"Oh god, Ollie. I've missed you. I've missed this." Hayden went in for another kiss before continuing. "I forgot what it's like to have someone to talk to, someone whom I can trust, whose intentions are pure. I didn't realize how much I needed this, to be able to show all sides of myself, especially a vulnerable one–I could *never* say this to Rei. But I have you, someone who believes in me and cares about me, genuinely. What am I going to do when you're gone?"

Liv paused and moved away.

"When I'm gone?"

Hayden sighed, leaning back on his pillow, putting his arm around Liv and bringing her closer, where she belonged, even if everything was trying to prevent it.

"Nothing is final yet." Hayden stated bluntly, but not assuringly. "Let's just enjoy this moment while we can."

But Liv's mind was racing. How could it be that the night was so perfect and within one question, her dreams turned back into a real-life nightmare?

"Hayden. What are we supposed to do?" She cringed at how desperate her voice sounded. But she had just gotten him back. She couldn't lose him again.

Hayden remained calm. "I think this is when we fall asleep in each other's arms, like lovers do." He playfully bit on her ear and tugged, then kissed her forehead. Liv's mind naturally eased in feeling his smile.

Liv smiled back, but not fully. "But what about us?"

Hayden sighed. "Ah. Us." He succumbed to Liv's pressing, knowing a lost battle when it came to her determination. "Well, I'll need to talk to my father. See what can be done. He won't be happy, but he may come around. Best case he accepts, worst case I get executed."

Liv shuddered, appalled. "Your father would actually execute you for loving a human?"

"I don't think he would, necessarily." Hayden shrugged, but did not sound promising. "History leads us to believe that the blackbirds are the ones who do it. They're the wise observers who ultimately enforce balance among the Gods. They listen, guide and hold order through punishment. Superstitions, mostly."

Liv felt chills trickle down her spine, remembering the guidance *she had* received from the blackbirds on campus.

Hayden felt Liv freeze, so jokingly nudged her–trying to bring her attention back to the light from the darkness he saw in her eyes as her mind unraveled with possibilities.

"Nobody has actually seen the blackbirds murder a God–and I don't believe in it. Understand that most of these Gods have never existed anywhere else. This world is all they know, unlike you and me. My father would most likely 'leave it up to the blackbirds' to decide my ultimate fate or punishment, so on that front, I'm not too concerned."

It was eerie how freely Hayden spoke of his potential death.

"What about Arlo? Is he a threat?" If Liv was going to do this, go full-heartedly again with Hayden, she needed all of her facts before she completely let down the cage around her heart. "Do you think he'll actually build an army large enough to wage a war against the Pure Gods?"

"Well, my father says pillars are being influenced to go Dark. We don't have any confirmations yet." Hayden had a great poker face, and to most, could get away with it, but Liv had spent the better part of seven years looking at his expressions, conversing with him about everything and studying his reactions, so could always sense when Hayden was masking his true feelings.

"Well, what have you heard?" Liv pressed on, needing answers.

Hayden smirked; admiring her perseverance and remembering what a force his innocent bombshell could have. "From what I've observed, the Pillars of Agriculture and Commerce are Dark now, but they haven't proclaimed their loyalty yet."

"But what exactly do the Dark Gods *want?* What are they fighting for?"

"They believe Gods should be present amongst the mortals again. It's been over two millennia since we interacted with them, during the Greek and Roman empires. We've just managed humanity from afar."

Liv took in this information and contemplated it, not exactly understanding why that could be a *bad thing*, or at least, the point of starting a war to prevent it from happening.

Confused, she finally asked, "Hayden, playing devil's advocate here, but what would the problem be with that? Couldn't it be useful to have the Gods involved again? Even Professor Montagnes said mortals are living in the Race of Iron, also known as pure destruction."

"But that's the thing–the Dark Gods don't want interaction to help the humans. They want interaction to help the Gods." Hayden furrowed his brows, struggling with a thought internally and then continued. "They want to force the humans to act and work in accordance to their will, whether the mortals want to or not. Control them."

Liv gulped, "Like slaves?"

Hayden remained calm, sensing Liv's fear in her widening eyes. He sat up to look at Liv directly to explain. "There's a fine line between governed power and authoritative power. If the Gods interact with mortals, the humans could never fight back. There's no balance if the humans knew about us, they would be at our complete mercy. Some time ago, our power over the humans got out hand–the Gods had too much control over the human race–forcing mortals to make unnecessary sacrifices, live in fear if they did not obey us. Did you ever hear about Dionysus turning a group of pirates into dolphins, just because they kidnapped him?"

Liv took a deep breath, trying to wrap her head around this mythology coming to life. But, what she did know were pirate tales, and that pirates were not the best sort of human race, so she continued with that theory.

"I'm sure the pirates deserved it."

Hayden chuckled, amazed at Liv's stubbornness. As a mortal, Liv was not permanently destined to remain with the Gods, so Hayden had anticipated she would be more inclined to support the moderate Dark Gods cause. But Hayden needed to open her mind, make her see and understand the dangers of the radical Dark Gods' vision.

"Ollie, even if the pirates deserved *some* form of punishment, was turning them into dolphins really the just way to do it? I don't think so, and neither did most of our ancestors. So, we removed ourselves from the human race, to be born into myth. Zeus ultimately decided it–the first Pure ruler of the Gods–we would still keep a balance in the world and over mortals, but remove ourselves from their day to day. Some, the Dark Gods who took Prometheus' side, are in favor for championing humans, but that mentality transformed into wanting to restore power of Gods over humans, not just for interaction, but for control, for total enslavement."

Liv shuttered at the thought. She finally understood this war was bigger than she and Hayden, bigger than just the Gods, themselves–it impacted the universe, depending who would triumph in the end.

FIFTEEN

The following week, Liv was finally beginning to enjoy her life at Puerdios University. She started getting into a routine, understanding her classwork and workload, and pictured herself staying on campus for quite some time.

Liv appreciated Piper's company, but Hayden's increased presence in her life helped tremendously. Although strictly appearing as friends in public and keeping their interactions minimal to prevent any speculation, Hayden would come to Liv's room every night and stay with her, and Liv had never been so excited to see the sunset in her life.

Their nights together were intimate, peaceful and provided exactly the time Liv needed to reintroduce herself to Hayden, and he to her–to learn about his world, understand who he was in these unknown circumstances and explore the man he was becoming through it all.

To Liv's delight, Hayden also preferred to sleep shirtless, which was not a sore sight for dreaming. The two spent their evenings always wrapped in each other's arms, mentioning the smaller, unimportant moments they encountered during their day, supported each other through the difficult times and laughed at the silly ones.

And each night, as she fluttered her eyelids and suppressed the urge to fall asleep, Liv would slowly doze off into a comforting slumber, wrapped in Hayden's strong arms, dreaming of his unexpected but radiant laugh. It was her favorite part of the night.

Once Liv finally closed her eyes and gave into her inevitable sleep, Hayden would watch her for a moment, enjoying the hint of a smile he saw on her face as she softly held on to his hand. That was his favorite moment of the night.

For them, it was as if a puzzle had finally been solved, each piece perfectly fitting into place and together creating the most extraordinary picture–they were finally whole.

But, puzzles are never permanently solved, and can be easily separated. For even when they appear beautiful and complete, the cracks still remain, visible, waiting to be torn apart again.

Liv and Piper were sitting on the patio at their favorite table for lunch. The sun was shining brightly, exposing Piper's luminescent skin and a soft hint of auburn to her dark hair. Liv secretly wished today, it were fashionably acceptable to wear shorts and a tank, as she sat in the shade trying to adjust her gold sequined shift dress and grudgingly noticed that the heat seemed to not affect her immortal colleagues. Even with short sleeves, a high hemline and sandals, Liv felt and probably looked much warmer than her friend appeared to be across the table, seemingly unfazed in the blaring sun, despite her peacock-feathered pencil skirt, navy satin peplum top and oversized metallic tweed blazer.

Liv had never been so appreciative of iced tea and began chugging her beverage as soon as it arrived at their table.

"Slow down nymph, don't drown in that beverage over there." Piper joked, gracefully squeezing a lemon wedge into her ice water.

"Can't you snap me a cool breeze, or something, please? This desert climate is sucking out my soul." Liv begged, placing the chilled glass next to her neck for relief.

"Sorry, Liv." Piper genuinely looked sad, shrugging, "Weather control is an Elite Elements thing, so I don't have the powers to change it. You know I would in a heartbeat, otherwise."

Liv sighed, "I understand." She felt a sliver of guilt for requesting such a ridiculous demand–she would have never thought of controlling the weather at her other school–and felt even worse for being disappointed that Piper couldn't deliver.

Per usual, Liv automatically turned her head, anticipating Hayden's arrival, her body gravitating toward his presence as she spotted him walking toward their direction.

Hayden swiftly sat down, smirking at Liv playfully as he mocked. "A little warm for your preference today?"

Liv glared at Hayden in return, trying to keep a platonic face, but noticed how gorgeous he looked in his pearl blue hoodie and a navy blazer, which matched his perfectly fitted white pant, all of which accentuated his sexy cerulean stare. She wanted to grab him then and there and kiss him passionately. Soon, she forgot why she was mad at him in the first place, but instead thought about how great it would feel to put her hands through his wavy curls, beautifully reflecting gold in the sunlight.

Piper rolled her eyes, luckily ignoring Liv's dramatics-turned-passionate-need. "Mortal can't hang in the heat."

"Easy." Hayden stated, smugly.

And with the quick snap of his fingers, Liv suddenly felt a chilly breeze on her neck, cooling down her entire body, immediately.

Stunned, Liv turned around, finding no device working magic, then smiled. She hadn't realized just how powerful Hayden was until this very moment. Who knew the value of air conditioning could be so quantifiable.

"Thank you!" She beamed, pulling on her camel cashmere coat.

"Cold already?" Piper asked, amazed. Then turning to Hayden, jokingly assessed, "You can never win."

"Well, I promise tonight I'll have climate control–I'm hosting a Symposium in my room tonight–do you two want to join?"

Liv blushed, not wanting to seem too eager at the opportunity. Fortunately, Piper jumped in before she needed to respond.

"You're inviting *us* to your social gathering?" Piper inquired, astonished. "As in, class reject and mortal missile?"

"Uh, yeah." Hayden just smiled back, cockily.

"Okay. This is weird." Piper muttered to herself, then took a deep breath as she continued, "Why do you all of the sudden want to hang out with us? Is it because of what happened last week? Look, you don't need to be nice to us; we'll keep your secret either way. We don't need pity invites to maintain loyalty."

Although fortunate for Piper's grandeur defense, Liv felt guilty that Hayden needed to be on the blunt receiving end of it.

Hayden looked at Liv, trying to fight his grin as she shrugged in return.

"Wow," Hayden jokingly stated, mischief gleaming from his eyes, "I cool down your lunch space and this is how I get treated in return? Well," he stood up, grinning cheerfully at Liv, "It's the least I could do for you both covering me last week in Humanities. If you do want to stop by, my dorm is in the north tower–starts at 270* SS, er–9pm," he looked at Liv, who gushed gratefully for the translation, "and the password is White Anemone."

Hayden subtly winked at Liv, but then smoothly added, "Hope to see you ladies there," and walked away.

Liv stared dreamily at Hayden's cute butt, sighing at the sight as he headed toward his friends. She wished she could have hugged him, or stayed near him longer–his short encounter left her yearning for his touch. And although she appreciated the invite, Liv was not exactly exhilarated at the idea that she wouldn't be alone with him until much later in the night, if at all.

"Liv. Holy snap. What was that about?" Piper looked panicked.

Liv popped out of her daze, "What do you mean?"

She tried to look confused, but Liv felt guilty and knew she looked it, so gave in almost immediately, with a new strategy of conscience reasoning.

"I don't know. He's trying to be nice, Piper. Maybe we accept his olive branch and just make peace with everyone."

Liv wasn't sure she sounded convincing, but Piper looked as if she was contemplating the notion, so Liv pressed on. "We could always stop by, just to see what it's like and make an appearance. We don't have to stay long–and you're always talking about wanting to fit in, so here's your opportunity. Why throw it away?"

Piper asked curiously, "Will you be *okay* with being near Hayden, let alone in his room? I mean, talk about jumping into the lion's den…"

"I'll manage." Liv rolled her eyes, excited for victory approaching. "I mean, it'll obviously suck–but having you there, and alcohol, will make it tolerable. And I'm totally willing to go and support your social endeavors."

Piper bit her lip and then nodded in decision, "Okay, I'm in."

"Awesome." Liv smiled, "Now, I'm assuming a campus symposium isn't as fancy as a royal one–even if it's held by the Prince–so what do you wear to these things?"

"Beats me." Piper shrugged. "What did you wear when you went out in college?"

Liv now grinned, finally being able to take the lead, for once.

After finalizing her Thanksgiving plans with her mom and sharing the white lie that she was going to Peyton's house instead of home for the holiday break, Liv sighed.

While drinking a glass of red wine and getting ready for the symposium, she felt guilty all night for not telling her mom the truth, and dreaded the inevitable discussion of upcoming winter break plans. But what could she do? Knowledge of Gods was forbidden to mortals, and she was only an exception to the ancient rule.

So, finally putting her conscience aside, Liv took a final gulp of wine and determined she and Piper looked *hot*. Correct attire or not, they would definitely have all the male deities drooling at their feet tonight.

Liv was wearing a silk plunging neckline dress, with an even higher slit up her left thigh, adorned with olive green, navy, silver and gold sequins so that the material almost appeared like a stunning velvet reflection of the rainforest at dusk.

"How do I look?" Piper asked insecurely, automatically going for her glass of wine and taking another sip.

"You, my friend, look amazing." Liv nodded assuredly, and she wasn't lying.

Her partner in crime for the night was dressed in a short burgundy glass-embellished dress with long sleeves. Her matching dark lip and shaggy bob was the perfect addition to her badass look.

"Really?" Piper lit up, eyeing the back of her dress speculatively, "Are you sure the length in the back is long enough?"

"Oh, definitely." Liv nodded her head confidently, trying to edge out the momentary relapse that she, in fact, had *no* idea what the dress code for this type of event was. But, Liv figured shorter would be better, if her college experience had any influence.

"Ok, let's go before I change my mind." Piper anxiously nodded in confirmation.

So with the grab of Piper's hand, Liv rushed them out of the room before she, too, lost her confidence for the unknown social scene in which they were about to embark.

As Piper led the way to Hayden's dorm room, Liv was both glad that she had no idea where it was located in order to pull off her unbiased demeanor genuinely in regards to getting to the party, but simultaneously hated the thought that she had never been there either and that this was a whole other part of him in which she had no connection.

Now they stood in front of two-oversized industrial-styled antique oak doors, assumedly Hayden's. Liv took a deep breath, willing herself to stay calm and composed, as she looked to Piper and clearly stated, "White Anemone."

As the doors slowly began separating, a handful of thoughts crossed Liv's mind. At first she assured herself that it was just another room–so what it if it was Hayden's? That she looked great and it would be a shame to let such a good outfit go to waste. Then Liv thought, *screw it*–she did not belong here and would rather hide under her comforter tonight. She started caving into her doubts when luckily, Piper grabbed her hand and jerked her inside before the doors shut behind.

Liv was officially in Hayden's loft, and would not be leaving anytime soon.

At first glance, Liv flooded with relief that her stab at anticipating the dress code paved out to be a success. Girls were dressed in various risqué dresses and guys wore chic blazers mixed with unique, edgy formal street-wear–but all in all, resembled a high-end version of a Las Vegas nightclub.

It didn't take long for Liv to find Hayden across the room. He immediately turned in her direction too, seemingly aware of the same pull that brought their gaze together, freezing the room and eliminating everyone else in sight so that it was only the two of them in the universe. Hayden politely excused himself and headed over in their direction, beaming.

"You came." Hayden smiled, hugging Liv first and then awkwardly adding an informal one with Piper to recover and not seem as controversial.

"Of course." Liv nodded, looking around. "Nice place."

"I'll have to show you around later–you guys showed up just in time for the opening story. Symposium tradition–Rei's going to do the honors." Hayden smirked when he saw Liv's reaction to the shocking idea of Rei speaking publicly, and then pointed to his left. "Drinks are over there, and bathroom is upstairs." He turned in the other direction to point toward a spiral staircase. Hayden then leaned into Piper and Liv, slyly sliding his arm around Liv and giving her a squeeze of appreciation. "That's more of a private bathroom, so just don't tell anyone I mentioned it."

And with another dashing smile, Hayden promised to find the girls later and ran over to prepare for Rei's performance.

"So they're actually going full-on traditional Symposium." Piper stated, nodding her head, "I'm impressed."

The girls worked their way over to the bar and grabbed glasses of wine. Liv was trying not to gape at his place, but the interior was exquisite, and a little unexpected to how he had blandly decorated his boarding school dorm room each year prior.

The majority of the walls were painted concrete grey, but he had exposed brick on the same side as the entrance. The first level was split up into three sections, the middle being a beautiful kitchen-turned-bar, with a large steel and rustic wood counter encircling the cutting edge stove top and appliances. Behind the kitchen displayed a large wine rack and open shelving unit, showing an eclectic collection of books, sculptures and paintings against the wall. On the third nearest the entrance, a long family-style wooden table paralleled the brick, with steel chairs surrounding it. On the same side, but in the opposite quadrant, served as an office area. And across from the kitchen were ceiling-high windows, to what Liv believed led to an outdoor patio, but it was too dark to tell. She debated looking through the glass to confirm, but figured now was not the time to be a creep.

Liv so desperately wanted to make acquaintance with this space and read through the books Hayden held close in his miniature library, understand his wine preferences and taste his favorite bottles, and see if her secret boyfriend actually enjoyed cooking recreationally or if the grandiose kitchen was just an interior décor element forced upon him.

Instead, Liv obediently followed Piper into the opposite side of the loft where a large black leather sofa curved around a brick fireplace, displaying what seemed to be a beautiful red Mark Rothko painting above. Liv turned her head back toward the kitchen, spotting the Jackson Pollock lookalike painting as well. She instantly took another sip of her wine, assuming they were most likely originals than fakes, and self-doubtedly wondered if Hayden had secretly enjoyed collecting art this entire time, too?

To make matters worse, as soon as Liv and Piper took their seat on the couch, Liv found Cleo sitting directly across from them, with her permanent scowl in attendance, per usual. Cleo had a silver bedazzled onesie on, covered by a see-through grey chiffon skirt. On either side sat her minions, Elsa and Brie, but Liv honestly always got the two confused.

"Which one is which, again?" Liv turned to Piper, asking for help.

"Elsa is on the left, with the velvet jumpsuit, Brie is the one on the right, in the black trouser, X-shaped silver satin blouse and oversized tuxedo blazer."

"Why do they always look like they're up to no good?" Liv was already beginning to panic by their facial expressions, looking vindictive in her direction.

"Beats me. They're part muse, so they supposed to spark inspiration, but maybe they're also Nemesis' descendants, so they also naturally inspire vengeance?" Piper giggled at the thought. "Either way, look at whose company they're forced to keep. I would be angry if I had to spend every day with Cleo, too. That's for sure."

"Cheers to that, sister." Liv grinned, raising her glass.

Hayden then jumped on the miniature fireplace awning, commanding his guests' attention.

As the crowd silenced, Liv happily sighed, looking forward to the next minute or so in which she could watch Hayden without worry of causing too much speculation.

Tonight he was wearing a metallic blue trouser, a loose grey flannel button-down shirt and casual olive green satin bomber–very *Rebel Without a Cause* James Dean, from Liv's perspective. He looked happy, almost fratty as he welcomed his friends for the first Symposium of the school year.

"Thank you, everyone, for coming." With a cheer from the crowd, Hayden cockily laughed, quieting the rambunctious group down again. "Okay, okay, I'll make it quick! Tonight we gather to celebrate our ancestors–tradition passed down from each generation. A way to remember those who can no longer be here with us and learn about those who are but... we didn't want to invite." Hayden grinned, raising his glass, "So, first, we exchange a story and then we drink!"

Liv blushed as Hayden stared at her, his eyes intriguing. They intensely raised their glasses to each other in acknowledgement and sipped from their respective glasses in celebration.

Rei jumped up on the fireplace, jokingly pushing Hayden off as he soaked up his glory as Symposium storyteller. Decked out in a bright mustard yellow velvet blazer and wrapped with an oversized chunky cashmere scarf, he calmly commanded the room, to Liv's surprise.

Once Rei had grabbed the guests' attention, he coughed and then recited.

"Sing to me of the man, Muse, the man of twists and turns
driven time and again off course, once he had plundered
the hallowed heights of Troy.
Many cities of men he saw and learned their minds,
many pains he suffered, heartsick on the open sea,

fighting to save his life and bring his comrades home.
But he could not save them from disaster, hard as he strove—
the recklessness of their own ways destroyed them all,
the blind fools, they devoured the cattle of the Sun
and the Sungod blotted out the day of their return.
Launch out on his story, Muse, daughter of Zeus,
start from where you will—sing for our time too.
By now,
all the survivors, all who avoided headlong death
were safe at home, escaped the wars and waves.
But one man alone...
his heart set on his wife and his return —Calypso,
the bewitching nymph, the lustrous goddess, held him back,
deep in her arching caverns, craving him for a husband.
But then, when the wheeling seasons brought the year around,
that year spun out by the gods when he should reach his home,
Ithaca —though not even there would he be free of trials,
even among his loved ones —then every god took pity,
all except Poseidon. He raged on, seething against
the great Odysseus till he reached his native land.
But now
Poseidon had gone to visit the Ethiopians worlds away,
Ethiopians off at the farthest limits of mankind,
a people split in two, one part where the Sungod sets
and part where the Sungod rises. There Poseidon went
to receive an offering, bulls and rams by the hundred —
far away at the feast the Sea-lord sat and took his pleasure.
But the other gods, at home in Olympian Zeus's halls,
met for full assembly there, and among them now
the father of men and gods was first to speak,
sorely troubled, remembering handsome Aegisthus,
the man Agamemnon's son, renowned Orestes, killed.
Recalling Aegisthus, Zeus harangued the immortal powers:
"Ah how shameless —the way these mortals blame the gods.
From us alone, they say, come all their miseries, yes,
but they themselves, with their own reckless ways,
compound their pains beyond their proper share.

Look at Aegisthus now . . .
above and beyond his share he stole Atrides' wife,
he murdered the warlord coming home from Troy
though he knew it meant his own total ruin.
Far in advance we told him so ourselves,
dispatching the guide, the giant-killer Hermes.
'Don't murder the man,' he said, 'don't court his wife.
Beware, revenge will come from Orestes, Agamemnon's son,
that day he comes of age and longs for his native land.'
So Hermes warned, with all the good will in the world,
but would Aegisthus' hardened heart give way?
Now he pays the price —all at a single stroke."

And sparkling-eyed Athena drove the matter home:
"Father, son of Cronus, our high and mighty king,
surely he goes down to a death he earned in full!
Let them all die so, all who do such things.
But my heart breaks for Odysseus,
that seasoned veteran cursed by fate so long —
far from his loved ones still, he suffers torments
off on a wave-washed island rising at the center of the seas.
A dark wooded island, and there a goddess makes her home,
a daughter of Atlas, wicked Titan who sounds the deep
in all its depths, whose shoulders lift on high
the colossal pillars thrusting earth and sky apart.
Atlas' daughter it is who holds Odysseus captive,
luckless man —despite his tears, forever trying
to spellbind his heart with suave, seductive words
and wipe all thought of Ithaca from his mind.
But he, straining for no more than a glimpse
of hearth-smoke drifting up from his own land,
Odysseus longs to die . . .
Olympian Zeus,
have you no care for him in your lofty heart?
Did he never win your favor with sacrifices
burned beside the ships on the broad plain of Troy?
Why, Zeus, why so dead set against Odysseus?"

"My child," Zeus who marshals the thunderheads replied,
"what nonsense you let slip through your teeth. Now,
how on earth could I forget Odysseus? Great Odysseus
who excels all men in wisdom, excels in offerings too
he gives the immortal gods who rule the vaulting skies?
No, it's the Earth-Shaker, Poseidon, unappeased,
forever fuming against him for the Cyclops
whose giant eye he blinded: godlike Polyphemus,
towering over all the Cyclops' clans in power.
The nymph Thoosa bore him, daughter of Phorcys,
lord of the barren salt sea —she met Poseidon
once in his vaulted caves and they made love.
And now for his blinded son the earthquake god —
though he won't quite kill Odysseus —
drives him far off course from native land.
But come, all of us here put heads together now,
work out his journey home so Odysseus can return.
Lord Poseidon, I trust, will let his anger go.
How can he stand his ground against the will
of all the gods at once —one god alone?"

Hayden jumped back on the couch, attacking Rei with a friendly hug. "Great job, as suspected." Then, turning back to the group, yelled "Cheers, friends. Now, let the party begin!"

Suddenly, the lights turned off and electric dance music started playing, the only visible light coming from strobe lights placed throughout the space. Hayden's loft turned from a cozy flat to a nightclub in a matter of seconds. Students danced in a mosh pit area by the couch, others raced back to the kitchen for more alcohol and Liv ran over to the glass window, now knowing she could finally see what was outside to solve the big patio debate.

As she stared out, confirming it was indeed a barbeque and patio sitting space, Liv sighed as she turned around realizing the current state of Hayden's room. She wasn't exactly expecting everyone to hold hands and sing kum-bay-yah, but the pre-story vibe was a little more her beat than what the party had turned into.

"What are you doing!?" Piper appeared, handing Liv a new glass of wine. She looked outside, "Hm, nice patio!"

Trying to change the subject, Liv pointed to where Rei had previously stood during his recitation, commenting sarcastically, "Nothing like dactylic hexameter to get a party going—The Odyssey, how original!" But, with the music volume increase, her delivery seemed more excitable than mockery as the two resorted to yelling in efforts to hear each other.

"Hey! This is my first symposium! Don't ruin it with judgment!" Piper joked, still yelling. "Besides, what's basic is that they chose the Robert Fagles' translation!"

"What?!" Liv screamed, the music had grown louder.

"Robert Fagles! Although eloquently written! It's the more common version! But not nearly as challenging as Alexander Pope's!" Piper shouted, and then sighed, as she saw Liv shaking her head and signaling she couldn't hear anything. So giving up on the possibility of any intelligent conversation, Piper pointed to the dance floor, "Want to dance!?"

Liv wasn't aware, but had apparently already chugged her entire glass of wine, and looked down to find her holding an empty cup.

"I think I need to switch to vodka—I'll go make myself a new drink, and meet you there?!" Liv insisted, still shouting.

"Sounds good!" Piper grinned, then leaned in to Liv's ear, still talking loudly, but the most feasible version of a whisper she could implement. "You know, if you want to leave, all of you have to do is say the word. Okay?"

Liv nodded, appreciatively. "I'll come find you!"

Heading to the kitchen, Liv slowly worked her way between the crowd, groups of people either dancing, conversing or inevitably trying to maneuver themselves to a new location. It was like a traffic crash on a four-way street, complete mayhem. Liv actually appreciated when she landed in the kitchen and noticed the music lower immediately, almost as if a sound room existed to balance out the noise.

"There probably is." Liv concluded with a sigh, finding the vodka bottle.

She poured herself a glass, then looked around and realized she easily could be the most sober person here. Liv took her drink as a shot and began her mixology again for round two.

"You know, vodka might be a little stronger than Fireball. Don't go too crazy."

Liv smiled, recognizing the voice and immediately jumping on Peyton with excitement.

"You're here?!" Liv asked, excited.

"Obviously." Peyton curtsied. She was in a beautiful lacy gold silk dress, almost appearing like lingerie, with an oversized sweater that fell off her shoulder.

"So, I see you and he-who-must-not-be-named are doing the whole 'friendship' thing. How's that going?"

Liv couldn't help but sense a bit of judgment from Peyton's eyes. Or maybe she was just self-conscious and the last shot of vodka was hitting her.

"Yes. Friends. Trying to be, at least." Liv shrugged, instinctively looking around for Hayden. Her eyes widened in disappointed shock to find him chatting with Cleo, which sent an automatic pang of jealousy through her spine and caused her stomach to drop.

Peyton turned around, finding Hayden with Cleo, and then looked at Liv, immediately resenting her previous tone.

"Hey," Peyton lightly hit Liv. "It wouldn't be a night out unless we celebrated with Fireball, right?"

Captivating Liv's attention again, Peyton turned to the counter, grabbed two shot glasses, and handed one to Liv.

"Where did you get this?" Liv took the tiny glass, amazed at finding it full of her favorite cinnamon concoction.

"Seriously, have you not gotten used to our Godly powers yet?" Peyton grinned, clinking her shot glass with Liv's before knocking the alcohol down with one swift gulp. "Fuck. Let's dance."

She grabbed Liv's hand, pulling her onto the dance floor. Liv found Piper on the way and grabbed her arm as they continued toward the center.

Now, it was just Liv and the beat—and if there was anything she could do better than the Gods, it was dance. Adrenaline rushing through her blood, she jumped, turned, shook her body and pulled out her favorite moves. She felt sexy and knew she had caught the attention of her peers, but just tried to block out the thought of whether Hayden was looking, too.

Rei joined the girls and grabbed Peyton so they could start dancing; Liv blew a kiss at Rei jokingly just to make him blush as he took her friend away. Having too much fun playing with Rei's shyness, Liv felt unconquerable, like this world had no control over her tonight.

After a handful of songs, Piper asked Liv to get more drinks in the kitchen. Liv obliged, needing more of this opportunity to feel less. She hadn't been expecting to spend much time with Hayden tonight, but now experiencing it in the flesh, she hadn't really prepared herself for how much it would hurt, now realizing that they could never act like a normal couple, in front of their friends, ever again. For Liv, she just wanted to distract her thoughts, she didn't want to be selfish and ask for it all, because she had always thought Hayden would be enough—but could he be?

"Hey, I'm-a-run to the bathroom!" Liv yelled, a little embarrassed at the notice of her slur. She took another shot of vodka—she was either going need to pass borderline tipsy to no longer care about her drunkenness and continue to have fun, or she would need to try to sober up, which sounded less exciting and too responsible at the moment.

"Okay! I'll stay here." Piper nodded.

On her way to the spiral staircase, Liv noticed a line nearby the closed bathroom door downstairs, secretly appreciating Hayden's tip about the private space, but then got mad at herself for thinking of him again.

Liv carefully held onto the railing, focusing on stepping up each stair, not falling backwards—or forwards for that matter—and refrain from thinking about how dizzy she was getting near the end of the trek. Successfully standing on the second level, Liv noted it would be a bitch to get back down, but ignored it and continued on her mission.

Liv looked left, finding a slightly cracked door nearby the staircase, and then turned to her right where she spotted the bathroom down the hallway with a white sink brightly inviting her inside. Curiosity getting the best of her, Liv decided to enter the closed entrance instead, anticipation building in her chest as she opened the door to reveal Hayden's bedroom.

It was simple, with only a large king-sized bed against an exposed brick wall, a couple windows for light and a simple industrialized wooden dresser. For the most part, the room more so matched Hayden's previous boarding school dormitory spaces than the remainder of the loft, comforting Liv with a form of familiarity in this intimate space.

She went to the door to leave the room in peace when she found the only piece of art hanging against the wall. It was an antique map of the sky, roughly sketched and with very faded outlines of various constellations, aside from a newer ink mark depicting a more recent constellation, hers: Ollie.

Liv smiled, softly touching the glass and tracing the new markings. She softly looked in the corner, noticing the map dated back to 1660 and was signed by its creator, Galileo Galilei. Liv's eyes widened as she almost pressed her nose to the map, staring down at the handwritten claim.

Stunned, she took a step back, appreciating the work of art even more, with Hayden's soft touch–even if he had decimated the original map with his meaningful scribbling.

"I was hoping you'd venture up here."

Liv jumped, caught in the act of snooping through the uninvited territory. She mentally interpreted the sentiment and turned toward to Hayden, clinging her palm to her chest as her heart still raced.

"You scared me." Liv sighed, beaming at the intrusion.

"You found my room." Hayden observed, playfully jabbing at Liv.

"You desecrated an original Galileo drawing." Liv poked back in return.

"You look beautiful tonight." Hayden said sincerely, grinning as he walked up and kissed her cheek. "And, besides, he's not going to miss it anytime soon."

Liv smiled, enjoying being alone and close with Hayden, but unable to switch off her self-conscious thoughts from earlier in the night.

"Do you cook?" Liv looked up at Hayden, inquisitively

"Cook?" Hayden, thrown off guard, looked into Liv's eyes, trying to find her reason for asking such a random question.

"Your kitchen, wine collection–it's a spectacular sight, and I just never knew you enjoyed doing that?" Liv shrugged, embarrassed. "And, your library is massive, have you really read *all* those books?" Liv, a known-book worm herself, couldn't help but control her voice cracking at the last question, wondering why her boyfriend never wanted to share that part of his world with her.

"Oh, that." Hayden let go of Liv and headed toward his bed. He sat down on the edge, patting the seat next to him for Liv to join.

"Why didn't you tell me? Why have you never invited me to your place before?" Liv pushed, as she took the seat next to him.

"You're here now." Hayden confirmed, grabbing Liv's hand in comfort, but it wasn't enough.

"Hayden, what are we doing?"

"Look," Hayden stood up, grabbing Liv again, trying to pacify her. "I've always come to your place because if we were to get caught, it would be a hell of a lot easier for me to escape and get back to my dorm than you. That's all. This is why I'm throwing this whole thing, I wanted you to be here, with me."

Liv looked up at the surrounding room and then back down, biting her lip. This space did feel more like Hayden, more familiar, more feasible, but what the hell did downstairs say about him now?

About them?

"Look, I know it's not ideal–"

"Ideal?!" Liv huffed, standing up. "Hayden, this is far from ideal. We can't even talk to each other in public without our friends getting suspicious or angry! I just wish we could go back to how things used to be, when it was simpler."

They stared at each other, both unsure how to continue, or what path the conversation was forming.

"Liv, what are you saying?" Hayden finally asked, looking worried.

"I don't know." Liv gasped, "Half of the time I don't know what's going on here, and the other half I feel like I'm drugged up in some psychiatric ward because I don't believe half of the things that are happening. *None* of it makes sense to me, Hayden." Liv looked up at her boyfriend, unsure where she was going, but she just needed to get it out.

"Like, how you supposedly love me, but support the cause that bans Gods interacting with humans. That male Gods literally think I am a toxic virus and ignore me at all costs. That you are prophesied to be with Cleo and so have to appear as if you two are together in public. And these clothes! Why does everyone always dress like they're going to the fucking Met Gala!?"

Liv didn't realize she was screaming until she stopped and there was an absolute contrasting silence. Hayden was just staring at her, unsure what to do next.

Liv sadly chuckled, point taken. "Hayden, I don't feel like myself here, and the only time I feel like myself is when I'm with you." Then in reflection of the two of them, how she wanted *more*, and knew Hayden wouldn't be able to give it to her, she sadly added, "And it just feels like I'm chasing an unattainable dream. And that I'm dragging you down along the way."

Liv looked up at Hayden, trying to stay strong as her world was once again crumbling around her. "What if we aren't the main characters in each other's love story? What if we're just the supporting characters who ultimately move each other individually toward that bigger, one of a kind romance. What if we're just helping each other find that infinite person, and this is all prelude?"

"No, Ollie, don't say that." Hayden ran over to Liv, grabbing her hands and kissing them fiercely. "I was an absolute mess when we broke up, Liv—my world ended when I lost you. You're the reason why I amassed that collection—all of those books are your favorite titles and I only started reading them because I was trying to stay connected to you, somehow. It's pathetic." He walked away, ashamed that he was too proud to have shared that part of him with Liv before.

"And the cooking, it's a silly hobby, too. Yes, I can cook, but only basics, grilled cheese sandwiches and stuff. I only started learning when I knew you were coming here." He looked back up at Liv, and walked over to her again, eyes sparkling. "I wanted to make sure that you wouldn't feel homesick, or I don't know, maybe it was just the idea of being able to do something normal, like make you dinner and have a glass of wine while we talked about our day. Stuff you see in the movie–"

Before Hayden could continue, Liv kissed him. She was so thankful for everything he had done for her, or tried to do so far. How could she have been so selfish, so insecure?

"I'm sorry." Liv blurted immediately after, wishing she hadn't consumed so much alcohol to cloud her judgment. "I'm glad I got everything off my chest, but, I'm sorry I did it here and in this way. Tonight."

Hayden only smiled at Liv in relief, as if finding his long-lost treasure once again.

"You were right on most parts. I'm asking a lot from you with all of this. And, I probably should have thought this whole Symposium plan through a little more thoroughly; however, not to toot my own horn or anything, but my plan did eventually work, didn't it? Even if I had to watch your very captivating body dance for an hour, but hey!" Hayden laughed, running away as Liv jokingly tried to hit him again, "I'm not complaining!"

Liv sat on Hayden's bed, re-looking at his Ollie Constellation map, then back to Hayden, beaming. "Can we go back to how you read Jane Austen to 'feel connected' to me?"

Hayden smiled, coming at full force to tackle her on the bed. "That is to stay between us, and only us. You hear?"

Liv smiled. "Surely, I would never tell a soul. But you? Oh, you'll never hear the end of it!" She grabbed a pillow and hit him with it, ducking under his arm and escaping triumphantly, and then stared at Hayden with exhilarating pride.

"I said I read them, I never said I liked them. So don't go on thinking I will be quoting Jane Austen or Gone with the Wind anytime soon." Hayden explained, playfully chasing Liv around the room.

"It's a truth universally acknowledged..." Liv began, difficulty exasperating through heavy giggles, all while dodging Hayden's attacking-jump, which forced him to land on the bed.

Hayden rebounded quickly, finally getting ahold of Liv as he tickled her while rebutting with, "Frankly my dear, I don't give a damn!"

After many shrieks and playful grabs, Liv finally wiggled her way out of his trap. For a moment they just smiled at each other from across the room; Liv taking a couple breaths to calm her happily beating soul; both relishing in their secluded paradise.

Finally, Liv approached Hayden again, wrapping her arms around him in joy. "So you're a book critic now, amongst your many new accomplishments?"

Hayden grinned, "I must admit, I can make a pretty killer grilled-cheese, and I'll be quite happy to host you for dinner, but that's about as far as my accomplishments go. So, unless you take on mastering that kitchen, set your standards low. Cooking is definitely not a talent of mine, even when I use my powers."

"Deal. So grilled-cheese sandwich it is. I can't wait."

They sat in the room for another moment, enjoying the silence and simply being together, alone.

"Hayden," Liv sat up, "Won't faculty be able to hear your Symposium?"

"One of my better hobbies." Hayden smirked, "Er–rather Rei's idea, a perk of having a Security Elite as your friend–only those who know the password can hear the music."

"Brilliant." Liv looked at him, nodding her head, impressed. "We should probably get back downstairs. People will wonder where we are."

She stood up and started to leave, but halted when Hayden grabbed her hand and went to open the door around her.

"Shouldn't we exit separately?" Liv cautioned.

"Nah, another brilliant idea, and this one was mine. Alcohol."

Liv rolled her eyes.

"Everyone's so drunk that nobody will even notice. Come on. I owe you at least one dance, and if I remember correctly, you may appreciate some guidance with getting down the stairs in one piece?"

Liv rolled her eyes again, but as she embarked on descending the stairs, Liv appreciated having Hayden leading the way as a strong base, in case she did tumble. As they approached the dance floor, Hayden refused to let go of Liv's hand or let her get away.

Liv was relieved to find that Hayden was right–by this time, everyone had either passed out from too much symposium fun, or were focused only on dancing with their partner of choice. None of the guests had even turned their head when Liv joined the floor and started dancing with Hayden.

By now, Liv was feeling the perfect buzz. She felt confident, sexy, and influenced by alcohol in the most positive ways–and she wanted Hayden, now.

He looked casually cool as he continued to dance, slowly sliding his hands from Liv's shoulders to her waist. Together, they were in perfect sync. Liv getting aroused by his touch, wanting more as she leaned her body against his front and spun herself around, enjoying the touch of his hard abs, and then migrating her hands behind to his strong back. It was just the two of them, in their perfect world, where nobody could pull them apart.

Dancing with Hayden was pure erotic torture. Liv wanted him, badly, so took it upon herself to taunt him in return, softly sliding her backside against his front, turning around and pushing her chest against him, touching his body all over with soft hands, slowly intensifying her movements as her need took over his body. To her content, Liv could feel Hayden's urge strengthen in response, as his movements became more passionate, craving in lust.

Finally, Hayden spun her around and kissed her deeply, madly and softly at the same time, grabbing her everywhere. The touch of their lips was everything, sparks of electricity radiated through their bodies as the desire subsided, their hunger for each other satiated for now, but only for the moment.

They separated in a daze, Liv on ecstasy at the sight of him. She went in for another kiss almost immediately, but suddenly was getting pulled in the opposite direction, away from Hayden, away from her bliss.

SIXTEEN

"**What are you** doing?!" Piper shrieked at Liv, a force whom was not letting go of her friend's arm until she pulled her right off the dance floor and through the kitchen.

"I knew it!" Piper muttered to herself, shaking her head.

Liv immediately spotted Cleo, giving her a nasty, disapproving look, uglier than her typical frown. Liv panicked, wondering if Cleo had witnessed her and Hayden's stupidity tonight, too.

"I knew it. But noooo, I chose to trust you. Believe you when you said, 'I understand the rules. Hayden is a God, and I'm a mortal. That's forbidden. We're just friends!'" Piper ended her rant with jazz hands, consequently making the entire situation all the more bizarre.

"Is that really your impression of me?" Liv asked, stunned.

Piper shot daggers through her eyes; an intensity Liv had never encountered from her friend before, but she had finally seen a deity come to surface. Piper relentlessly gripped her wrist as she opened the entrance door and directed Liv through it, commanding, "Let's go. Now."

Liv rolled her eyes as she grudgingly stepped into the hallway.

"Okay, happy?"

"No." Piper pointed her finger and then continued pulling Liv through the hallway. "I can't believe you could be so stupid! Do you not understand the consequences of Hay–" Piper coughed, catching herself as she worriedly looked around, hoping nobody was nearby to hear her added whisper, "–Of a God loving a mortal?"

She turned to Liv, making direct eye contact again. "Do you!?"

The intimidating force her friend was continuing to ensue impressed Liv–she noted to herself internally never to cross Piper again.

"I do, actually." Liv crossed her hands, determined to stand her grounds and make her friend understand. "Legend says the black birds will determine punishment for the cause, but there's no proof that they've ever implemented it before!"

"Never been implemented, huh?" Piper dramatically pretended she was considering Liv's proposition.

"Okay, spill it." Liv ordered. "That's what Hayden told me but if you believe otherwise, tell me now."

"Well, Hayden is probably unfamiliar with The Fallen Element. Did he ever mention that story to you?"

"What story?" Liv asked, a bad feeling, growing in her stomach with apprehension.

"Come on." Piper grabbed Liv's wrist again, pulling her down the hallway.

The two girls had turned a couple of corners before Piper started talking again.

"I, unlike Hayden, have studied the histories of the Elements Pillar my entire life. I know every legend, myth, story, fact and fiction associated with the Elements."

Piper finally stopped in front of a white marble statue, presenting a melancholy sight.

"The Fallen Element." Piper bluntly stated, letting Liv absorb what the sculpture gruesomely depicted.

It was a man bleeding out, limp against a rock, dead. On his shoulder, a blackbird sat, beak wide open as if calling out victory, surrender–punishment dually given.

Piper's voice softened. "Legend says that the Element Elite was murdered by black birds for falling in love with a human. The Pure God's rule, descending from Zeus, forbids it in our world and constitutes death if one breaks the code." She turned pleadingly to Liv, "I know it's legend, but the Element Elite *died*, what's speculative is only *how*. He sat on the top of our pillar, not that long ago–for I saw and witnessed his rule upon my creation, along with his death."

Liv was speechless, not knowing what to think or how to process this additional new version to her and Hayden's story.

Piper continued, "Don't you see? All we may know are facts, but what we do know is that an Elite fell in love with a mortal, and he *died*, Liv. The coincidence is too close for me, and it should be too close for you, too. You're risking Hayden's life and your own right now."

Liv lay in her bed, staring at the fire embers as they crackled, watching the flames go up and down. She wanted to look out her window, search for her constellation and will Hayden to come, but she wasn't sure she wanted his explanation, just yet.

If the Fallen Element myth were true, wouldn't the black birds have already come and captured her? Or worse, destroyed Hayden by now?

Liv shuddered at the thought, focusing back on the flame, listening to the soft crackling sound instead. The fire was warmer, easier, and simpler to focus on, and yet a deadly, dangerous force to play with. Funny how the thing that brings you the most comfort in life can also be the thing that easily destroys you.

A lifetime of mindless staring to her kryptonite, Liv heard a soft knock on the door. She quickly pulled on a flannel button-up shirt over her loose grey tank top and hopped off her bed to see who was unexpectedly visiting her.

As she opened the door, she sighed in relief as Hayden swiftly pulled her into an embrace.

"Are you okay?" he asked, softly.

"Of course." Liv mumbled, already feeling like she was in trouble for doing something wrong, but not knowing exactly why.

"I'm so sorry." Hayden added, letting Liv go. "I was stupid."

"Me too." Liv blushed, heading over toward her couch, inviting Hayden to join.

"I just always feel drawn to you, Ollie. It takes all that I have in me to stay away, even now."

"Even now?" Liv shyly smiled. She knew she shouldn't be flattered, not in the current circumstances, but observing the beautiful specimen in front of her, hearing his confession, and being the recipient of Hayden's longing gaze gave her all the feels, and in all the right places.

Hayden sat down close to her, grabbing her hand. Liv smelled his intoxicating scent, gravitating closer to him in response.

"I always want more of you, Liv. You are more than enough for me, but I can never get enough of you." He kissed her forehead, softly.

Liv took a deep breath, absorbing him entirely before she looked back to her fireplace, heat radiating from the flames in unison with her own body.

"You mentioned you don't feel like yourself here, earlier tonight." Hayden calmly reported. "What if I took you somewhere this weekend–a familiar place–so we can talk and just, be away from all of this?"

Liv looked up, intrigued. "Where would we go?"

Hayden smiled, "That would be called a surprise, Ollie."

Liv rolled her eyes and looked out her window, seeing the stars and her constellation. For some reason it gave her courage; this was what she needed.

"Okay." Liv turned back to Hayden, affirmatively radiant with her decision.

"You might want to put on a jacket, though, it'll get cold." Hayden added, looking hungrily at Liv's bare legs under her make-shift t-shirt dress.

Liv grinned as she headed to her armoire, "But no pants?"

"Well, selfishly speaking… don't think that'll be needed, or at least, not for very long." He flashed a seductive smile as Liv hit him with her denim jeans.

Now layered with her favorite wool socks, boots, jeans, grey shirt, flannel shirt, quilted vest and grey beanie, Liv was set to go.

But, *how* they were going to get there, Liv wasn't quite sure.

Hayden led Liv to her window, opening it as he crawled through the space and extended his hand to her. A cool breeze hit Liv, chilling her immediately and making her appreciative for the additional items she wore.

"Here, there's a ledge you can step onto." Hayden held out his hand as Liv took a lunge onto her office desk and ducked her way through the window to meet Hayden outside.

Liv looked at her boyfriend for guidance on next steps, but he stood there a minute, looking out across the campus and then back at Liv, eyebrows furrowed as he took a deep breath.

"So, what's the plan now?" Liv placed her hand around Hayden's torso, tucking herself under his arm – more so for heat and balance, but also to reassure him that she was there, and not afraid. She avoided looking down at the steep drop to the ground, just to be safe and refrain from fainting.

Hayden looked back out to the dark horizon, taking a deep breath before he blurted, "We'll fly." His gaze went down to Liv, assessing her reaction.

"Okay." Liv stated, surprisingly not as shocked as she had been to the other revelations. Maybe she was starting to get used to her boyfriend's powers and this supernatural world, after all.

Hayden looked relieved, buckling his right arm under her knee and picking Liv up. "Just hold on to my neck, we're going to go pretty fast."

He casually took a step off the ledge, and Liv immediately closed her eyes in return, automatically squeezing Hayden tighter as her body reacted to the upcoming drop.

But when they didn't hit the ground and burst into a million pieces, Liv opened her left eye, squinting cautiously to assess the situation; they were gliding through the air.

Liv looked up at Hayden, laughing, as adrenaline pulsed through her veins.

She noticed Hayden had bright white-feathered wings, bigger than himself, pulsing strongly against the wind–but she admired them at work; they were beautiful. Liv then looked down, seeing large green hills rolling out to the ocean, which glistened with the moonlight's gaze.

They were picking up speed, as Hayden turned left and headed away from the ocean. He seemed to be unfazed by the wind, but after hitting an unthinkable speed, Liv chose to duck her head back into Hayden's chest for protection. In return, Hayden rubbed her back, a mutual understanding that this was not ideal means of travel for a mortal.

After an hour of flying, Liv was beginning to tire. She was sobering up from the symposium, and it was getting pretty late. As she broke out into her tenth yawn, Liv wondered how Hayden had the endurance to fly for so long, let alone carry her in the process.

"You can fall asleep, Ollie–we have about another hour or so before we get there." Hayden whispered into the cozy nook Liv created with his chest.

And with that blessing, Liv slowly dozed off, welcoming sleep

"Ollie, wake up." Hayden softly nudged her neck with kisses, "We're here."

Liv came to her senses as soon as she realized they were static, Hayden was standing on solid ground and she hadn't even felt their apparently smooth landing. Opening her eyes, Liv looked around, but only saw trees.

"Where are we?" Liv wiggled her feet to the ground, still holding onto Hayden's arm for support as she continued waking up from her slumber.

"You'll see. Come with me." Hayden smiled, taking her hand and walking her over to the clearing of trees.

Ahead of them was a lake–the beautiful lake where they had celebrated Liv's birthday the year prior. She turned around, finding the cozy cabin where they had spent playing board games and reading books with their friends.

Everyone has his or her happy place, and this was hers.

"Hayden, how did you get us here? We must be miles away!" Liv ran into his arms, hugging him tightly, ecstatic and overwhelmed by the considerate thought.

"More like thousands, but I figured if you needed a break from Puerdios University... there's nothing better than the great outdoors." Hayden grinned, giddy that Liv liked his idea. "Come on, let's set up the fire pit."

They walked toward the lake and found the fire pit with an oversized love seat facing the lake. Liv sat down and watched Hayden walk over to the firewood stack and grab some logs.

"You're actually going to build a fire?" Liv asked, perplexed, "Can't you use your power for that?"

"Normal, Ollie. That's the theme for tonight, right?" Hayden explained, throwing the logs into the pit. "Don't tell me you actually enjoy the perks of dating a God?" He joked, smirking, as he snapped his fingers to ignite the flame.

Liv raised a confronting eyebrow at Hayden in return.

"You can't make a fire with nothing to burn, anyway." Hayden admitted.

"Compromise. I like that mentality." Liv smiled, nodding in approval.

"In that case..." Hayden reached into his pocket, pulling out a large, oversized wool blanket and tossing it to Liv.

"Okay, that was weird. But appreciated." Liv wrapped herself in the blanket. "How did you do that?"

"Simple shrinking trick. But now it's big enough for the both of us. Give me some of that blanket."

Hayden sat down next to Liv, wrapping his arm around her and pulling the blanket around him. Liv cozied herself up in Hayden's arms, appreciative for his natural body warmth. Together, they were already heating the blanket's insulation.

Looking up at the sky, Liv smiled, seeing her constellation.

"Just look to the stars for guidance." She mumbled to herself, resting her head on Hayden's chest, then paused, as a thought ran through her mind. "What does it feel like when I look at my Constellation but I'm already with you?"

"Pure Bliss. But only because you're with me, it has nothing to do with the stars." Hayden kissed the top of Liv's head, sending chills down her spine.

Liv didn't want to ruin the moment, but she needed to ask Hayden about what she had learned earlier in the night.

"Hayden, have you heard of the Fallen Element?"

"Of course. Why?"

Liv wasn't expecting that response, it caught her a bit off guard. "Do you believe in the legend? That he fell in love with a mortal and the blackbirds killed him?"

Hayden sighed. "It's all speculation. Like I said, I don't believe in it."

Liv bit her lip, not entirely accepting his perspective. "But, it's a bit coincidental? Doesn't that worry you?"

"Ollie, what's more coincidental is that he was an Elite and got murdered. Everyone wants power, and as an Elite, you're always a target. My father told me that his brother wanted the throne–he was hungry and desperate for power–so, it's also very possible that the Elite's brother murdered him to ascend to the Elements Pillar's throne."

Liv paused in awe at the idea of a God willing to murder his own brother in flesh and blood, and how casually Hayden had mentioned it, as if they had been propelled back in time to a Shakespearean Tragedy.

"Who was the brother that you think killed the Element Elite?" Liv asked, cautiously. She looked to her right, staring into the dense forest ahead, sensing as if they were being watched, but could only see darkness between the trees.

"You actually encountered him the other day. The Fallen Elite's brother was Arlo–the Lord of the Dark Gods."

Shivering at the name, Liv wasn't sure what bothered her more–that Hayden was in danger with her, or that he would still be in danger, without her.

SEVENTEEN

Liv squinted her eyes to sparkles of peach sunlight peaking through the window. Smiling at the beautiful sight, she turned over on the bed and planted her face into the soft pillow.

Then she jolted upright, now aware that she was sleeping indoors, and indeed, on a bed. She frantically looked around, instantly relaxing as she recognized the furniture and room she was in. Liv must have dozed off during their late night fire pit, not realizing Hayden carried her indoors to finish her sleep. But, if that was the case, where was Hayden?

Liv got out of bed and stretched, checking herself out in the mirror, in horror. Her heavy makeup from the night before had smeared, giving her raccoon eyes, and her hair was a nest, resulting from the sweaty dance floor and windy transit to arrive at the cabin.

She ran to the bathroom and quickly washed her face. Shortly after, Liv decided nothing could be done with her hair, so threw it up into a messy bun.

Slowly descending the stairs, she could smell pancakes coming from the kitchen. Hayden was quickly moving around the kitchen, flipping pancakes and grabbing plates simultaneously as he saw Liv and greeted her with an infectious smile.

"Smells delicious," Liv sat down at the kitchen counter. "How long have you been up?"

Hayden ignored Liv, instead grabbing a coffee mug and sliding it in front of her.

"Americano."

Liv grabbed the mug, tasting the hot beverage, which was delicious.

"How did you make this?" She asked, impressed.

"There are *some* perks to dating me." Hayden smiled. "Compromise. Remember?"

Liv smiled, but as she looked around, couldn't help reminiscing about how much fun they had at this cabin the last time they were here. It seemed like a lifetime ago.

"Do you ever miss it? The world we lived in? You know, football practices, movie nights, and jeans as an acceptable wardrobe option for class… that life?"

Hayden sighed, plating a stack of pancakes and handing it to Liv.

"It was less complicated, sure, and there was less responsibility, but– I'm where I belong now, Liv." He asserted.

Liv drizzled maple syrup on her pancakes.

"Yeah, but do you miss it? Would you go back, you know–if you could?"

Hayden snuck a bite from Liv's pancake stack. She gave him a joking glare and then took a bite for her own. She could taste soft banana slices; he had made banana pancakes, her favorite–and they were deliciously orgasmic.

"I don't know." Hayden shrugged. "It was just a completely different way of being than I was used to. I always thought of it as traveling to a different country. They have their own customs, culture, lifestyle, and yeah you adapt to get the experience, or just fit in, and try to appreciate it for what it is. But, it's not yours. And just because you're not there anymore doesn't mean you don't love it, or appreciate it any less. But for me, that world always just seemed like a vacation, not my reality."

Liv thought about that concept, and how it applied to her life as she took another bite of her pancakes. Did she feel as if she was on vacation right now? Away from her reality? Would she miss this world if she returned to her normal one?

Liv glanced over at Hayden as he carefully poured more pancake batter into perfectly tiny circles on the griddle. She appreciated how he had cut up bite-sized banana slices for her favorite breakfast meal and reflected on how he always made her feel so special, even when she couldn't offer anything in return. Then, noticing his grey sweats that hung perfectly on his hips, and his dewy skin, she sighed–Hayden was so beautiful. Liv could only think to herself: *How did she get so lucky to find him, and what did she do to deserve getting him back?*

She would miss him. Liv knew that–she had already experienced a life without him and it was not a survivable one. Hayden *was* Liv's reality–her past, present and future.

Hayden sat down next to Liv, with his very own hot stack of pancakes. He cut off a small portion and dropped it on Liv's plate.

"I believe I owe you for one stolen bite?" He grinned, as he plopped another piece into his mouth, looking up at the ceiling, then back at Liv, face serious. "But truthfully, Ollie, I think I only belong wherever you are. Because with you is the only time I feel like I'm in the right place. You're my home."

Liv smiled, leaning in for a kiss. Hayden gravitated toward her direction, responding with his lips. He lifted Liv up and placed her on his lap, wrapping his arms around her, beaming.

"Hayden," Liv looked into Hayden's eyes, finding her mirrored soul. "I love you."

Hayden kissed her in return, passionately and deep. "I love you, too. Always have and always will."

He picked her up, and carried her back upstairs to their room, as if she were light as a feather. He kissed her neck, and her chest, and urgently rushed her through the hallway as he came back to her lips. The tension from the dance floor returned, the longing, the need–but this time they could do something more than just touch. They could do so much more.

Hayden gently laid Liv on the bed, and took off his zip-up hoodie, exposing his glorious abs and rock hard physique. Liv tremored inside, as she threw off her flannel shirt, excited for their skins to collide. Hayden leaned over her, their mouths magnetically finding each other in response.

Hayden lightly touched her neck and then grazed her chest, sending chills down her legs. Every touch was electric, and when Hayden grabbed her and lifted her onto his lap, Liv welcomed the new, closer position. He grabbed Liv's grey shirt, and paused to look at her for permission, which she granted by rocking forward on his lap, rubbing the bulge she could feel growing underneath. He softly lifted the shirt, and touched her silk navy bra, in awe.

Liv's nipples grew hard in return; she needed more of him, and wanted him, now. She softly groaned in response to his touch, breathing harder, and moved into another passionate, yearning kiss.

Hayden quickly unsnapped her bra and laid her back on the bed, all in one swift and gentle movement. Liv grabbed his sweatpants, pulling them down, as her hips shifted in position, full of desire.

Soon, Hayden was pulling off her silk panty and kissing a following trail down her legs, making Liv scream internally with yearning. When Hayden returned to look at Liv, she opened her legs and glided her fingers down his back, pushing his hips toward her as she felt his strong butt.

Liv was breathing heavily, yearning for what was to come. Hayden thrust himself inside her, and she moaned in pleasure, loving the feeling of him, her insides unraveling as they continued to pulse against each other. He touched her neck and arms slowly with his hands, but simultaneously sped up his pace, causing an uncontrollable sensation through Liv's body, as her insides convulsed in pleasure. His hips rose in delight, her arms grabbed his neck to bring him closer to her, to feel her boobs pressed against his strong torso. Liv hadn't felt this alive in a long time.

Hayden's breathing deepened with Liv's soft moans, soon she got even more turned on by hearing Hayden's pleasured voice, and soon, she was climaxing, along with Hayden, as he pushed himself forcefully one more time inside her.

They both took a deep breath, relaxed and beamed at each other. Hayden slowly lifted himself up and placed himself next to her, wrapping Liv in his arms, welcoming her to relax.

"I love you, Ollie." She heard him whisper after sometime, as she began dreaming of their future together and the days to come in their cozy private world, their little piece of home, in each other's arms, where they belonged.

Hayden and Liv spent the weekend enjoying peace, calm and each other. After a couple days of bliss, Liv was actually disappointed with the reality that they would need to return to Puerdios University when Sunday evening approached.

"We both have classes tomorrow, and if neither of us show up, that will cause for some speculation." Hayden insisted, as Liv crossed her arms in defeat.

"Can we come back here soon?" Liv asked, looking for a thread of hope to hold onto.

"Of course. Anytime." Hayden shook his head as he pulled her into a hug.

"Next weekend?" Liv suggested, jokingly. She stood on her tippy-toes to kiss him.

"If next weekend is what you want, next weekend it is." Hayden laughed, bending over to replenish her pouty request. "But, I may need to get a mileage program to support these long travels..."

Liv smiled, feeling a little better at their departure, knowing a return was possible in the near future. Everything had been so perfect for the past two days; she wasn't looking forward to reuniting with the bizarre world of Puerdios, one that constantly caused so many issues between Hayden and her. They were able to act oblivious to their surroundings this weekend, relish in each other's solitude, reconnect–it was like old times and exactly what Liv needed after such a rollercoaster month. She temporarily could forget the dangers she and Hayden faced for a moment; a much-needed break after learning about the Dark Gods war mission and Hayden's never-ending potential massacre.

Hayden and Liv left in the evening, so as they flew over the gorgeous woods, Liv watched the sun set over the horizon, glowing the fields with a bright amber and soft hue, her eyes mirroring the sun's departure, as she slowly relaxed into a blissful dream.

By Monday afternoon, everything had gone back to normal. Piper acted as if nothing had happened on Friday night, or she accepted that she had done all she could do to warn Liv from her own, or Hayden's, potential demise. They sat through Astronomy per usual, answering Professor Deligne's questions about resources from other planets and extra terrestrial sub-particles.

Liv was surprised when she even answered two questions successfully, but aside from that, Piper responded for the majority of the class, as usual.

The two girls headed to Environmental Science, which Liv had minor precautions about facing Cleo for the first time since Hayden's Symposium. She secretly wished that Cleo hadn't seen her and Hayden kiss and was very worried about what Cleo could do with the information.

Liv and Piper sat down in their seats, and although Piper was talking about a God she had met at Friday's party, Liv was a little preoccupied, still watching for Cleo to enter the classroom.

When Cleo didn't show, Liv's concern spiked even more.

Anxious to tell Hayden about Cleo's absence in their next class, Humanities, Liv barely paid attention to Professor Claredon's lecture about Global Warming. And when the bell rang, Liv raced to lunch, as if she could speed up time by accelerating her pace.

"Hey! Wait up friend!" Piper chased after Liv, catching up to her immediately.

Although Liv had gotten used to walking in stilettos on the regular, she was no competition to a God – they were pros in the catwalk category.

"Where are you running off to?" Piper asked curiously. "Or are you sick of me already?"

"Sick of you?" Liv was thrown off by Piper's remark.

"Well, I didn't see you all weekend, and after I showed you the Fallen Element Statue, I feel like, things have been off between us."

Liv hadn't even thought about Piper since Friday, which made her feel bad. "I'm sorry, I'm not mad or anything, my mind has just been a bit distracted since the Symposium."

Piper jumped in, relieved. "I totally get it. I figured you just wanted space to think everything through. Accept the inevitable–"

"The inevitable?" Liv interjected.

"I mean, you and Hayden. Obviously you guys can't be together, so you had to process it this weekend, I understand." Piper explained.

Liv shook her head, angrily. "No. That's not it."

Piper turned to Liv, "Wait, you didn't end it with Hayden?"

"No." Liv said, shocked at Piper's assumption. "I talked to him about the Fallen Elite, and he told me that he's in danger just for being royalty. Like the Fallen Elite, he's a target for any power-hungry God who wants to take over. Especially with Arlo and the Dark Gods wanting to usurp the throne, he's already in danger and has other things he needs to worry about."

Piper looked shocked, but more genuinely concerned for her friend. "Are you sure about this, Liv? It puts him, and you, at more risk, too."

"So what?" Liv yelled, a little too aggressively. "I'm already at risk! And you are as well. Arlo tried to kill me barely over a week ago, Piper. And, you're my friend now–right? You care about me, so that also puts you in danger, too– for caring about a mortal. And at the end of the day, unlike you, I am mortal. Either way, I'm going to die, eventually. But I'd rather live a life that I'm in control of, instead of living one that's depicted by fear."

Liv stomped off, ignoring the thunderous clouds that hovered over Puerdios University. She refused to acknowledge them, for in the back of her mind, she dreaded an omen that was warning her something bad was about to happen.

Sitting by herself at lunch, Liv was actually relieved to see Cleo's entitled scowl enter onto the patio deck, but quickly tensed up when she found Cleo headed in her direction. Cleo's eyes looked darker, more dangerous than before.

"Mortal, where's your lame sidekick? Or should I say parasite?" Cleo scowled, glaring at Liv up and down. "Was she too embarrassed to be sitting by you because she realized you're a throwaway, not even worthy to be taking up space? Everything about you, your personality, your outfit and your existence, screams desperate."

Not letting Cleo get into her head, Liv knew she looked good–she was wearing a long-sleeved cream crop top and matching pencil skirt with her gold strappy heels. And she was *not* desperate.

Standing up, Liv jabbed back, "Oh I'm sorry, but I think you were describing yourself? Or has no one told you, nobody cares what you think?" Liv was nose to nose with Cleo, refusing to back down.

"You should leave now, mortal. Before I make your life a living hell." Cleo snarled back.

"Is that a threat?" Liv was shaking internally, but commanded herself to remain strong in this battle. Cleo could have something on Liv, and she was more than completely aware of it, but Liv's internal stubbornness refused to lose.

"Obviously." Cleo growled, teeth clenched, and then looked around to notice her peers were starting to stare, so she stepped back.

"Consider yourself warned." Cleo threatened and then swiftly turned away, hitting Piper's shoulder purposefully as she headed back toward her posse.

Piper looked back at Cleo, confused, and cautiously approached Liv.

"Are you all right? What was all of that about?"

Liv rolled her eyes, exasperated. "Ugh! Cleo–she literally ticks my every last nerve."

"What's new?" Piper muttered rhetorically, sitting herself down at the table.

Liv paused, unsure if it was fair to bring her innocent friend into the mess she had created.

Piper raised her hands in surrender. "Disclaimer, I get what you said earlier. I'm on your side, Liv. You're my friend and I care about you. I'm prepared to be massacred, if it comes to it. You can trust me." She confessed, apologetically.

"I think she saw Hayden and I … on Friday night." Liv whispered, cautiously.

Piper's eyes went wide before she quietly and eagerly asked, "Did you tell Hayden?"

"No, I, wanted to be sure it was a possibility before I brought him into it."

"Liv! You need to tell him. He may have wiped her memory before, but she's vindictive, and if she noticed any sign that you and Hayden were a thing, she'd probably be pretty pissed that you're swooping in on her soulmate and her key to ultimate power over us peasants."

Liv automatically grinned at Piper's reasoning. She raised her lunch menu slyly to look back at Cleo behind it, with whom Liv found was still staring at her from afar. Cleo's face was stern, clearly with vengeance painted on her mind.

After one glance, Liv agreed with Piper. She confirmed her evidence (even if speculative) and needed to tell Hayden as soon as possible.

Liv wasn't very hungry during lunch, so as soon as she saw Hayden leave the Dining Ballroom with Rei, she sprinted toward the exit to catch up to them.

Nearing Hayden, Liv began to call out his name, but Hayden must have sensed her behind him and turned around before she could make a sound. Hayden shot a fierce glance at Rei, commanding him to leave, so Rei obediently departed without a word.

"What's wrong?" Hayden asked quietly, but sternly as he approached Liv.

"Cleo. I think she saw us on Friday." Liv panted. Her heart was racing.

Hayden took a deep breath in; Liv could tell he was not happy about this news.

"I'll handle it." Was all Hayden said, forcefully.

Before Liv could ask how, Hayden had turned away, stomping back toward the great hall, toward Cleo. She immediately felt relieved, but also guilty for putting all the weight of her troubles onto Hayden–he already had enough on his plate. Liv just wanted Cleo to leave–she wished her enemy would just jump off a cliff or something, and then angrily remembered she couldn't even die from *that*. Although Hayden had affirmed many times that Cleo was on their side, and that she was a Pure God, Liv did *not* believe that for a second.

Liv stomped off to her next class, angry and anxious–a very caffeinated feeling–and just hoped Piper or Professor Montagnes could distract her from her angst during Humanities.

Liv found Piper immediately, running over to her friend and plopping herself down onto the seat next to her.

"I'm sorry." Liv blurted out.

Piper looked surprised by Liv's outburst.

"For everything." Liv continued, "It's a mess. I know it. And thank you, for just accepting me. And being there for me and caring about me. I'm sorry I got angry, I know you're just trying to be my friend and help, so I'm just sorry for dragging you into all of this."

Piper smiled. "Thank you. But you're my friend, too. And I wouldn't have you any other way." She nudged Liv, accepting her apology. "How did everything go with Cleo?"

"Hayden said he'd handle it." Liv shrugged, feeling much better than 45 minutes ago, when her entire world felt turned upside down and infinitely spiraling out of control.

As if being summoned from hearing his name, Hayden swiftly sat in the seat next to Liv. Piper quietly began freaking at his appearance, sending silent stabbing daggers in his direction from her cold stare.

"Everything's fine." Hayden stated, ignoring Piper. "I found Cleo and commanded her to forget Friday night. She remembers nothing."

"What if she's already told someone?" Liv asked, apprehensively.

"I willed her to tell me, she hadn't. All is okay." Hayden confirmed, and then looked at Liv, smiling, still ignoring Piper's astonished dramatics. "You look beautiful, by the way. I forgot to mention that earlier, but I couldn't stop staring at you during lunch."

He got up from his seat. "I'm going to sit by Rei today. It may be better, for now." He nodded towards Piper, finally acknowledging her glares.

When Hayden left, Liv turned to Piper. "How does that work? I know he can command Gods and Mortals, but is that something all Gods can do?"

Piper shook her head, "No that's a unique power, only blessed upon the royal bloodline. It helps maintain the balance – anyone who has pledged loyalty to their reign has no choice but obey any commands the royal family gives."

"But where's the balance, then?" Liv asked, intrigued.

"Well, anyone who rebels against the Pure Gods cannot be controlled by them. That's probably why the radical Dark God uprising is such a threat." Piper explained, "Yes, the King still has authority to the conservative Dark Gods – those who still obey the Pure Gods rule, but the radical Dark Gods, those who want to overthrow the system, the royals can no longer control."

"And humans?" Liv asked, intrigued.

"Royals have absolute power over mortals. It's a little tricky how they manage it, because they're unknown to that world, it's not really possible for mortals to rebel against them." Piper shrugged. "Might not be the fairest, but they don't abuse the power, I don't think."

"You don't think?" Liv hadn't realized how much power her boyfriend potentially could have over her.

"Well," Piper hesitated, biting her lip, "I guess my opinion is based on choice – and of course this perspective is completely objective, but by refraining to give mortals the knowledge to choose, like the Gods are able to, and refraining from educating them on the Gods and our powers, that's not necessarily democratic, is it? It's just controlling from afar, which in scientific terms could be concluded as abusive."

Piper made an extremely valid point, again forcing Liv to ponder the blurred lines between right and wrong, dark and pure. It truly was a fine line, and one she struggled with, for she saw both sides, and felt herself residing between the two contrasting beliefs.

Soon, Humanities concluded and it was time for Study Hall. Liv was happy to have the day almost over with; there was only one more study hall class before she could be reunited with Hayden for the night. Liv adjusted her cream skirt automatically, already feeling fervent with anticipation for their reunion. All she wanted was the security of Hayden's warm, comforting embrace.

It had been a day.

By the time Piper and Liv got to the Galleria Library, most tables were full with students, already diligently reading or trying to complete their assignments for the week. To Piper's dismay and Liv's excitement, the only table with available seats was the one where Rei and Hayden were sitting. A blessing in disguise, Liv could sit by Hayden for the next two hours. She instinctively went over to take her rightful seat, but Piper was too quick, and slid in next to Hayden before Liv could, and nodded toward the opposite side of the table, prompting Liv to sit by Rei, and as far away from Hayden as possible.

Liv rolled her eyes, succumbing to her friend's inconvenient choice. She felt Rei tense as she plopped down into the seat beside him, prompting another eye roll.

The four studied in silence, per study hall rules. Usually, Piper and Liv would pass each other notes, but whether from being near Hayden and Rei or just the day's unusual activities, they all kept to themselves, needing a break from the seemingly always complex world at Puerdios University–everyone was aligned with the notion of needing simplicity for a moment, effortless solitude.

Liv joyfully worked on her Chemistry homework, which focused on balancing chemical reactions. She had never had an interest in chemistry before, but found she was actually pretty good at understanding atoms, molecules and the periodic table, so overall enjoyed that class. For her, it became more of a fun game to figure out how to keep the balance on paper, possibly because in reality she seemingly had no control of her life at all.

She had just finished her final equation, which was balancing: copper sulfide + hydrogen nitrate = copper nitrate + copper sulfate + nitrogen dioxide + water ($CuS + 8HNO3 => CuSO4 = NO2 + 4H2O$), when the doors burst open with a thundering 'bang!' and caused all of the students to turn their heads, almost in unison, at the intrusion.

Many jaws fell open as King Rowan strode through the room, followed by a mass of guards, directed toward Hayden, who had already stood up with concern and confusion.

"Father, what's going on?" Hayden commanded.

"What the hell do you think you're doing!?" King Rowan yelled back at his son, grabbing his arm.

As if on cue, the guards separated, revealing Cleo, faking a look of distraught.

"I can explain." Hayden stated, quietly.

"Explain what? Seems very clear to me. You're blatantly trying to prevent the prophecy from coming to fruition, putting all of your subjects in *danger*, AND, interacting with a mortal!? That is forbidden! What more do you have to *explain*, Hayden?"

Hayden bowed his head, shamefully.

"That's what I thought." King Rowan nodded, softly commanding to his guards, "Seize her."

Without a second to process, Liv was suddenly being grabbed by both arms and lifted from her chemistry equations.

"No!" Hayden fought his father's grip. "Don't put this on Liv. This is entirely my fault, not hers. Take me instead!"

"Oh, no—you're staying with me." King Rowan muttered coldly, then growled to his guards. "Take her to the dungeon."

"No!" Liv screamed in panic, trying to fight off her captors, but it was no use – they were too strong. She refused to give up, and for a moment almost thought she had rid herself of them, but then another handful of arms grasped her limbs and she was again restrained.

As the guards pulled Liv away, she was still making weaker attempts at escape when she caught a glance at Cleo, whose evil smirk pulsed through Liv's core, a malevolence she had never felt before.

And in an instant, Liv knew.

Cleo had gone Dark.

EIGHTEEN

Liv stayed in the dungeon all night, and when she woke up chilled from the damp, concrete, soulless cell, she shivered. Out of all days, why did she have to wear her two-piece crop top and skirt, with the thinnest cotton fabric today? She tried pulling down her skirt to make it longer, wishing there was a way she could will the air to heat around her.

Liv looked through the one small window in the cell, out of habit. She had peaked out about every hour throughout the night to see if the earth had rotated, in hopes she could see her constellation. Around 11:30pm (her fifth time checking since sunset), she finally spotted Ollie, and sadly stared at it, guilt filling up her soul as a single tear emerged.

Hayden didn't come, which made her feel inferior, filled with even more remorse. She wasn't sure what was worse, that he physically wasn't able to come to her rescue or the possibility that he no longer wanted to.

Sniffling, she laid herself against the cold hard stonewall, resting her head in her hand as she started gasping for air. How could she be so stupid? She knew she was putting Hayden in danger, but she was too selfish, too needy, to do the right thing and keep him safe.

In the loneliness of the night, by the time Liv noticed her cell lightening and welcomed the new day, hoping it would bring an opportunity to allow her to do the right thing, defend Hayden, even if at her own cost.

She heard faint footsteps growing louder, so Liv stood up, trying to look composed and strong for whatever she may face.

When a familiar face appeared around the corner, decked in his beautiful camel coat and thick grey cashmere sweater, Liv welcomed Kai with a deep sigh of relief.

"Kai, thank god you're here." Liv walked toward the barred entrance, eager to hear what her friend's plan would be to get Liv out of her current hostage.

"You shouldn't thank 'God' in the presence of a god, Ollie. It's degrading." Kai mocked, sardonically.

Liv was a little thrown off; Kai had never called her Ollie before.

"I'm sorry? Are you here to help get me out of this situation, Kai? I can leave. I'll go back to my world. You can will me to forget this entire life–I just want to keep Hayden safe–"

"Hayden. But do you *really* want to leave him?" Kai snarled.

Liv's trepidation was building; this wasn't the same Kai who swooned her with kind charm at the Symposium a couple weeks back.

"Kai, if you're angry that it didn't work out between us, I'm sorry." Liv pleaded, "But I really need your help right now."

"Between us?" Kai scorned, "Do you really think you are worthy enough to deserve a God's love? Is that why you fell for the Prince? Do you really think the Pure Gods would just dust off a rule enforced for over two millennia? For *you*? A *mortal*?"

Liv lowered her head, ashamed at her foolishness.

"You're worthless. My sister's brave confession was for the best. If the Pure Gods ever had a chance to defeat the Dark, you cannot be here." Kai's voice tremored through the dungeon.

Soon, Liv could hear security guards marching down the corridor, toward her cell. Kai looked satisfyingly happy as they arrived and opened her cell, seizing Liv for her next destination.

Liv, eyes open wide, looked at Kai for an explanation, something to assure her she would be all right.

Instead, Kai walked right up to her and glared into her eyes. Liv noticed his gaze was smokier, more of a chocolate brown, when before they were a caramel amber. A subtle change, one that may not have been noticed if it hadn't been weeks since the last time she saw him. As Liv studied his hair, she also noticed it looked darker, almost like a wintered season hue.

Kai was becoming darker.

"You've turned Dark." Liv accused, strongly lifting her chin up, with all the dignity she could amass. She looked down on him in disgust.

Kai smirked, whispering, "The Darkest of Darks, actually. But, too bad there's nothing you can do about it now, mortal. Nobody will believe you."

He looked to the guards and nodded at them in command, then turned back to Liv as they started forcing her out of the dungeon.

With a devilish smirk, Kai glared evilly into Liv's eyes and made only one last announcement before leaving.

"Time for your funeral, Ollie."

Liv's heart was racing as she was dragged outside onto the pavilion of the royal palace. She noticed a wooden platform, similar to what she had seen in old historic movies, where criminals got hanged or their head chopped off. The security guards stopped, so she remained behind the crowd, another witness to the show.

With the sight of Hayden walking onto the wooden stage, Liv's mouth dropped as she lost her breath.

No.

She could not watch this. Hayden was facing his execution, and this was all of her fault.

If only Liv had the strength to stay away from him, like he had tried so hard to stay away from her. She couldn't grasp the thought that Hayden, his caring soul, intelligent and kind, and his handsome smile–that all of him was about to be removed from the world, forever. He still had so much potential and so many things he could have accomplished if it hadn't been for Liv.

No, this cannot be happening.

This past week had been everything to Liv; she could not lose him again, she *would* not lose him again.

She needed to do something, but as Liv looked around, with all of the security gods surrounding her, restraining her, with her hands bounded tightly by rope, Liv realized she couldn't.

She was only human.

So instead, Liv watched, grief-stricken.

As Hayden approached the center of the stage, Rei's father Silas bound his hands to a stone disk with a saddened face.

Frantically trying to remember every part of Hayden, Liv watched, stared and examined him so she could assess a memory to keep forever. She studied the small details and his entire feature all at once, noticing just how beautiful he truly was, inside and out.

Hayden bowed his head down, in defeat, stirring more hysteria within Liv.

She desperately needed to see his stunning eyes, just one more time to remember the life, wisdom and unconditional love that emitted whenever Hayden looked at her, as if into her entire being. Just one more time, if this were to be the last time she could see his glorious soul.

Always connected, Hayden heard her silent plea from afar and looked up and saw Liv. His gaze filled with a look of regret, defiantly apologetic, in defeat.

They had royally screwed up with this unforgiveable mistake.

A man came up behind him, with a rope that seemed to be on fire. It was happening. Hayden lowered his face back down, again.

"No..." Liv whispered, eyes panicking from Hayden to Silas.

I cannot lose him again.

The guard raised his arm, to position the whip and began the motion.

I will not lose him again.

"NOOOO!" Liv screamed, with everything she had, her entire soul and being, reaching forward.

She broke her wrists apart.

As the man released his arm to strike, water and lightning burst from Liv's hands, emerging out of her palms, each its own individual rope, ready for battle. The lightning hit the stone, in which with Hayden's arms were bound, disconnecting his bandage, while a gust of wind simultaneously blew him away; Hayden missed the impact of the fiery whip by only a thread of distance.

The water attacked next, extinguishing the rope and its flames entirely, until it remained nothing but ashes, and fell to the ground like sand.

But nobody was concerned with Hayden anymore; they were all staring at Liv in amazement, wonder, disbelief and shock.

Oblivious to the crowd's astonishment, Liv was more alarmed by her hands, gazing at them with wide eyes and confusion.

Kai ran up to her, first angry and then bewildered. "How did you do that!?"

The King ran up to Liv's side, staring at her in a studious wonder as he called off security from trying to restrain her again. "Not just any God could overpower the enchantments cast by the Candor and Security Elites."

Liv felt weak. Falling to her knees, she continued to stare at her hands, shocked.

"Explain yourself." King Rowan commanded sternly, showing no compassion.

"I–I don't know, I've never done that, I…" She looked up, her eyes immediately darting to Hayden, who was breaking through the crowd.

Once he got to her, Hayden dropped to Liv's side and pulled her into an embrace, assuring protection.

"Are you okay?!" Hayden breathed, holding Liv tight against him, giving her the security and strength she needed.

"I'm… I'm fine…" Liv didn't recognize her voice, it was jittery and soft, and almost an octave higher than usual. But then Liv's mind finally registered Hayden next to her, alive. She grabbed his head, frantically, "You're not dead."

Liv just needed to say it out loud to believe it. Looking into his eyes, relief flooded her at the sight of his wondrous gaze, feeling even calmer when his smile radiated back at her. She beamed back at his beautiful, living soul.

Kai broke up their reunion, almost immediately.

"Who are you?!" He boldly asked, interrupting. "Are you a spy? Do you work for the Dark Gods? Declare yourself!"

Hayden immediately stood up to defend Liv, face to face with Kai, scorching with anger.

"She is NOT a spy!" Snarling, Hayden threatened, "How dare you."

King Rowan cautiously stepped between the two infuriated Gods. "No, she's clearly pure. The question is, *how*?" He knelt next to Liv, softly putting a hand on her shoulder. "Tell me, Olivia, who are you parents?"

"My..." Liv tried to answer. Her mom was just her mom, nothing close to an anomaly, and as she tried to think, her mind went blank.

Hayden interjected, automatically aware that Liv was upset. "Her mom is an accountant. Mortal. I've met her–she's harmless. Her dad..." He stopped, tilting his toward Liv, asking for permission to go on.

"My dad died before I was born. I didn't know him." Liv finished Hayden's explanation, her voice shaky but starting to feel a bit stronger.

"Curious." King Rowan cocked his head, still looking at Liv like she was a science experiment. He looked back at Hayden. "Well. It seems for the moment, punishment may not be required. Please take Miss Olivia to her room–she may need rest with all that has transpired."

Hayden immediately went back to Liv's aid to help her up, but Kai interrupted, holding King Rowan back with his arm.

"We aren't going to take her into custody!? She interfered with the security proceeding for punishment! That's clearly a crime and we need answers. This is unacceptable!" Wide-eyed and fuming, Kai pleaded with the King to seek justice.

But King Rowan simply looked back at Kai, with a subtle glare. "The truth will come out, in time."

The King gently removed Kai's hand from his arm and walked away.

With his dad gone, Hayden immediately scooped Liv into his arms and flew her back to his room at Puerdios.

Once they arrived, he gently sat her on his couch, making sure she was stable and comfortable; Hayden kneeled down and put his hand tenderly on her knee.

"Liv, do you promise to be honest with me?" He asked, softly.

"Hayden, I've never lied to you before. Why would I start now?" Liv replied, bleakly.

"Can you tell me everything you know about your father?"

"I… I never knew him. My mom barely even knew him." Liv hung her head low, so confused, trying to remember any detail that she could. "They met before I was born, sorry–that's obvious. I'm thinking out loud."

Liv looked up at Hayden and shrugged, "I believe she loved him, she always looked so wounded when she mentioned him."

"Mentioned him?" Hayden softly asked, sitting beside her on the couch, encouraging her to go on.

"Only common phrases, ones that I gather mother's have to say to their daughters when their father is dead. 'Your father would be proud, your father loved you, you have your father's eyes...' that sort of stuff." Liv shrugged, fiddling with her necklace.

"Okay. Did she tell you how he died?" Hayden sounded defeated, but still determined to find some form of a clue.

"Supposedly he was attacked, murdered and found on a beach, but that's human enough, isn't it?"

"Supposedly?" Hayden prompted, curious.

"Well, she heard from a friend, but my dad didn't have any relatives or friends for my mom to contact, so she had to go off that guy's word. She knew nothing, all she had left of him were memories and–" Liv stopped fiddling with her necklace, pausing to look at it, curiously, "And this."

Liv held onto the necklace in her hand. "He gave this to my mom, and she passed it along to me on my eighteenth birthday." She quickly unfastened it from her neck and handed it to Hayden, feeling a hole develop in her being upon its departure, a piece missing from her soul, somehow attached and in transit with the necklace.

Hayden inspected the necklace, looking at it from every angle; Liv impatiently inspected Hayden and awaited his response.

"So?" Liv couldn't take the suspense any longer.

"I have an idea, but it's a stretch. I need someone who knows their history to confirm what I think this could be…" He was still looking at the necklace, eyeing its every crevice, in awe.

Liv had an immediate solution, "Get Piper. She's a researcher–she'll know."

Hayden nodded. "Done."

A minute later, Piper knocked on the door.

After Hayden opened the door for her to enter, Piper ran to Liv, yelling, "You're OKAY! And you're free? Thank Zeus! I was so worried!"

Liv smiled, embracing her friend in a hug, but remembered the unfinished business Hayden and she needed Piper's expertise on.

"Can you look at this necklace and let us know if you've seen it before?" Hayden handed over the heirloom to Piper, but she looked confused.

"Liv, isn't this the necklace you wear, every day?"

"Yes. But can you take a closer look?" Liv prompted, eagerly.

Piper shrugged and closely examined it, and then as if something clicked, her mouth dropped open, and Piper looked both at Liv and Hayden with incredulous eyes.

"Where did you get this?" Piper whispered.

"So, you think it's The Druzy, too?" Hayden asked.

"Think? The Druzy of the Elements? Um, yeah. It definitely is." Piper looked closely on the left side of the necklace, "But the question is how? It hasn't been seen in…"

"Eighteen years." Hayden confirmed.

Piper brought the necklace to Liv's eyesight and pointed to the side of the stone, "Can you read this?"

Liv took the necklace, bringing it closer to her eyes, so she could depict the small writing.

"Yeah, it says 'et virtutem elementorum'?" Liv read, uncertain to what it meant.

"The power of the elements." Hayden translated, still staring at the necklace incredulously. "Let me see that."

He looked at the side of the necklace, confused. "I don't see anything?"

Piper rolled her eyes, "Obviously. That's because only those who belong to the Pillar of the Elements can see it, and pending how much power you impose on the pillar, it becomes more legible. I only see scribbles because... I'm so low in the hierarchy." She blushed, trying to play it cool by shrugging it off. But then Piper recovered and turned to Liv, ecstatically, "But, Liv—you can actually *read* it. That's HUGE. You could be an heir to a Head House or an Element Elite or something..."

Hearing the phrase Elite, Liv suddenly remembered what she had discovered before exiting her dungeon cell. She told Hayden and Piper about her encounter with Kai, before everything went down.

"An extreme Dark God infiltrated the Elites?" Hayden asked with strife cut across his face.

"But, if you're the true heir, you can overthrow him!" Piper shrieked, excitedly.

Hayden gave a scowling look to Piper.

"Yes, she could be the rightful heir, and yes, she could be extremely powerful, but we don't have *any* facts, and she doesn't even know how to wield her power, let alone control it." He looked at Liv, cautiously, and grabbed her hands. "This information that we have here is *very* dangerous, even if just speculation." Hayden looked to Piper and then back to Liv. "We cannot tell anyone about this conversation. If any Dark God, especially Kai, heard this theory, they could come for you, Liv."

Liv rolled her eyes, sarcastically stating, "What's new?"

Piper was more anxious. "So, what do we do?"

Sternly, Hayden decided, "I need to talk to my father."

"Your father!?" Liv turned her head to Hayden, shocked. "You would actually trust him? Even though he just tried to have you executed?"

"Executed?" Hayden huffed, in a laughable shock at the accusation. "My father didn't try to have me executed." He contemplated the statement, shrugging, "Or at least to my knowledge."

Liv lifted her brow at him to continue.

"He knew the Fallen Element before he died, so he may be able to bring light to this." Hayden turned back to Liv, "You actually thought my father would try to kill me?" He looked back to Piper for support.

"But, the fire whip! Doesn't that kill Gods?" Liv was beginning to doubt herself in ever being able to understand how this world worked.

"Liv, I told you–Gods cannot be killed, only sent to the Underworld." Hayden explained.

"Then what does the whip actually do?"

"It inflicts a strong beating, one worse than I could imagine. I feel pain just thinking of it." Hayden automatically rubbed his arm as if it had been struck. "Thank you for preventing me from that, by the way."

"No problem." Liv responded automatically. "Although, I'm not sure I could do it again. How do I even figure out if I actually have powers, or if it was a fluke?"

Piper interjected before Hayden could respond. "It definitely wasn't a fluke. I am a God, and even I couldn't do that. But, we do need to get you in training. If you don't learn how to control your powers, it could be really bad."

Piper then noticed Liv and Hayden sitting next to each other on the couch, unconsciously holding hands, and smiled.

"On that cue, I'm going to go and start processing your paperwork for classes. I can take a hint when two lovers are reunited and realize they won't actually be killed for spending some quality time together for once, if you know what I mean." Piper winked, very obviously.

"Piper–she'll need to be enrolled in defense and combat training. Please make that a priority. Contact Rei and Peyton immediately, but only them–no one else." Hayden added sternly, not taking his eyes off Liv.

"Of course." Piper quietly confirmed, obediently. Before running out, she turned so only Liv could see her, and winked again.

Liv looked at Hayden and smiled. It was all going to be okay. With him here, and safe, she knew that now. They could take on the world, together. She was at peace, and suddenly yawned, with the previous night and all the days' activities finally catching up to her.

"You're tired. Can I get you anything?" Hayden asked automatically.

"If I'm really a God, aren't I not supposed to get tired?" Liv yawned again.

"You start inheriting your powers when you turn eighteen, so you're still adapting to them. It'll take time. It's mostly mental, too." Hayden confirmed, smiling. "And you have eighteen years of thinking like a mortal to combat."

"Oh, okay. Well, I am tired, but I want to stay up anyway. With you." Liv went over to grab a blanket, and then came back to Hayden on the couch, spreading the blanket over them.

Hayden followed obligingly, wrapping Liv into his arms.

"The only thing I need to say, is that I may be able to order every God around, but you must realize, I am at your complete mercy, Ollie. Tell me what to do, and I will do it with pleasure." Hayden kissed her cheek, softly. "I will never command you to do anything out of your will. Please understand that."

Liv smiled. This was exactly where she needed to be.

"So, if I wanted to light up your fireplace, do you really think I could?"

"Of course," Hayden affirmed, whispering in Liv's ear and sending chills down her back, "but this may turn into a dangerous first lesson." He chuckled in her ear; Liv could feel his comforting breath, warming her neck.

"How do you do it?" Liv asked, intrigued as she stared at the fireplace.

"Well, I've never really thought about it, I guess." Hayden's eyebrows furrowed. "You sort of just will it to ignite, and it happens. Of course, if your power is weaker, you may have to use Latin to spark the process, but really it just helps you focus on what you're trying to do by saying the command. I think the koine phrase is Ignis."

"Okay. I'll try to just 'will' it?" Liv questioned, repeating what Hayden said.

"Stare at the fire and concentrate. See what happens." Hayden instructed.

Liv looked at the fireplace, feeling her core igniting as she lifted her palm up and toward the fire. The heat rose from her chest and through her arm, as if her blood were a liquid metal. Then the warmth touched her palm and a light burst out of it, igniting the fireplace with a flame.

"Whoa." Liv responded.

"Whoa, for sure. Are you sure that was your first try?" Hayden pulled his head forward to look at Liv in the eyes.

"First try, I swear!" She lifted her hands up in surrender, laughing.

"Well, this calls for celebration." He snapped his fingers and suddenly two oversized mugs flew to the table and a kettle appeared hanging in the fire. "Spiked apple cider?" Hayden grinned mischievously. "Word on the security force is you have a taste for Fireball."

"Did Peyton tell you?" Liv laughed.

Hayden poured the cider into the mugs and handed one to Liv.

"Cheers." Hayden raised his mug, sitting down on the couch, facing Liv and smiling. "To young power."

"To young power." She clicked her glass and grinned back at him, unbelieving that the beautiful soul in front of her was entirely hers, and hers alone. "So, can you tell me something about yourself, Hayden?"

"Sure. What do you want to know?" Hayden took a sip of his cider.

Liv smiled, "Anything, really."

Hayden raised his eyebrow.

"How about something I should have known by now, but you couldn't tell me because I was a human and you weren't allowed to."

"Well, there are a lot of those." Hayden confessed, apologetically. "I need more specific." He smiled, nudging her playfully, but his words cast a dark cloud in Liv's mind, which Hayden immediately noticed.

"What's wrong?"

"It's just that, I've known you for nearly seven years. I thought I knew you so well, but even now it's unraveling new secrets that make you still feel like a stranger sometimes."

There was a long silence as Liv stared into her delectable apple cider.

"Hey," Hayden nudged her again. "You know who I am, I'm the same guy. There's just more to learn about me, just like now there's a lot more to know about you. That's all. And," he lifted Liv's chin, so she would make eye contact, "The best part is that we have forever now. And Ollie, you have to believe me when I say forever with you is all I have ever wanted."

"But…" Liv still wasn't entirely comforted

"But, it will just take time, which we have. If you'll still have me now that you're a powerful deity, of course."

Liv sat up, putting her hand on Hayden's cheek, assuredly.

"Always."

The couple chatted late into the night talking about Hayden's child-hood, his real one. Liv learned about his family, how he *really* spent his summers (Hayden boasted that he did, indeed go to football camp, which is why that's all he ever shared with Liv about his summer, so he had never lied in that regard).

Liv learned that because Hayden's mom, Daphne, was an Elite of the Candor pillar, his sister, Joss was in line to take her throne. Hayden also explained that there were 10 pillars, and Candor specifically covered every-thing from education to law. (Hayden even showed Liv a copy of the *In Diurnus*–their daily newspaper–and proudly read his sister's most recent article about the politics of humans and how it affects the God's day-to-day ruling decisions and efforts.)

It was a night of new beginnings–the most obvious being Liv's first sleepover at Hayden's. They eventually headed up to his room, where Liv crawled into Hayden's satin bed sheets, exhausted from the day, and fell asleep smelling her favorite blend of basil verveina, cedar and leather musk–the smell of her love, Hayden.

NINETEEN

The next morning, Liv woke up early, welcoming the soft sun lit glow as a new day began, a new beginning. Eager to go on her usual morning run, Liv was ecstatic when Hayden offered to join her, like old times. They ran up through the forest to the top of the mountains, to watch the pale sunrise lift the hills up with a soft glow, admiring the quiet cotton candy landscape in the sky.

Liv sat at the top of the hill, telling herself to remember this moment, the moment of calm–when everything in the universe seemed to make sense and presented life's true beauty to admire. *Moments like these,* she thought to herself, *are ones some people spend their entire life chasing.*

And because some things change so drastically, Liv was anticipating just how much her world would catapult into something new. But for now, it was serene and assuring to find that even as some things may venture into the volatile unknown, others–like the mountains and the cyclical, beautiful process of the sky–could remain exactly the same.

The view was a spectacle, both the one in front of her, trees spiraling up and down over the hillside for miles, a soft dewy glow from each branch that sparkled and changed color as the sun continue to breathe its beauty and warmth over them. The second, to her right, the strong and handsome man who had stayed by her side and fought to keep her safe with all that he had. Hayden–he was hers, and now would always be.

There were so many questions, so many unknowns in Liv's life, but for now, all was still, beautiful and kind. She leaned her head against Hayden's shoulder, marveling at how wonderful life could be, if one only took the time to admire it every once in a while.

"You know," Hayden nodded to the valley below them and surrounding trees, and then to the far beach, with the ocean sparkling in excitement at the light, "This could all be yours, one day." He turned to Liv, beaming at the possibility, "If you're the true heir of the Fallen Element, the Elite–you could control all of this."

"All of this?" Liv sat up, wondrous at the concept as she stared over the skyline.

"Earth, wind, fire and rain." Hayden explained, "Simply speaking, of course. There are many branches underneath that, but you would essentially control the sun–fire," he nodded to the sunrise, and then over to the sea, "and the ocean–water." Hayden looked up at the sky. "Air, the clouds could be moved at your demand," and then he gazed out at their view, smiling at the strong forest ahead, "and earth, with all of the magnificence it grows."

Liv took a deep breath at the potential responsibility, mesmerized by the power she never knew she had.

"So, if I was feeling happy, and wanted sunshine to warm up the sky, I could do that?" Liv inquired, her mind racing internally.

"Exactly; however, I wouldn't recommend switching the weather patterns based on emotion, there's a cycle and consequence for whichever schedule is implemented."

At that moment, Liv felt guilty for all her internal rage against Oregon's stormy fall season. "Might explain all the weird thunderstorms that seemed to follow me in the past month." She shrugged, admitting her fault.

Hayden laughed in agreement. "That would make sense." He turned to Liv, lifting her chin in his direction, "But you *can* learn to control your powers, Liv. They're a part of you, just like your mind, your hand and your lips." Hayden softly kissed each body part after mentioning it in his speech. "You learn to identify it, understand it and mold it to your desire."

Liv stared into Hayden's eyes; appreciative for this generous soul she had been so lucky to meet seven years ago.

When Hayden and Liv descended from the mountain for the second portion of their morning jog, Liv felt alive. No step was too long as she leaped over rivers and rocks, and similar to her previous runs, whatever pace she ran ceased to exhaust her–she just hadn't quite noticed it before.

When the two finally finished their jog and arrived to Liv's room, they were surprised to find Peyton, Rei and Piper already there.

"Can I cast a personal lock on my door?" Liv muttered to Hayden, wondering just who else he had given access to enter her room for whenever they pleased.

"Of course." Hayden grinned, walking over to Rei and giving him a friendly hug.

Liv blushed as she noticed Rei wearing the light grey trench coat she was infatuated with a couple weeks before. *Had that really only been a month ago?*

"Well, I personally should apologize for not catching onto your obvious divine ways." Peyton laughed, jokingly bowing down to Liv, her gold and silver bandeau dress shimmering with a statement necklace that's iridescent strings hung in the motion. She then ran over to Liv and tackled her with a hug. "Like, seriously, how did I not figure it out? I only lived with you for a month! I blame the 'emo' outfits."

"I should apologize, too." Rei came over, and to Liv's surprise, actually looked cheerful. "I'm usually not such a dick." He laughed, astonishing Liv even more. "But the whole Fallen-Element-Ban-On-Mortal-Deity-Interaction thing sort of freaks me out."

Liv smiled, fully appreciating being exposed to this new Rei. "No worries, I completely understand."

Peyton put her arms around Liv and Rei, smugly looking around as she said, "See!? I knew we'd all get along, eventually."

Liv looked over at Piper, who sat in the corner, quiet. She had an eager smile on her face, excited to be included, but still a little anxious at the actuality of being near two Elites, including the Prince. To keep herself tasked and occupied, she quietly adjusted her satin navy cutout dress.

But, now that the joyful reunion had transpired, Peyton was ready to get the meeting in order. She strutted over to Liv's desk, grabbing a piece of paper and handed it to Liv.

"Here's your new schedule. I also brought your new books." Peyton happily smirked as she added smugly, "Figured it was tradition now, so I had to come and help with the onboarding."

"New schedule?" Liv raised her eyebrow at Peyton and then glanced down at the paper.

WARFARE & DEFENSE
1 / 3 270* SR
EAST LAWN

METEOROLOGY
1 / 3 330* SR
NORTH TOWER BELOW LEVEL

DEITY POWER-I
1 / 3 60* SS
NORTH TOWER

CHEMISTRY
2 / 4 270* SR
SOUTH TOWER BELOW LEVEL

MYTHOLOGICAL CREATURES
2 / 4 330* SR
ELITE MUSEO HALL

ENVIRONMENTAL SCIENCE
2 / 4 60* SS
HERBOLOGY WING 9A

DEITY HISTORY
5 270* SR
AUDITORIUM

STUDY HALL
1 / 2 / 3 / 4 120* SS
GALLERIA LIBRARY

"One more class than before?" Liv looked up, slightly panicking. Friday was designated for going through each class' weekly reading material–and it usually took her all day.

Hayden walked over and put his arm around her for a hug, immediately calming her. "And afraid you're still stuck with Professor Deligne for Meteorology, but dropping her Astronomy class. Don't worry about Deity History–it's basically just going to be us, sharing information that you should know, or would have known if you grew up in this world." He pointed to Liv's schedule, "That's why Humanities is removed–you most likely already know everything, or are familiar enough to go without it. But in our world, you're starting from scratch."

"But isn't this a bit pre-emptive?" Liv questioned, staring at her newly confirmed schedule, still hesitant if she was capable of the distinguished workload, or the expectations that came with it. "I haven't been proven to be a God, or if it's even possible with my heritage?"

"Well, about that…" Piper spoke up, then immediately went wide-eyed when she saw the room turn to her direction, realizing she had voluntarily commanded a room to listen to what she had to say, lest behold *two Elites* to notice her. She paused in panic.

Liv walked over, assuring Piper that it was okay and put her hand on her shoulder, prompting (and eager for) her to continue.

Taking a deep breath, Piper finally composed herself, and terrifyingly squeaked, "… I did some research last night, and Liv–the facts align in your favor."

"The facts?" Liv was already invested. Had Piper discovered the history she never had access to until now? Her heart raced in anticipation of learning about that mysterious half of her soul that she had always wondered about: who was her father, where did she come from, and who she could be?

"I traced Monaco, your mom's lineage, and your bloodline traces back to Thebes." Piper walked over, handing Liv a huge folder of documents. "It's all in there, and the history proves the possibility that you're capable of inheriting the deity powers of our kind."

Liv impressively flipped through the papers, seeing diagrams and files of her family from over the past two centuries, all compiled and noted in Piper's very thorough documents, proving her thesis for Liv's immortal case.

"Er–would it be possible to share the condensed version of your findings?" Liv asked, apologetically. Between her current schoolwork *and* additional workload her friends were giving her, she would not have time to read this encyclopedia of information voluntarily anytime soon. Plus, she couldn't wait another minute longer to learn the truth.

Piper smiled, amused. "Your lineage goes back to Kadmos–the first hero before Heracles."

"And who is Kadmos?" Liv looked around the room, feeling as if she should know this common knowledge of her ancestry.

"He is the founder of Thebes." Piper said matter-of-factly. "When Kadmos took a wife, the favor of the gods smiled upon him, so he was able to marry Harmonia, the daughter of Ares and Aphrodite. Their wedding was blessed by the Gods and their union produced five children. Between the Sown Men–those who grew from the teeth of a monster Kadmos had defeated–and his children, the population of Thebes was said to have grown from the combined seeds of animality, humanity and *divinity*."

Piper nodded, then walked over to Liv. "You have divine blood in you, blood blessed by the Gods. It's rare, and unheard of since the time our kind made themselves known to the earth's mortals, but ultimately possible."

"And my father's side?" Liv asked eagerly, helplessly wondering what she could learn about him.

"Well, the necklace you have is a uniquely rare treasure, and one that your mother would not have come into possession to without an Elite Element or some powerful God being involved, somehow." Piper explained.

Liv instantly touched her necklace; beginning to understand the unexplainable connection she had felt with it, ever since her mom had gifted it to her, and ultimately, her dad too.

She thought the sentiment had grown only because it reminded her of her father, but had never realized just how unordinary the connection had felt, almost as if it was a part of her, physically completing and enhancing a person within that she had never known existed or been missing before. It was seemingly, and literally, a part of her dad, and all of his powers, being passed onto Liv.

Liv took a deep breath, still questioning the possibility that she could be a divine power. She still felt the same, aside from her unnoticed growth in physical endurance. Was she really a powerful entity? Could she be?

"So, my first class. What is that going to entail?" Liv asked curiously, fighting the butterflies and queasiness in her stomach.

"You'll be fine." Rei assured her. "Hayden and I will be there, and we'll make sure you're not overwhelmed."

"And Piper, too." Hayden added.

Piper raised her head in alarm, unaware of the shift in her new schedule, too.

Hayden laughed. "Piper, you clearly already know more about the Elements Pillar than the Element Elite himself, in fact–you know more about *every* pillar than their respective Elites combined. And, being friends with this one," he pointed to Liv, "You're going to need to learn how to fight, to defend yourself."

Although Piper somehow accomplished to appear like she was about to throw up and dance in celebration at the pillar-promotion simultaneously, Liv was relieved. Piper had been with her from the start, and knowing that Piper would be by her side as they mapped their way through this new life, brought Liv peace and confidence. Whatever was about to come her way, Liv knew that they would be able to face it, and with help from Hayden, Rei and Peyton, they would conquer it, together.

Liv departed for her first class with Piper, Rei and Hayden, unsure of what to expect. Peyton had suggested she wear more pliant-clothes, to get used to the quick movements needed for training, so tasked herself with picking the necessary outfit. Unlike Liv's typical running clothes, Peyton's selections demanded a little more of a runway element than Liv would have ever chosen for herself with a workout in mind.

Now, Liv dawned a very tight rose-gold body suit, bonded and structured with a large golden band, acting as a corset and keeping everything restrained, but surprisingly pliant, too. She was thankful for the thigh-high boots she sported–although beautiful, they were sturdy and the only practical element of her entire costume.

On the other hand, Piper chose a short navy romper with long sleeves, also structurally designed for intense support. With her gold choker and navy thigh-boots, similar to Liv's, she appeared like a force to be reckoned with.

Liv appreciated the attire, it made her feel more powerful and she felt like she would need all the help she could get. But as she looked at Hayden's equally intimidating wardrobe, charcoal jogging pants and an olive green tightly fitted ninja-inspired hoodie, she realized her peers would quickly challenge her personal edge in comparison. If Hayden's height and muscles weren't threatening enough to begin with, the silver zippers designed strategically to look like open cuts throughout his body, communicated quite clearly she would not want to mess with him. Luckily, she remembered, he was on her side, and Liv would definitely prefer he *defend* than battle her.

Rei was donning a metallic cameo bomber jacket and tight gold jeans. He may have looked the least prepared to fight by wardrobe, but Liv had already been on the receiving end of his neutral scowls, showing a rage she'd be pretty okay with never having to fight against, ever.

When the group arrived on the East Lawn, it had transformed into a boot camp course, which appeared to be their first class. But to Liv's terror, it was not a typical boot camp that she had ever seen before.

Approaching the obstacle course, Liv gulped, noticing the 20-yard wide canyon they would have to jump across, *to start*. She was too scared to imagine how deep it would be. From there, a handle bar swing ascended 50 yards high, where she presumed a jump of unrealistic length would need to take place to maneuver between 10 redwood trees, and then cross a wall filled with randomly placed rocks, none of which proved to be a reachable distance between–so Liv gathered she would have to propel herself in order to climb, but how was that even *possible*?

Liv took a deep breath, seeing a 500-meter track that followed, wondering if she would be forced to sprint, and hoping if she ever made it to that point, she could actually attempt something she knew she could handle. Her confidence deflated more when she then saw a salmon latter, with only one bar to climb upward, which seemingly concluded with a jump to a rope swing and ledge (presuming she would make it), to then face the final task of crawling through a destructive laser bridge to the finish line.

Liv turned to Piper, relieved her friend had matching wide eyes filled with terror. Liv ran up to Hayden, comforted that Piper also found this class to be absolutely insane.

"Um, Hayden. A question." Liv casually requested.

Hayden turned to Liv, with a smug grin on his face. "You and Piper are coming in midway through the quarter, so today is more of a crash course, but a test for the other students. Don't worry; I'll help you get through it. I promise. I'll be with you the entire way."

"You actually expect me to get through this!?" Liv yelped, secretly hoping it would have been a joke.

"Exactly." Hayden confirmed. "All while combating dark curses."

Liv froze. "Hayden, I don't even know how to cast defensive powers, let alone do it while I'm suspended from a 100 foot redwood tree!" Liv hushed her accusation toward the end, not wanting her new classmates to overhear her trepidation as they approached them near the start of the course.

Hayden grinned. "You'll be fine. It's only a simulation, so you'll only be slightly wounded or bruised if you're unable to conjure the proper protection."

"And what about the falling 100 feet and landing on my neck part?"

"Well, that'll be the easiest way to determine if you're immortal or not." Hayden dryly confirmed.

Liv hit him in response, but Hayden was too quick, so she missed. She scowled, but then consequently, laughed at herself.

"And the professor expects *me* to get through *that*? And he's okay with you helping Piper and me?"

"Of course. We were able to arrange something." Hayden grinned, mischievously.

Rei walked in front of the students, commanding the class' attention. To Liv's surprise, Hayden reactively walked over to Rei and faced the class, too.

"Today is the first simulation of the year," Rei began, firmly. "Learn what we've taught you, and *survive*. A point will be deducted for every hit you are unable to deflect."

Hayden continued, sternly looking out at the group in front of him. "But remember, outside of class, you will not be so lucky to simply receive a failing grade. Complete the course as if you are fighting for your life; we may be immortal, but there is no return from the Underworld. If captured by your enemy, you become powerless to controlling your fate."

Liv felt chills down her spine. Between the two encouraging sentiments from her friend and boyfriend, she felt undoubtedly ready to fail and be taken to the Underworld. Liv hadn't been immortal for a day, if she even *was* immortal, and was already accepting her powerless demise.

"Please welcome our newest students, Piper and Oll–I mean, Liv." Rei corrected himself and then continued, "Hayden will take Liv through the simulation, and Matthias you'll go with Piper. They will leave last, and please respect that this will be a crash course for them. And, students," he added, "Time will influence your grade, but extra credit will be provided for those who also protect each other. You cannot defeat an army with just one person. We are a team."

Aside from one young man, each student left to begin his or her simulation. Liv walked over to Hayden and the stranger clad in black leather, unsure of what she was supposed to do next. Piper followed at her tail.

"You two *teach* this class?" Liv exclaimed. "You could have mentioned that."

"Oh, sorry Liv." Piper jumped in, apologetically on the men's behalf. "It's kind of common knowledge that each Pillar Elite work with the Candor Elite to appoint whom to prepare and teach the curriculum for their Pillar. Usually, it makes the most sense for the throne's successor to handle, since they're naturally the most experienced and powerful; it's sort of their own version of training for succession."

"Piper, this is Matthias." Hayden smiled, appreciating her defensive explanation and also wanting to change the subject. Introducing her to the man beside him, he added, "He's one of our most promising security guards in training, and top of his class. You'll be in good hands."

Staring shyly while blushing, Piper seemed infatuated with this new God. He swept his dark auburn hair to the side, revealing bright sea-green eyes. Liv had to admit, she could see where her friend was coming from–he definitely looked like a promising fighter, and had swoon-worthy looks. But really, was there a God who didn't? Matthias was almost as tall as Hayden, with a sculpted physique easily seen through his olive shirt. But Liv was speculative with his attire; Matthias was dressed like a Dark God, with dark red furs and a bonded black leather outfit.

With a nod from Hayden, Matthias grabbed Piper's arm, and they headed toward the starting line. Liv decided to let it go, clearly Hayden would have a better grasp on whom and what was safe than she.

Rei nodded, inviting them to start, and jumped into the sky to start patrolling the course. Liv figured it would be to score his students, but anxiously tried to block the grading part out of her mind.

"So, you also instruct classes?" Liv quietly asked Hayden once they were alone. She felt slightly hurt, just because it was another insight to Hayden's life that she hadn't known, and was getting a little tired of all of these surprises. Would it ever stop?

Hayden put his arm around Liv, reassuringly. "Rei instructs the class, but yes, as Prince I work with my Dad, Mom and Silas to ensure everything runs smoothly for training. You're going to be in great hands." He smiled, interpreting Liv's reserve to the obstacle course, not her heart.

"Okay, let's do this," Liv said determinedly. If she would ever fully be on Hayden's level, well, she needed to get there somehow, and this was the starting point.

They approached the canyon and waited for Piper and Matthias to cross. When Piper took the plunge and leapt, Liv saw an eagle fly overhead, projecting lightning bolts of attack. When she looked closer, Liv noticed the bird had a tail—looking almost like the backside of a lion. Piper shielded herself and Matthias in a brightly illuminated bubble when she jumped, so was able to run away with him after he yelled some form of incantation and projected a deadly burst of fire to the creature's tail.

"See, it's simple." Hayden grinned, to Liv's horror. "That's a Griffin, a very strong creature. One of the simpler ways you can impair it is by attacking its tail. You already know how to will fire, so that should be fine. For this part, we'll practice the shielding charm. You physically have to feel the protection coming out of you or else it won't work, but if you say 'Sphaera Tutelae,' then it can help divert your shield outward. Try it."

Liv said, "Sphaera Tutelae." But nothing happened.

"You have to feel it, Liv." Hayden pressed.

Liv tried to imagine the feeling of security erupting from her soul. It was a bizarre concept, but she focused on the idea and said, "Sphaera Tutelae."

"Will it, Liv." Hayden remained calm, patient, but stern.

Liv closed her eyes, trying to source a feeling of protection from within, any strength, and in frustration, yelled, "Sphaera Tutelae!" Pausing, she slowly opened one eye, to see if anything had happened, but all she saw was Hayden, evaluating her attempt, lips pursed.

He looked across the canyon, studying the situation, then back at Liv with narrow eyes. He took a step forward toward the canyon; Liv quickly darted toward him in response, grabbing his arm, and pulled him back with fear.

"Hm, let's try another method." Hayden nodded, resolutely. "Ready?"

"Sure." Liv replied, a little discouraged. She hadn't realized that understanding how to wield her powers would be this challenging.

Without warning, Hayden sprinted toward the canyon, but Liv already knew what he was doing. She sprinted after him, terrified and panicked as he leapt into the air, unprotected and in the Griffin's attacking peripheral range.

When she saw the Griffin shoot his first bolt of attack toward Hayden, Liv pressed as intensely as she could off her last limb to propel herself through the air following him, and without thought, yelled, "SPHAERA TUTELAE!"

There wasn't a feeling; it was just an action–a need.

She needed to protect him.

A translucent sphere encircled her body and amplified to Hayden, covering him just in time to deflect the hit. Liv felt a jarring pain thud inside her chest, but nothing, she expected, that would have compared to Hayden taking the full blow without protection.

Liv landed on the other end of the canyon, falling onto the ground and rolling across it from the momentum, so quickly jumped up to regain her footing and attack the Griffin.

The monster yelled an angry cry, annoyed at its failed attempt of murder. Liv didn't even realize the feat she had just accomplished by leaping 20 yards because she was too distracted by the task at hand. Liv ran over to the edge, meeting the Griffin head on as it darted toward them for the next round of attack.

"IGNIS!" Liv strongly yelled, concentrating on the Griffin's tail for her target. Fire emerged from her hand and spiraled directly toward the beast, catching on his tail and burning the tip. The creature croaked in pain, and immediately flew away.

"Great job, Ollie!" Hayden ran over to her, smiling with pride.

"Are you crazy!?" She screamed in return, pushing Hayden away by hitting his chest while recovering from the intensity she had just encountered. "How could you do that to me?!" She fell onto her knees, trying to compose herself.

Hayden immediately turned from impressed to apologetic as he put his arm around her, gently pulling Liv up to steady her.

"You needed to will your power and understand how it feels. My method may have been extreme, but it *worked* Liv. You did it!"

Liv turned back, looking at the obstacle she had just completed, incredulous in retrospect. She could *do* this.

"I did it." She exasperated in relief, turning back to Hayden, with a sudden burst of energy from her radiated excitement.

"An element-related spell will naturally come easier, it seems to be in your blood." Hayden explained, "But the other powers that are not within your pillar are going to be more challenging to command. I will have to push you Liv, if you're going to learn and get stronger."

Liv nodded, still in shock, but ready for the next lesson. She looked ahead, upward to the handle bar swings, trying to figure out how she would be able to will herself through the extensive distances between each handle. She looked to the pole, trying to identify if there was any leverage she could use to pull herself up to the starting swing.

"Mind over matter." Hayden called out behind her.

Liv turned, intrigued.

"Care to expand on that thought?" Liv asked, puzzled and also eager for any additional advice he could give.

"Your biggest obstacle will be learning how to think like a God, not a mortal." Hayden nodded up to the starting point. "You have unlimited powers, Liv. You can endure and do *anything*, you just have to believe you can do it and wrap your head around it. On the rare account it's not possible, I'll let you know. But really, the sky isn't even the limit–you can go farther. Just put your mind to it."

He nodded to the rings, "The handlebars will burn your palms, and so will need to battle the sting with a cooling power to keep your grip and hold on. Think of your hands in a bucket of ice and focus on repeating 'Glacies' in your head. There's also a heightened gravitational force below, so every time you leap, the earth will fight to pull you down against your will. That part of conditioning incurs pure determination to stay up. You can think, 'Volatum,' but afraid it won't help much."

Liv gave Hayden a nod, trying to absorb the instructions. She stared at the first ring, thinking of her hands numbing from ice, and felt herself slowly lifting toward the handlebar. She wasn't necessarily focusing on trying to levitate herself, but instead focused on just doing it, like moving her fingers. She felt the air below her expand, and taking advantage of the elements, willed it below to push her to the higher destination. Liv's intrigue heightened when it worked and she quickly propelled upward with the help of her self-created wind flow.

As soon as her hand latched onto the ring, she cried in pain. Her palm pierced with heat as if she voluntarily placed it on a stovetop. She wanted to let go; she needed to let go, but something inside her sparked, and she refused. Stubbornly, she pictured ice, imagining she was holding a frozen bag, chilling her hands, and began swinging herself for the first leap.

Mind over matter.

She began swinging for momentum, and propelled herself to the next ring, commanding the wind to work on her behalf and keep her on an accelerated airborne course. Liv grabbed the next handle bar, laughing with joy at her accomplishment, remembering to focus on ice and rely on her strengths – earth, wind, and water were perfect for this portion. She managed to swing and fly her way through the obstacle, maintaining the heat of each ring on her hand.

Toward her last set of rings, Liv's arms began aching, not being used to enduring the aggressive strength training of carrying her body weight, but she refused to give in. She could do this. Liv knew it and she believed it.

Finally, when Liv grabbed onto the last ring, she smiled and propelled herself onto the small wooden platform, preparing herself for the next challenge and ignoring the ache in her shoulders.

Hayden wasn't far behind her and landed immediately after.

"Great job Ollie." He beamed, "Pulling the wind to your aid was quite the innovative solve. I'm impressed."

Liv cockily shrugged. "Mind over matter, I've heard?"

Hayden ignored her, moving on to the next obstacle ahead.

"This upcoming station is all about listening and anticipation. You must face the wall and listen closely for any indication of attack. You won't be able to see where the power is coming from, or which direction it's heading, but if you think it's coming near you, shield it with a retracting curse and send it back in the direction it came from. 'Reversus' is the koine phrase."

"Reversus." Liv repeated.

She hopped on the wall, clinging to two rocks, trying to silence her breathing so she could concentrate on the surrounding sounds of the woods. Aside from the rustling branches, nothing out of the ordinary could be sensed, so she propelled herself to the next set of rocks, 10 yards away. This one had an inconveniently located foot stand, but luckily one nonetheless. Liv closed her eyes, hoping to hear some indication of something malicious heading her way, so she could anticipate and be prepared to combat it.

She heard a whoosh on her left side and whispered, "Reversus!" meaning it with all of her might, and heard in response a heavy wind recoiling the sound and altering the power in the original direction. Liv allowed herself to breathe, understanding now her senses could be heightened, she had just needed to allow her body to adjust.

Liv thrusted herself to the next set of rocks, again thankful for another miniscule, barely-there foot rest. Her arms were growing tired, her mind exhausted from all of the intense concentration and catapulted danger – her body was weakening, not being used to this excruciating mental and physical activity.

Liv heard another whoosh on her left side, and immediately sourced its location. With another whisper of "Reversus," her power syndicated toward it, challenged it and sent the attack back in another direction. Liv took another deep breath of relief and looked to her right for the next set of rocks.

Her ears picked up another whooshing sound that she sensed on her left side again, so she whispered, "Reversus!" But instead, a piercing jolt hit her right arm, immediately causing her right hand to let go as she cried out in pain. An excruciating sting throbbed through her right limb, heating up her arm with fury delivered from the attacking bolt. Liv bent her arm close to her chest hoping to mediate the pain, with no luck.

"Liv, you must keep going! You have to stay focused!" Hayden yelled, from behind.

Motivated, Liv tried to reach her hand out again and fight the tormenting condition of her arm, but with no luck, another wave of unbearable agony shot through her arm, forcing it to recoil in response.

"Hayden, I can't!" Liv cried, unable to go further.

Another power attacked her right shoulder, causing Liv to scream louder at the torture. She lost her footing temporarily, only hanging by one arm before she scrambled to a recovered position, clinging against the wall.

"Liv, in our world, the only way you can be defeated is if our opponent temporarily decapitates you, whether they numb you, capture you or wound you beyond immediate repair. You cannot give up your control!" Hayden yelled, trying to encourage Liv, and bring her unconquerable determination back to surface.

Liv could hear another power approaching, she tried to deflect it, but all she could focus on was her right limb, intolerably heated with raw aches and strong pulses. She knew it was coming, that it would hit her left side and that she wouldn't be able to hold on much longer afterward, if at all. She closed her eyes, frozen in fright, agonizing in her inevitable physical defeat.

But instead, a bright blue laser blasted it before impacting Liv; and soon Hayden was right next to her.

Shocked, Liv turned to Hayden, very appreciative of the small protective gesture.

"We're a team, Ollie." Hayden assured her while deflecting another curse, allowing Liv to recompose herself. "I won't let you lose. But you have to give this your all and get through it–I'll always do my best to protect you, but I can't always be there. You have to prove that you can protect yourself, too. I believe in you. You can do this."

Knowing Hayden was with her gave Liv a new boost of confidence. Sure she was in agonizing pain, exhausted, terrified and clueless, but internally Liv began to remember what she was capable of, her determination surfacing once more.

Liv reached out her arm, grabbed onto the rock and pushed away the deep ache from her mind, focusing her attention back to the sounds of the powers in the woods. Liv caught one on her left side and blocked the curse before it hit her left foot. She quickly leapt to the next set of rocks, wincing as she used her right hand to help attach herself back to the wall. She recoiled two more powers and looked to the last set of rocks before the finish. She took a deep breath and lunged herself once more, yelling "Reversus!" mid-air to attack a power headed in her direction. She almost went airborne in the process, but willed the wind to help her make it to the last rock. Doing one last assessment for sounds nearby, Liv happily soared to the Redwood tree and waited for Hayden, which wasn't long. He jumped onto the branch a moment after she did.

"Great job!" Hayden gushed, immediately inspecting her arm for damage and solutions. "Levare Apud Gelidus." He touched Liv's arm and relieved the warm throbbing with a calming coolness. "It will be sore for a day or so, but that should help temporarily. We can bandage it more thoroughly after the course–you'll want full movement until then."

"What's next?" Liv asked, fearful that there was more she would need to endure. How could this be her *first* class?

"You must propel down the redwood, but you have the choice as to how. It's stimulated with a sleeping aid, so you'll need to fight slumber. When you get to the ground, a sphinx will try to capture you. They're wicked fast, so you'll need to sprint while combating the creature's speed with defensive and offensive powers. If you don't, she'll catch up to you. You cannot outrun her, but you can try to prevent her from catching you."

"What's your version of a sphinx, Hayden?" Liv felt like she didn't want to know, but figured it was better to be prepared than surprised.

"Head of a human, body of a lion, wings of an eagle and tail of a serpent. They're quite intelligent, so you have to be creative if you want to avoid capture. Typically then, your life or death depends on the solving of a riddle, but you only have one chance."

"Any suggestion on how to outwit a mythological genius?" Liv looked to Hayden, warily. She didn't even know what a sphinx was and now was expected to out think one?

"Stick to your strengths." Hayden responded, non-chalantly. "I have mine, and I'll be there with you the entire way if anything goes wrong."

Liv felt dizzy, trying to strategize, but came short of any ideas. She had already used fire, air…

"Water?" Liv looked at the ground, "Do you think that could suffice, if the flow was forceful enough?"

Hayden smiled. "If I'm correct, humans, lions, snakes nor eagles enjoy getting sprayed in the face much."

"Okay." Liv nodded, trepidly. And jumped.

Liv caught on to the last branch hanging above the ground, growing more tired. Hayden followed, seizing the branch, beside her.

"Stay alert. Ready when you are." He confirmed, with heavy eyes–he was struggling with his own advice, but tried to hide it.

Liv had swung herself from branch to branch, fighting the slumber that the Redwood eluded. Her mind was becoming cloudy, yawning as she looked down to the track and slowly processing that the longer she hung, the more lethargic she grew. Liv finally let go and fortunately landed on both feet, slowly moving into a sprint. She heard Hayden drop behind and easily catch up to her pace. Soon, he was beside her.

Liv got the subtle message, now wakening up from her induced coma, so quickened her steps, elongating each stride, so she could go faster and keep up with Hayden.

About 25 meters in, Liv heard a loud hissing noise, followed by a terrible high-pitched screech, and she knew their captor was on their tail now. Fully awake, Liv kept running, pushing herself farther, ignoring her throbbing arm and aching legs. Instead, she focused on the sound, trying to identify where the Sphinx would be, or anticipate where the creature was going.

A rumbling of footsteps approached Liv and Hayden, the sphinx was behind them and quickly diminishing the distance between her targets and self.

Liv fervently picked up the pace, turned and pointed her left hand toward the Sphinx.

"AQUA!" She thundered, feeling her entire being diving into her mission. A blast of water attacked the sphinx, discharging the creature off the track, 100 yards away.

"Bloody hell!" Hayden yelled, impressed at the result, and picked up his pace even more. "Try to push yourself to go faster, Liv–the sphinx is not going to be happy about that attack and will retaliate even more aggressively next time!"

Liv charged forward, adrenaline rushing through her veins. She had not expected that blow to be so strong, so purposely mindful with delivery beyond expectations. She was beginning to understand just how powerful she could be as long as she put her entire soul into the action.

Hayden was correct, Liv could hear the pounding of the sphinx's paws quickly approaching; the monster was back on course, angrily hissing from afar.

The sphinx was getting closer, but Liv was waiting for exactly the right moment to attack again. She wanted the monster to come nearer, so her explosion could be even more impactful.

Hayden turned to Liv, a minor hesitant expression crossing his face as he cautiously looked to Liv to confirm what she was up to. In return, Liv smiled and shot her hand back, fully and completely, feeling her internal body power through the demand she cast in her head.

Bigger and stronger.

The fountain burst out of her hand, an explosion that blasted the Sphinx, shooting it up into the air like a tornado, over the mountain and out of sight. The power was addictive.

"Holy shit." Hayden's jaw dropped, turning to Liv in awe.

They ran through the finish sans another sphinx sighting and approached the salmon latter.

Liv looked up hesitantly, her arm still throbbed intensely, and if there was another dangerous warfare component to this portion, she was not sure how she would successfully hop the bar up to each bracket. She went to raise her arm up and winced, recoiling it back to her chest.

Ultimately deciding what she needed to do, Liv muttered, "Glacies," over her forearm, icing it over and numbing the pain. Then, she raised her arm straight up into the air and grabbed the pole, crying out in pain as her muscles extended. She commanded, "Glacies Intenso," over her shoulder, freezing her entire arm in place, but ultimately, reducing the pain to a tolerable level.

"What are you doing?" Hayden exclaimed, shocked at her now immobilized ligament.

"I learned this power anticipating I would need to use it on you." She added with a determined huff, now that her arm could no longer move. "I would never have been able to hang with this arm without some support, let alone propel myself upward. It hurts too much." Liv stated, a little worried she had just done something reckless and hoped there was a way to numb her arm back its normal state.

"What does this task entail?" Liv asked, trying to avoid panic by focusing on the next obstacle at hand. Her arms were already growing weary from her weight.

"Simple, each pole will identify your fears, challenge your self-confidence, and prick you where it hurts most. It's built for you to fight and defeat yourself. No matter what you hear or see, keep going and face the next scenario. They'll get progressively worse."

"Great," Liv muttered, rolling her eyes. "Something to look forward to."

She swung her body, raising the pole up to her first bar, "Will you have to do this, too?"

Hayden smiled, awkwardly, "No, I'll be skipping this one, thankfully."

Liv rolled her eyes again and then focused on propelling herself to lift the pole onto the next latch. It stung to get the momentum she needed, but soon her arm had settled into its new locked position (not that she had a choice in it anyway).

When she successfully ascended upward to the first latch, a voice echoed.

"You're not as pretty as the other Gods."

Liv blushed, more embarrassed than hurt. She shyly turned to Hayden to see if he could hear that superficial insult. He snorted and tried to hide his laughter by pretending to cough, causing Liv to turn a brighter shade of red.

"Well, if you're trying to kill me from embarrassment…" Liv mumbled, focusing on the next bar and trying to swing her body again to maneuver another bar raise.

Upon her success, the voice echoed, "You don't belong here. You will never fit in."

Liv saw a projected film ahead, showing her future. She was sitting by herself as Hayden, Piper, Rei and Peyton walked by, ignoring her as she longingly wished to be granted back into acceptance.

Okay, that bar had a point, Liv thought to herself. She did worry that this wasn't the world she was supposed to live in, and that one day she would wake up from a dream, torn from this reality and returned to Oregon–still ignored by Hayden and sentenced to live the remainder of her life in miserable solitude once again.

Liv looked to the next bar, a little scared of what was to come.

The one thing that kept her relatively sane was the knowledge that she could have never dreamt up the bulging pain she felt in her right arm. Unless her arm had fallen asleep while she was passed out in a dorm-room coma…

Liv shook the idea out of her mind, focusing on propelling the bar to the next latch.

"You'll never return to your regular life."

The film projector changed to a scene with Liv staring through a window at an old woman in her mom's house.

Who was the lady?

"Liv always wanted to be a meteorologist." The elderly woman sadly muttered to herself, staring at a picture of Liv. "It's a shame my daughter died so young."

Liv reached out to the film projector longingly with her left arm, now recognizing her mother, but recoiled as soon as her right arm shot a subtle ache to her chest, reminding her that physically, it still wasn't strong enough to support her entire weight.

Liv heard a distant voice shout, "Keep going, Liv!" but she was too preoccupied with the thought of her mother, saying she died at a young age. Would Liv get sent to the Underworld and be unable to visit her mother like what had happened to her father, Liam? Or would she be banned from seeing her mother once she passed an age that she could no longer attribute her immortality to being blessed with youthful genes? Would she never know what it was like to save for retirement, or work a nine-to-five job in the city? Was her envisioned future, everything she knew and had imagined for her life, obsolete? Could she even be a meteorologist in this world?

Liv felt a tear trickle down her cheek, mourning the death of a life she would never live.

But after having her moment to grieve, Liv looked up at the bar, forcing herself to leave the sorrow here and move forward. She had to move forward.

She swung for the next bar, starting to feel numb throughout her entire body, and not because of her spell.

"You were never good enough for him, you will never be enough for him. You're only temporary; he won't love you forever." The voice snarled.

Liv fought not to believe her inner demon, but she was completely absorbed into the picture painted in front of her. She was sitting by herself, watching Hayden and Cleo, happy together. The prophecy coming true. If the previous film showed her mom, a fraction of Liv's inevitable future, would this be inevitable, too? Liv tried to scream, yell at Hayden for choosing Cleo, after all she had put them through, but nothing came out. He went in and kissed Cleo, joyfully, happier than Liv had ever seen him be. She felt a concrete slab hit her chest, weighing her down and shrinking her soul. Her pain was raw, and too familiar.

Was this her destiny? Eternal heartbreak, and having to watch her love, be in love with somebody else, forever?

Liv didn't want to watch anymore, she couldn't watch them anymore. If this were her fate, she would need to accept it and move on, eventually. She had done that this summer, Liv reminded herself. She may not have lived, but she survived. Liv at least learned how to numb the pain from that experience and she knew that she needed to, now.

Closing her eyes, Liv focused on Peyton, Piper and Rei, ignoring the soft tear trickling down her cheek. She thought about the people who had been good to her, cared for her and had risked their lives for her safety. She had friends who would get her through this, who would help, whether she liked it or not. When Liv opened her eyes, she breathed a deep gasp of air, empty and numb, wincing at her aching frozen arm, and simultaneously relieved for the reminder of her reality coming back to life.

Picking up her messy pieces, she ignored her blurry wet eyes, her stuffed, sniffling nose, and looked up to the last bar. The finish. She pulsed herself up for the last time, relieved when no more visions, voices or negative thoughts attacked her mind. Liv rotated her left side, staring at the rope swing 10 yards away. She refused to look down at Hayden, still recovering from those lifelike visions. But, with her arm still ice, there would be no way she could propel herself that far, powerful God or not.

Well, the sky isn't even the limit. Liv lightly joked to herself, thinking that maybe she *could* just jump, but she'd prefer not to risk it–that felt more like a dramatic suicide mission. Instead, she focused in on the air behind the rope, willing it to breeze the line in her direction. With a smooth blast of wind, the rope came as if called by Liv, and she grabbed it with her left arm.

Liv wanted to look down at Hayden for encouragement, applause for her cleverness and action, but she still couldn't bring herself to make eye contact with him, not yet. She needed to do this without him, just so she could prove to herself that she could.

She ungracefully slid down the rope. Having only one arm for the activity and another sticking up in mid-air eliminated any possibility of elegance during the process.

When she landed on the ground, she mumbled, "Resitutire," and was thankful to feel her arm numbing, restoring itself to a nimble form. Once it was back to its throbbing state and recoiled back to her chest, Liv closed her eyes, took a deep breath and prepared herself to finally look over to Hayden. He had witnessed her raw emotions and deepest fears, and she felt embarrassed and exposed, as if she stood naked, beaten down in front of him.

She cautiously looked up, knowing he was already concernedly watching her from afar–she could feel his gaze upon her. So, when she finally locked her eyes with his, Liv knew she had unintentionally wounded him, too. She shrugged, apologetically, but couldn't find exactly the words to say. She didn't want to apologize for how she felt, but she also wanted to acknowledge that she was sad Hayden had been exposed to her internal demons.

Liv expected Hayden to run over to her side, so they could continue on the course and forget what had just transpired, but he stood still by the latter, keeping the distance between them.

Instead, Hayden observed the obstacle, contemplating its existence. He looked back to Liv, and shrugged in return. Hayden summoned the bar down and grabbed onto it, forcing himself to embark on the battle through his fears for Liv to witness. Liv smiled, sadly appreciating Hayden's gesture, but was also having a hard time imagining his fears being as intense as hers: Hayden was fearless and confident, and he was immortal–what could he be scared of?

But, if he were able to witness Liv's deepest fears, it would only be fair that Liv have the opportunity to do the same for him. And she loved him for wanting to be fair in a world that never was.

Soon, a thundering voice commanded her attention. Hayden had begun his simulation.

"You'll never defeat the Dark Gods."

Liv crossed her arm, annoyed. Of course his first fear was gallant, non-narcissistic nor self-involved, unlike hers.

Hayden pushed himself upward onto the next latch.

"You will be a terrible king."

Liv could see Hayden struggle with his first vision. He swung around, as if looking for something that wasn't there. If only Liv could see the picture presented before him, but she could only see a dark cloudy blur from where she stood.

After a moment of searching, Hayden moved on to the next bar with an angry groan.

"You'll never live up to your father's expectations."

He looked like a child, innocent and vulnerable, as he was absorbed into his first virtual reality. Liv frowned, wanting so desperately to affirm that he already had accomplished that. His father had to be proud of him—Hayden was the best person that Liv knew. But from her experience, Liv knew Hayden wouldn't be able to hear her, no matter how hard she yelled. So instead, she wept, for all that he was and for all he would be, with or without her.

Hayden shook his head, forcing himself out of the reality, and swung onto the next bar.

"You're going to be defeated, captured, and drowned for eternity."

Hayden yelled, "No!" And suddenly stopped his breath, going limp. He looked like a corpse; Liv started panicking. What on earth could he be experiencing?

"Hayden!" Liv shrieked, not liking the sight of him decapitated, so tried running toward him. But when Liv stepped forward, she was forced to cover her mouth and bend over, feeling saltwater fill her lungs. She quickly moved back to where she was, spitting out the disgusting liquid, not understanding what had just happened, or why.

Liv looked back, worried. Hayden had groaned, coming back to life and spitting out water in the process, as well. He had been drowning in his simulation too.

Hayden looked absolutely miserable, but alive and determined, to Liv's relief. He bounced to the top, the last and most challenging section of the obstacle.

"You'll never be worthy of Ollie's love."

Hayden broke down, shouting, "No!" and tossed his head back and forth, as if in a vivid nightmare. Then, he stopped, with an eerie calm, as if he had given up on life, completely. Liv looked at him solemnly, waiting for him to fight the trance, but after a couple of minutes, he remained defeated.

Something didn't feel right.

"Hayden!" Liv yelled again, desperately. She wanted to run forward, but didn't want to risk the consequence of stepping over her boundary again on this level.

She needed to get to him, somehow.

Liv lifted her left hand, not knowing if what she wanted to do was even possible, but needed to at least try. Liv focused on Hayden, her love for him and how much he meant to her. She felt it through her soul, and pushed it out, willing her feelings to be shared with Hayden, needing to establish a connection. And as she saw an electric light pink spark leave her hand and whimsically fly over the pathway, she held her breath, hopeful and terri- fied–Hayden still hadn't woken up from his simulation yet.

The sparked power danced around the course towards Hayden and finally absorbed into his chest.

After contact, Hayden took a deep breath, as if his soul was being sucked back into his body, and came back to life, looking around terrified.

He quickly bounced up to the final bar, summoned the rope and swung himself over to Liv.

Upon impact with the ground, he swiftly pulled Liv into an embrace, and without a word, kissed her passionately, as if he hadn't seen her for a decade and it was their first reunion.

When Hayden finally let her go, his remembrance of what had trans- pired came back. He looked at Liv, who noticed his vulnerability breaking through, although he tried to contain it.

"You didn't have to do that." Liv said, openly.

"Figured it wasn't fair for me to know all of your inner demons and not reciprocate by sharing mine."

"You're going to be a great king, you know, someday." Liv affirmed, needing to make sure he knew his worth. "And, we'll defeat the Dark Gods, if it comes to war. I won't ever let you get captured or drown for eternity." She paused, softly smiling at the last thought, then shyly looked up at him to confirm, "Are you really afraid of drowning?"

Hayden laughed, lightly. "Thanks. And not drowning, specifically–Gods can't drown, but it's a fear of being confined for eternity, mostly."

There was a silence between the two, still absorbing all the internal doubts they had learned about each other, what lived at the raw core of each other's being. Somehow the drowning fear felt like the easiest one to tackle first, but now that they had discussed it, Liv was at a loss.

Hayden was the first to break the silence, "I'm not sure what I can do to make sure you know how much I care about you. But, you aren't temporary, Ollie. Not for me–you'll never be temporary. I can't promise our future will be easy, and we have a lot of burdens to overcome, but I hope we can figure it all out, together." He said sincerely, with a hit of shyness.

Liv looked up to Hayden, appreciating his initiation to talk about her fear. "I love you, Hayden. So much, that when I lost you, a part of me felt like it literally died. I fear not having you in my life, because honestly, I don't think I could survive without you. I can't explain it, and it scares me, but I only feel complete when you are with me. You are selfless, kind, smart, funny... you are the best person I know." She shrugged. "I can't guarantee what we'll face, but I can promise I'll always be there for you, because you're worth all of this. Having you in my life is worth everything."

"And without you, none of this is worth it to me either." Hayden confirmed, smiling. "It scares me, too."

Liv recalled Hayden's defeated sight during the simulation, like he had died. "What happened to you?" Liv asked. "There were times when you seemed immobile."

Hayden sat down, contemplating his response. "I'm not sure exactly. It was almost as if the simulation had a darkness cast over it, a stronger effect, permanently locking me into the abyss."

"Is that typical for this challenge?"

"Possibly," Hayden contemplated the feasibility. "However, I cast the simulation and I definitely did not formulate it to have such an effect as it did for me."

"What made you go limp?" Liv asked, curiously.

"Well, the drowning one is more understandable–I was confined, trapped in a chest, sinking to the bottom of the ocean. So, unable to move, breath, see–only exist."

Liv remembered the saltwater fiasco she had experienced in the process of trying to save Hayden, so shared it with him.

Alarmed, Hayden looked back over to the ladder. "That definitely shouldn't have happened. You were unable to get to me?"

"It was like I was choking on salt water. I couldn't breathe."

Hayden studied the platform they were on. "I need to tell Rei. This simulation was tinkered with Dark Powers and somehow was trying to capture my soul in that alternate world."

"Is that even possible?" Liv's eyes grew wide at the possibilities of danger seemingly awaiting their very next step. Nowhere was safe.

"Ollie, anything is possible when you're a God." Hayden said sternly. "Come on, let's get through this course and find the others, quickly."

They headed toward the laser bridge.

"Hayden, what about the final time you went immobile? I had to attack you with my power to get you out of the trance."

Hayden looked out ahead into the forest. "Probably dark magic, but the result is a little more explainable." He shrugged, "Like I've said, before, Ollie, I don't see the point in living in a world in which you aren't apart of. Without you, I'm nothing."

TWENTY

The last course, thankfully, seemed to be the easiest yet. Liv quickly crawled through and achieved the goal of the task: Don't touch the lasers.

Granted, there were some interesting angles and ninja moves she executed to avoid getting burned by the obstacle, but between her dance flexibility and not having a mythological creature attacking her, the whole process was cathartic, mindless.

When she emerged from the final army crawl, she saw the rest of the students already working on their next lesson. For a moment, Liv felt a burst of energy from her successful completion of the course, but immediately shrugged, weakened, when she realized that simulation was apparently only their warm up for the class.

Rei walked over to Hayden and Liv, looking enthusiastic.

"Great job, Ollie!" He exclaimed, giving her an encouraging pat on the back.

Liv winced, it was the shoulder that had gotten damaged during the course.

"Oh, let me heal that, now." Hayden confirmed, touching her arm, lightly and sending cool chills down her shoulder and arm.

Liv slowly extended it, a little in shock. It was still a little sore, but had regained its full dexterity without ache. Now mostly healed, she punched Hayden with it.

"You could have done that an hour ago!?" She angrily shrieked.

"You're welcome." Hayden smugly responded, rubbing his arm and ignoring her accusation. "Ouch, Ollie. You are getting stronger."

"It's a part of the test," Rei defended Hayden, backing him up. "It makes the simulation more realistic, if you're combating a God, you may not have time heal yourself, but would still have to fight."

"Of course." Liv nodded, rolling her eyes, still pissed.

"But, now it's time to teach you combat." Rei optimistically added, sending Liv over to the battle line. "First, observe."

Liv stood, watching Piper and Matthias fighting each other. Matthias was clearly more experienced, but Liv stood proudly as Piper handled her own as she attacked back.

Matthias would cast an opposing force, and Piper would leap to deflect it, immediately reversing the power back in his direction, followed by sending another attacking power in his direction. Unfortunately, Matthias seemed to be an expert at combat and would easily block and relinquish it entirely.

Hayden leaned toward Liv. "You see how Matthias only blocks with his right side? If Piper cornered him to his right, and directed her powers to his left, she could sneak in a double power attack on his left, forcing him to use his weaker side. It could throw him off balance and then she could gain the upper-hand."

Liv observed, watching Matthias predominantly use his right side for defense. He was clearly more comfortable on that side, and when he did cast a spell with his left, Piper had more control in her deflection.

"The key to successfully defeating your opponent is to study them while you fight, so you can anticipate their next move. Defensive reflexes come too easy for Gods, so you have to be one step ahead of them at all times, or else your spell could become more dangerous for you than for them, if countered properly."

"So, how do you ultimately defeat a God in battle?" Liv wondered out loud.

"The best way is to enclose them with matter or space, but we need to see how powerful you are in battle before I recommend that strategy."

Liv thought of Hayden's fear–being contained for eternity, shivering at the thought, as she understood it could apply to her now, too.

"If you're not strong enough, your opponent may be able to fight the forced confinement with their power. I suggest just weakening the Gods enough, so you can get away for now, until we determine just how well you can capture Deities."

Matthias had just successfully restrained Piper against a tree; she was enclosed and although attempting an escape, remained stuck. The class was all watching.

"Why doesn't someone help her?!" Liv asked, taking a step forward to join the fight and help her friend.

"No." Hayden countered, grabbing Liv's arm and gently pulling her back.

Liv viciously looked at him, alarmed that he would prevent her from helping her friend. Did Hayden still think Piper was a Dark God, and this was his secret motive? Punish her through a gruesome warfare course in which she had no chance for victory?

"Liv, hitting a God from behind is frowned upon, Dark or Pure–it's a universal God code–possibly the only one everyone agrees upon. It needs to be a fair duel to be considered a win. If you step in and attack Matthias, you may be defeat one battle, but soon you'll have every witness, Dark or Pure God, against you."

"Oh." Liv shrugged, feeling guilt from the slight doubt of her boyfriend, but also wondering if he had also just confirmed her speculation that Matthias was indeed a Dark God.

"Don't worry," Hayden whispered behind her ear. "I'll interject if anything gets out of hand."

By then, Piper had stopped fighting the restraints, and fell limp against the tree. Matthias immediately removed his curse and she fell to the ground. Hayden let go of Liv's arm, giving her permission to finally check on her friend.

"Piper!" Liv shrieked, running over to her lifeless body. "Are you okay?"

Piper eye's fluttered open at Liv's touch. "Yeah. Fine." She pushed herself up onto her knees. "Feel like death though." She shrugged, weakly.

Matthias walked over, grabbing Piper's hand to help her up in a truce.

"Sorry for the last blow," Matthias said sincerely. "I wanted to make sure you knew what you were getting yourself into and to see if you could actually handle it. Plus, it's not like I could let you off easy, I have a reputation to live up to. My grandfather was the Security Elite, and well, you have your status."

Piper sadly smiled, trying to cover her shock. She nodded in polite agreement, "Yeah, of course. I totally understand," before walking away.

Liv, on the other hand, was livid for her friend.

"I'm sorry? You think that just because your grandfather was a powerful God, you can be a dick?" She said bluntly, angrily at this stranger who humiliated her friend.

"Liv, it's fine." Piper had come back at Liv's retort, grabbing her friend's hand and pulling her back.

"No. It's not!" Liv said, aggressively toward Matthias. "Piper is a good person. And even you just admitted that she's strong. You're just scared."

Matthias laughed, "I'm not scared."

"Okay, so you're too proud to be defeated by a God, but what about the possibility of getting destroyed by a half-mortal?" Liv instigated. Her anger and competitiveness was relentless.

"Liv, you do not have to do this. Seriously." Piper pleaded.

"Yes. I do." Liv determinedly insisted.

And honestly, Liv was tired of all of the hierarchy bullshit. Just because you came from a good family did not automatically make you a good person, deserving of whatever is handed down to you, power or wealth or status. The smaller things, like how you act when people aren't looking, or how you treat others no matter what the situation may be, should determine your value in society.

"Challenge accepted, mortal." Matthias grinned.

He let go of Piper's hand, (which Liv hadn't realized he had been holding during their altercation), and walked toward the center of the field. They found themselves encircled by their intrigued classmates, who all seemingly had forgoed their personal battles to watch this spectacle.

Hayden ran over to Liv, his eyes incredulous.

"What are you doing?" Hayden asked, sincerely.

"I didn't really think that part through." Liv gulped, realizing this was her first battle, ever.

Hayden sternly looked at Matthias, and then back to Liv, which did not help the tension rising in her throat.

"This may be your first battle, but you fought off a Sphinx, remember?" Hayden offered, encouragingly. "Remember what I said–anticipate his next move. If you push him to those trees, he'll be forced to use his left side more."

Liv nodded, registering the plan. The bigger question was how she would force him in that direction.

"Liv?" Hayden gently grabbed her chin, curiously looking into her eyes, trying to gauge her courage. "He also steps his right foot back whenever he is about to send an attacking spell. That's how you'll know when to block." He kissed her forehead, gently. "I believe in you."

Liv knew this was only class, but she felt like she was walking into her demise. Where was that courage she had 5 minutes ago when she challenged Matthias to this duel?

"You can still back down, you know." Matthias smirked.

As quickly as it had departed, Liv had found that anger again. She wanted to destroy this pompous dick.

"And you can still find your balls, if you want them." She threatened back.

Quiet laughter and gasps slithered amongst the crowd.

Liv walked to the center and maintained eye contact with Matthias, refusing to look away. He bowed, so Liv bowed in return, really hoping it wasn't a ploy to attack in advance.

Luckily, it wasn't. Hayden was right, there was a level of civility between Gods, even between Dark and Pure during warfare. Well, aside from the extremists, Liv reminded herself, recalling Arlo's unjust attack.

That slight loss of focus almost cost Liv her life, or worse, dignity. She barely blocked Matthias' curse, not just from timing but also brute force. She sloppily recovered, gathering her footsteps when he sent another power in her direction. She obstructed it again, with a little more composure, being prepared for the strength this time and immediately cast another fiery blow in his direction, trying to push him over to the right and limit his stronger side.

Matthias barely flinched as he drowned her fire blast with water, but Liv was internally impressed to see he had, indeed moved a step in the right direction. Trying to recall the attacking powers she briefly studied before class, Liv shot a bolt of lightening, curving it so it came directly to his left side, forcing him to move back a couple steps, closer to her target location.

Liv saw Matthias step his right foot back, she was prepared to defend his attack this time, so when he launched an offensive attack, she reflected it and sent it back even more powerfully in his direction. He struggled to block it, but she was too quick. Liv shot another blow to his left, but purposefully missed Matthias so he could jump back to avoid it. Matthias was exactly where Liv wanted him, so she moved forward, sending more fireballs to his left side as he struggled to block with a now limited movement on his right side, Liv cast a binding spell directed to his left wrist, easily wrapping his unfocused limb and tying itself to the tree branch above. Matthias tried to break the rope, but Liv had willed that only she would be able to command release when she cast it.

"Alligando." Liv casually commanded, releasing another bind that too easily wrapped itself around Matthias, hanging him entirely from the tree.

Shocked, Matthias turned to Liv, completely at her mercy. He smiled and laughed in return, which confused Liv.

Nodding to Hayden, Matthias chuckled. "You've got a strong one there."

Liv lost focused, releasing him while still pondering his lighthearted response; Matthias dropped to the ground.

Piper ran over to Matthias, shouting, "Are you okay?!"

Matthias nodded his head in response, but continued walking toward Liv.

"Point made, mortal." Matthias reached out his hand as a friendly gesture, smiling. Liv shook it, not sure why she was so glad to have his approval.

Matthias then turned to Piper, grabbed her neck and pulled her in for a passionate kiss.

Liv's jaw dropped.

"Sorry I was a dick." Matthias said, both to Liv and Piper, but mostly Piper. "I was only joking earlier, but I'm never one to refuse a challenge."

Piper was beaming.

"It's fine." Piper smiled, shyly.

Liv coughed, very confused and in need of an explanation. Hayden had arrived, putting his arm around Liv.

"So, you two?" Hayden smiled. "What a surprise," he added, sarcastically.

Piper blushed.

"We met at the Symposium." Piper explained to Liv, "On the dance floor. Liv, he was the one I was telling you about." Piper grinned, blushing shyly.

"And I was stupid about how I handled it." Matthias added, turning to Piper. "I like you. And I've been an idiot for ignoring you. I was reading too far into my family politics, not wanting to cause any more tension since I declared my loyalty to the Dark Gods."

"So you are a Dark God?" Liv interjected, cautiously confirming her original observation.

"Not a radical." Hayden answered on behalf of Matthias, turning with Liv. "You can trust him."

Liv was beside words. Between finding out her outcast best friend had a secret lover, who was also a Dark God, that was one thing. But to hear Hayden verbally say the notion out loud and confirm that they could trust a Dark God was possible, that was another thing.

Deciding not to ruin her friend's obvious joy from Matthias' proclamation, Liv bit her tongue. She was still tired from the excruciating course, and still had no idea as to what would be up next, she let her concern go–if her friend was happy, Liv would be, too.

"Thanks for going easy on me." Liv stated, her own offering of truce to Matthias.

"You've got some good moves too, mortal." Matthias smiled, jokingly.

"Well, I've got a good coach." Liv placated, beaming to Hayden with admiration.

"Come on. We still have more training to do." Hayden nodded, pulling Liv with him as he called out for the students to continue their exercises.

"We have more?" Liv moaned.

"Defensive exercises, you'll just be blocking my attacks. Now it's time for the fun to start, let's see how strong you really are."

Hayden placed Liv across the field, stepping back as he took his position. Standing across from Hayden, Liv suddenly felt defenseless and exposed, unsure if she would be able to protect herself from his powers.

"Aren't you going to give me any more tips?" Liv yelled.

"You seem to be doing well enough for your first day." Hayden hollered back, amused. "My only advice is to not get hit."

"Thanks!" Liv mockingly yelled back, playfully adding a vulgar gesture and eye roll.

Hayden bowed, initiating the beginning of the exercise. Liv followed suit.

Liv watched Hayden immediately begin to cast an offensive spell and then caught himself. He looked at Liv, wanting to make sure she was ready.

It was as if for a moment, Hayden had forgotten that his girlfriend was on the receiving end, not an actual opponent. Someone he did not actually want to destroy.

He slowly raised his arm back, signaling Liv to prepare herself. He spiraled a blue lightning bolt in Liv's direction. When she blocked it, the collision caused her to fall backward. She immediately got up, just in time to notice Hayden raising his arm for another attack. She blocked the next fireball with a stronger force, but still had to take a couple steps back to regain her balance again. He sent another attack in her direction, almost hitting her left foot; Liv had to squat to block the power in time. Another blue lightning bolt was heading toward her right side–she ducked underneath it and jumped over another fireball, eyes widening as she saw another bolt headed in her direction. She blocked the incoming power and spiraled it back toward Hayden with all her might, sensing both the fireball and blue lightning bolt returning in her direction from behind. Using the wind, she forced them to collide together, an explosion erupting in front of her.

Liv was panting, her arms felt weak, but Hayden was relentless. He hadn't even moved from the spot where they started. Liv rolled her eyes, knowing he was just showing off and evilly thought to herself he was a sadist who was secretly enjoying her struggle.

He hit the redwood tree on her right, causing it to timber in her direction. She willed herself to stop it from falling and held it above her, and although she wasn't touching the tree, using her power felt like she was physically holding it up. She was stuck with both arms in the air, unsure where to go from there. If she lost focus, or pulled away from weakness, she'd be crushed.

She summoned the flame within her to burst, lighting the tree on fire and feeling it slowly burn as the branches lightened in weight and crumbled to soot. She was shaking, trying not to let go of her will to keep the tree upright. She focused on the fire, on holding the tree in position, and tried to strategically stretch her mind to will water to combust the fire and prevent burning down the entire forest. She yelled in pain, resulting from her soul attempting to focus so intensely on three different things at once. But soon, the tree was merely a long stump, and she threw it across the other way, exasperated.

If only Gods could win wars by rubbing their stomach while simultaneously tapping their heads. That she could do. Her soul and mind felt like it had split, like a tree stump getting axed into kindling.

Liv turned to Hayden, disgruntled, breathing heavily and trying to catch her breath.

She faced him head on, not exactly sure if she was ready to keep going, but knew she had no choice.

Hayden nodded, awaiting confirmation to start again.

Casting "Ignis" silently in her head, Liv powered a fire blast toward Hayden in response, smiling as she watched the Prince of Gods thrown off his guard and block the spell with less dignity than he had casted his powers earlier.

In response, Hayden smirked, sending a blasted lightning bolt in Liv's direction.

She blocked it, and reversed the bolt back toward his left side, following up with a fireball power of her own toward his right. He blocked it, swiftly and nimbly, turning it to dust with a snap. Liv sneered, her competitiveness getting the best of her.

Hayden lifted all the pines and sticks from the ground nearby him, throwing them in her direction, like knives ready to attack. Liv built a shield of fire, burning the plants on impact. She wiped her forehead, tired, but before she could compose herself, she was blasted with water, unexpectedly, and fell to the ground from the blow. She heard a tree falling in her direction again and she looked around in panic, impulsively ducking for cover under her arms for protection–as if she knew a baseball was flying overhead in her direction, but unable to spot it in the sky.

"Liv!" Hayden grasped, immediately by her side and holding her in his arms.

Liv's conscious came back to the present. She hadn't been smashed. She cautiously looked up, to find the tree a foot above her, held up by Hayden's other arm.

Without effort, Hayden catapulted the tree in the other direction.

"Are you okay?" Hayden asked softly.

"I–I'm fine. I was just caught off guard. I panicked. I'm sorry."

"Don't be sorry. That was completely normal. You have been exceeding my expectations all day, and they were high to begin with. I'm so proud of you." Hayden pulled Liv into an embrace.

Liv melted into his arms, not realizing just how tired she felt from her first class.

"Most of this is mental, Liv. Your powers and your control are solely based on your focus. It's okay to retort back to your mortal thought-process at this stage. You've been a human for eighteen years of your life, and a God for a week. It's going to take time to re-sculpt your mind."

Liv relaxed, comforted in Hayden's embrace.

"Well, when I have my energy back, I want a rematch." Liv stubbornly mumbled, her head heavy on Hayden's shoulders.

TWENTY-ONE

The remainder of Liv's new schedule had been less eventful. In fact, in her beginner Deity Power course, Liv was actually disappointed. Her first lesson had been more about thermodynamics and physics rather than power—and only explained how her powers worked and what was impossible for a God to accomplish.

"You may think Gods are all-powerful, but indeed they are not." Professor Ellasie mentioned in Liv's Wednesday course, filled with a handful of Gods who also had just become of age in receiving their powers. "Olivia, and class," (Professor Ellasie always enjoyed calling out Liv before she made any mortal references), "similar principles in the mortal world apply to us. We cannot transfigure objects, nor make objects appear from thin air. You can transport objects at a very rapid speed, almost as fast as light itself, granted no obstacles lie between the starting point and destination, but alas, you cannot evaporate objects and make them magically reappear at command."

"But what about the fire I can combust, or lightning I can produce?" Liv asked, eagerly trying to find a loophole. She secretly wished her powers seemed a little more impressive than what she could have done as a mortal, just with time and speed being the only factor.

"Great question, Olivia. Your body is static, so can continuously produce electric particles for use. It's also able to create friction for fire by rubbing such particles together."

Liv shrugged, disappointed. Learning the science behind her powers made it seem a little less mysterious, less compelling. But, perhaps that was a good thing, so she could better understand how to command and control them.

"Your first task is to will an item from your room and transport it to this classroom. And quickly–you don't want a God to intercept anything you are summoning. Just think of the word 'Kalo' and imagine the course your desired object will need to embark upon to arrive here. Really, the only stipulation you need to know is the beginning location of the object and the end destination, and rough be able to identify its path–but that part can be a bit more blurry, depending on how fast you summon it."

Liv wasn't sure what she wanted to bring from her dorm to the North Tower, lest she fail. Liv couldn't even remember where she left half of her things in her room, since she had stayed at the cabin, in the dungeon (she shivered at the recollection) and Hayden's in the past week. She thought back to Hayden's abode and smiled as she commemorated his bigger space, grandiose kitchen and the ability to fall asleep and wake up to his delicious scent and glorious abs; however, once she remembered the task at hand, and unfortunately her inability to retrieve her boyfriend for the class assignment, Liv came back to the present, assessing what state her dorm would be and the objects in it.

Liv unconsciously tugged at her embellished silver sweater dress, trying to remember where she would have left her hairbrush before settling on a purple Lisianthus that she knew would be in a floral bouquet near her fireplace. She imagined the flower as she remembered it, really hoping it was still there, and muttered, "Kalo," as she became apart of the flower, envisioned it opening and shutting her door, and then flying across campus in her direction and through the tower window to her desk.

But nothing came.

Frustrated, Liv looked to Professor Ellasie for an explanation.

"Let's start with something easier." Professor Ellasie prompted, setting a pen down at her desk. "Summon this."

Liv focused on the pen, willing it to come toward her. The pen shook, but refused to rise.

"Well, some things will take practice, Olivia. Your assignment for the week is to practice summoning. No using air or wind to help push things your way, either. I've noticed you heavily rely on your powers within the elements and we need to work on that balance."

Professor Ellasie turned to the remainder of the class, whom all had successfully summoned their desired objects.

"Quiz on Monday, everyone. Class dismissed."

Liv grabbed her books and left, heading toward the Galleria for Study Hall, discouraged.

When she entered the West Corridor, Liv noticed Hayden radiating light in her direction, so naturally calmed down, instantly feeling brighter, happier in his presence. Hayden could help her with summoning; Liv always felt stronger when he was nearby, anyway.

"I believe this belongs to you?" Hayden extended a single purple flower, the Lisianthus Liv had tried to call during class.

"Did you snatch my class assignment?" Liv gently grabbed the stem from Hayden's hand, smelling the intoxicating floral scent.

"I saw it exit your dorm room and head down the hallway, so grabbed it to make sure a less friendly God wouldn't hex it. Other than that, I'm innocent." Hayden grinned. He was in a cheery mood, happier than usual. Although he had been much more like his normal self since Liv had actualized her deity powers, his smile was much too genuine for a Wednesday–or 3–afternoon. Liv even grimaced when she remembered how sore she felt from her earlier excruciating security and warfare class.

"Are you okay?" Hayden inquired, examining Liv from head to toe.

"Yeah, I'm fine–just recovering from my new classes." Liv honestly replied, rolling her shoulders in a stretch.

"Good." Hayden replied obliviously. "My parents have invited us for dinner Friday night, would you want to go?"

Liv froze, not expecting such a friendly parental gesture from the King and Queen, who had seemed cold toward Liv at every prior encounter.

"If it's too much, we can bail." Hayden covered, trying not to pressure Liv.

Once Liv had gotten over the initial thought, she observed how hopeful Hayden was, and how he was trying to contain his boyish excitement. His joy was contagious, and Liv began to feel delighted, too.

His parents wanted to meet her.

That was a good thing.

"No, I would love to go." Liv affirmed with a genuine smile.

"Great." Hayden took a breath in. "I figure it could be the perfect time to ask my dad about... everything. He and my mom are both really looking forward to meeting you–and Joss will be there, too."

"She will!?" Liv felt genuinely relieved and excited at the news of Joss' attendance–she practically felt like her own sister.

Hayden grinned wider in response to Liv's reaction.

Liv spun around in front of her mirror.

"Do you really think this is 'visit the parents' appropriate?" Liv asked Piper, hesitantly.

She was wearing a navy crewneck fitted dress, with a cutout slit that revealed a gold pleated fabric underneath. She was hoping it helped package simple, sophisticated, adorable and beautiful into her appearance.

Piper leaned back onto her bed, "Of course it is! Have I led you astray before?"

Liv took a big gulp, not sure what she was expecting from tonight nor completely understanding why she felt so terrified.

On one hand, Joss was a delight. On the other, King Rowan had been against Liv since she came to Puerdios, and had almost punished his son for the purest act of love. Her head was dizzy, and thankful when she heard a soft knock on the door, announcing Hayden's arrival.

"Don't be nervous." Piper assured Liv. "I've heard 'meeting the parents' is never a fun venture. So, just remember that they raised Hayden, and you like him, so they can't be all that bad?" Piper shrugged encouragingly, running to the door to let Hayden in.

Liv immediately felt more at ease at his sight. He smiled enthusiastically, radiating vibes that were the complete opposite to what Liv's insides were going through. But his hug calmed her, giving Liv some of his happiness and excitement to pacify her feelings holistically.

"You look lovely, Ollie." Hayden said, beaming.

"Thanks." Liv smiled shyly and then felt a pair of eyes gazing on their intimate moment.

Liv turned back to her friend, remembering Piper was still there.

"We'll be going." Hayden announced to Piper, who sat smugly on Liv's couch, smiling.

"Don't stay out too late, kids." Piper called out sarcastically.

And with that, Hayden led Liv out of her room and into the hallway.

"Do you ever get used to the glamour of this world?" Liv asked, admiring the iridescent candles that sparkled throughout the hall.

But turning her gaze back to Hayden, Liv remembered that even *he* was a mesmerizing sight, and almost made the castle look dull in comparison.

"Just wait until you see the view I've arranged for tonight." Hayden deviously hinted, leading Liv out into the pavilion.

Hayden had arranged a stunning silver carriage to transport them to his parent's castle; the sparkling vehicle flew whimsically in their direction and softly landed in the pavilion in front of them. Getting into the carriage with Hayden's assistance, Liv had to admit, she slightly preferred this option to his solitary means of transportation, especially when she needed to look presentable at their arriving destination. Plus, in the carriage, she could keep her eyes open and still snuggle close to Hayden. At the sight of a champagne bottle and two flutes, Liv was even more excited for the ride, courtesy of her boyfriend's thoughtful romantic gesture–it was all too perfect.

But she couldn't help but have a sense of déjà vu when the carriage landed in front of Hayden's castle, looking out to the transcendent palace, an outsider once again. Large torches lit grandiose pillars, two great steel doors still blocked their entrance, and many windows appeared laminated, shadowed with secrets. Would this place ever feel less intimidating, and more welcoming to her?

Hayden grabbed Liv's hand, looking out of the window, too.

"Home." Hayden stated with contemplation, "The beginning of one's story, but never the end."

"You don't see yourself living here when you're crowned King?" Liv asked curiously.

"Possibly." Hayden contemplated with an underlying scorn, as he stared out. "But I'll always see the hallway as the place I got punished for playing with a statue as a little boy, or the bedroom I was sent to when I behaved improperly. It's home, but not ours. Not yet, at least."

Liv smiled, appreciating Hayden bringing humility to the fortress. To him, it was just where he pulled Joss' hair, tried to sneak in an additional chocolate for dessert or drew on the wall with crayons—or whatever Gods did to get into trouble as kids.

Liv snorted, imagining an adult Hayden innocently drawing on a Manet painting with crayons in the corridor.

"Do I amuse you?" Hayden grinned.

"Always." Liv confirmed, regaining her composure and putting down her flute. "I think that's enough liquid courage for now."

Hayden hopped out of the carriage, extending his hand to Liv. She grabbed it, appreciatively, feeling calmer than she had all night. His gaze was too assuring, promising and comforting. He truly was her everything.

"After you." Hayden softly put his hand around her waist, guiding her forward toward the palace entrance and unintentionally sending an assuring musk of cedar and verveina.

Upon ascending the staircase and without hesitation Hayden clicked a button and commanded, "Aperta."

Without a glitch or use of much effort, the entry doors opened.

"You make it look like anyone could easily break in." Liv observed.

Hayden smiled, "It's cast with a link to royal blood and our crest–only our family is able to command it open."

"Of course." Liv agreed, turning back at the doors in amazement.

She wasn't able to speculate for long; however, because as soon as the two had crossed into the corridor, they were greeted by Joss.

"Liv! Brother." Joss ran in to hug Liv first, ignoring Hayden. "I'm so glad you could make it tonight. Mom has been putting on quite the fuss to make everything go perfectly–you would think she were hosting for the Pillar Elites!" Joss rolled her eyes, leading Liv into an elaborate sitting room.

Hayden followed quietly. Liv could feel his mocking grin linger behind as they all walked into the new room, causing her to smile coyly in return.

Opposite to Liv's conservative dress, Joss was adorning a striking gold gown, with a high neckline and fitted to her every curve, adorned with a bright lip and topknot. Liv looked over to Hayden, thankful he was dressed in a traditional silk navy suit with a simple white collared shirt.

"Would you like a cocktail, Miss Olivia?" A lady maid approached Liv cautiously. Liv almost mistook her for another guest, but noticed a similarly dressed woman approaching Joss with a cocktail. In a glistening silver high-wasted pencil skirt, white silk tank and satin black blazer with matching stilettos, the woman looked more like a CEO than a maid.

"Um, a French 75?" Liv asked inquisitively. She wasn't sure why she recalled the drink, but for some reason the Editor-in-Chief like persona reminded her of a fashion magazines, 'Best Cocktails,' article she had read over the summer.

"Wow, you fancy, huh?" Joss giggled as the lady maid magically returned with Liv's flute.

"Nothing compared to all of this." Liv raised her glass to cheers, absorbing the rococo decoration filling the ornately designed room.

"How are classes going?" Joss changed the subject quickly, catching Liv off-guard. "I only mean, is it proven? Are you succeeding at a deity level?"

Hayden came in for the rescue, wrapping his arm around Liv, protectively. Liv wanted to respond, but *how could she know how to evaluate herself after a week?*

"She is doing wonderfully–in fact, she's a quick study."

Joss clapped in return. "Oh, I am so grateful!"

The doors burst open before Joss could finish, immediately draining the lighthearted conversation to a burdening mood, as Hayden's parents stood in the doorway, silent.

Hayden turned immediately toward them, gracefully pulling Liv along his side and not letting go of her as he greeted them.

"Mother, Father–you remember Liv?"

Hayden's mother smiled quietly, nodding.

Hayden's father spoke first. "Olivia, it's such a pleasure to have you here tonight. We did not get to acquaint ourselves properly at my ball."

Liv frowned; surprised that he would so easily skip over his whole stint of trying to imprison her.

Queen Daphne kindly placed her hand on Liv's shoulder, with a devious glare over at her husband's ignorance. "What my husband means, my dear, is–we are terribly sorry for how our initial introductions ensued. You must understand, as leaders we are sometimes needed to act on procedures we do not fully agree with–but we do hope that we can start anew tonight."

Between Hayden's warm touch and Daphne's soothing cool hand, Liv felt almost forced and fully persuaded to succumb to their wishes.

"Of course." Liv smiled, awkwardly, but hoping she appeared as graceful as Daphne conducted herself.

"Wonderful." Daphne smiled, then nodded toward the lady maid, eagerly awaiting her upcoming orders. "The usual cocktails for us, Sybille."

With the initial encounter over, Hayden led Liv back into the sitting room, squeezing her arm as they sat down across from his parents.

"Olivia, Hayden tells us you have quite the natural talent for the elements?" King Rowan asked, nodding in approval.

"Really?" Joss blurted out, and then blushed at her outburst, explaining, "It's just the more difficult curriculum to master. Took me an entire year to wield fire. How impressive!" Then as she countered back glares from her parents, she added, "But, I'll let Liv tell us all about it," prompting Liv to continue with a chuckle and nod.

Liv blushed, appreciative for Joss yet again lightening the situation. "Mostly everything is difficult curriculum to me, but yes, it seems I'm catching on, in general, thankfully."

Liv tensed, wondering if that sounded spiteful?

She wanted Hayden's parents to know she had already forgiven them for their misjudgment and vindictive punishment resulting from Hayden and her desire to be together, but squirmed as she tried to recover from the awkward pause.

"Actually, it seems my father may have been an expert–" Liv continued, but Hayden quickly cut her off.

"She's more than catching on–she passed our defense and warfare midterm without a day of studies." He nudged her, letting her know it wasn't the time to bring up her heritage theories.

"Well, we may have an Elite in training!" Daphne huffed impressively. "Are you sure you didn't mark her with favor, Hayden?" She jibed, smiling kindly at her son.

After sharing more small talk for a while, Liv noticed her glass was still full and that she had never actually noticed the lady maid Sybille refilling her French 57 during the entire conversation.

Still perplexed at her beverage revelation, Liv looked up to find Daphne standing to announce that dinner was ready. Liv got up immediately, relieved to have something concrete to fidget with other than sipping on her cocktail, when Hayden softly pulled her back, nodding to his Dad.

"A word before dinner, Father?"

Queen Daphne looked inquisitively at Hayden, and then her husband. Their icy stares at each other worried Liv, who did not want to be in the same room once the politely subtle glares could turn into something bigger. An unspoken word transpired through the group, and Daphne quickly, yet gracefully, rounded up the lady maids and Joss into the dining hall.

"I didn't mean to catch you off-guard." Hayden began explaining, "But I felt there would not be a proper time after dinner to chat."

"Of course, of course. I understand." King Rowan nodded to the door. "Let's go into my study. It'll be more private there." He tersely looked over at Liv, questioning her attendance, but Hayden held onto her, insistent.

"This has more to do with her than it does me, Father."

King Rowan was silent in response. He merely nodded and walked over to the door, leading the way.

They entered King Rowan's study across the hall. Resembling what Liv expected to be a refined gentlemen's club, she naturally felt like she smelled hints of cigar and pipe tobacco in the background, but figured it may be her imagination, or French 75, playing with her senses.

King Rowan turned away from them, looking at a photo on a shelf behind his desk.

"You must admit the resemblance speaks for itself." Hayden began, nodding to the same photograph.

"It can't be." King Rowan turned back, pain and awe revealed on his face as he looked at Liv directly. Staring her down, she felt her body burning from his glare.

"Once you place the pieces together, it's a wonder I was so blind." King Rowan sadly confirmed, his gaze enlightening a story of words unspoken to Liv. "I'm still not entirely convinced, one can never be in my position, but you do remind me so much of him. I just hope it's not wishful desires of the past playing games with my conscience."

Liv shrunk at his words, unknowing what to say, or how to respond–she barely knew this man, and had no sense to the one he was speaking of. All she really desired was for King Rowan to remove himself from her direct sight immediately because she was eager to finally see her father's image behind him.

"Look at her necklace, Father. She was able to wield air, fire and water with her initial power. That alone should give us enough hope. If Kai truly has joined the radical Darks, and the Elements Pillar has fallen, Liv may be our only hope of reclaiming their Gods." Hayden insisted.

"How could a half-mortal ever defeat a Pillar Elite?" King Rowan snapped. "You put her in more danger by the second. Why do you suggest such a thing?"

"She's powerful." Hayden insisted. "She defeated Matthias in battle during her first training session!"

"She was not born Elite!" King Rowan growled, walking over to Hayden to continue his case.

Ignoring the terror unfolding in the study between the two men, Liv only had focus on one thing–her father. Instinctively, she darted over to the photo, intoxicated by the opportunity. She saw her eyes, staring back at her–inviting her in. She picked up the frame, tracing his smile–so much like her grin that she had seen in photos of herself. And Liv did get her height from him; he stood nearly as tall as King Rowan–looking so joyful and carefree in the photo. A father Liv would have loved unconditionally, if she had the chance to have known him. Seeing him wear the necklace she currently bore, the piece that completed her soul upon reuniting, she only felt one thing: light.

For so many years, she had wondered what his story could be, why a man so important in a child's life could be pulled so morbidly from her existence. Suddenly, looking at this memory of her father, it all clicked–everything made sense. He did it for love. He did it for her.

Liv was his descendent, his disciple. Training or not, this was her rightful place; she was meant to be here. Liv was destined to carry on his legacy–somehow he must have known it and somehow fate had brought Hayden into her life, and for whatever reason–started this war, all so she could be reunited with her people, so she could take on her designated responsibility. She was fighting for something more beautiful than she could have ever imagined.

Liv turned toward Hayden, excited to share her revelation, to find both father and son about to blow up the study with their ludicrous power-struggle.

"Hayden, you are asking too much of Liv!"

"Just watch her and you'll eventually agree!"

"Stop!" Liv commanded, still clutching the photo in her arms.

Both men turned to Liv, silenced. King Rowan did not look pleased, but simultaneously impressed at her natural ability to command the room.

"Yes?" He finally prompted, encouraging Liv to continue her thought.

Liv took another moment to compose herself from her outburst before beginning.

"Look, I understand both of your concerns. King Rowan, yes this world is completely new to me and I know little next to nothing."

King Rowan huffed in agreement; Hayden glared back at his father, but knew Liv was strong, so remained quiet and let her continue.

"But this is my father." Liv pointed to the photo. "I can't explain it, but every piece that has led me to this exact moment, has made me feel more complete. And right now, I have never felt more whole or stronger in my entire life. His legacy was cut too short, and who knows why. All we know is it was too soon and unjustified, but I must fight to continue it–and when the time comes, I will."

King Rowan stood impressed, finally seeing an immortal Elite shine through this mortal exterior.

"And Hayden–we cannot fight your father every step of the way. He may have his disagreements, but at the end of it–we're in a war–and we need to stick together. Who else can we trust if not our family?" Liv pleaded, hoping to move on from their petty bickering. She had forgiven King Rowan for his mistakes and understood his intentions–they seemed pure.

"Liv's right." Hayden agreed.

King Rowan nodded his head. "Arlo is doing more than building an army, my guards are sure of it. But, we can't figure out what exactly. And if what you say is true–the Elements Pillar has gone dark, then Hayden–it's only the beginning."

"We need to figure out what Arlo is up to." Hayden whispered frustratingly with his eyebrows furrowed. You could visually see his internal debate, contemplating all of the options to solve their handful of current problems.

"In time, my son." King Rowan put his hand assuringly on Hayden's shoulder. He turned to Liv, grinning. "Liv, if you thought being at Puerdios University as a mortal was tough, you're in for a reckoning as a God."

The three left the study much more amicable than they had entered, to Liv's surprise. She felt more at ease now that they had cleared the air, and could finally see King Rowan as Hayden's father rather than the intimidating powerful leader of the Gods.

Before entering the dining hall, King Rowan held Liv back as Hayden began simultaneously greeting and apologizing to his mother and sister for the delay.

"Liv, I feel I need to disclose a bit of pertinent family history, if you are indeed Liam's descendent, and the rightful Element Elite."

Liv paused, staring speculatively at what King Rowan could possibly divulge. She was still wary of their newfound camaraderie.

"I know Hayden has emphasized the importance of keeping these, heritage discoveries under wraps," King Rowan hesitated at whispering even that, "But I must stress just how precarious you must be–you could find yourself in much more trouble if this information were to become public knowledge or in the hands of a less trustworthy souls."

"I am aware." Liv confirmed, skeptically wondering if this was a ploy to discourage her from challenging the Elite throne in the future.

"You see, Liam had a younger brother–you have an uncle."

"I have an Uncle?" Liv gasped. "Who is he?"

"Unfortunately not a friend, but our greatest enemy–Arlo."

Liv bent over involuntarily, grabbing the door for stability. She had forgotten all that Hayden had disclosed about the Element Elite, but finally connected all the dots at the revelation. Liv had been so excited about the prospect of figuring out who her father was that she had overlooked everything else, or just refrained thinking about it.

But, after hearing King Rowan confirm the name Arlo, Liv felt the full circle of life–her uncle being born and dying within a second with her life. He was a traitor, and she could never forgive him.

"Upon the death of The Fallen Elite, er, your father–Arlo was assumed to be the next heir to the throne. But due to one of my better judgments, I had already sensed his extreme loyalty to the Darkness. I knew he was longing for power, and not the responsibility that comes with authority–that is, he was not sufficient for the role to lead his people. I'm afraid granting Kai's late grandmother the position was the trigger which sent Arlo to declare his independence to the Gods."

Liv nodded, trying to absorb this piece of family history she had not expected.

"I'm just trying to look out for you Liv, and be completely honest with your current situation. If Arlo were to discover your patronage and a chance for the Elements Pillar to be overthrown and returned back to Pure, it will put just another target to the many you are burdened with already."

"So, do you truly believe that Liam could be my father?" Liv hadn't expected to need King Rowan's blessing, but now she longed for it. This man standing before her, aside from her mom, was the only other encounter she had with a soul who knew her father, so Liv desperately wanted to learn his truth and hear his final jurisdiction.

"The prophecy was heard by a direct-descent of Apollo, from his oracle at Delphi over a millennia ago. 'Only when the heir to the King falls in love with a daughter Elite, do the Pure Gods stand a chance at defeating the Darkness once and for all.' I was very close with the Fallen Elite, he was like a brother to me–so I would be honored if Liam's daughter were the one fated to fulfill the prophecy with my son."

Liv nodded, appreciating King Rowan's blessing.

"You do remind me so terribly of him," King Rowan observed, sadly. "I should have known, or been more receptive to the idea, when I first met you at my birthday and believed that I had seen him reincarnated." He finally turned to Liv, "I never formally apologized for trying to keep you and Hayden apart, and I am sorry. This whole world, it's bigger than both you and Hayden can imagine. But, I'm grateful you have each other. For now, it may just be the fate of the Gods fall in the hand of you and my son. And that is a burden I would never wish upon anyone."

King Rowan nodded, finalizing their secret exchange, joining his family in the dining room with Liv looking in, wondering if she would ever be prepared for what she was to face in this world in which she now so desperately belonged.

After sharing rich stories over wine and lighthearted banter, Liv was almost disappointed when dinner had concluded. She gave Joss a long hug, filling her with warmth and gratitude before the journey back to Puerdios.

"Visit me any time. I would love to see you soon!" Joss gushed, going in for one last hug before departure.

"Truly, Liv–you are welcome anytime." Queen Daphne offered sincerely, adding dryly, "Hayden, I suppose you can come back, too."

Liv laughed, joy radiating from Daphne's unexpected and dry humor. She could see parts of where Hayden and Joss got their lovely personality beginning to emerge through Daphne's poised exterior, built from many years of burdening the responsibility of her subjects.

"Sadly, you may get your request, Mother–I'll be back soon. Father and I have our next trip planned in a few days."

"Next trip?" Liv asked, surprised.

"Recruiting mission–we'll need to start affirming loyalty for the Pure God's cause, if the Dark Gods are indeed on the hunt to convert pillars." King Rowan interjected.

Liv appreciated their newly formed open trust and honesty, but felt the weight of potential responsibility growing–was this how ruling would feel if she ever were crowned to lead with Hayden? Could she bear it?

"Please tell me you two are amping up security at the University while you are away?" Daphne pleaded to Hayden. "Liv, I am so glad you are one of us, but I must applaud with wariness my dear. You are in great danger with your current status. Not many Gods will welcome you as a potential royal, even if it's your rightful place to be ranked among Elites."

"Come on, Mother–female deities aren't as petty as that. They won't get jealous that she's with me." Hayden retorted back.

"I know I'm not," Joss chimed in, sarcastically. "I actually feel *sorry* for Liv that she has to put up with you."

Queen Daphne gave both her children a stern look, trying to resist the urge to smile, but Liv noticed her sparkling eyes gave her away, just like Hayden's.

"I'm just being cautious. I went through the very same thing with your Father at Puerdios, so I just want to let Liv know that she's always welcome here and should feel safe." She put her arm invitingly around Liv while giving one final nod to her children to conclude her lecture.

"Puerdios is different now, Mother. It's not like we're not in high school." Hayden argued.

"Aren't we?" Liv huffed in response, remembering the many glares she had received from Cleo just for interacting with Hayden.

"Your mother makes a good point, son." King Rowan agreed. "Continue defense and combat training, but I insist you give Liv additional lessons outside of class. Petty Puerdios Gods are the least of your worries. In fact, pull in Rei to help while you are gone–tell him I gave permission."

"And me too." Daphne smiled, grabbing Liv's hand in assurance and adieu. "Come back, darling girl. Please send me a sign that you have arrived home safe tonight."

And with a kiss on the cheek, Daphne glided down the corridor and out of sight.

"Good night, you two. Be safe." King Rowan added, but before he said his final goodbye, whispered, "And remember, for now–it may just be the fate of the Pure Gods rest in the hands of you two."

In shock, Liv stiffly hugged Hayden's father–the King of all deities, still trying to come to peace with how easily he spoke of the fate of their entire world being their responsibility. The same girl who less than a week before, had thought shots of Fireball were her savior. How could *she* be *the savior* for an entire deity world?

Liv didn't even notice that Hayden had steered her outside into their cozy carriage. He had taken off his blazer and covered her shoulders, warming up her body from the remaining body heat within his coat.

"Sorry about my family. Intense and peculiar cannot be avoided with them. Plus the outlying circumstances don't help the inevitable awkward first parent encounter. If only they were dentists…" Hayden began rambling, unsure how Liv would respond to the unusual dinner.

"I love them." Liv blurted out. Turning to Hayden, liberated. "They're everything I wanted your parents to be, and more. Kind, funny–they understand this world and can give parental advice, and they're graceful, smart, caring–and well, what could be better than having that for your mom and dad?"

Hayden gave her a speculative look, unexpecting her excessive appraisal.

Liv burst out with laughter. "I'm sorry, I'm intoxicated from tonight. It's just that, I was so nervous to meet them. And granted this was a night for the books, but it was almost as if I had known them my entire life. They welcomed me so openly, after the initial meeting, of course. I feel as if I'm a part of your family now, just as you're a part of my small one. And they knew my Dad, Hayden. It's just… it all came together. You get your humor from your Mom and your genuine care for others from your Dad–and your competitive spirit from Joss. It was just all so wonderful."

Liv sighed in delight, leaning against Hayden's chest and setting her head comfortably on his shoulder. She could feel his grin growing as he rested his head on top of hers, squeezing his arm around her shoulders in joy. Two pieces perfectly fitting together.

"I'm glad you enjoyed yourself. My family seems quite fond of you, too."

Liv smiled in return, but came off her high when she remembered Hayden's upcoming trip–away from her.

"How long will you be gone next week?" Liv asked, somberly.

"Hopefully back before the weekend. We're visiting the Pillar of Humanities to speak with their Elite. Depending on how the conversation goes, I could be back mid-week."

Liv could sense hesitation in Hayden's voice.

"What else? Come out with it." Liv demanded, but not as intensely as she had wanted. The champagne and wine was beginning to catch up to her cozy position in Hayden's arms, she was peacefully calm and had eerily begun accepting their ongoing danger as normal.

"Well, my father has an inclination to what Kai may be after."

"What is his hypothesis?"

"You know how you cannot kill Gods?"

Liv nodded groggily.

"We're immortal. Destined to never die; however, cleverly enough–Zeus created the Underworld, secured by a series of powerful lock keys and protection powers. So powerful that Gods can enter but are unable to escape. Some go willingly, either to be with loved ones or because their time has passed, but most are forced–either commanded as punishment or trapped reluctantly through. That's where all of our ancestors go once they pass, either way. My father thinks Arlo wants to open The Underworld portal, to release all Gods–those who lived among the mortals, those who were banished as punishment–all of them, to help build a following to his cause."

This discovery caught Liv's attention.

"Hayden, is that where the Fallen Elite exists?"

Hayden paused, reluctant to answer.

"But Hayden, if there is a chance I could see my father, ask him the questions we're all wondering, we may be able to finally get some answers."

"Liv, I know what you are thinking and you cannot even begin to explore that option. The Underworld serves as a place for those who are no longer present in the living one, a loophole to our immortality. Even if you are able to open the gates, who knows who or what could emerge. There are over a millennium's worth of souls trapped in the underworld, and most were sent from force, and for a reason–plus, only a fraction actually chose to go willingly. It would be complete chaos–or worse, you could be forced in and never able to return. The closer you get to the portal, the more vulnerable you are to being trapped and commanded through it for eternity."

Liv knew a lost fight, and was too tired to try to go head to head with Hayden tonight. Instead, she figured the best tactic would be just to understand the whole concept before making her decision.

"Okay, point made. But I'm just surprised nobody has figured out a way to break through, yet."

"Most avoid the challenge—it's a dangerous venture because there's no control to the portal, unless you're Hades. Once opened, anyone can exist—friend or enemy. It's not a select and choose situation. Not a known soul has attempted. If anyone had—they ended up there from failure to open the gate. And now, it'll be harder than ever—my father upped security to help protect The Underworld, and all are instructed to show no mercy for breaches. So, many would prefer not to take the risk, if you understand."

"Understood." Liv sighed, shutting her eyes and succumbing to her drowsiness.

In her slumber, she dreamt of Hayden kindly laying her in his cozy bed and removing her dress, only to replace it with a soft cotton t-shirt that smelled of him—basil, verveina and cedarwood, allowing Liv to fall further in a comforting, deep sleep.

Her last memory was soft lips touching her forehead, wishing her a peaceful slumber before she woke up to find herself in Hayden's room, alone.

TWENTY-TWO

Liv should have been used to the notion of Hayden leaving without notice by now, but was still too relieved when she saw an envelope in place of his head on the pillow. She immediately felt more at ease knowing he had time to draft a note, although she wished he had just woken her up instead to say goodbye.

OLLIE-NEEDED TO LEAVE ON MENTIONED TRIP EARLY. DON'T WORRY-WILL EXPLAIN WHEN I GET BACK. (HOPING IT WILL BE EARLIER THAN MY PREVIOUS ESTIMATE) PLEASE STAY HERE WHILE I'M GONE-IT'S SAFER.

I LOVE YOU.

--- H

Although appreciative for the note, Liv wasn't quite as assured as she had hoped to be from it. He clearly wrote it quickly–sticking only with the essentials and keeping the facts as obscure as possible. Liv knew he was on his way to the Humanities Pillar, but where that was located and why it became so pertinent to leave during the night remained unknown.

Luckily it seemed that with his early departure he would return sooner–which comforted Liv. Although in Hayden's room and surrounded by him figuratively, Liv still felt disconnected and a little off without knowing that he was nearby.

She shook her head, removing herself from that mind space. She refused to be vulnerable or needy–she was powerful and belonged in this world now. Gone were the days where she would allow herself to sulk or feel weak. If the Gods were on the verge of a war, she needed to start thinking with a survival instinct.

Liv jumped out of bed and ran over to Hayden's drawers, finding a grey cashmere cardigan to pull over her oversized white tee. She guiltily smiled, happy that it smelled of him. Folded neatly on top of his cabinet, she found a pair of destroyed denim looking rather too tiny to be Hayden's in any capacity. Lifting them up, she breathed a sigh of relief, thankful for her clever boyfriend who did not leave her stranded to the previous night's cocktail dress for a calm weekend morning.

She also spotted his fuzzy slippers, and feeling rather devious, slid her feet into them, stomping her way quite ungracefully down the stairs and into the kitchen to make coffee.

After setting the coffeemaker to brew, Liv casually walked over to Hayden's bookcase, perusing her favorite titles and debating if she should revisit a classic or study some new curriculum on her lazy Saturday. Turning over her shoulder to notice her books placed neatly on the kitchen table, the outdoor patio view caught her gaze. The sunlight was sparkling, with such an innocent cotton candy palette, the dewy sight enticed her to pause and appreciate the calm before the storm. Looking around the quiet apartment, Liv felt at peace–still. She turned back to the bookcase, finding *The Odyssey* amongst the titles, and opened the introduction to find Alexander Pope, whom Piper had recommended at the Symposium, translated it. Liv grabbed the book, looking around the quiet loft and figured compromise could be best–perhaps there may just be some learning to be had from Homer and his translating acquaintance Alexander.

Once the coffee had brewed, crying for attention at its preparedness and demanding to be divulged, Liv grabbed an oversized dark grey porcelain coffee mug and danced her way to the couch, pulling on a heavy blanket and commanding the fireplace to light (and successfully, with a conceited grin).

The man for wisdom's various arts renown'd,
Long exercised in woes, O Muse! resound;

Who, when his arms had wrought the destined fall
Of sacred Troy, and razed her heaven-built wall,
Wandering from clime to clime, observant stray'd,
Their manners noted, and their states survey'd,
On stormy seas unnumber'd toils he bore,
Safe with his friends to gain his natal shore:
Vain toils! Their impious folly dared to prey
On herds devoted to the god of day;
The god vindicitive doom'd them never more
(Ah, men unbless'd) to touch that natal shore.
Oh, snatch some portion of these acts from fate,
Celestial Muse! And to our world relate.

Liv continued reading on, and after a couple hours of meticulously studying any historical fact that could present itself in the Greek epic, she was out of coffee at last.

Staring at her warm mug and cozy hibernated space, Liv turned to the kitchen, dreading her upcoming venture, so instead stared at the coffee-pot longingly when she had an obvious epiphany: powers.

To begin, she practiced sending her morning novel back to Hayden's bookshelf, carefully filing it back into place. Simple. She could do this with more breakable cargo.

She sent the coffee mug over to the kitchen, concentrating on its landing, making it smooth–like an airplane. She turned to the pot, focused on lifting it up above the cup, as if her hands were physically there, but instead her mind completed the task. The pot turned over to pour the dark roast slowly into her mug. Her brain ached, as if she were physically holding the pot with her unmuscular organ–like the feeling your arm gets when you're forced to hold something upright for an undesirable period of time. No matter what size object, it inevitably weighs on your extended muscles, eventually.

Thankful to put the pot back onto the counter, Liv began her most challenging task yet–bring the filled mug back while keeping it levered, balanced and steady to avoid spilling.

She lifted the mug, carefully practicing levitation over the counter and after eliminating imbalance, began its journey toward the couch.

Liv had gotten it midway when the door to Hayden's loft burst open, causing her to deflect her attention to the intruder and drop the coffee mug simultaneously.

"Good morning Liv!"

"Fuck!"

Liv scrambled off the couch, looking at the mess she had just created and ignored her visitor, which she presumed to be Peyton.

"What happened?" Peyton turned the corner to gaze around the kitchen. "Oh, that bites." She said nonchalantly as Liv began brushing the scattered pieces of the mug into a garbage bag. "What are you doing?"

"What does it look like I'm doing?!" Liv shrieked, in overwhelming panic.

"Okay, first–just because your power caused this havoc, doesn't mean you aren't allowed to use it to clean up the mess." Peyton explained, pacifying Liv. "It's just a broken mug, and yes you may have murdered it, but it's not like you killed someone or did something actually destructible."

Peyton knelt down, putting her hand on Liv's shoulder. "You're still learning–and consequently are bound to have hiccups. But that's how you learn."

Liv paused, staring at the broken mug, wiping a tear from her eye. "I was doing so well. And yeah, it was a mistake, but it's not one that you, Rei, Hayden or even Piper would make. And we're on the verge of a world where mistakes will become a matter of life or death."

"How deep." Peyton mockingly responded, grinning.

"It's not funny, Peyton!" Liv yelled. "I need to pull my weight. You can't be watching over me or taking care of me forever, you need to focus on taking care of yourself first, instead."

"We get that, Liv." Peyton sternly confirmed. "There's still time. And all you can do is practice and get better. Which you *are*."

Liv shrugged, still feeling down but also realizing how odd her outburst must seem. "I'm sorry. I guess sometimes you do cry over spilt milk," she added with a soft smile.

"No, you cry over spilt coffee. Which in my opinion is completely justifiable!" Peyton offered as a truce. "Now, is that a pile of all the mug pieces? Let's put it back together."

Peyton stood up as she flipped to instructor mode. "The key to repairing anything is simple–you just need to have all the pieces. The mug is actually quite a perfect example for this lesson. See? Silver lining."

Liv stood up, staring at the mug and willing it to piece itself back together. The mug obeyed and swiftly magnetized back to its prior form. You could still see all the cracks from the break, but overall seemed functional once again.

"Try to replenish your brew, may the prior rest in the piece." Peyton prayed solemnly, but ended with a huge mischievous grin.

Liv rolled her eyes, thankful for her weird former roommate's humor. She poured another pot (physically, with her arms) and took a sip.

All seemed okay until Liv felt a warm prick sting her palm. She saw a light brown drop on her hand. Turning to Peyton, she questioningly raised her limb to showcase the leak.

"Easy–that just means we missed a piece. Maybe under the couch or something." Peyton skipped over to the mess and leaned perpendicular to her legs. "There." She pointed under the couch, to a spot that was definitely *not* visible to Peyton's eye from where she was currently standing.

"Kalo." She muttered, holding out her hand. Liv noticed no movement, except her roommate coming back with her palm closed tight. "Here's the missing piece–here you go."

Liv eyed the tiny crumble–it couldn't have been bigger than a grain. "How did you find that?!" She asked, looking up in amazement.

"Perks of my powers–I'm the God of Discovery. I'm quite good at finding lost things, especially searching for those in which do not wish to be found."

Liv took the grain and willed it back to the cup. Then she turned back to the coffee mess, which luckily looked much less intimidating to clean with the broken shards now removed. She willed the spillage to the sink and then turned on the faucet to rinse the crime scene down the drain.

"Nice." Peyton observed, impressed.

"Water is *my specialty*." Liv confirmed, mocking Peyton sarcastically.

"Well, it's a good damn element to have on your side." Peyton commended. "It's one of the few that can replenish and destroy–consider yourself lucky."

Liv paused, unsure if she should have highlighted her power so nonchalantly. She would need to practice hiding her strengths if she were to keep her Element history safe.

"Don't worry–I'm on your side, Liv. Hayden sent me over to bring you some clothes." Peyton nodded to the kitchen table behind, a tidy stack of metallics and beadwork in view.

"Thanks." Liv said, apologetically. "What other tasks or duties do you have to complete today?" She asked, kindly.

"Nothing crazy." Peyton shrugged, "You?"

"No plans. I was thinking of studying a bit." Liv paused, curious for more insight, "Peyton–what do Gods do on the weekends here? For fun?"

"*Fun?*" Peyton asked, aghast. "Nonsense! None of that can be had in this world!" Peyton dramatically overreacted, her extreme sarcasm made Liv smile. Then, calming down as if she never had an outburst, Peyton added, "I was going to go hang out with Rei, want to join? We have to check out a historic site, but we could make a day out of it. Promise Rei and I will throw random attacks at you so you can practice your defense during the trip. That should be bloody fun for us."

Liv smiled, thankful for her friend. "Sure–er, should I grab anything?"

Peyton looked around, then back at Liv. "Not at all. Although, you may want to change into something a little, er–more presentable."

Liv looked at her outfit, laughing internally. What would be a rather solid weekend outfit in her world, apparently looked like rags to her peers, here. Peyton's casual weekend-wear included a brilliant maroon sequined short sleeve dress and bronze pumps.

"Noted." Liv laughed. "I'll go change."

After changing into a more 'appropriate' leisure outfit of a golden-feathered bodice with a sheer tulle long skirt underneath–Peyton and Liv headed over to Rei's dormitory on campus, running into Piper along the way. As Rei, Peyton and Liv were Piper's only speaking colleagues on campus, she also had no plans and was quite eager to join the excursion.

Piper, on the other hand, donned a futuristic power suit, with sharp white shoulder pads contrasting the silver ombre sequined core of her blazer that slowly merged into a midnight blue, matching her navy satin trousers.

Liv was only a bit surprised upon sight of Rei, who had a grey cotton motorcycle jacket with black trousers and a thin satin lime green evening scarf. He was the most casual out of the girls and still looked ready to walk a red carpet or pose for the cover of Rolling Stone.

"Where exactly are we headed?" Piper asked as Peyton and Rei led the group into the courtyard.

"Mount Lykaion." Rei confirmed, disinterested.

"Any particular reason why?" Piper pressed, anxiously. Liv could sense a terseness in her voice.

Rei annoyingly turned to Peyton, demanding she continued the conversation.

"Your familiar with the histories?" Peyton asked, nonchalantly.

"Of course I am." Piper confirmed, indignantly.

Liv interjected, "Er, mortal until recently here. What's the myth?"

Piper turned to Liv, "Legend says it is the place where Lykaoin was transformed into a wolf for his wickedness."

"A wolf? And we want to visit this memorial mountain why?" Liv was growing apprehensive by the minute. *Was this really Rei and Peyton's version of Saturday fun?*

"He sacrificed a human child on Zeus' altar–it didn't please the Gods. So he was punished, and don't worry, it's not like we'll do any sacrilegious act–we just need to investigate." Peyton nonchalantly explained.

Rei's eyes, like daggers, cut Peyton off from further explanation.

"Investigate what?" Liv asked cautiously.

Rei took over the conversation. "More so conduct research, Peyton means. To see if there is any inspiration or odd occurrences happening. You don't have to come if it sounds too boring, Liv."

Liv was even more confused, now. She contemplated leaving, going back to her haven of Hayden's loft, but really she felt like this was a personal test. She needed to do this–she couldn't run away from everything that terrified her or else she would never leave Hayden's loft again.

"Not going to pass this opportunity down. Ancient ruins? I'm in. So, how do we get there?"

"Fly, of course." Peyton nonchalantly confirmed.

"Fly?" Liv gulped. First challenge, apparently accepted.

"Liv hasn't quite learned that part of transit." Rei smugly replied. Liv wanted to hit him, but also felt an immense relief from his teasing. It meant she was in and had his approval.

"It's easy." Piper interjected, putting words into Peyton's dropped jaw. "Just like jumping in our simulation, but think long term. Your wings will do most of the lifting."

"How do I get my wings?" Liv asked, straining her neck to look over at her shoulder blades. How was she supposed to will a structure she had no idea existed in her body?

"Oh! You don't grow wings." Piper laughed. "It's a tool we invented."

"Like a bicycle or skateboard," Peyton interjected. "We usually just shrink and attach them to ourselves so we have access at all times. I guess I could see how it would look like they magically appeared. If you don't have a pair yet, we can borrow something. Right, Rei?" Peyton nodded to her boyfriend, requesting the source that Liv was missing.

"Done." Rei mumbled, pausing a moment and then holding out his hand to reveal a pair of tiny white wings.

Liv cautiously grabbed them, delicately placing them in her palm for further inspection.

"By the way, act surprised when Hayden gives these to you, officially. For now, we'll just pretend they're borrowed."

Liv looked at Rei in surprise, unbelieving that these were actually *hers*. But of course Hayden always thought five steps ahead–knowing she would need wings, eventually. Liv brought her hand to her head, in awe at the tiny spectacle. They flapped a friendly hello, as if the wings had a mind of their own, but still felt as if they already belonged to her. The wings had gold tips and sparkled as they eagerly awaited instruction from their new master.

When Liv looked back over to her friends, they each had tripled in size, now with their own wings fully extended.

Like Hayden's wings, all of theirs were white. Piper's had a silver shine throughout hers, Peyton's literally sparkled like diamonds were glued to each feather and Rei's were plain white, but the back showed a more unique design–light blue metallic feathers mixed with white, as if resembling the sky above.

"Will them to get bigger and become apart of you. It'll feel weird at first, but you'll get used to it." Peyton kindly explained, understanding Liv's naivete.

A moment later, Liv felt her wings attach–fitting perfectly to her back, as if they were meant to be one.

"Hayden did a good job in pairing–must have done his research all right." Rei stood, surprised at how quickly the wings had listened and latched. "Finding a pair that fits and obeys is quite the messy ordeal, usually."

Liv smiled, feeling comfort in her wings. They supported her, and she already felt a bonding connection. She wouldn't have trusted anyone else with the task of finding her wings. If anyone knew her better, possibly more than she knew herself, it was Hayden.

"Now, let's see if she can fly with the things." Peyton smirked, gracefully raising herself up into the air; Rei and Piper swiftly followed.

Liv felt her wings obeying her command; she acted as if they were just an extension of her body, as if she were raising her arms up and down, but instead forcing the foreign limbs that sprouted from her back to conduct the movement. Liv rose above the ground, first cautiously and only a couple feet, but soon she was gliding through the courtyard, frantically trying to learn how to steer as she barely dodged the fountain and was heading straight toward an oak tree.

Bang!

With a mix of terror and blackness from her skull smacking against the tree stump, her face landed in the wet grass below. Liv took a breath and assessed the damage.

"Are you okay Liv!?" Peyton was the first to her rescue, delicately lifting her up onto her feet. "I didn't realize you would go so fast! I couldn't catch you! I'm so sorry!" She continued frantically examining Liv's body, looking for any injury. Piper and Rei finally landed a moment after.

"Speedy Hermes!" Rei laughed, assessing Liv was all right. "Well, we don't have to worry about you out-flying your enemies, that's for sure."

Liv smiled, regaining her senses. "That was incredible."

"Direction tutorial, first." Peyton kept her hands on Liv's shoulders. "It's sort of like sailing, or canoeing. You need to work off the wind–if you want to turn right, you'll need to either lean into your left wing, so it catches the wind on the interior, or lower your right wing so it blocks the wind on the outside. And vice versa."

"And if there is no wind?" Liv asked, curiously.

"You're a God–you make it." Rei answered bluntly.

"And to slow down, you just need to add resistances to your wings head on." Piper added matter-of-factly.

"How do you land?"

"That's up to you." Peyton shrugged. "Some prefer the 'slow walker' or 'the airplane.' I prefer the first–it's a little less intensive. You sort of just have to wing it and learn by trial, unfortunately."

"Well, I'm sure anything will be better than my last." Liv agreed, rubbing her head and beginning to feel a very sore bump on her head. "Who's leading the way to Mount Lykaion?"

Once in the sky and above any and all obstacle objects, Liv found flying quite enjoyable. Unlike her previous flight with Hayden, she felt more in control with the wind and speed—which resulted in her ability to see, so she could witness the captivating new scenery surrounding Puerdios from her elevated view. She sprinted through the sky without exerting any effort—she was simply *being*.

When Rei signaled landing was upon them, Liv was relieved to see an open space, almost her own personal runway of grass. She also appreciated the lack of trees or objects that she could collide into during the process.

She darted down toward the ground, deciding to attempt the 'slow walker' and will the air to soften her fall.

As she followed Rei's lead downward, she looked around in confusion. Aside from a bland hill and some deserted concrete fixtures outlines, Mt. Lykaion was underwhelming—only the appearance of rocks and weeds remained.

Finally, it was time to land, she held her wings up against the wind, fighting the strain in the resistance they faced, slowing down her speed. She watched Rei's graceful landing ahead, and tried to mimic his movements, with little success.

As she approached her doom, she willed the air to catch her about 1 inch above the ground, and then dropped softly onto the grass.

"Good job, mortal." Rei applauded from afar. "Impressive."

"Thanks." Liv muttered, looking around the deserted space. "And what exactly are we looking for here?"

Rei turned toward Peyton upon her landing, Piper followed shortly after.

"Any trace of Dark God powers, anything that looks out of place, or something that could just be interesting to note." Rei carried his voice, so Piper could hear his instruction too. "Piper go with Liv, Peyton and I can stick together."

"But what is this all for?" Liv asked, trying to get any direction for what the purpose of this excursion was–between the abandoned land and lack of any sign declaring they stood on a historic site or sacred grounds– Liv would be worthless if sent out to achieve anything.

"Hayden sent a message this morning–we're not sure of the details exactly." Peyton cautiously explained. "He'll probably enlighten us when he gets back and probably didn't want to risk communication getting intercepted by the wrong God. But we can expect it has something to do with Arlo and being able to check off this space from inspection."

"He was heading to the Humanities Pillar last night." Liv added, trying to be helpful. "Could that have anything to do with his request?"

"Possibly." Rei nodded up the hills, "Peyton and I will examine the mountain if you two can stay level. Let's report back in 180 degrees."

Liv took a step and already regretted her choice of changing into strappy-heeled sandals this morning as she clunked around the unlevel ground. By the time she got to Piper, she had almost sprained her ankle twice.

"Where do you suggest I hide my wings in the meantime?" Liv asked angrily, unbuckling her sandals to go barefoot for the remainder of their adventure.

"I attach mine to my ring, because I wear it every day, so it's an easy place to store." Piper held out her ring to show Liv.

Liv had never noticed Piper's ring, but now that she saw it, wondered how she hadn't admired it before. The piece of jewelry was brilliant silver, matching the lighter specs of her friend's eyes. In the center was an ocean blue stone and wrapped over were her beautiful silver wings.

"Got it." Liv focused on shrinking her wings to the size of a pearl and also willed them to enclose on the backside of her father's necklace.

"Are there any other weapons that Gods sneak within their wardrobe that I should be aware of?" Liv asked jokingly. "Grenades? Pistols? Magic wands?"

Piper laughed. "Not the Pure Gods, I can assure you. But Matthias does keep a pocket knife?" She rolled her eyes, "No idea why, I've never asked."

The girls walked in the direction where they saw the most promise, some light grey rocks in a square shape about 40 yards ahead.

"I'm sure we're here to see if there is anything wicked or cursed over the land. I mean, why else would we be looking around unless Arlo chose a place to do Zeus-knows-what, but where a dark soul was transformed for his wickedness? There couldn't be any other parallel."

Liv stared into the horizon, unconvinced.

"It feels too deserted. Has there ever been anything excavated here before? Does Lykaoin even still exist on this land?"

"Humans have found skeletons, but none that would have questioned a full mammal–mostly were from spiritual rituals done in Ancient Arcadia." Piper sighed as she willed the rocks out of the way for a flatter pathway.

Liv followed suit, clearing the pathway to make a softer path for her bruised feet. She willed her shoes back toward her, now understanding how to make due with her inconvenient footwear.

But as Liv went to grab her shoes, she found a pebble–no bigger than her palm, with an obscure shape carved on the surface, vague from centuries of aging.

Instinctively, she picked up the stone to examine it, with immediate regret. A vision hit her head, forcing her to black out and witness a lightning bolt strike her soul before she regained consciousness.

"Liv!" Piper shrieked, running over to Liv who was now on the ground, one of her heels uncomfortably wedged into her leg. "Are you okay? What happened!?"

Liv took a breath, trying to recollect what had just occurred. Her head hurt, which she couldn't determine if from the bolt of vision she just received, or if it still lingered from her previous fall. She assumed a combination of the two.

"Rei and Peyton will be here any second." Piper stated, looking around. "That was a really loud blast–so much for trying to keep a low profile..."

A low growl erupted among the darkened horizon. Piper warily looked at Liv, eyeing her to confirm she heard it too, and then slowly turned her head behind her, into the darkness.

Liv spotted two slanted yellow eyes among the night, with white fangs snarling at its future prey.

"Succendam Caeli!" Piper yelled, blasting the creature into the moonlight and away from the girls.

It looked like a wolf. When it howled from the attack, Liv turned to Piper.

"Shit. Was that Lykaoin?"

"I hope not." Piper exasperated, looking toward where the monster used to be. "But let's not stay here to find out!" She stood up, pulling Liv with her.

Liv stumbled a bit before regaining her footing.

"Wait! I found a coin, that's what caused the noise... it should be here..." Liv muttered, frantically crawling over the ground. "I think it's a clue!" She continued, trying to spot the rusted metallic sphere, with no luck.

Thankfully, Rei and Peyton were flying down in their direction.

"What happened?" Peyton demanded.

Rei was distracted and stared curiously off into sky.

"Liv found a clue, we think." Piper explained, also bent over, searching for the treasure in the ground. "And then Lykaoin–or his reincarnation–paid us a visit and so we think we should–"

"Leave. Now." Rei commanded, completing Piper's thought unexpectedly as he pulled out his wings. "Dark Gods are approaching. Let's go!"

"One second!" Liv yelled, frustrated. She ran over where she had collapsed, willing the coin, as she vaguely remembered it, back to her and prayed her weak summoning would work.

"Kalo."

Like a magnet, she caught the metallic object in her hand.

"Quick!" Piper advised, "Attach it to your necklace. We'll figure it out later!"

Liv willed the coin to her necklace and simultaneously her wings to grow and attach to her back. Following Piper, Rei and Peyton with a running start, she began acceleration immediately.

"Sphaera Tutelae Maximus!" Peyton screamed, deflecting an attack in Piper's direction. Piper turned in gratitude and summoned her own safety shield shortly after.

Another red flash passed Liv's ear, barely missing her wing.

"Sphaera Tutelae!" Liv commanded, joyfully feeling her protection shield expand. As she turbulated through the air, she began panicking as she debated looking back to see the magnitude that was causing the attacks, or if she should simply focus on getting as far away from whatever it was, as soon as possible.

Another red flash hit her sphere, causing a slight ache near Liv's calf. It hurt, but she could manage another strike if needed, so chose to turn her head and consequently slow down, to see what she and her friends were dealing with.

Her eyes grew in trepidation. About 100 yards behind, an intimidating large group of black masses paralleled. Their black wings flapped in the moonlight, looking like magnified bats. Liv gulped, and turned back around immediately, willing her wings to flap harder and catch back up with her friends.

Sensing another attack in her direction, Liv yelled, "Reflecto!" and with a smirk, felt it retract and head back toward the black bats.

But then another bolt hit her protection shield near her torso, hurting a little more than before. Liv focused on strengthening her protection power than retaliating the curses, holding onto her torso as she continued to fly in the distance.

"We need to descend into the forest for coverage!" Rei yelled. "Liv– can you manage?!"

Liv gulped, eyeing the outskirts of a forest approaching on the horizon. She knew they couldn't remain in the clear sky, as the attacks were increasing and Puerdios was still too far away to manage through. The only chance they had of dodging their attackers was to find coverage so their track could not be followed. Liv wasn't positive how she could maneuver through the obstacle ahead, but she couldn't put her friends through any more risk at her expense.

"I'll figure it out!" Liv nodded determinedly.

"Peyton start the trail, Piper follow her and Liv go behind! I'll be last!" Rei shouted as he strategically flew between the girls to carry his voice through the wind.

Liv gulped. If she tanked–Rei would know and stay behind with her. She had to succeed–she could not put in him danger. Not now, when he had risked so much for her to keep her safe this whole time. Crashing was not an option anymore.

Peyton darted downward, finding a giving entrance, to Liv's relief. Piper fit herself in between Peyton and Liv, and Rei followed suit to form a line.

Liv concentrated on Piper's stunning silver wings, mimicking every angle they moved, hoping that would suffice enough as a guide to get her through the upcoming maze.

Piper's wings pivoted downward on the left, Liv followed suit, barely missing a tree, then turned them the opposite direction to dodge the next. Before she had a chance for recovery Piper angled herself downward beneath a branch, which Liv clumsily mimicked, almost steering directly into the ground. To her luck, there was an open lake crossing that allowed Liv to regain control, but as she passed over, she saw the shadows of their followers above in the reflection. They had spotted them through the clearing, sending more attacking forces below the tree line.

Sphaera Tutelae. Liv thought in her mind, finding a small force without giving too much luminescence away. It blocked an attack near her neck, sending a painful stab through her spine.

Peyton and Piper had darted sharply to the left to find cover. Liv followed, but heard a large splash behind, turning quickly to see a big wave, with Rei no longer behind her as the attacks increased overhead.

"Sphaera Tutelae Maximus!" Liv yelled, turning herself around to try to spot Rei across the lake.

"Liv, we need to keep going!" Peyton demanded ahead.

Liv ignored her friend and focused on protecting Rei. Her shield, spread across the entire lake, was getting attacked every second, sending aches through her entire body. She wasn't sure how much longer she could hold on.

"Liv, we need to go!" Piper screamed.

Where was Rei?

"Come on Liv, Peyton wait!" Liv heard Piper call ahead, her voice diminishing as she flew away to find Peyton.

But Liv remained behind. She had to, what was happening to Rei under the lake?

Finally, a strong force emerged from the water. Rei looked bloody, but functioning enough to fly back to the edge of the lake. Liv spun, maintaining her extensive protection shield as she darted in the direction Peyton and Piper had gone. She sensed Rei nearby behind, but unfortunately couldn't find any trace of Piper through the cluttered forest.

How on earth would she get back onto their trail?

Rei smoothly passed below her, yelling, "I'll lead the way back!"

Liv felt the weight lift until she started following Rei's guided path. He looked beaten for the worse. His wings had a blend of red spots, and his usually pristine conditioned attire was wet, ripped, and revealed dark blots seeping through over his scraped skin.

His right wing appeared broken–it was struggling to pull its weight; Liv was just thankful to know it was not actually a body part, and hoped none of his actual limbs were in a similar state.

Rei's current path was not as giving as Peyton's before the lake, he chose blunt turns with little notice; Liv figured it was an attempt to lose the attackers in the forest, rather than get back to Puerdios as directly and quickly as possible.

After one turn, Liv accidentally didn't recover fast enough to avoid another tree branch and tumbled to the ground from the unexpected collision.

"Are you okay?!" Rei was at her side, immediately helping her up.

"Thanks–yeah I'm fine." Liv shook off her dress, the tulle skirt now filled with leaves and caught in sticks. "You didn't have to stop for me."

"Least I could do after what you did for me earlier." Rei shrugged, "Plus, Hayden would kill me if I returned without you."

Liv laughed, almost forgetting their state of danger until she saw Rei's eyes widen once again.

"Damn. I thought we lost them–we need to keep going. Now!" Rei turned and flapped his wings. Liv turned around, spotting flames erupting amidst the trees.

The forest was catching on fire.

"Easier to spot us if they eliminate our cover!" Rei shouted ahead, running to take flight.

A fireball dropped beside her, a flame catching onto her wing.

"Aqua!" Liv commanded, blowing out the tip with a burst of water immediately; internally, she wanted to scream a lot more.

Rei continued to speed through the forest's obstacles, but Liv noticed a slightly less aggressive directional change. He must have remembered, or finally noted, her extensive lack of flying capabilities.

Soon, they had escaped the falling fireballs, and Rei began a more direct route once again. The trees began thinning; Liv understood they were about to leave their terrestrial safety net. He pulled back to fly by her side and share further instructions.

"After the forest, it's a direct line to Puerdios–all we can do is fly directly and rapidly. Think of 'Homer' if you see the entrance gates without me–that will grant you access through!" He shouted as they flew, but almost sounded mute to Liv because of the intense wind that carried his voice away as they sped through the trees. He darted forward through the clearing, setting the pace Liv needed to maintain.

"I won't get to Puerdios unless you're with me!" Liv promised in return.

Liv willed her wings to flap harder, wielding her protective powers in case of attack. When she saw the sky and horizon once again, she held her breath until realizing that without being immediately attacked and with no visible threat nearby, that they must have escaped the Dark Gods.

As they flew, there was also no sign of their two friends further ahead in the clear sky. Had Piper and Peyton escaped? She turned her head back, looking back into the forest.

Rei came closer to Liv, assessing temporary safety, and nodded to a hill up ahead. He turned towards it, insinuating they fly over to the landmark and take temporary refuge.

As they approached, Liv began descending when she saw two pairs of white wings erupt. She immediately sighed relief.

Peyton and Piper were safe.

Rei landed with a running sprint towards Peyton; Liv noticed Rei also had a limp in his leg as he pulled Peyton into an embrace.

Liv landed a little more cautiously and further than she had expected to, but still on two feet, so deemed it a success and ran uphill towards her friends.

"What happened to you?!" Piper shrieked, running over to Liv.

"Not what happened to me, more like what happened to Rei," Liv nodded to Rei, wanting to hear his underwater crisis. "And what happened to you?!" She demanded, ignoring Piper and accusing Peyton. "Why would you just leave Rei like that?"

"Don't get mad." Rei grunted.

Liv glared at his defense but was secretly happy to see him returning to his standoff-ish ways–that meant he felt they truly were no longer in immediate danger.

"Peyton and I are under oath to keep you protected," Rei continued explaining, battling Liv's accusation, "she did what she had to do, and you were supposed to follow. You shouldn't have stayed back for me, Liv. That was dangerous."

"Well, I did." Liv crossed her arms, indignant.

"And I owe you a thank you for that, no matter how stupid it was for you to ignore Peyton's orders." Rei chastised Liv, but then sighed as he admitted, "But who knows where I'd be if you hadn't." He nodded to Peyton, adding, "They commanded Charybdis to attack from below the sea."

"No…" Peyton whispered, looking up at Rei with her hand covering her mouth. After a deep breath for strength, she distracted herself by examining Rei's wounds and began healing them, as she could suffice.

"What's Charybdis?" Liv wondered aloud.

"A terrifying sea monster, almost like a whirlpool that sucks you under his spiral indefinitely and usually with no return." Piper interjected. "We've never been able to confirm if you ultimately pass onto the Underworld or if it's another sphere Gods get trapped in for eternity."

Liv shuddered. "And that means Charybdis is in allegiance with the Dark Gods?"

"Afraid so." Rei muttered. "We should have expected it with the Elements Pillar going Dark, but it sort of puts the repercussions in a new, more precarious light, I suppose."

"So, how *did* you escape?" Liv pressed.

"Well, your protection spell helped alleviate the battle taking place below sea, because I didn't have to focus on the attacks above." Rei explained. "But, honestly, it was almost like the water protected me from the sea monster's whirl pool; I wasn't getting pulled under. Charybdis got a couple strikes at me with its fangs, but luckily, I was able to propel myself out of the lake before any serious damage could be done."

Piper walked over to Liv, pulling her aside and whispering quietly. "It's because you're the rightful Element Elite–don't you get it? The water listened to you and obeyed your protection command. Kai may be the Element Elite, but the physical Elements have a stronger loyalty to you–the true Pillar heir."

Liv stared at Piper, incredulous but still radiating fury when she jibed back, "I would have preferred my friend's loyalty over the water back there, but I guess in this case blood isn't thicker than water then, is it?"

Piper looked back, shocked. "Liv, I begged you to come. You didn't follow! By the time I looked back you weren't there, and we had no idea where you had gone!"

"I stayed back with my friend!" Liv defended, raising her voice and gaining Peyton's attention. "Unlike the both of you!" And with a final 'hmph!' of disapproval, Liv marched off into the night, away from her friends.

TWENTY-THREE

Staring at the night sky, Liv refused to make eye contact with her constellation, Ollie. As she adamantly looked at Polaris, she mentally could identify where it was in the sky and could almost sense Hayden's presence lingering, waiting for her to summon him–but she couldn't. She wouldn't.

He was busy and had more than enough on his plate. The last thing he needed to worry about was flying across the world and exposing himself to danger, just to get to Liv and console her.

She knew Hayden would drop everything in a heartbeat to be there for her, too, but she couldn't allow him to do that. And for now, the thought of his pure intention and care was enough–it had to be. She had to be stronger tonight.

Liv smiled at the thought, she could do it. As she wiped a tear from her cheek, the excitement from the day came back to her and she realized she had made it through *that*. But that was just one day.

Would there ever be a dull moment in this world? Could there ever be, now? Would she be strong enough to survive?

She heard quiet footsteps behind her, expecting Rei as he slowly and steadily walked up behind her, each step softly rustling grass, almost silent if not for the wind carrying the subtle noise. Pausing near Liv's left side, he looked down hesitantly, almost as if asking permission, but before Liv could nod or tell him to leave, he was already setting up camp. Sitting himself down, one arm leisurely rested on his knee as the other supported him upright from behind, Rei looked out into the dark horizon.

"I've always preferred the stillness that lives during this time of night. That one moment when it feels as if every soul in the world is asleep, with thoughts drifting to their own dreams, living in their very own crafted world of slumber, and you truly feel alone in yours, too. It's a shame that Drex has to command the light to come back every morning."

"I prefer the sun." Liv retaliated back immediately, not even knowing why. She wasn't entirely mad at Rei, but knew that was exactly why he had been selected to check in on her, which still irritated her desire for solitude.

Rei tilted his head, giving Liv a disapproving glare that ultimately gave her amusement.

"I mean, I love when the sun returns," Liv sarcastically stated, saving her previously stubborn moment as she mockingly explained, "The serenity of watching it slowly rise above the horizon, the color that it brings, the 'dawn of a new day', some say..." She bumped into him playfully, rolling her eyes at her cheesiness. Liv paused, composing her thoughts before honestly expressing, "I admire the sunset, too–it is always so stunning. But I feel too many have the privilege to watch that beautiful act of nature, so for me, the sun's return is a quiet connection, one that when I watch it, feel as if it, too, is only me living in the world and enjoying it, and I wonder how I ever deserved to witness such a wonderful sight."

"And alas, the next night takes over the earth, and you get your undeserving view yet again." Rei added unenthused. "The world continues on."

Liv was expecting Rei to begin lecturing her on how the optimized time to return back to Puerdios, safely in the dark, was passing, but he didn't press nor direct the conversation back to security. They were truly just talking like friends for once, which Liv appreciated.

"You can't stay mad at them forever, you know." He stated bluntly.

Liv glared to her left, eyeing her companion with her eyebrows raised and challenging his statement.

"I'm not holding a grudge. And they left me, not you." Rei continued insistently, "But, you also disobeyed our command and not to follow them when they were only trying to lead you safety."

"It's not that." Liv muttered, quietly. "I'm just angry that everyone holds me to this higher podium because I'm Hayden's girlfriend. They feel like I need more protection–but my life shouldn't be more important than anyone else. And, I guess I'm just frustrated that Piper and Peyton think like that. To me, I'm just Liv, and all of your lives are equally important as mine."

"I volunteered to keep you safe, Liv. I'm a Security Elite, so it is my job to protect you, not the other way around." Rei grabbed Liv's hand. "And as thankful as I am for your help, it shames me that you had to sacrifice yourself to do it for me. And next time, I insist you leave Peyton, Piper, or me. If you were to have been captured or worse, exiled–it would be the utmost black mark on my duty and soul."

"But why me? Why can't Piper, or Peyton or you have the same value?" Liv pleaded, still not understanding where Rei was coming from with his request.

"Because we are not the fated ones to defeat the Darkness." Rei replied bleakly. "And yes, I was quickly observant to your natural connection to the Elements. Plus, you are the image mirror of your Father."

"You knew my father?" Liv asked, intrigued.

But Rei cut her off before she could anxiously ask another question.

"Not now, we're too exposed to discuss details." Rei explained. "But what it means is–it will be an honor to die in the effort to keep you safe, but a tragedy if I do not succeed in keeping you alive in the process."

Liv finally looked up the hill, feeling the weight of responsibility and burden heavy on her chest. She needed to remember that she wasn't in high school anymore, where petty ideas like grades or what you wore to homecoming mattered, but in a new world with different processes and structures that were on the brink of war, and she was a core target. She needed to keep her friends close and not push them away for the simple act of caring about her and the fate of their world.

Liv needed to stop being so self-involved and see the bigger picture. Peyton, Piper and Rei weren't just fighting for her, but for the existence of the deities as they believed it should be.

And so with a big sigh, Liv stood up and walked back up the hill.

Peyton looked up hopefully, nudging Piper as Liv approached them.

"I'm sorry I overreacted." Liv muttered apologetically. "And for not listening to you when you were only looking out for me."

"It's okay. I didn't have an Americano on hand to pacify the situation this time." Peyton joked, shyly.

"We're sorry, too–Liv. We're just under orders." Piper squeaked out, too.

"So, should we head back to Puerdios University now?" Liv asked softly, turning to Rei as he joined the girls again. "Are you feeling up to it, Rei?" She asked softly.

"Me?" Rei asked amusingly. "I've been fine this entire time." He smirked. "I just figured if I kept the three of you stranded in the middle of nowhere, you eventually would have to say *something* to one another."

Liv's eyes grew wide in amazement. "Rei, *a schemer*? You shock me! Who knew?" Turning to Piper and Peyton, Liv giggled as Piper and Peyton burst into laughter simultaneously.

"I told you he'd come around." Peyton joked, kissing Rei's cheek.

"Is the route clear back to Puerdios?" Piper asked cautiously, looking out above the flat plains.

"Who knows?" Peyton muttered blandly in response. "As soon we exit the perimeter of my invisible confinement and soundproof enchantment, we'll be in plain sight with no cover. And I doubt the Dark Gods have given up so easily. They're probably spread around the perimeter of the forest and hidden sporadically throughout the path back to Puerdios, as well."

"So what do we do?" Liv asked, staring trepidly at the seemingly still journey ahead.

"Exactly what I told you before we ran into Peyton and Piper." Rei explained nonchalantly.

"Just fly through them, head on?" Liv confirmed, eerily calm compared to how her insides were reacting to the suggestion.

"I'll go first with Piper, we'll test to see what extent of blood share we may run into." Rei turned back toward the forest, trying to spot any unexplainable movement, with no success. "You'll follow behind with Peyton. If we run into anything, Piper and I will divert away from the trail, and Liv–you must *promise* not to follow us if that is the case."

Liv clenched her jaw, not wanting to promise anything.

"I will make sure I stay safe." She responded, thinking there was some wiggle room without breaking her word.

Rei eyed her in disapproval, easily seeing through Liv's schematics.

"Promise you will obey Peyton no matter what." Rei commanded.

"And if I don't?" Liv challenged back.

Rei sighed. "Peyton, extend your security spell. Seems we'll be staying here for a little while longer, or at least until Liv chooses not to defy a Security Elite!" Rei intensely growled the final phrase, startling Liv.

Sensitive and understanding Rei was gone, intimidating and angry Rei was back.

"Liv can you please just agree that you'll do what Peyton says?" Piper whispered desperately. "Remember, we may think you are an Elite, but you are not quite one yet, and refusing to oblige one is a crime." She turned to Liv pleadingly, "And I promise I will stick to Rei and do my best to protect him. And he, me–it'll be like a buddy system?" She suggested encouragingly, turning to Rei for approval.

Liv paused, eyeing Piper's sincere Switzerland attempt. She wanted to get back to Puerdios, after all, and sooner would be better. Her stomach was already turning enough at the anticipation of their journey back, and her body was getting more jittery by the second.

"Did I mention that I summoned Hayden to meet us back at Puerdios, tonight?" Rei added, nonchalantly.

Hayden.

Hearing his name aloud brought to mind just how desperately Liv missed him, her insides ached from longing–she needed him. Everything would feel better once they were reunited, she would no longer feel so utterly lost.

With her dignity high and chin up, Liv conceded. "I promise under the stipulation that you all promise to keep your promise and protect each other, too."

"Promise!" Piper squealed, nodding to Liv. She looked as terrified for their upcoming journey as Liv felt.

Liv turned to Peyton and Rei for their agreement. They nodded, although reluctantly. Liv understood she was the priority, and hated putting her friends in more danger, but she was determined to get back to Puerdios and do whatever it took to be reunited with Hayden–he would be there, and that's all she needed.

To appease her guilty feeling of dependence, Liv added mindfully that Piper brought a good compromise to the table, too. And everyone wanted to get back to Puerdios, sooner than later. So, Liv would determinedly let nothing get in between her and her desired destination now, so her friends wouldn't *actually* need to risk their lives for her–she could fight her own battle.

She nodded to Peyton, quietly insisting, "Lead the way." Stubborn, and relieved to be at least heading toward safety (instead of further into danger), she watched Rei and Piper take off and prepared her wings for flight.

As soon as Rei and Piper crossed Peyton's security perimeter, black figures began swarming after them, flying over the mountain.

Peyton grabbed Liv's arm, barricading her attempt to step forward and fly to their rescue.

"Going alone will result in capture, I warn you. We will have our own battle to fight when we eventually cross, too. Save your strength."

Liv held her breath, trying to make out their figures, but she could only see a black hole ahead.

"They have an advantage of distance and they're skilled flyers. They may have distracted a handful of the Dark Gods but only that." Peyton spoke quietly, in a monotone voice and without her usual energy. Cautiously looking around their hill and beyond, Peyton concluded, "The bulk must be waiting for us, but possibly still remain around the perimeter of the forest."

Liv stayed quiet. Peyton turned around, quickly trying to analyze what could come, calculate a plan and discover any helpful hints to influence their next steps. With her jaw clenched and eyebrows furrowed, Peyton's intense focus pacified Liv as she awaited further instruction.

Soon, Peyton looked out ahead in the sky.

"We must fly. There may be four or five Dark Gods at the ready for attack, but they do not know where we'll emerge. Let's switch clothes quickly and I'll pin your hair up so it looks shorter, like mine."

"No. I will not let you!" Liv pleaded anxiously. "They'll want you just as much as me. There's no point. If we're going to be captured, we're going to be captured together."

"Liv—now is NOT the time to challenge me. And you just said we'd be captured together, anyways. So we're switching to divert them. Remember: you're the target. And they'll be even more inclined to attack you knowing that you're less experienced in combat. If you fall under, then we're both screwed, because I will not let you get captured alone."

"Well, I won't let you get captured, either." Liv stubbornly added.

"Great. Deal. So, let's go."

Liv quickly followed Peyton's orders, handing the chiffon skirt and gold bustier top to her friend and noticing how damaged and depleted her gown looked with all the unexpected mayhem it had encountered.

In return, Peyton gave Liv her own maroon sequined dress to put on. As she finished zipping up her new dress, Liv felt her hair being pulled and tugged as if a professional were styling her hair, but when she turned around, she only saw Peyton sliding into her heels, now donning an oversized messy bun to make her hair appear look much more like Liv's.

"Not my best disguise execution, but it'll have to do." Peyton mumbled decidedly. "Hopefully they won't recognize your wings, yet. We need to head North—you'll see a hillside and lake paired together, that's when you'll divert North West. Fast will be your friend, Liv. Don't look back. Are you ready? We need to go soon."

"Go ahead of me." Liv nodded ahead.

"Are you crazy?" Peyton asked, eyes wide. "I need to make sure I can see you safe to Puerdios University. Pun intended!"

"Exactly. If I'm to be you, and you me–I need to be behind 'Ollie.' Otherwise they'll see right through it."

Peyton grimaced, looking ahead in the distance as she contemplated her decision. Time was wasting and their status getting more dire by the second.

"Okay." Peyton agreed. "We leave together. And I'll pull in front when necessary."

"Great." Liv said sarcastically, turning to face their battlefield and extending her wings. "Count on 3."

Peyton followed suit. "1… 2… 3!"

Both girls took a running start to ascend into the air, forcefully beating their wings to build momentum and gain as much speed as they could before being caught visible in the open fire.

Liv felt herself passing through the vortex, a slight buzz shook her entire body with a sense of being encompassed in lighter air–the feeling of one's first emergence outside after being locked in a house during a storm. She knew she could easily pick up more speed with her lighter weight.

Moments after, whirling winds stirred behind her. Liv knew what storm was brewing in their dust. Still focusing on maintaining her speed, Liv willed her protection shield, not realizing just how exhausted she was until the burden of implementing a constant power came back into play. The feeling reminded her of moving into her dorm room at Oregon. Carrying the heavy boxes, bins and luggage was fine until her mother kindly asked to take a break for lunch (understood), but after they had relaxed and lay on her bed for an hour, returning to the task at bay seemed daunting. Liv had realized just how heavily she had exerted herself earlier as soon as she needed to get up and grab the next load of the car to unpack.

But this was different. She could survive a term without her favorite sweaters, but not her soul captured for eternity. So she kept fighting, and continued to remember that Gods didn't get tired, hoping to fuel her weakening body.

A small bolt hit her ankle, her first attack. Luckily it was weak–either her attackers were also feeling drained (unlikely) or they were too far away for a strong, targeted strike (more likely).

"Murum Electrica!" Peyton yelled, casting a force behind her. A large neon yellow wall began to grow, static and bright, looking like the sun itself. Liv turned back into the darkness, trying to adjust her pupils to the night again. She wondered just how intense of a bolt that substance would electrocute to anyone who touched it, but gathered it would be at minimum, a deathly amount.

"Are you okay?!" Peyton screamed, diving toward Liv.

"Fine!" Liv nodded with a thumb up–fine that the electric wall of death was behind them, and not an obstacle *they* needed to face.

As Liv looked ahead, her eyes adjusted back to the darkness, and she noticed only a slight movement in the distance. Only until the dark blurs were becoming exponentially closer, Liv worried about Piper and Rei. Hoping they were safely en route to Puerdios University, Liv tried to block out the other infinitely dark possibilities.

Sparks headed in her direction, luckily far enough for the moment for Liv to anticipate deflection, but soon she would need to go on offense, if she and Peyton were to get through the attack.

If only they could force them aside, nobody needed to get hurt, and Peyton and Liv wouldn't be any worse off than at the present.

"NOVIS!" Liv yelled, catching a spark coming too close for comfort, and sending it in the opposite direction.

Liv turned her head around, keeping their following predators and the distance between them in mind. They were getting closer, too. She flew over to Peyton, looking for some devised plan and blocking a couple more attacks along the way. Each power she forcefully re-sculpted hit her hard, and even when it hadn't actually hit her, the blow still felt like an ache she was fighting against, just from afar. But luckily each pain was only temporary, unlike an actual power attacking her because of her protection shield.

Peyton was amidst her own battle, blocking an unkindly higher amount of attacks. Her disguise seemed to be working; their attackers clearly thought she was Liv.

But, feeling responsible for Peyton's struggle, Liv started assisting her friend.

"I think we should force them out of our path... divert them East!" Liv shouted, in between blocking an attack, which had increased since approaching the targeted line of fire 'Fake Ollie.'

"I have an idea... that may eliminate both sides... of our new friends!" Peyton shouted, also in between a handful of blocking curses, "When... they approach... Novis! We'll need to..."

Peyton was struggling, Liv could tell, so she expanded her protective shield over to Peyton for an extra cushion, absorbing more of the blows as Peyton cast her deflective powers.

"Thanks!" Peyton shouted, blocking one more curse. "We'll need to turn sharply west!" Peyton blocked one more. "And since you said water was your specialty–can you send a fucking tidal wave to push them east?! You'll know when!"

A handful of powers came toward Peyton. Liv got hit in her arm, causing a momentary relapse of protection. Liv recovered her shield, but they were unable to fully deflect the influx of curses. One hit Peyton's arm, which immediately cut open as she screamed in agony. Luckily, it was not as harsh as it would have been without Liv's protective spell–Peyton probably would have blown up–so Liv knew that meant it was time to execute their plan. She just hoped Peyton had something good up her sleeve.

"Cover me! I'll cast now!" Peyton shouted.

Liv began deflecting all the powers she could, but in efforts of prioritizing Peyton's defense, she got blasted on her own left leg, causing a huge gash that split open down her thigh. It felt as if a steak knife had cut through her entire ligament. She screamed in pain as she spun, holding onto her leg as if it would fall off otherwise.

Trying to regain momentum, Liv looked up and noticed a blast of powers headed in Peyton's direction.

"Soli absorbuit!" Liv shrieked, commanding the dirt below to rise in a protective shield in front of Peyton. The soil from the ground formed a large sphere around her friend before being blasted suddenly upon impact from absorbing all the cast powers at once.

"West! Now!" Peyton commanded to Liv.

Liv knew it was time to prepare for her diversion as she sharply cut left, harshly turning her wings downward to catch the wind and steer west.

"MAGNES!" Peyton screamed, focusing on her powers as she followed Liv's suit and changed her direction. Liv saw a dusty grey sphere appear, attracting any dirt or object nearby to its core. It was getting bigger as it pulled more objects to it. Peyton had created a magnetized sphere; Liv felt a soft tug drawing her in, which she fought as she continued to head north.

"NOW!" Peyton screamed.

With the magnet already pulling wind toward its core, Liv focused on that instead of water, to help give her the momentum she'd need. She pushed the wind behind their approaching attackers, shoving them forward at her command. Peyton and she headed west, as Liv forced their enemies into Peyton's black hole, continuously growing stronger and larger by the moment. Luckily, once they were closer to the magnet, it slowly relieved Liv's combative struggle with the wind and the dark god's will.

"Let's go! That thing is going to explode!" Peyton yelled, looking back. Liv thought she could see a hint of a smirk appear on her friend's face, proud of the work they just accomplished.

Liv looked forward as they flew ahead.

She could scarcely see the collision behind, but heard many angry Dark Gods cursing as they crashed into each other, uncontrollably and repeatedly from the magnet sphere's pull.

Peyton flew closer to Liv. "We should be safe unless we run into any other undesirable strangers on our journey back. The sphere should keep retracting any offensive spells in our direction at least until we're far enough away and have distanced ourselves from sight." Peyton took a deep breath, looking more tired and weak now that immediate danger was behind them, at least for the time being.

Liv breathed a sigh of relief, as if it were the first one she had taken since they had departed an hour ago.

"How far away are we from Puerdios University?" Liv wondered.

"With our tiny detour, I would say a little under two hours." Peyton responded, wincing as she readjusted her arm, which was entirely covered in blood. She tried to hold on to her side hip without success due to Liv's decision to wear a constricted, corseted garment today.

Liv looked back at her leg, gagging at the sight, also covered in bloody gashed crosses throughout, with a long, deeply exposed cut down her thigh.

"Peyton, I think we should switch our outfits back. If we run into anyone, I can take the next round of blows–you did an amazing job protecting me with the last attackers, so I'm barely wounded. Plus, your dress is looser, it'll give you more breathing space."

"Liv, I don't know." Peyton whispered. She was clearly too weak to fight, which meant she was worse condition than Liv suspected.

"Up there by the tree. Let's land for a moment and quickly dress your wounds."

"Okay." Peyton sighed.

The girls landed on the hillside, and Peyton slowly sat herself against the tree trunk, wincing during the entire process.

"Let's see your waist." Liv demanded, willing the dress to remove itself from Peyton as she threw Peyton's original dress off herself, simultaneously.

It was as if Peyton's skin was red; she had so many cuts and scrapes everywhere with luckily some dried blood, but her torso was nowhere near to fully healing.

Liv ran over, ripping a line of tulle from her gold dress.

"Agua." She commanded, cleansing the wound as best as she could, and tried a new power with all her focus and will. "Kalo... plant sanitatem," she guessed, focusing on the expansive forest and valley, in hopes the earth would grant her command.

"It's okay, I'll heal... eventually." Peyton panted. "Removing that corset has already done wonders."

Suddenly, a batch of leaves flew into Liv's lap. She looked around in awe, wondering if it was just a coincidence or Mother Nature had actually listened to her request.

"You'll heal either way?" Liv confirmed, observing the deep cut. It didn't seem to look like it was getting better, only worse–but the large quantities of blood could have resulted from the water cleanse Liv attempted.

"Yeah, let's go." Peyton started getting up.

"Wait." Liv pushed her back, to stay in place. It was too easy, and that's what worried her. She grabbed some leaves, placing them strategically across the cut and pressing them in place gently by wrapping her tulle around Peyton's torso.

"Feel better or worse?" Liv asked, after securing the wound underneath her makeshift gauze.

Peyton took a deep sigh or relief. "Loads better. I no longer feel like my torso is slowly burning into ashes. What did you do? Don't tell me you have a long-lost ancestor who was also a Medicine Elite?"

Peyton's humor was back. That was almost a better sign than her word. Liv was so happy, she didn't even want to ask Peyton how she discovered her heritage secret, too.

Liv helped Peyton into her red dress; happy to see it did fit with more accommodation. She threw on her skirt, now at various lengths, and clipped the golden corset over her core, taking a small breath–it really was the worst outfit she could have chosen for today and felt even more terrible Peyton had to put up with it during one of her worse hours.

"Okay, we need to go." Peyton demanded, getting herself up without Liv's permission. She was still holding onto her side and wincing, but trying to at least disguise her pain more than before. That meant she was indeed, on the mend.

"Agreed." Liv propelled herself up to stand, and then collapsed.

TWENTY-FOUR

"Shit."

"Are you okay!?" Peyton leaned over Liv, curious.

"I think something's up with my leg, but I didn't realize how bad it was until now–it just collapsed."

"Can you get up?"

"Yeah. I was just in shock at the unexpected pain. I think the fall hurt even more than the initial wound." Liv shrugged, holding onto Peyton's extended hand for leverage as she tried again, standing up with the weight on her left leg, instead of the injured right.

"We're a mess." Peyton chuckled, after successfully helping her friend up. The sun was rising.

"Can barely stand, look like we rolled around in dirt. Just a typical weekend adventure." Liv smiled in return, trying to put some more weight to her right side. "It's like we brunched… only without the 'brunch' part."

"Next weekend, I demand mimosas!" Peyton pleaded. "At least give me a valid reason to look like I napped in a bush!"

Liv exploded with laughter. Whether it was exhaustion, relief, or simply forgetting what it felt like to smile, she couldn't help it.

"Maybe the Dark Gods' hit us with shots of alcohol," she hypothesized. "I certainly feel elated."

"Always makes for a better flight." Peyton confirmed, looking out into the sunrise horizon. "Come on. Let's go. Luckily you don't need your leg to fly."

Liv nodded, growing her wings and getting ready for flight.

The remaining distance was much more enjoyable. Although still in danger and making great speed, Liv felt more relaxed–whether it was the reunion of morning light and new beginnings, or knowing at the moment they were no longer near immediate threat. Liv could breathe and absorb the beauty of the sun welcoming its light to be shared across the sparkling ocean in view. Just the dew and brisk chill of an early morning was comforting, knowing warmth was on its way. It was a different world from the one she lived through last night. A new day was always the most promising sight to instill hope once again.

As Peyton predicted, after two hours of enjoying the sunrise and various colorations to the valley they flew over, the girls could finally see the medieval castle glisten in the horizon.

Liv felt Hayden's presence growing stronger as they approached. She always felt him, whether faint or literal, and questioned if it were a deity trait or a connection truly unique to them. The sight of Puerdios confirmed the increase in her abstract ability to identify his location in relation to her as they approached. And Liv could tell that he was waiting for her, anxiously.

They flew over the gates, Peyton signaling with an accepted motion by security to let them through. Liv thought of the password, "Homer," upon crossing and from remembering Rei's previous instruction, desperately wishing that he and Piper were alight.

It didn't take long for Liv to spot Hayden in the plaza waiting for her. She landed, fighting her painful limp to run right into his arms. He was the perfect landing support, easily stopping her descending momentum with his sturdy strength by holding her into a long embrace.

Happiness, relief, worry and all of Liv's emotions came to surface, as she cried with joy at their reunion.

"Are you okay?" Hayden whispered, quickly looking at Liv's body for any immediate wounds needing care. "What happened to your leg?"

"I don't know. I think the cut's too deep." Liv mumbled, going back in for another hug and his support. She wanted to hide in his arms. Now that she no longer required being strong, Liv felt weak. She has used up all of her strength for the day, maybe the year.

Hayden remained silent, letting Liv stay in his arms and absorb his strength for a moment longer.

She knew she needed to think like a God, that her functionality did not depend on energy, strength or any mortal compass of exhaustion, but with her leg throbbing in pain and feeling so lost and scared for too long, she just needed a second of humanity. Liv wanted to feel like herself until she rebuilt and could focus on conquering the next challenge ahead.

"Where's Peyton, is she okay?" Liv lifted her head, only enough to look around and assure her friend's comfort. Liv sighed in relief at the sight of Rei holding Peyton at a distance away. She spotted King Rowan and Silas behind the two, but one person was missing.

"Where's Piper?" Liv came alive, fully alert once again and pulled away from Hayden, looking around for her friend, protectively and anxiously.

"She will be okay." Hayden quickly confirmed. "We took her to my loft immediately–my mother and Joss are tending her now. A strong current of Dark Gods attacked her and Rei."

"We were able to deter most of them, too." Rei angrily sneered, more at himself than to everyone else. "I'm sorry that some slipped through to you both." He eyed Peyton's arm and shook his head, trying not to disturb the gentle support he gave as Peyton still clung to her side.

"You did the best you could." Peyton nodded assuringly.

"We should join the Queen, Princess and your friend." Silas encouraged, looking around suspiciously. "Anyone can hear us out here."

"Agreed, good call Silas." King Rowan nodded, "Let's go."

Hayden picked Liv up gently as if she were cotton.

Rei started helping Peyton walk, but both, equally injured, winced in silent pain at the process.

King Rowan turned immediately, "Peyton, do you need assistance?"

"You're too kind, but I can manage. Thank you, your Highness." Peyton smiled in return, pausing in movement.

"Nonsense. Tonight, I'm simply a concerned parent. Not your King." King Rowan softly lifted Peyton, relieving Rei, who instantly took a deep breath after no longer being a support system. As he followed, Liv saw he was still limping–he could barely stand himself.

"Son, here." Silas also took quick notice, putting Rei's arm around his shoulder.

Hayden slowed his pace, letting Rei and his father pass ahead as they entered the castle's corridor. Liv understood, Hayden wanted to take advantage of a moment alone before joining everyone in his room.

"I'm so glad you're okay, Ollie." Hayden mumbled, in relief, agony and pain. "How do I keep failing at keeping you safe?" He looked at her, helpless.

Liv grabbed his face, bringing his lips to hers. There was nothing to forgive.

"You don't need to always worry about me, Hayden." Liv started. "I can take care of myself."

"Why didn't you call for me?" Hayden persisted, still hurt, lost and desperately looking for an answer in Liv's bright blue eyes.

"You have enough on your plate, and I was with a Security Elite." Liv calmly combated back.

"But you still could have alerted me." Hayden furrowed his brows, "At least to let me know you were okay, that's the whole point of the Constellation, Ollie."

"But we *weren't* okay." Liv retorted, rhetorically asking, "And then what, Hayden? You would have tried to find me–putting you in more danger than Rei, Peyton, Piper and I combined. That's what the Dark Gods want, Hayden–they want to get to you through me. And I refuse to put you in that much danger voluntarily at my expense."

Hayden remained silent. Liv couldn't help chuckle at her boyfriend's stubbornness.

"–Plus, I'm strong, Hayden, and getting more powerful every day." Liv added encouraging, trying to pacify the last brutally honest statement.

"But if anything happened to you, Liv...." Hayden broke, taking a deep gasp and gently putting his forehead to hers, his eyes closed and relief flooding his body at their safe reunion.

"And same with you, Hayden." Liv whispered back, taking a deep breath as she added, "But you have to remember, I chose to go on this crazy adventure. So it's in no way your fault and you need to stop blaming yourself for every conundrum I get myself into."

Hayden chuckled. Liv radiated to hear his infectious smile come back.

"Crazy adventure?" Hayden mimicked sarcastically, raising his head and eyebrow as he questioned, "Are you talking about this weekend or your choice to be with me?"

"Both, I guess." Liv giggled back. "But does it matter? Either way, I'll keep choosing it, as long as it means I get to be with you. So you can take my safety off your list of responsibilities–you simply can't control me and you have enough to worry about as it is."

Hayden smiled adoringly at the beautiful soul he carried. "But, that's the thing, Ollie. I'll always worry about you. That's the beauty of love." Hayden laughed, starting for his loft as he gently flopped another kiss on her forehead. "And worth every minute."

By the time Hayden and Liv returned to his apartment, Peyton and Rei seemed to have already recovered as they energetically recounted their quest: how Liv found the coin and their dangerous escapade back to Puerdios University. Piper lay on the couch, smiling with her eyes closed and holding an ice pack to her head.

"... That's when Piper selflessly took the entire lightning strike so I could missile the Dark Gods halfway across the globe." Rei added, nodding to Piper in salute. "She went unconscious, as you all know, so I flew her back to Puerdios. So, aside from a lack of company to chat with on the way back, it was relatively uneventful from there."

"Liv, do you still have the coin you found at Mt. Lykaoin?" King Rowan asked gently, as Hayden lowered Liv onto his couch and sat protectively next to her. Liv smiled at the fact Hayden had refused to lose touch with her since their reunion in the courtyard.

"Yeah, it should be… here." She grabbed her necklace, relieved to feel the cold coin emerge at her request, and handed it to Hayden.

"Tell them how you blasted across the mountain and awakened Lykaoin's reincarnation." Piper bluntly added, not moving as she continued to look at the ceiling, still blindfolded with her ice patch.

"Well, yes–but not intentionally of course." Liv admitted, embarrassed. "It was sort of the beginning to our challenging journey back."

"That's the understatement of this millennium." Piper muttered across the room.

Liv looked at Piper in shock.

"Sorry," Joss whispered to the room, "Forgot to mention we gave her some strong sedatives earlier to help relieve the pain, so she's pretty heavily medicated at the moment."

"Why did you send us to Mt. Lykaoin in the first place?" Liv asked, absorbing Piper's newfound influenced confidence.

"You?" Hayden jokingly asked, and continued with the clarification, "We asked *Rei and Peyton* to visit Mt. Lykaoin."

Liv glared at her smug boyfriend.

King Rowan interjected, "My son and I went to the Pillar of Humanities to request they claim loyalty to the Pure Gods, and found that Arlo had visited earlier and invited the Elite to join the Dark Gods with a seemingly very persuasive case. Although the Humanity Elite was not yet fully convinced where his allegiance lay, he gave Hayden and I the same riddle to solve as he challenged Arlo to prove where their loyalty should go."

"Find what humanity has lost." Hayden explained, "Whoever God solves the riddle first, will receive his pledge."

"So we sent Silas to Ithaca, asked Peyton and Rei to visit Mt. Lykaoin, and Hayden and I visited Pompeii." King Rowan added.

"I was on my way to Athens when I heard the message of your peril." Silas explained, "So came here directly instead."

"But, we may be a step ahead now, if what Liv found is truly a clue to Virgil's riddle." Hayden said energetically.

"Wait, like Virgil of The Aenaid?" Liv automatically interjected, eyes wide.

She only received uninterested nods in return.

"As in, the poet of one of the most famous Epic poetries was actually a God? Er–I mean–*is*?" She turned to Hayden, shaking her head in shock and trying to wrap her head around this new discovery.

"He started documenting our human encounters before the restructure. I'll tell you all about him later." Hayden offered, and then insisted, "But back to Mt. Lykaoin…"

Liv nodded, understanding that she needed to rein in her focus for the task at hand, but one piece of the puzzle didn't yet make sense.

"But, why Mt. Lykaoin?" Liv asked, genuinely confused and still trying to lay out the clues she had learned so far so she could help figure out if what happened with the coin was actually credible. "Pompeii, Ithica, Athens–those are all very common geographical areas within human history. What made you think of Mt. Lykaoin?"

"Well, that was Hayden's idea." King Rowan explained, looking at his son.

Hayden took over. "I figured with Arlo's head start, he probably had started with the obvious locations–and we still needed coverage there, in case he missed a clue, but if there was to be any chance we could find a clue before he did, we needed to gamble on lesser-known locations as we looked at the bigger places simultaneously. Really, it was luck from there. I remembered Professor Montagnes mention the story of Lykaoin wickedly sacrificing a human child on Zeus' altar… from one of the very few Humanities classes I attended this year."

"Another understatement of the century." Piper muttered. "And I told you that history, *not* Professor Montagnes, when I helped you with your midterm. Next time tell me and I can give you the relative facts you need, instead of sending us on a death mission based on luck."

"At least her memory seems to be functioning?" Joss added encouragingly before snorting into laughter.

Liv wasn't smiling, but recollecting her own memory of interacting with the coin instead. "When I found the coin, there was a blast of lightning when I grabbed it. Maybe there's a connection there?" She nodded to the coin, now static in Hayden's hand.

"The coin does have an engraving of Zeus." Hayden confirmed, handing the coin over to his father for further inspection.

"Indeed, it does." King Rowan confirmed. "And Mt. Lykaoin is supposedly where Zeus was born, but Zeus as a clue doesn't narrow our search much, it may possibly expand it more."

"And every day, more seem to succumb to Arlo's wrath." Silas perilously added, turning to Liv with a softer tone to ask, "Are you sure you didn't see or witness anything else?"

"Afraid not." Liv shook her head, trying to re-live the beginning of her terror-filled night. "The bolt blasted me across Mt. Lykaoin, loudly–giving away our location to the approaching Dark Gods and thus, beginning our escape."

"There was no more time to search the premise further." Rei confirmed, backing up Liv's case.

"Is there any way to identify who has joined the Dark God's Army?" Liv whispered, chills running up her spine at the thought of her suggestion, "Could we not arrest them, to diminish the Dark Gods cause? At least in numbers?"

"I recognized a few–like Aria and Jaxon of the Arts Pillar and Benjamyn from Agriculture," Rei muttered to his father, who looked shocked at the names.

"But there's no proof." Hayden stated.

"Exactly." Rei shrugged, wincing. "Just to note for those we can no longer trust."

"So what can we do?" Daphne finally spoke, cold and crisp, daring but kind. Her eyes sparkled through her anxiously calm tone. Years of wisdom radiated out of her few words; she did not exist on speculation, but of a millennium of action and observance.

"For now, we need to ensure the majority of the Pillars stay in favor of the Pure Gods, and that our Pure Elites do not lose control of their subjects." King Rowan confirmed bluntly.

Hayden turned cautiously to Liv, explaining, "We run a democracy system, if enough pillars were to turn Dark, then we could be reinstated. Or, at least, the Dark Gods could build an army large enough to overtake the Pure God rule."

"Win by eliminating the majority vote and forcing it to be the minority." Liv nodded, understanding just how delicate the Deity politics were, as they very much mirrored the structure her world's government dealt with since the beginning of time.

"And you're sure the Dark Gods heard the blast?" King Rowan asked Rei.

"Peyton and I heard it easily from the other side of the mountain." Rei confirmed.

"And it wasn't quiet for us with our distance, either." Peyton added.

"If that is the case, Puerdios University is no longer safe. They will report to Arlo, who will come here soon and try to retrieve what you discovered, through force or whatever means it may take."

Daphne stood up, looking at Liv and Hayden sorrowfully. "It has begun." She turned to King Rowan, whispering, "I feared this would happen, but had hoped we would have more time…"

King Rowan grabbed her hands, pleading silence as he looked into her eyes with sadness. "Whatever is to happen–we must ensure we protect Liv and Hayden."

"Father," Hayden jumped up defensively, staring at his parents, "That is unnecessary. Do not ask our people to sacrifice themselves for us."

"Son, we know you can fend for yourself, but if the prophecy is true," King Rowan turned back to Hayden, making eye contact with him and then

Liv, "Then you two are our only hope–I will gladly sacrifice myself if needed to keep you two alive."

"No, I will not ask of it!" Hayden battled.

"Not for discussion." King Rowan nodded toward to Silas, heading toward Hayden's door to exit, Daphne and Jocelyn magnets to his lead.

"Silas–command more guards to the grounds immediately, time is of the essence." He led Jocelyn and Daphne outside, pausing before he added, "You know how to summon me, Hayden. Alert Silas and me immediately if anything goes amiss," before leaving with Silas and slamming the door behind.

TWENTY-FIVE

Shortly after Hayden's family and Silas departed, Peyton and Rei helped Piper return to her room, leaving Liv and Hayden alone to enjoy the rest of their Sunday afternoon.

After Hayden walked their friends out and whispered something to Rei that Liv couldn't hear, he shut the door with a big sigh and turned to Liv.

"Would you like some tea?" He asked, still holding the door closed.

"Got anything stronger?" Liv teased back.

"Hot toddy it is." Hayden slightly grinned, then paused, taking another breath before heading toward the kitchen.

He was subtly limping; and with his terse, concentrated glare toward the kitchen, Liv knew he was trying to hide it.

Liv figured it wasn't the time to press, he would tell her what happened when he wanted to, so she let it slide for the time being. Instead, she watched as he concentrated on squeezing a freshly cut lemon, and then carefully measured the Pendleton whiskey to pour into her mug. His sexy lip was naturally pouting, asking to be kissed.

Liv bit her lip, as she glared down his front side, wanting him to take off his chunky grey knitted crewneck sweater.

As if Hayden knew her lustful gaze was upon him, he smiled, looking up at Liv.

"I never realized you could get so excited about Pendleton Whiskey." He smirked.

"Something like that." Liv smiled coyly, gazing at his firm, muscular backside while Hayden turned to grab the steaming water from the whistling pot.

Finally, walking over with both mugs, Hayden's limp was even more noticeable. Liv's concern was beginning to grow when he held his breath to extend his arm and hand her the mug.

Watching Hayden slyly wince as he cautiously sat down on the couch next to Liv was the last straw; he was hiding his apparently excruciating pain and Liv needed to know why.

"You've heard all about my adventures this weekend, why don't you tell me about yours?" Liv demurely asked, nonchalantly taking a sip from her hot totty.

"Nowhere near as exciting as your past 24 hours." Hayden muttered, following Liv's lead and taking a sip from his drink.

"Okay, then how did you hurt yourself?" Liv responded bluntly.

Hayden glared at her, taking another sip of his tea, before putting it down and wincing in the process. "I was trying not to alarm everyone earlier."

"How noble." Liv breathed, exhausted and eager to cut to the chase. "What happened?"

"Arlo had his followers on the perimeter of the Humanities Pillar, expecting our arrival. So we were attacked before crossing the borders to sanctuary."

"Where did you get hit, and why didn't you say anything!?" Liv moved forward, reaching toward Hayden to begin her thorough search, but he caught her hand mid-way, cursing from pain in the process.

"I'm the Prince of Gods, Ollie. I'm not allowed to show weakness." Hayden explained. "It's one thing for an Elite to get wounded by the Dark Gods, but I'm the Pure Gods and the Elites' leader. We're the prophecy to defeat them, and if I can't protect myself against the Dark Gods, then who will follow our reign?"

"But you were among your family, your closest friends, Hayden–you cannot fight this alone, you need to let us in." Liv pressed.

"I let you in. But just think–Mother, Joss, Peyton, Rei, Silas–they were all in a state of panic tonight, even if only under the surface. And Piper too, if it weren't for the heavy dosage of drugs she was on. The Dark Gods were able to hurt all four Pure Gods on a mission together, not to mention a Security Elite with another top ranked Security Guard in the mix. Your entire group, badly injured–and that wasn't even a proper battle! We were just trying to gain the loyalty for a neutral pillar. If I showed injury under the same premise–that does not rest for a strong case against defeating the Dark Gods. They may be family, but the one thing my father taught me is that nobody can doubt our ability to accomplish this, Ollie–everybody needs to have hope. One word of doubt can ignite like a fire in a dry forest. And I won't allow it to happen, not under my rule."

"Okay, Winston Churchill. Point taken. Show me the battle wound."

Hayden scowled, wincing as he attempted to remove his sweater.

Liv gasped as she saw his skin underneath. Quickly lunging forward to help him gently remove his clothing, she shuddered at his burnt skin, raw and broken.

"It goes down through my leg." Hayden muttered, more closely examining the extent of his burns, grimacing at every subtle movement his left side encountered. "But it's improved since I've arrived." He added, bleakly.

"Kalo glacies." Liv commanded, willing ice to come in a large zip-lock bag from her mind.

Successfully receiving her medicinal goods in hand, Liv looked upstairs, hesitantly turning back to Hayden.

"Let me take off your pants. Can you get to your room?"

"In another circumstance, I'd request you repeat that phrase." Hayden smirked, standing up, then cringing immediately at his legs extending. "On second thought, maybe I'll resume my humor at another time."

"In another circumstance." Liv smiled, unbuttoning his pants, and then sadly observed his torn up leg–red, black and blistering–scarred and looking like fury itself. She sighed, refusing to let her mind go to her weaker side, and shifted her weight to her good leg as she stood up beside him, holding the bag of ice in her hand.

"Let's go." She nodded to the staircase, hopping behind him as she followed Hayden to his bedroom.

"Any chance you can summon anything stronger than ice?" Hayden inquired, scowling with each step up the stair. "I'd love a dose of whatever Piper was on tonight."

"I'll see what I can do." Liv painfully replied, although trying to sound upbeat. She hated seeing Hayden hurt, again. "Why is it that whenever you leave me, you come back in pieces?" Liv joked; gently putting her hand on his less destroyed side for support as she joined him on the second floor.

"Maybe I like my nurse." Hayden grinned, pausing for a moment to lean in and kiss Liv as a thank you.

Liv tried to ignore his soft wince from the romantic gesture and smile back positively, but now done with the stairs, Hayden's eyes sparkled a little brighter than before.

"So, about that another circumstance…"

Liv rolled her eyes.

"Let's work on getting both of ourselves back to one piece, first."

Witnessing Liv and Hayden's state as they both lay in bed, one would never believe they were immortal, all-powerful Gods.

Hayden was face down, sprawled out on top of his covers and naked, while Liv gently iced his burns with cold cloths, sitting next to him with her leg wrapped up in gauze and icing her sprained ankle, too.

She could only chuckle at the sight, now thankful to see Hayden's burns no longer blistering with wrath.

"Do you think all we accomplished was worth this?" Liv asked aloud. "All for a coin?"

"If wealth is what humanity has lost, then yes." Hayden joked.

"That's what I don't get. If the riddle is to find what humankind has lost, wouldn't we need to find a more abstract interpretation of some belief or value?"

"Maybe the coin represents something less obvious." Hayden suggested, "The location, for example, related to a history where the human race defied the Gods."

"So perhaps the next place we look should involve Zeus again, and another history of humans interacting with Gods where they either disappointed or defied them in some way–possibly where they challenged Zeus, perhaps?"

Hayden's head bounced up from the pillow, "I think you're right. It must be something with mortals interacting with Zeus–that would explain the coin…" He lowered his head back against the pillow, his mind running. "And possibly a connection to where we should look next."

"Any ideas?" Liv adjusted the icepack on her ankle and added more healing herbs to her boyfriend as she adjusted his bandages.

"A couple." Hayden shrugged. "I vaguely remember Zeus being angered by the King once at the City of Elis–we'll need to go to the library tomorrow to do more research."

Liv sat up. "Shouldn't we go tonight?"

Hayden turned his toward her, eyebrows raised in confusion.

"We need to rest, Ollie. At least for the night."

"But Arlo's army could already be at Elis!" Liv argued.

"Ollie, we know Arlo's after us–so I don't believe leaving Puerdios University is a good idea when we can barely leave my bed." He chuckled, as he turned back, sighing in silence as he fought the pain. "We must plan accordingly to make sure it's safe–or even the right location to risk transit."

"So, let's go to the library now. Come up with more concrete ideas, a strategy. Then we'll be prepared once we can make the trek."

"Today, we were able to throw off his spies by sending you, Rei and Peyton–but now they'll know you're working directly with us. Arlo will have Puerdios surrounded, trying to barricade us. Besides, Arlo doesn't have the first clue, so we have some advantage with time to figure it out.

And for the moment, I'm also not sure I could handle another adventure quite yet." Hayden winced as he turned over to sit himself up on the bed, summoning a bag of ice in his direction to ice his waist.

"Can't you use your power to eliminate the pain?" Liv asked, concerned.

"Sometimes it's nice to just mend it the traditional way every once in a while." Hayden explained, taking a deep breath, "Nothing ice can't fix."

The next morning, Live woke up, realizing she and Hayden fell asleep holding hands. He was still sleeping, but Liv noticed his burn marks were now only faded bruises, almost obsolete. Her leg still ached, but she was also impressed by her already miraculous recovery, now only seeing scratches down her leg.

She quietly got up and headed to the kitchen to make omelets. For the time being, nutrition was her priority – she and Hayden hadn't eaten since Saturday morning, and it was now Monday.

Then, Liv laughed to herself when she remembered that to Gods, nutrition was not actually a thing to be concerned about. But at least breakfast was comforting, and that's really what she wanted to feel: safe, secure and at ease. And that could always be found in America's favorite meal.

After chopping up her favorite ingredients (bell peppers, onion, ham, avocado) and Hayden's (sausage, mushrooms and tomatoes), Liv grilled the eggs and added the mix of their favorite toppings into the pan. All while brewing her favorite roast, the smell filled the kitchen, energizing Liv with an intoxicating scent. Caffeine: another human must-have that she was not so willing to give up just yet.

As soon as she poured her first cup of coffee, she smiled as she heard slight footsteps upstairs.

"Yum. What are you making? Smells delicious."

Liv looked up to find Hayden descending the stairs.

"Thank-you-omelets." Liv replied, smiling as she flipped the egg to a new side.

"Thank-you-omelets?" Hayden approached Liv, pulling her in for a hug and giving her a kiss on the cheek before heading to the coffeepot.

"Yes. They're the utmost delicious." Liv grinned, walking over the now completed omelets to the counter. She heard Hayden grimace and turned to find him reaching for a coffee mug.

"Hold on–sit." Liv gently grabbed her boyfriend and led him to the barstool, before willing the mug herself and pouring him a cup of coffee. Handing it over, she commanded, "Now don't move. Enjoy. Relax." She ended with a smile as she slid the plate of eggs in front of him.

Confused, but not in the mood to challenge Liv with his aching body, Hayden took an obedient bite as Liv joined him on the barstool next to him.

"Thank you for my wings." Liv held onto her necklace, the soft feathery back touching against her thumb. "They're beautiful and perfect."

Hayden looked surprised, but not shocked as it came to fruition. "I'm glad you like them. Although sad I missed seeing your reaction to them. How did you do on your first flight?"

"I'm actually quite fast." Liv whispered proudly, then remembered the bump on her head, as it instinctively ached to remind her of its existence. "But not so good with turns or direction."

"I'm sure you're a natural. You survived your first very dangerous encounter with the Dark Gods, so that's all I can ask. They served you well." Hayden took another bite.

"So, Elis. Did you think about it any further?" Liv pushed, wondering what the next steps could be.

"I have, and I think I need Piper–if her medications have worn off by now." Hayden joked, chuckling, but inconsequently hurting Liv, a little.

"Piper?" Liv asked casually, even if internally her heart was racing. Why was she heated on the inside with insecurity and adrenaline? Hadn't she found the clue? Wasn't she helpful enough?

Wasn't *she* enough?

The last thought sent an ache through her soul. But she was so focused on her internal insecurities, that Liv didn't catch what Hayden had started explaining, oblivious to her unfocused facial expression.

"... To bring every book on Zeus she can think of–then we can try to find any legends or histories that involve him and mortal disobedience to either confirm my inclination of Elis..."

Hayden paused, finally catching Liv's blank face.

"Ollie–do you need more coffee? You look out of it."

Liv snapped out of her trance.

"Oh, sorry. Yeah, you're right." She shook her head, grabbing her cup of coffee to take a diligent sip. "Continue." Liv added lightheartedly, immediately wiping away Hayden's concerned glare.

"Well, if it's not Elis then we can at least research other options to guide us in the right direction for the next location to visit. Who knows, maybe she'll have some ideas off the top of her head before class."

"Of course." Liv felt ashamed for her previous doubts, but it was true–Piper was the brain of her friends. How long would it take Liv to learn a lifetime's worth of the God's histories and worldly culture? She felt so helpless, which she had never experienced before, and did not like at all.

Piper showed up shortly after Hayden summoned her, to Liv's surprise, bringing with her a large stack of books as Hayden had requested.

As she set the dozen books on the table, Piper immediately asked how Liv and Hayden were doing, profusely apologizing for whatever she had said the night before.

"I have no idea what your family gave me, but once Peyton put me to bed, I didn't move until sunrise!" She squeaked, blushing as she shook her head in embarrassment and naturally dove into a book to cover her own social deficiencies.

Hayden kindly chuckled. "Don't worry about it–sassy Piper was actually quite refreshing. Are you feeling better?" He asked sincerely, putting their guest at ease.

"Much. Thank you. So what can I help you with?" She asked in a high-pitched, nervous tone and anxiously gulped.

Hayden explained his theory about the city of Elis to Piper as Liv poured herself another cup of coffee and asked if anyone wanted anything before cleaning up the kitchen.

"It's definitely a good starting point, but I agree we should try to source all the facts before attempting another visit to a location outside of school parameters." Piper offered, automatically grabbing her head to soothe the pain inflicted from the night before.

"Do you need ice?" Liv offered, sliding into a chair next to her friend.

"No, I'm fine," Piper shook her head. "But thank you, Liv–why don't you start with *History of Ancient Greece*? Hayden you can tackle *Government in the Pure Rule* and I'll refresh my memory on these books in the meantime."

An hour later, Liv was almost completed with her current book, after noting various locations and flagging any mortal interaction tales, but remained solemn to find no account of the City of Elis in her set of textbooks. Her brain felt as if it could no longer retain or comprehend any more information–they had gone through at least 25 books on Zeus, and another handful where he was in only a section or received a bleak mention.

"Well, what about the other options?" Piper asked, speculating curiously at all of their post it tags and contemplating new theories or possibilities throughout their mini-Zeus library scattered throughout the table.

Hayden shook his head. "None of them feel right–not like my inkling toward the city of Elis."

"Well, where is this city? Is it far? If you feel like it's the place, it can't hurt for us to go there." Liv insisted.

"It's in Western Peloponnese." Hayden sighed, exasperated as he looked at the books, disappointed.

"Like the Peloponnesian wars?" Liv asked, remembering Rei's Trojan War mention during the Symposium that had sparked her additional reading of The Odyssey during the prior weekend.

"That never actually happened. It's just a myth, made up by the mortals. That's one thing the race of humanity lost–their sense of truth." Hayden lazily explained.

Liv was a little hurt, only because he was insulting her people–well, she guessed they weren't her kind anymore, but her mom was still mortal. Before she could open her mouth to defend her family and friends, Piper interjected.

"That's it!" Piper jumped up. "Of course–how could we have not put that together before?"

Liv and Hayden looked at her curiously. Only Piper's brain would have the fuel capacity to solve a puzzle after getting knocked out in the skull and a full morning of studying.

"Don't you get it?" She squeaked, "We're solving for the Humanities Pillar–of what the human race lost–so we have to think like the Humanities pillar. Of course! We need to be reading Zeus histories documented by the human race–not our kind!"

Excitedly, Piper ran to the window, summoning a handful of more books, but nothing compared to the extent of the collection she originally brought.

"Makes sense why I'd remember the story," Hayden explained to Liv. "Since I was inbred with mortal schooling." Hayden shrugged, adding, "I always had a keen interest in Greek mythology since it was the only thing I could remotely relate to from a historical standpoint."

"There aren't as many textbooks on campus, but we can start here." Piper ran back with her tiny collection of books and assigned one to each.

Liv glanced at her book, *Introduction to Greek Mythology*, and looked up puzzled.

Zeus would be mentioned in this book, he was like one of the few massively recognized Gods in her world, but the chance Elis would be mentioned, too? Slim to none. She had never heard of the place until last night. Liv sighed, turning to the back of the book to the index page, searching E for the city to be listed, when she gasped.

Elis, 74

"It's in here!" Liv exclaimed, quickly turning the pages to find the mention. She scanned the page with her finger, quickly glancing over for the gold world.

"The king of a city in Elis claimed to be Zeus himself, imitating the lightning by hurling torches into the sky, and making thunder by dragging bronze kettles behind his chariot. Zeus was furious with King Salmoneus, so took his lethal thunderbolt and wiped out both Salmoneus and his people."

Liv looked up, happy to see excitement on both Piper and Hayden's face–this was what they had been looking for, but she was a little surprised at how brutal a punishment those innocent of his kingdom had to endure, so she continued.

"This was a case where Zeus stepped in to vindicate his own personal honor. But on another occasion, in an altogether more complex myth, Zeus intervened to maintain the general integrity of the divide between gods and humans. Apollo's son, Asklepios, was a great healer–but one day took his medicinal prowess too far, by raising a mortal corpse to life. Zeus' thunderbolt restored the status quo, blasting the doctor and patient simultaneously. According to myth, Apollo retaliated by killing the Cyclopes, who made the lethal thunderbolt for Zeus, angered for his son being sent to the Underworld without consent…"

Liv looked up, shocked. "Is this also false?" She asked, hoping it was. What sad, vindictive stories to occur, all done by her apparent ancestor, who only found a solution in more destruction and terror.

Piper looked up somberly. "That one sadly is more true than not. But Apollo only killed one Cyclop–not all of them?" She added, offering a silver lining–although a weak one.

Hayden looked saddened, too. "That took place in Epidauros–there is an alter at the Asklepios theatre for Asklepios for remembrance. The Gods aren't perfect, Liv–as you are witnessing now, we don't always agree on a moral compass. And it's bad enough without mortals involved, and will only get worse if they do." He sighed, "But I don't think Asklepios could be the location. It's too intertwined with other deities and the parallel with Elis is too connected–it has to be the place we go next."

"I agree." Piper added, looking to Liv next.

Liv nodded her head.

"Then it's settled. I'll summon Rei and Peyton to plan our route. You two should get to class, and keep researching during any breaks, just in case."

"Wait–are you insinuating that we're not going?" Liv asked, shocked.

"It's too dangerous, Ollie." Hayden insisted.

"No." Liv countered back. "We went with Peyton and Rei last time and were the ones who found the clue, *and we* just helped solved the riddle–where would you be without us?"

"We're supposed to keep you safe at all costs, you heard my father last night." Hayden calmly explained, but Liv could feel his agitation growing.

"He said to keep both of us safe, Hayden. So are you going to stay back with me as well, so Piper can babysit us?" Liv stood up before Hayden could interject, "And, for the record–your *father* also said the fate of the Gods rests in our hands. *Ours.* Not yours. So I'm coming Hayden, whether you like it or not."

Liv heard a thunderstorm raging outside, and she was proud of its impact, helping make her case even the more.

"You should really learn how to control that power, Ollie." Hayden responded, not challenging her demand, to Liv's surprise. "You don't want Kai catching on to what you are capable of."

"What I am capable of is so much more than he could ever imagine, Hayden. And you best remember that, too. So let the thunder roll, that's only the beginning of my storm." Liv declared, internally happy to have won the argument, for once. There was no way she would ever let Hayden into danger without her there to protect him, again. They were a team, and if they didn't stick together, it had already been proven–they could never survive apart.

"Piper, let's go to Warfare & Defense class. We need to prep for our next excursion." Liv commanded, leaving Hayden's loft with her head held high. "And I expect to see you there, *Professor*," she added, scornfully.

And without looking back, Liv followed Piper out, slamming the door behind her and praying to all the Gods that she be given the wrath for her fury to fight this battle ahead.

After a long day of class, Piper, Rei and Peyton joined Hayden and Liv at Hayden's loft; it was decided to head to Elis the following evening. Peyton and Rei were in charge of figuring out an exit strategy from Puerdios, Piper and Hayden were to learn the terrain for Elis, (and exactly what they could encounter in the process of traveling there), and Liv stuck to Piper's mortal textbooks, hoping to find any additional clues or helpful information in the process (while also building her case for why she would *not* be staying behind).

"The guards are at the front interior, but they're more sparse on the north end. We can use a back trail that leads through the mountains–it will at least give us coverage." Peyton explained, pointing to her makeshift map of Puerdios' Campus.

"There's a tunnel through the mountain?" Liv speculated. The mountain by campus always looked untouched and stunning, wild and beautiful.

"Not exactly." Peyton explained, "It's a makeshift and handmade path, but nonetheless a secret exit route if Puerdios were ever in danger."

"Who knows about the trail?" Hayden asked. "Is there any chance the Dark Gods are aware?"

"I believe only Silas, your father and the Candor Elite–your mother." Peyton looked around, "… And now everyone in this room. Honestly, I've been using entrance without issue so far, but it's not completely hidden. At times you are exposed between the mountain and Puerdios, so there are chances to be spotted and attacked. We will all need to be stealth and very careful to keep the pathway safe."

"And I assume there are no other options?" Liv asked.

"Rei and I have been over this map a thousand times, ever since our escapade this weekend. Puerdios has become safe-locked. Nobody is to enter, and therefore, nobody is to leave. With the perimeter guarded by Dark Gods, we cannot risk open exposure."

"So it's settled. We'll start through the mountain, and then we fly to Elis." Hayden confirmed. "Everyone should get rest, we have a enduring journey ahead of us. Meet back here tomorrow at 180 degrees sunset."

Although Liv agreed with Hayden, she continued perusing, yawning at the beautiful thought of sleep. She only had two more books to read through and wanted to make sure she didn't miss any pertinent detail.

"Ollie, you should rest." Hayden gently put his hand on her shoulder.

"I have one more book," Liv said determinedly, shutting the one she just completed and opening her last book to the index and quickly began scanning for Elis and Zeus.

"Okay." Hayden shrugged, bending over to kiss her cheek. When he stood up, he made a small exhaling moan, becoming stiff as a board.

Liv turned away from her book to examine him properly. "Hayden, promise me if you still don't feel 100%, you'll consider staying back."

"I'll consider it." Hayden replied, turning to his room to lie down.

Liv watched as he exited and headed upstairs, sighing as she turned discouragingly back to her last book.

No Zeus mention, no Elis listed.

At least she did all she could; now it was time to prepare for another long day of classes and the adventure unknown. So, Liv shut the textbook and dragged her feet up the stairs, her eyes getting heavier after each forced step.

When she got to Hayden's room, he was already asleep. Watching him lay in peace, with his soft caramel skin against his grey sheets, now showing only faint scars, Liv could relax. Hayden was healing, and that was all the comfort she needed for the time being.

No wonder both felt agitated with each other, they were both in physical pain from the day before. Tired and anxious, even deities experienced emotions, perhaps even stronger than mortals themselves.

Liv quietly tiptoed to his bed, carefully and silently resting her body next to his, so she didn't disturb his slumber.

After another day of class, Liv decided she should take a quick nap before they left for the night's journey. Her friends seemed fine with their lack of sleep, but Liv still hadn't mentally accepted the concept of not needing rest, so was physically exhausted and barely could keep her eyes open during Chemistry, Mythology and Meteorology.

Liv awoke to find herself alone in Hayden's room, with only a faint glow of sunshine remaining, confirming it was almost time for departure. Leaving the warm bed, she stood in the room, feeling a breeze of solitude, which left a lingering of sadness.

Shrugging it off, she walked toward the closet, looking for a more travel-appropriate outfit, removing her grey cashmere sweatpants and white sweater for a metallic dark grey leather pant, black crewneck sweater with gold studs and olive green wool jacket that contained an oversized hood, which wrapped around her collarbone and would prove warm for a chilly drop in temperature at nightfall. She eyed her stiletto collection with a chuckle, immediately grabbing her favorite black leather boots instead.

At this point, she didn't care that she technically looked like a Dark God. If anything, it could serve as a good disguise if she was captured and either way, she'd blend in better with camouflage. But after assessing her look and feeling guilty at her rebellion to the cause, Liv added some gold eyeliner to heighten the gold details on her olive coat and gold studs that peaked out from her sweater's embellished wrist detail underneath.

Before leaving, she took a considerate look at Hayden's room, trying to remember every detail of what had become her home for the past month, just in case she were not to return. Maybe it was the trauma from her last adventure, but she felt unsteady and weary about the upcoming departure and even more unconvinced about her return.

Emerging into the open area of Hayden's loft and hearing his voice downstairs chatting with Rei put Liv's melancholy thoughts at ease. She sighed, tasking one last breath of uncertainty before preparing to build her stronger façade fortress for her friends.

She headed downstairs, happy to see Hayden's eyes sparkle upon making eye contact with her. He was also dressed for their journey, wearing a thick knitted grey turtleneck with a navy field jacket, dark metallic navy denim jeans paired with a loose charcoal beanie and scarf. He also had a pair of dark leather brown boots that Liv hadn't seen before.

"You're up." Hayden smiled, "I was hoping you would rest a little longer, but I'm glad you came down. Would you like something to eat, or drink?"

"No, I'm okay. But thank you." Liv shyly smiled, not sure why she was acting so reserved.

Hayden pulled her into a warm hug, and Liv felt at home again.

"How are you feeling?" Liv asked. "You're in wool and jeans–which are not forgiving fabrics, so I assume your skin is healed?"

"You assume correctly." Hayden chuckled, kissing her forehead.

"How much longer until we leave?" Liv asked, pulling away from Hayden to welcome Rei, who was awkwardly looking out toward the patio to give them privacy.

"Fifteen degrees or so, just waiting for Piper." Rei called.

Rei had a white cashmere hoodie underneath his gold bomber jacket and sported metallic olive green jeans with tan combat boots.

"Wait, is Peyton here?" Liv asked confused, turning around to find her friend standing by the couch.

"The one and only." Peyton smirked, "Although, you'd think that you gave zero shits about me since you were too busy being entranced by your lover boy's gaze than notice your best friend. I'd be offended, but not really my biggest concern at the moment."

Liv smiled, instantly comforted by her friend's relentless egotistical humor.

Peyton was dawning a tribal printed dress, mostly bronze with hints of silver, coral and metallic turquoise jacquard woven throughout in stripes. As Liv approached Peyton for a welcoming hug, she saw it was actually a bandeau top with a pencil skirt connected by straps that were a part of the skirt, and so only exposed only an inch of her torso to appear like a cut out dress. Peyton also donned a cross body bag, fierce turquoise gladiator sandals, and a gold and black leather headband that matched her black leather strapped gloves.

Liv turned back to Hayden, and he immediately caught her gaze. She bit her lip, wondering if he could read her mind–that if he was feeling better, then she wanted him before they ventured into the unknown. He subtly nodded in approval, walking in her direction, but didn't lose eye contact in his conquest.

Liv extended her hand to take his and started with an excuse to head back up to Hayden's room.

"We're going to go upstairs to grab–"

But Hayden didn't care to share a reason, instead picking Liv up and determinedly throwing her over his shoulders–he was on a mission only for Liv.

Liv squealed in shock, losing her breath in laughter as Hayden carried her up the staircase.

Before Hayden entered the room and shut the door, Liv faintly heard Peyton mutter to Rei, "Can you blame them? We did the same thing an hour ago."

After successfully re-touching her makeup and hair, Liv changed back into her clothes, eyeing Hayden out of the corner her eye with even more longing than before. He smiled at her; the same look of desire reflected back.

"Every time you get redressed, I just want to tear the clothes off you again." He walked over, holding her into an embrace, softly brushing his hands down her spine and sending chills down Liv's back as he kissed her collarbone. "You're too sexy, Ollie."

Liv blushed, biting her lip. "I'm glad the sentiment is mutual, Hayden."

"And what is that?" He inquired.

"Love, Lust, Longing–all the L's and more." Liv added with a joke, noticing her unexpected alliteration.

"Speaking of L's, we should probably leave soon." Hayden sighed, with a hint of disappointment. "But I would hold you here forever, if I could."

"A very lame segue, but I'll give points for effort and concluding sentiment." Liv joked, standing on her tiptoes to give Hayden a kiss. "I love you, Hayden. Don't ever forget that."

"I love you too, Ollie." He smiled back.

These moments, this moment, even the simplest of things—made everything Hayden had been and was fighting for, worth it. Her anticipated touch, the earned soft giggle, her comically stubborn eye roll, and sometimes just the intoxicating smell of her—jasmine, violet leaves and strawberry—was a beautiful thing in pieces and as a whole, and he knew experiencing this world was only beautiful if Liv were in it with him.

Vincent Van Gogh once said, "Great things are done by the a series of small things brought together," and Hayden couldn't help but admire that this moment was one of those small things, and smiled, knowing that Liv and he were one of the great things.

When they got downstairs, they found Piper in the kitchen packing her bag with textbooks while chatting with Rei and Peyton.

Piper was in a dark charcoal wool jumper, with a silver and white turtleneck that popped out underneath and was visible on her sleeves and the jumper's shoulder cut out. She had dark navy booties to complete the look.

"Apparently, you and I both learned our lesson from the last adventure." Liv giggled at their much more practical outfits, as Piper placed the last book into her bag and swung it across her body, shrinking it in the process."

"Much more prepared." Piper nodded proudly. "I packed the books that we found with any and all mention of Zeus and Elis, medicinal herbs and gauze for emergencies, pillows and tents plus sleeping gear, and water—just in case." She shrugged, tightening the strap.

"I think we're all set to go, then?" Peyton asked to everyone, but mostly Hayden for confirmation.

"Yes, it's time." Hayden nodded, heading over to his front door.

"Let's do this." Liv agreed, following behind and trying to battle the burst of anxious energy erupting inside her.

They left the Puerdios Campus fairly easy, only running into a handful of students, thankfully Pure Gods, as most were at study hall with their designated professors. They simply acted as if they were running late to study hall, to reduce any suspicion.

"We can't have any DGs speculative to what we're up to, they could easily send word to alert the camp, and then we'd be really screwed upon departure." Rei whispered to Liv and Piper. "The only thing we have going for us is that they are only anticipating we eventually cross, so there is still some element of uncertainty."

Liv gulped, eyes wide at Piper as they hurried across the north courtyard, with the desire to enter the forest for camouflaged cover as fast as possible.

Liv ducked under a tree branch, resting her back against the tree facing away from the school, her heart still racing.

"And that was the easy part." Peyton shrugged, walking ahead for a better view of their upcoming trail. "We'll continue north. Stick to the trees for cover. The cave entrance is straight up from here, by that clearing." She nodded upward, toward the sky.

Liv bent low, trying to spot the 'clearing' her friend referred to, only to find sporadic trees without pattern. She quickly ran and took cover at a tree closer to Peyton, not wanting to get left behind.

Sliding her coat's hood over her head to hide her blonde hair, she continued on, swiftly dashing from tree to tree, mimicking Peyton's personal trail for cover, with Hayden, Piper and Rei following behind.

They continued upward, until the trees lessened and coverage became more faint by each higher foot of elevation.

Liv heard a *whoosh* overhead, carefully unhooking herself from her tree stump to see what was above her, spotting a black blur immediately. She wanted to believe it was a wild eagle, but her gut told her otherwise, so she leapt back underneath the tree for coverage, her heart racing.

"Are you okay?" Hayden whispered, jolting Liv with terror from the surprise guest.

Liv took a deep breath. "It's you." She whispered, relieved.

"We're almost there. We'll be in the mountain soon." Hayden coaxed, putting his hand on her shoulder assuredly as he stepped toward the next tree.

Liv still heard wings flapping, air being forced to move above. "Wait!" She whispered, eyes closed against her tree trunk of safety, keeping its touch like it was a lifeline.

Hayden turned back, confused.

"There's something overhead, I can hear it. I mean, I can still hear the wind it's flying through."

"Flying?" Alarmed, Hayden turned around, a sense of calm gone and urgency in full-mode as he grabbed Liv's shoulder, demanding she stay against the tree branch (as if she had even planned on moving in the first place).

"I saw a black object overhead, before I retracted," Liv whispered.

"I need to go warn the others." Hayden confirmed.

"Be careful!" Liv whispered, but he was already gone.

She kept her eyes closed, trying to focus more on the sound in the sky rather than her heart pounding. She felt as if she were home alone and could hear an intruder, but too scared to move and face it. So she remained still, not even sure how much farther she was from the others anymore. She was alone.

Thankfully Hayden was back five minutes later, grabbing Liv and pulling her out of the tree. She would face the intruder, whether she liked it or not.

It all happened so quickly. They had sprinted to the next tree before Liv even registered she had left her previous one.

"What is going on?" She asked, panting.

"The Dark God might have already spotted us, there's no way to tell. The only chance we have is to try to get through the tunnel before more join, in hopes we can escape before they find the tunnel's path." He confirmed, remaining calm. "Let's go!" He grabbed her hand this time, nodding to a far redwood on the left as they dashed to the next cover.

"Piper, the others?" Liv whispered, once safely under cover again.

"Executing the same strategy now." He nodded, looking around to see if the coast was still clear. "Run!"

They made it to the next tree.

"You call this a strategy!?" Liv snapped, hissing with her whispering tone.

"Okay, survival tactic, then." Hayden challenged, unamused.

He sprinted to the next tree, almost 15 yards ahead; Liv followed. She could hear the wind above flapping more loudly, which told her they had been spotted, and more were heading their way.

"We've been found." Liv confirmed, trying to look up through the trees for any sign of movement or shadows covering the faint sunset glow.

"We're almost at the mountain entrance–it's only 200 meters or so away."

"Hayden, what happens when we get to the mountain?" Liv asked, warily.

"We'll figure it out *if* we get there."

Liv didn't appreciate that clarification. She went forward to the next stop but Hayden pulled her back.

"Not yet." He looked out of the clearing first and then said, "Now."

Liv took a deep breath, rolling her eyes in the process, before sprinting to the next landmark that could help conceal them. She knew where she heard the wind in the sky, and Hayden had just lost them 10 seconds for their next escape.

"Keep going!" Hayden murmured, giving Liv a gentle push toward the next tree.

They found a rock, which didn't conceal them very well, but in retrospect also allowed them to see the mountain's entrance, which proved to be only a handful more sprinted zig-zags away.

They continued with increasingly longer sprints between each concealing landmark, until suddenly they found themselves making a 50-meter dash through the mountain's entrance with greetings from their friends.

"Did you run into any trouble?" Piper asked immediately, cautiously looking out the tunnel entrance, squinting back into the sunlight.

"Celare." Peyton whispered, already concealing the entrance. A light pearly liquid drop emersed from her hand and blew up to the length of the entrance, looking like the oversized bubbles Liv used to blow with a large wand as a child. The liquid attached to the edges of the mountain and blocked the entrance, but remained transparent enough so the group could still vaguely see out.

"There." Peyton nodded happily. "At a minimum, they won't be able to find this entrance, nor enter. But we'll be able to pop through the concealment charm on our way back. Pun intended." She smiled, adding a more serious, "Lux!" to begin emerging light from her hand, glowing like a flashlight to clear a visible path ahead.

Liv followed suit, as her friends also brightened up the dark tunnel, and proceeded through it.

An hour later of climbing rocks, walking through narrow pathways, and hiking steep curvy turns, Liv noticed a lighter, fresher smell in the air and a hinted glow of silver luminescence naturally reflecting off the cave walls.

"Now's the fun part," Peyton grinned devilishly. "We fly around the mountain, back south and then head southwest toward Elis."

"The region of Elis is pretty expansive. Any specific location you are aiming for us to cover?" Liv asked, remembering her difficulties in understanding how ancient Elis related to Greece topography in today's modern world.

"I have some ideas. Archea Ilida makes the most sense, that's were the original city of Elis stood when the king experienced his... difference of opinion with Zeus." Peyton paused, trying to find the appropriate word to describe the standing myth.

"But the Temple of Zeus is in Olympia–" Piper began.

"Exactly." Peyton agreed. "Which makes Olympia just as strong a contender."

"But the original Olympics were held in Ancient Elis," Piper added.

"Which were held in honor of Zeus." Liv nodded, understanding the complication. Zeus seemed to be literally related to any and all mythology.

All the Gods turned to Liv in surprise at her factual addition.

"How do you know that?" Peyton asked, speculatively.

"It's common knowledge. In my world–the Olympics are sort of a huge deal, so when we learned about the origin, I guess the fact stuck during 6th grade ancient history," Liv shrugged.

"The games weren't made to just honor Zeus, Liv. They were made at his request; Zeus helped create the games." Piper explained, "But knowing that mortals know of the connection ties back into our theory on the Humanities Pillar's logic for this quest."

"But we also know about the temple of Zeus, too. Olympia is like, one of the biggest travel destinations in the world for Greek mythology, apart from Athens." Liv contended, now again confused to which would be the better option to stop by first, from a strategic standpoint.

"Mortals know about the temple, Liv–you forget that you no longer fit the description of humanity." Hayden added, jokingly.

Liv was annoyed with his correction, so sarcastically replied, "You forget, *Hayden*, that I spent eighteen years believing I was human. So, it's going to take more than one month of being a deity to alter my entire perception of my world."

"Okay, let's stop bickering, love birds. We've got bigger issues to worry about, in case *you both forgot*." Peyton smirked.

"So, conclusion: we'll need to split up." Rei confirmed.

"Eventually. Let's stick together for now, until we reach the border of Elis, like we *originally planned*." Peyton was getting impatient. "Five Pure Gods together are better than less if we encounter any enemies on our journey."

Rei looked outside of the mountain and up into the sky. "The coast is clear. The Dark Gods knew we were leaving Puerdios tonight, but now none are in sight. They must be planning something." He observed, turning back to Hayden for confirmation, and with a nod from the Prince, added to the others. "We need to be extra cautious when we return tonight."

"Why not plan to go back to the royal palace, instead?" Liv asked.

"Without the heads up, it would be impossible to attempt arrival without getting murdered by security," Rei explained.

"Besides, we'll need to get back to school eventually, and it'll be easier to sneak back in tonight during the dark, than tomorrow morning." Hayden added, "You still have classes tomorrow, Liv."

"Is school really more important than everything going on?" Liv battled back, remembering how irrelevant her Deity Power I class seemed yesterday, in the scheme of things.

"Learning how to harness and control your powers are." Hayden countered back.

"Okay, that's another argument for tomorrow." Peyton stepped between Hayden and Liv, noticing Liv rolling her eyes mockingly behind Hayden. "It's decided, once we get into Elis' borders–we'll split up. Liv and Piper, you can go with Rei to Olympia and I'll go with Hayden to Archea Ilida."

"No, Liv stays with me. She insisted we're in this *together.*" Hayden replied tersely.

Liv rolled her eyes again.

"Okay, Liv comes with us." Peyton quickly caved, to Liv's surprise, as she looked hesitant in the process of confirming. "Ready?"

"After you." Hayden requested, looking at Rei, Piper and Peyton to start ahead.

When their friends had departed from the mountain, Hayden pulled Liv back, quietly commenting, "I could very easily command you to stop eye rolling at me Liv, you do know that." He looked ahead, refraining from making eye contact with Liv.

"You could have commanded me not to come, too." Liv agreed, slightly embarrassed that he had noticed her eye rolls, and terrified that he had the audacity to actually confront her about it.

"Yes, I could have–but I won't. I promised that I would never command you to do anything against your will." Hayden said quietly, "I just don't like when we're on edge with each other, Ollie."

"I don't like when you treat me like a child, *Hayden.*" Liv spit back.

"Do you think I enjoy this?" Hayden finally turned to Liv. "I'm not trying to demean you, Liv–I'm trying to protect you. And I love your fearlessness, but I'm not keen on the idea that with one mistake–you could be gone." Hayden snapped his fingers, catching Liv off guard. "I'm powerful, and I'll do everything in my will to keep you safe, but I'm not invincible, Liv. It terrifies me that you are here right now and about to fly into danger, literally. I cannot be in a world where you do not exist."

Liv had been staring at the ground, but finally looked up at Hayden. "Hayden, I exist–and it terrifies me just as much when you go on these trips, but the difference is I'm helpless in that case. If something happened to you," her voice cracked, making her angry for not keeping her strength at the front, "I wouldn't be able to do anything. And I could get kidnapped at Puerdios, you never know. At least if we're together, we can do our best to protect each other and make sure nothing happens to us in the flesh. At least when we are by each other's side, we know we're safe and have each other's back, so we don't have to worry or wonder about the could be's or infinite possibilities of destruction."

She looked up at Hayden, longing for his embrace. He responded by grabbing her in his arms, and giving her a passionate kiss, connecting them once again.

"We're stronger together, Hayden." Liv confirmed.

"I'm weaker with and without you, Ollie. You're my biggest distraction." Hayden grinned, pulling her in for another kiss. Liv melted in his arms, forgetting their mission for a moment of bliss. But then, reality came back as quickly as the waves hit the ocean shore.

"Okay, let's go. We don't want to lose the others." Liv pulled away, but Hayden didn't let go.

"Ollie, I'm the Prince of the Gods, I know exactly where all Pure Gods are at all times. We'll be able to find them easily."

He pulled her in for one last kiss, making her smile and relax. Liv realized she had truly had been on edge, anxious and scared for this entire trip, and had been taking it out on Hayden. Her lips felt lighter as they rose into an upward curve.

"Now, do you need any help lifting off or any guidance with your wings?" Hayden asked, cautiously, but Liv smiled even more when she saw only genuine love and concern on his face.

"Nah, this ain't my first rodeo." She smirked back, releasing her wings and attaching them to her back. "Let's go." She smiled and ran into the wind.

The group flew seamlessly around the cavernous mountain and southwest toward Elis without challenge. On edge throughout the duration of the entire flight, Liv felt something was eerily wrong and agreed to Rei's suggestion that the Dark Gods must be planning something bigger in store for them, which made her even more anxious.

After hours of flying through the sparkling sky, Rei shouted to the group, "This is where we depart! We'll meet you back here at 75 degrees sunrise."

Liv looked around, but all she saw were grassy hills with no trees to even help determine a landmark of some kind. She turned to Hayden, who anticipated her question.

"We use the stars as our map, not topography. The constellations and how they rotate is cyclical, so you can use their positioning to locate anything in the world, as long as you know the grid."

"That's how you can always find me with my Constellation?" Liv asked.

"Exactly, although it's more challenging during the day." Hayden shrugged, "It's not as accurate when the Constellation isn't as easily visible or located on the other side of the globe."

"Luckily most crime occurs at night then," Liv joked. "But, I would like to learn the astrological map, just so I can also understand Ollie's positioning during the day."

"Are you insisting that you want to be able to alert me to find you at any time of day?" Hayden smugly asked, pleasure radiating from his face.

"Can't you already?" Liv asked, remembering his mention of always knowing of each Pure God's location.

"Well, yes." Hayden admitted. "The difference is you could alert me that you needed, or wanted, to be found. It does take a lot of concentration to locate the correct deity, so it's not something I try to focus on all the time. Plus, it's not exactly normal to know the exact whereabouts of your girlfriend, all the time, God or not. I want to keep some trust in our relationship."

"Thank you." Liv turned to Hayden, genuinely touched that he didn't take advantage of his unique powers.

They continued on through the night sky, Liv gliding left and right and truly enjoying the remainder of the flight, until she spotted an enlarged ancient ruin ahead, which resembled an ill-kept amphitheater. She knew—they had arrived to Archea Ilida.

"Let's go to the North-East side of the amphitheater!" Peyton shouted, beginning her dissent.

Liv followed suit, hoping to land seamlessly, but instead shifted too steep, resulting in a miss-step that left her tumbling.

When she finally stopped, she took a deep breath, slowly moving each limb to assess any injury, but it seemed only her ego was hurt from the maneuver.

"Are you okay?" Immediately by her side, Hayden grabbed her hand.

"Yeah, just a couple more bruises," Liv sighed, taking his offering to stand back up. "So, this is where the first Olympic Games were held?"

Liv looked around, absorbing the desolation of the area and trying not to feel so depressingly connected to the abandonment of it all. How had the Gods, or humanity, let such a place with so much rich, beautiful and complicated history get to his desolate state? She was disappointed in both of her worlds at the sight.

Pushing aside her opinions, Liv started walking through the amphitheater, keeping an eye out for anything that looked suspicious or out of place.

"A little underwhelming after 2,000 years, you think?" Hayden observed. "It's all about the imagination of what used to be here. Picture it that way and not just a pile of rocks. It'll help."

Hayden continued his search, as Liv looked out, trying to imagine what the amphitheater could have looked like back in its glory days, but to no success. Sighing, she followed Hayden, trying not to feel sad for the mortals that once were, and for the architecture they had worked so hard to build.

She felt some unexplained connection to the souls as she continued on, trying to remove the urge to rebuild the amphitheater so their time and turmoil wouldn't have been wasted, and continued to fight for her focus to remain on the mission at hand. Liv felt suffocated by the sight from guilt, yet she had no idea why.

For the next hour, Peyton, Hayden and Liv walked in and out of the ruins, and around the circumference of the amphitheater, with no luck.

"Are you sure there isn't anything we're missing?" Peyton rhetorically asked, frustratingly looking out over the amphitheater. "We have found no sign, only desertion. Should we dig deeper?"

"I think that's our only option." Hayden sighed, "I may be biased, but all the clues come together too closely to think it's in error, now."

"Okay." Peyton shrugged, "Where do we start?"

Liv had been silent, observing the conversation, almost like she wasn't there. A gloomy ghost of years past fogged over her existence in the presence, like she was walking through Culloden Moor in Scotland, picturing all the bloodshed and lost soldiers resulting on the haunted ground instead of remaining in the present.

Peyton was already assessing the next task at hand. "Let's start with this section of seats, then move throughout the amphitheater." She started willing the rocks to remove themselves from the ground, causing more destruction, more desolation.

But once they were done with their excavation, Archea Ilida would be destroyed.

Why would the Humanities Pillar want the Pure Gods to destroy a mortal-built and seemingly God-approved site? What could really be found in the dirt underneath?

"Wait!" Liv cried, unable to accept the thought of what they were about to do.

Peyton stopped, turning questioningly to Liv.

"I just don't understand what good could come out of demolishing this historical place. And do you truly think you could find a clue under the rocks? It doesn't make sense."

"But that's just what this place is, a pile of rocks, Liv." Peyton countered, waving her hands around to prove her point. 'If there's nothing above ground, the only other option is below it."

Peyton's claim sparked an idea with Liv.

"What if that's the problem? We're taking this place too literally. Hayden, even you said to imagine what it looked like when the mortals used this amphitheater, but I couldn't. And Peyton, you just said this place is a pile of rocks. What if we need to think of the area as it was in its glory days? When it was newly built and used by mortals for its actual purpose, intended by Zeus?"

"You may be brilliant, Ollie." Hayden agreed, turning to Peyton for alignment.

"She had me at Glory Days," Peyton raised her hands up in surrender.

"Do you know of any altar or secret room that would have been dedicated to Zeus here?" Liv asked, hopefully.

"That's a Piper question." Hayden shrugged solemnly. "I'll command her–"

"No, we stick to the plan. They have their own area to cover, Hayden." Peyton argued. "Besides, instead of asking, let's just visualize it, instead." She walked to the edge or the amphitheater, waving for Hayden and Liv to follow.

Peyton closed her eyes, muttering to herself, "Reædificabo, rursum. Reædificabo, rursum." She continued to repeat the commands for the next 15 seconds.

"What is she doing?" Liv whispered to Hayden, watching a wind gust beginning to build near the ground.

"She's doing a duplex spell, when you conduct two spells at once. She's commanding the site to rebuild and rewind itself, so that it can reconstruct to what it once was in the past."

Suddenly, Liv could see the change. As Peyton continued her casting, stone pillars began to grow, seating redefined itself and marble statues started to resurrect themselves back to the beginning. They watched the rust and decay rewind, destruction grow. The broken down rock Peyton had previously thrown returned to its original location, growing into a brightly colored and new seat, its former self.

The site was magical; Liv stood in awe.

"Celare." Hayden muttered, shooting his arm around the perimeter of the newly built colosseum.

"Why are you concealing this? It's beautiful!" Liv asked, stunned.

"We cannot let mortals see Peyton's enchantment, what would they say if one of the greatest amphitheaters in history suddenly rebuilt itself overnight?"

"Solid point." Liv shrugged, "But it is a stunning sight."

Below them, the marble and stone came to life, reinvigorated and renewed, if only for the night. The structure sparkled under the sky, looking like a ghost returning to haunt its enemies.

"We don't have much time." Peyton warned, joining Hayden and Liv after taking a final look at her work with a self-nod of approval. "We need to meet Rei in 60 degrees, so we only have 30 degrees left."

"Let's split up." Hayden nodded. "Peyton take the seating, Liv take the ground floor, I'll go to the royalty and nobles' suite." He looked across the amphitheater to the box structure, regal and intimidating, covered in gold and lavish rugs.

"Sounds like a plan." Peyton nodded, flying over to her first section of the amphitheater seating.

"Ollie, if anything happens–good, bad or just an inclination that it might, can you promise to summon me?" Hayden pleaded to Liv, desperately.

"Yes." Liv nodded, although still not enjoying the prospect of being told what to do.

"Okay. Meet back here in 30 degrees, then." Hayden took a hesitant look at Liv, not wanting to leave her, but fought the urge and turned to fly over to his investigation site, eloquently and in one swift movement.

Liv ran down the steps. Since she was still sore from her last flying escapade, preferred to stay on foot. Besides, how many people could say they ran through the actual site of the first Olympic games? Her face broke out into a smile as she pretended she was competing in a stair flight race.

She won.

Jumping onto the gaming grounds, she felt surreal as she spun around looking at the entire structure, absorbing the moment that would be forever frozen in time, if only for a second.

Suddenly, Liv remembered the task at hand and immediately began looking for another clue–a coin, gemstone–anything that looked out of place–but found nothing.

Convincing herself to 'think like a mortal,' which was a weird concept to wrap her head around in the first place, Liv tried to think like her old self. What would she do if she had this experience without the whole deity responsibility? Liv looked back up to the stairs, her initial desire was to pretend she was competing, so maybe she needed to act like an ancient Greek game competitor?

She tried the discus throw–picking up a rock (after first observing it to ensure she wasn't tossing an actual clue) and throwing it as hard as she could, a little shocked that it went the length of the amphitheater. Was she really that strong?

Liv grew excited, deciding she couldn't have achieved that distance by herself. She hoped that she had figured it out and the rock would lead her to the next step. She ran over to her destination, picking up the rock to find nothing different, just more dirt. Shocked, she looked at the distance covered. Apparently, she was just that strong now.

Refusing to be discouraged, Liv decided to try the 100-meter dash. If anything, she was on the opposite side of the amphitheater as Hayden anyway, and she had already covered most of her designated territory. At this point, she was open to anything.

She marked a starting line and willed a finish line 100 meters away, and then with her own countdown, bolted across the amphitheater.

Moments later she crossed the finish and Liv felt more childish than ever when nothing happened. But another scenario quickly caught her attention, as Liv continued to walk forward, unable to stop. She turned her back to the sky, frantically looking for her constellation as she uncontrollably pulled out her wings. She finally spotted it as she began her ascent and internally begged that Hayden would feel her summon as she flew into unknown danger.

When she unwillingly approached the royal's suite, Liv became even more terrified. Something must have happened to Hayden–he was nowhere to be seen, even after her calling.

What was happening?

She flew through the entrance and into the suite, landing with an alert urge to find Peyton and Hayden calmly standing in the corner.

"Are you guys okay?" Liv asked in frenzy, quickly looking around the tiny quarters for any captors.

"Of course we're fine, what took you so long?" Peyton asked accusingly.

"It was Liv's first time being summoned." Hayden shyly explained. "Sorry, I should have given you a heads up, but I figured it was the quickest way to–"

"You summoned me?!" Liv's eyes grew wide as she took deep breaths in efforts to maintain her fury.

"It was the quickest way to get you both here and show you this!" Hayden interjected, spitting out his reasoning before Liv could turn any redder. "Look what I found!" He pointed to the wall, where a painting of a brunette lady resided.

"This has to be a clue. We haven't found any objects or decorations, only the architecture. This wouldn't be here unless it meant *something*."

Liv looked around the empty room, realizing Hayden had a point. She walked over to the corner, looking at the picture. The woman in the artwork was holding an embellished jar, but did it mean anything?

"Have either of you seen this painting before?" Liv turned to her allies, hoping they had more insight.

"No. But the artist's signature is in the bottom corner–Dante Gab... Ross.... it's a little hard to read." Hayden shrugged, "We can try to figure out his name and go from there." He walked over and grabbed the painting from the wall.

Liv gasped, her eyes grew wide as she stared at the location where the painting used to hang.

Hayden and Peyton turned back immediately.

Carved into the stone structure, they had found the direction they were looking for.

In 1871, the world's evil escaped. But what remained?
Babrios witnessed.

"Babrios?" Peyton repeated out loud. "Who's Babrios?"

"And you're sure you've never seen this painting nor heard of Babrios before?" Hayden asked Peyton cautiously. "Could you have conjured this subconsciously to any degree?"

"Confirming that I have no recollection of either, and I can vouch for that on a subconscious level." Peyton shook her head, "There's no way I could have compelled this in my spell."

"Let's take it all. It's nearly time to meet up with Rei and Piper." Hayden decided, shrinking the painting and carving the sketched-wall out from the structure.

Liv studied Hayden as he removed a tiny gold disc from behind his ear; it grew big enough to fit both items inside, and then shrank back to the size of a 1-carat diamond. He stuck it back behind his ear as his wings attached to his back.

Liv had never noticed the tiny gold plate before. Had it always been there?

With both clues now carefully secured, Hayden nodded to Peyton, "You know what to do next." He then turned to Liv and announced, "Time to go."

She obediently willed her wings to attach, wondering if her instant reaction to appease his command was because of his power or just because her heart hadn't stopped pounding since they had first left Puerdios. One thing she knew, she was ready to get the hell out of there and return to safety.

Hayden and Liv took flight, cautiously pausing a distance away as they watched Peyton's demolition of the amphitheater begin.

Liv couldn't help feel a twinge of guilt for each boulder as they crashed to the ground and once again became the dust of history's past.

"Are you okay?" Hayden asked, looking over to Liv.

"I'm not sure." Liv shrugged, looking at Ilida Archea with an empty sadness. Just like her, the site had no say in what happened to it. The Gods–Hayden–controlled it all. "I just, don't really want to talk about it right now."

"Are you sure?" Hayden supportingly grabbed Liv's hand, looking ahead at what Liv was staring blankly at, in silence.

After another moment of quietness, Hayden broke the silence.

"I'm sorry I commanded you tonight." He leaned in to Liv, looking apologetically into her eyes, desperately trying to understand her thoughts.

"Can you read the minds of your subjects, too?" Liv turned away, defensively.

"No," Hayden chuckled, "but I can interpret cues pretty well, especially yours." Hayden explained, pulling Liv back toward him. "And you seemed a little agitated when you learned that I had summoned you. And I'm sorry, in hindsight, I shouldn't have done that without letting you know, first."

"Letting me know? Isn't that just a more gentle way of saying command?" Liv whispered, almost rhetorically to herself. She shook her head, coming to her senses as she turned to Hayden full force, stronger and more confident, she needed to make a stand–he crossed a line, broke a promise, and consequently chipped off a piece of her trust. "What about asking me?"

Liv took a deep breath, calming herself down again. "Look, I understand why you did it–it was the right thing to do for the situation at hand, I guess. That's why I'm not sure why I'm so angry right now. It's just–you can't ever do that again Hayden, not without my permission. I don't like this idea that ultimately, you actually have complete control over me. And, that's not a relationship I can be apart of. You can't treat me like your subject."

Liv finally looked up at Hayden into his eyes; He looked broken, ashamed and regretful.

"I am so sorry." Hayden whispered into Liv's soul, "And you're right. I promise, I will never command you without your permission again."

"Thank you." Liv replied automatically, still not completely assured. It just felt like there was always *something*. Ever since learning Hayden was a powerful God, their relationship just seemed so much harder to maneuver in this world–and Liv wondered if they would ever figure it out, or if there would just continue to be new challenges that posed new issues of the deity caliber that she would have never imagined before.

Luckily, leaving the new gravesite was Peyton, who was now in sight.

"Let's go!" Peyton yelled, jokingly waving her arm in a circle, as if herding her friends to get moving.

Liv welcomed her friend's humorous dynamic, turning around in sync with Hayden and flying back towards Puerdios.

They met up with Piper and Rei seamlessly at their designated location, and a couple hours after, all five Gods were soon approaching Puerdios.

Rei signaled for the group to descend to a nearby forest for cover.

"It's been too quiet in the skies, tonight." Liv overheard Rei re-affirm to Peyton and Hayden.

"Alert and summon your father." Hayden agreed with a whisper. "Either way, we should show them what we found tonight."

"The mountain is just beyond that hillside," Peyton confirmed. "Stay low to the ground, under the trees. We'll go around again, but to the east side this time to avoid the school entrance." Peyton explained, just loud enough for only the group to hear. "And stay close to me–I'll reveal the entrance, but for only a moment. Liv, once we emerge from the trees, any chance you can cover the moonlight with clouds? Start now and make it look natural."

"Me?" Liv asked innocently.

"Yes." Hayden confirmed. "I would offer, but if the Elements Pillar has gone dark, I won't be able to command it. Since you have a natural connection to the elements, you may be the only one able to triumph Kai's powers."

Liv nodded, then looked up to the sky, to find zero clouds above. She continued to nod, but a little less enthusiastically, taking a gulp as she assessed the situation. She would need to create clouds starting from scratch, while still finessing her flying and steering to avoid natural landmarks, keep an eye out for any Dark God attacks, and all the while making everything look natural.

Peyton nodded, confirming it was time to take flight, and ran off into the sky with Rei and Piper following her lead. Hayden began walking over to Liv, but she didn't want to talk to him, so ran off to take flight, leaving him behind.

Unfortunately for Liv, Hayden was more skilled at flying than she so her avoidance efforts didn't pay off.

Hayden flew towards Liv, ignoring her deliberate escape.

"Can I help? You have the best chance of combating the Elements Pillar's powers if you are able to concentrate fully on them–do you want me to fly you, so you can focus on just commanding the sky?" He asked, wholeheartedly and sincerely.

"Then if a Dark God attacks, you'll be at a disadvantage." Liv countered, immediately regretting her curt response.

"If a Dark God attacks, we'll *all* be at a disadvantage." Hayden reasoned calmly. "It was just an offer. Let me know if there's anything I can do." He nodded, moving back up toward Peyton and Rei.

"It's not the worst idea." Piper added softly from behind. "The night shouldn't be like this tonight, Liv. I read the weather reports for the week and that clear sky is Kai's doing. And combatting it will not be an easy task, let alone making it look unforced."

Piper made a good point. Liv stubbornly bit her lip, internally debating between her ego and the practical, safer thing to do.

"You're also running out of time." Piper added, reasonably with a playful nod.

"You're annoyingly right." Liv rolled her eyes and sped back up toward Hayden.

"I've come to redeem your offer." Liv mumbled, quietly.

Hayden beamed, first grabbing Liv's hand and then her back, firmly pulling her into his arms; she shrunk her wings and placed them back behind her necklace.

She had to admit, being against Hayden's body did feel comforting. His warmth radiated through her, and she finally felt safe again, as if she no longer needed to worry about any attackers heading in their direction–she was home.

Liv looked up to Hayden, her lips lingering near his for a moment and whispered. "I love you."

Hayden inhaled with a big smile, kissing her immediately with a long, passionate kiss. "I love you, too."

Liv pulled her head back, smiling. "Okay, no more distractions, I need to change the stratosphere."

Liv focused, thinking through how to best and most naturally create clouds, or if fog would be easier with the ocean nearby. But then fog couldn't travel fast enough to their inland location without looking suspicious, so clouds it was.

She figured the perimeter around Puerdios was altered by Kai, but if she created the right circumstances nearby, she could move the clouds slowly to angle out the moon, and if she created enough, they could slowly dissolve naturally with Kai's powers as if nothing was forced, but allow enough coverage for her friends to get by. It was just a game of scientific calculation now.

Liv smiled, imagining her 6th grade science textbook and a picture-diagram showing how clouds were made, grateful that she had a bizarre interest in meteorology as a child as she recounted the steps in her mind.

First, she needed moisture, so Liv slowly increased the amount of water drops in the air and cooled the temperature in the sky to build ice crystals.

Looking proudly out at her army of condensed chilled moisture, she needed to warm up the sky, but that was easier said than done. She looked at the ground, wondering how warm the temperature could be in the air to not seem suspicious, and also contemplated just how much warmer her conflicting air would need to be. She just needed enough heat to rise so that all of the vapor could slowly condense into pieces of dust, but not too hot, so that the cloud would evaporate slowly. She willed the air particles from the ground to move around quickly, build energy and ultimately rise in temperature, before she sent it upward. Liv continued the process until she proudly saw the emergence of a thick cloudy sky. She repeated the process in another area of the dark night, and once her curated sky turned various shades of grey, with no star light breaking through, Liv created a natural wind source and direct the clouds near Kai's heat parameter, building more clouds in the process naturally by moving more cool-moisture air particles– that's where the ocean would come into play.

"Perfect, Liv!" Peyton exclaimed. "Team, time to blast around the mountain, now. Liv, can you give us five more minutes of coverage?"

Liv nodded her head, fighting the temperature above in the sky. Piper was right, it was getting harder to keep the area by the clouds temperate as they continued to hover around the moon, and soon she would need to them to dissolve. Not too quick and not too slow, so that it would appear normal to Kai and the Elements Pillar.

"You're doing great." Hayden whispered in assurance, holding Liv a little tighter as he accelerated faster.

Liv allowed the air by her clouds to warm up slightly. Using Kai's pre-cast atmosphere, the outer edge of the clouds began to dissolve slowly. Her friends and Hayden had just begun their journey around the east mountainside. Liv willed the air to warm up just a couple degrees more, letting more nearby clouds to dissolve. There were still enough in front of the moon, but they only had a handful of seconds before the moon would brighten their shadowed cover.

She fought the temperature for a moment longer, her brain aching and pounding with concentration. Liv only gave into a couple more degrees as she soon began battling her mental migraine. *Just hold on for a second longer...*

The moon broke through her cover, beams of light attacking the shadowed ground.

But then it was dark.

Hayden slowed his pace, from a sprint to a run to a jog to a walk, finally stopping and letting Liv down, but continued to hold her hand, protectively.

Liv stumbled, recovering from the unexpected turbulence, and let her eyes adjust to the blackness.

"You did it, Liv!" Peyton shrieked. "I don't think anyone could have seen where we went. The entrance is blocked, covered and out of sight now. We're okay."

A blast of light ignited ahead, Liv turned to Hayden, alarmed.

"Sorry! It's just me." Piper squeaked apologetically. "I may have gone a little overboard with my command… I really don't like the dark."

"We have about an hour until sunrise, think you can last until then?" Rei taunted, amusingly patting Piper as he jogged past her.

"Yes, let's go home." Hayden smiled, kissing Liv on the forehead, before he proceeded ahead, still refusing to let go of her hand.

TWENTY-SIX

They exited the cave, finding themselves happily back in the safe, protected grounds of Puerdios. All five continued to proceed in silence, still making notes of any subtle noises they encountered, staying cautiously aware to any undesired visitors as they quietly exited the forest and headed toward the pavilion.

After clearing the forest's border, Hayden stopped. He simultaneously pulled Liv behind him, blocking her from whatever lay ahead.

"Rei." Hayden whispered in a breath, standing still and nodding ahead as his friend came to his side.

Peyton and Piper stopped behind Rei.

"As we suspected." Rei tensed, looking back at Hayden.

Between feeling the immense pounding of Hayden's heart in sync with her own and understanding that whatever existed ahead were not welcome, Liv appreciated hiding in Hayden's protection, just for one moment to gather her composure before facing what lie ahead. She took strength from his strong grip, which still had refused to let go of her hand since entering the cave.

"Summon your father again." Hayden commanded. "I'll do the same. Tell them to come now."

"And what do we do until then?" Peyton thought out loud with a monotone voice, her mind was already spinning with strategy development.

"We should–"

But Liv never heard the end. In a blink, she was getting yanked away and pulled in a flash toward the courtyard.

When she landed on the grass, she stumbled while trying to maintain her balance and realized someone sturdy was helping her stand. Hayden. He was with her. He hadn't let go.

Hayden squeezed Liv's hand and nodded in assurance before turning his sight over to their captors. His gazed tightened immediately, a stoic statue surfaced; Hayden looked intimidating, scary and powerful. Liv felt chills run down her spine at the transformation.

"I should have figured you would join Olivia's little adventure." Arlo sneered, as he emerged from the crowd, ready to be seen. "Do you ever give each other breathing room?"

Hayden remained silent at the comment, his temper in control. "What do you want, Arlo?"

Liv looked behind Arlo, to find Kai, Finn and Cleo's faces amongst the Dark Gods. Her eyes locked with Cleo's, glaring with daggers as her insides boiled with fury.

"It's simple–hand over the Humanities Pillar's clues, and we'll leave." Arlo offered, a sly smile erupting from his face.

"Guess you'll be here for a while, then." Hayden taunted back, with a smirk.

"Is that a challenge?" Arlo stepped forward, curiously studying Hayden to call his bluff and then turned his sight over to Liv. "But, my innocent dear, are you ready to fight?"

Liv gulped, reminding herself to look unafraid, even if her entire being felt otherwise.

"You'll have to get through me first." Hayden fearlessly interjected, once again putting himself between Liv and Arlo, hiding Liv behind his strong, statuesque body.

"But rumor has spread of Olivia's powers–so why not duel tonight?" Kai stepped out, walking around so he could see Liv. "Reclaim your right to the Elite throne, and prove you truly are the proper heir," he added with a teasing snicker.

"Kai, not now." Arlo pacified, cutting in as he re-appeared behind Liv, causing her to turn around. He wickedly looked at Liv, observing first her head and then glared up and down her body. He walked over to her, grabbing Liv's chin and forcing her to look up into his blackened eyes.

"I should have seen the resemblance–you do look so much like Liam. But what would have been the point of imagining? He was destroyed before you were even born." Arlo let go of Liv with a scoff. "Now, Olivia you have a choice. I'll offer you this option only once, so choose wisely." He dramatically turned to his followers, pointing to them in show. "We believe humans should interact with Gods, and don't you want to see your mom again?"

Knowing she wouldn't be able to lie to Arlo convincingly, Liv remained silent.

Arlo slyly smiled. "That's what I thought. So why not join us, and fight for the beliefs that could reunite you and your mom once again?"

Liv looked up, only to find Cleo's condescending smirk, which made her even angrier inside, a fire catching flame in a dry forest and about to explode.

"Why? So you can have the true Element Elite at your beckoning call to do unnecessary evil in the world?" She tersely replied, "Never. I will *never* join the Dark Gods."

"Bold response." Arlo commented with a laugh. "Especially to think you may be powerful enough to challenge me, for it was I who made sure my brother would cease to rule the Elite throne in the first place." He turned, smirking at Liv's anticipated response. Her jaw had dropped at his casual confession.

"It's true, I sent your father to the Underworld years ago." Arlo paced back and forth as he eagerly shared his side of the story. "It was a simple solve, really. Liam had confided in me that he loved a human, and I simply wanted the throne. My brother was a traitor to the deities and all I needed to do was frame the black birds as responsible for his demise." Arlo conceitedly smiled, radiating pride at his mischievous plan. "Those who were even the slightest of superstitious clung onto that concept–for who could truly defeat the Element Elite? But alas, I did. And it was easy. I merely had to dangle the thought of killing your beloved mom, and he surrendered entirely."

Liv was boiling inside, all she wanted to do was tear Arlo's head off and burn his body.

Arlo turned to Kai, prompting him to come forward. "So, your father wasn't strong enough to defeat me, his less powerful brother in the end, but do you really have what it takes to defeat your subordinate?"

He nodded to Kai, slyly moving aside so that he was in a direct fire of Liv. Arlo returned his concentration back to Liv, willing her out from Hayden's protection.

"Now, you duel." He confirmed, with an evil grin.

"No!" Hayden yelled, again stepping in front of Liv.

Kai looked a little intimidated at the prospect of battling Hayden, but only for a moment.

"It's discourteous to step into a duel that's not yours, Hayden." Arlo sneered, pushing Kai aside with a subtle hand flick, so that he was again in sight of Liv without Hayden's protection, "You wouldn't want to break proper protocol, would you?"

Hayden stayed back, anger clearly building up as he held his hands in fists and started turning red, but was unable to step forward again.

"Oh, I'm so glad to see you prefer order."

Liv turned to Hayden, eyes wide at his restraint. She began to panic– she knew she was not ready to battle Kai, not yet. She had barely learned to control her powers, let alone fight with them.

"Pure Gods believe in dueling conduct, so as a Pure God, there can sometimes be minor flaws, and sometimes major effects, if you plan correctly." Arlo explained, smugly.

"And even the best of plans can sometimes find error." Rowan boldly interjected, landing in front of Liv so she was again blocked from Kai's sight.

Daphne, Jocelyn, Silas, Peyton and Rei all flew in after, strategically landing around Liv for protection.

Liv finally took a deep breath, looking around to find more Deities landing around Liv and Hayden, with Centaurs riding in from the forest to encircle the Dark Gods.

"Rowan, this is not your battle. Olivia wants to reclaim the Elite Throne, which can only be done by her fighting Kai directly." Arlo sneered, clearly angry that his plan was unraveling.

"Not tonight. And unlike my son, I determine the Pure God's conduct, so won't adhere to being moved with force. Kai will have to fight me first."

"But how will you battle him if you're forced to combat me, instead?" Arlo demanded. Without waiting for a response, he jumped into attack. "Impetus!" Arlo angrily commanded, launching a large fire bolt towards Rowan, who dissolved the attack by blasting a powerful stream of water.

Chaos ensued directly after as Dark Gods, Pure Gods and Centaurs all immediately broke out into warfare combat. On a vendetta, Kai automatically went for Liv with a lightning bolt, but Hayden intervened, moving a tree stump in front of her to block and absorb the high volt of electricity, automatically claiming the duel. Liv turned around to show gratitude to Hayden, but he was already on offense, going after Kai.

In her peripheral, she saw Piper battling Cleo, and couldn't help smile from the sight of Cleo sweating. After all of the bullying she had put Piper through, it was time the bitch got what she deserved.

In the distance, Liv heard King Rowan yell, "Protect Liv and Hayden, at all costs—they are the ones that need to survive the attack!" But as she watched him continue to fight Arlo, Liv noticed the King's lips had never moved and realized he sent the communication mentally to the Pure Gods so their opponent wouldn't seek them out as a target.

Liv deflected a curse in her direction, turning around in a panic for whom she should try to battle, or try to avoid fighting, when she spotted Finn and made eye contact. He determinedly set out in her direction with an evil, determined grin—one that could only be the smile at the prospect of vengeful destruction.

Rei relentlessly jumped in front of Finn to block Liv from him, sparking another offensive curse to delay him and ultimately command the duel.

A powerful blast erupted to Liv's side, blowing up the entire fountain in the pavilion. She turned to see who caused it and witnessed Arlo aggressively jumping through it toward King Rowan.

"If only you granted me the permission to succeed the Element Elite from my brother, Rowan! None of this would be happening." Arlo screamed, "And for what? The Elements Pillar has still joined my side, the right side, so you should cede to me now King Rowan, or you and your deities will fall tonight!"

Arlo shouted a command, causing a dragon to fly through the explosion toward King Rowan.

"Do you think I'm an imbecile?" King Rowan roared back, shooting icicles into the dragon like arrows as the beast came crashing down in defeat, shrinking to the size of a snake. "You know that all of this would have happened faster if you were ever granted power–but we have the prophecy on our side, now! The Pure Gods will not fall tonight, or any day in the future, as long as our powers exist in this world!" And with that, King Rowan cast a large curse, pinning Arlo against the fountain to be held hostage.

In that moment a thunderous blast exploded across the courtside, but all noise became muted and all combative activity ceased to Liv–all she sensed was Hayden.

He was in danger.

She sprinted towards where she felt him, desperately trying to find him, searching through the combats, cries and erupting sparks of powers crossing her path, to no avail.

Distraught, Liv deflected a curse, reversing it and forcing it brutally back in the direction it came, attacking its creator, who cried in pain from afar. Liv would have felt more satisfied, but her focus remained only on Hayden, panicking at the thought of what was happening to him to make her feel so terrified.

Recklessly running through the courtyard, defending all powers cast in her direction to keep moving as quickly as possible, finally Liv found him.

Hayden's hand was completely strapped down by one rope, so he could only helplessly deflect never-ending lightning bolt attacks from Kai with the other. He was strong enough to reverse them, but his confinement was limiting his power, and he was beginning to struggle. She saw a chest below, made for the sea. Recalling Hayden's greatest fear, Liv knew she needed to give him time to undo the binding, and fast.

She frantically looked around for some form of distraction, but fell short. Liv turned back to Hayden; his body was going limp from starting to get hit without full protection. There was no more time to lose; she needed to free Hayden as soon as possible.

Focusing on ice to cool the interior near his skin, Liv blasted fire to burn the rope, knowing it would command her will over Kai's power, because she had no other choice. This grasped Kai's attention, smiling as she made her invitation to fight.

"You know stepping into somebody else's duel is not of conduct to the Gods, Olivia." Kai mocked with a wicked grin.

"You see, I'm not entirely a deity, so I don't entirely follow the code." Liv snapped back, inviting Kai to battle. She just needed to stall long enough for Hayden's straps to unravel–but hoped she would be strong enough to endure the time needed to succeed. There was no other choice.

Kai blasted a lightning bolt in her direction, which Liv deflected weakly–she had not anticipated how strong Kai's force would be to block. The impact threw Liv up in the air to land twenty yards away, but she quickly stood up, even though her entire body ached. She had survived the first blow, reminding herself quickly that she just needed to focus. Liv turned back to Kai, and in the corner of her eye, noticed the rope confining Hayden was burning slowly, but thankfully managing to break through Kai's curse. She continued to focus on that mentally as she ran back toward Kai and blocked another lightning bolt attack.

"You'll never defeat me, Olivia!" Kai yelled, sending another bolt in her direction. "Electricity doesn't seem to follow your orders as you wish now, does it Olivia!?" Kai observed, sending another electric bolt in her direction. Liv was struggling to keep up with his speed and strength, each bolt slowly getting closer and closer to her before she retracted or absorbed it. Kai maliciously grinned, sarcastically adding, "How disappointing you're performing for an 'Elite' in battle, let alone a God! This clearly shows the difference between a deity and a *mortal*."

Liv ignored her desire to scream, scared that even the smallest thought for a clever comeback would distract her from expanding her mind to both focus on her powers for fighting Hayden's bindings and her survival. Instead, she powered through, using all of her physical strength to block another electric bolt, and all of her mental capacity to continue willing the fire to burn quicker. Secondary, was to remember keeping the coolness on Hayden' skin so she wouldn't burn him through it all.

Finally, the rope broke, releasing Hayden. Liv sighed relief, just in time to sense another bolt heading her direction, but this time she was ready and could fully focus on combatting it.

With her entire will, she commanded the electric ball to reverse, spiraling it even more forcefully at Kai, relentless in allowing him to block or redirect its path. Although drifting slightly off course from Kai's blocking power as it approached him, the bolt hit Kai's ankle, to Liv's surprise. He kicked his leg up, cooling it immediately, but when he looked up, Hayden was next to Liv, recovered and ready again for battle.

Hayden started relentlessly attacking Kai, causing their opponent to step backwards, with a look showing terror of what was to come.

With his wings appearing, Kai flew away for refuge and surrendering the battle.

About to celebrate their small victory, Hayden turned to Liv, but in an instant something behind her caught his attention. He flashed past her without explanation. Liv looked back to find King Rowan suspended in the air, black fire binding him against the tree, almost limp. Liv ran behind Hayden, shocked at the sight before her. King Rowan was bleeding out internally and quickly losing consciousness. As Liv's sight adjusted to decipher what was happening with Hayden's father, she realized he was not bounded by fire, but his own blood. She wanted to fight, but she knew the medicinal powers were not her strength, nor specialty. Liv had no idea how to fight this power. If it were fire, she would have tried, but she had no experience in combatting blood control.

Hayden started attacking any and all Dark Gods standing between him and King Rowan, a warrior emerging as he tried to get to his father as quickly as possible. His wrath was immense, causing Gods to cede immediately and fly away to safety. Liv followed in his trail, trying to help wherever possible, but all she could focus on was King Rowan, losing his conscious more quickly each second, surrendering to the vessel that pulled him away.

Finally, Arlo yelled, "Consider King Rowan gone from this world, for eternity." He looked to Hayden, "You're next, Prince Hayden! Or shall I now say, King?" And with an evil laugh, he catapulted himself with the lifeless body away from the grounds, sending the unconscious King Rowan to the Underworld, to exist in damnation.

"No!" Hayden shouted, determinedly spreading his wings to follow in Arlo's path and try to stop his escape.

Panicked, Liv quickly followed suit, in efforts to follow Hayden and make sure he was okay. Trying her hardest to dodge trees and keep her speed in flight, Liv exerted all of her concentration to keep up, but she was losing him–he was too quick at maneuvering through the forest's obstacles. He clearly had no desire to be followed–only Arlo, and revenge, was on his mind.

Finally, Liv dropped, in surrender. She could no longer see Hayden, nor Puerdios University's luminescence through the trees.

She was alone.

TWENTY-SEVEN

Finally, Liv gathered enough strength to fly high enough above the trees to spot the university and head back to the destructed castle.

It now felt lonely, empty. The grounds were dark. She knew Hayden hadn't yet returned, which sent chills through her arms as she stood frozen in the middle of the courtyard, trying to decide if she should return to Hayden's dormitory or her own.

He needed space, but he was already getting it–wherever he was now.

Liv just hoped he was okay. She automatically started heading back to his loft, mindless in route. She couldn't let her thoughts wander to the endless possibilities–whether he was captured, or worse. So her mind remained blank, empty, and she remained numbed. Liv prayed that Hayden would return sooner than later because she could not obliviously put her mind at ease much longer.

She willed his door to open, surprised when it worked and saw Daphne and Jocelyn huddled on the couch consoling each other inside. From the kitchen, Peyton, Rei and Piper turned their faces to the doors, alert and ready to attack.

Peyton took a deep breath when she realized it was Liv, and ran over in her direction for an embrace.

"Liv! Thank Zeus you're okay. Where's Hayden?" She peaked around, at the slight possibility Hayden just hadn't entered yet.

"I tried." Liv bleakly whispered, her lips quivering. "I couldn't keep up and I don't know where he is Peyton, I'm sorry–I tried. I'm so sorry, I'm so sorry..." Overwhelmed by finally admitting her defeat, Liv broke down.

Peyton immediately hugged Liv, softly combing her long hair while soothingly shushing her to calm, "It's okay. Rei believes Hayden went to Hades not too long ago. Security reported to Silas that Hayden was fine, but in a wrathful state... Oh gosh, Liv–you're freezing."

Peyton turned to Piper, who started pouring a hot kettle of water in response, handing Liv a cup of chamomile tea. Rei brought over a blanket, and Peyton wrapped Liv in it. Liv inhaled the scent of the blanket, smelling Hayden, which had a naturally calming effect over her.

Peyton brought Liv to the couch to join Joss and Daphne. Hayden's sister had blackened eyes and a red nose with stains of tears streaming down her face–making Liv feel even more bleak. Liv wrapped her arms around her, trying to stay strong and comfort Joss, when Daphne sadly smiled and placed her hand on Liv's, squeezing it.

"I'm so sorry." Liv apologized, more tears running down her cheek as she failed to keep her composure.

"Let's just hope Hayden isn't an idiot tonight." Joss retorted with a snort, leaning out of Liv's hug for a tissue.

Liv choked with a laugh. She grabbed a tissue as well, nodding in agreement and blotting her nose. Pulling her blanket around her, she headed back to the kitchen and found Piper eyeing her cautiously.

"I'm a little better now." Liv shakily said, not convincing anyone. She turned to Rei, "Why would you think Hayden went to Hades?"

Rei leaned in closer, whispering, "Security spotted him near Hades' residence and sent word to my father." In hopes of giving Liv a little more relief, Rei added, "He commanded they stay with Hayden for protection."

"But why Hades? Why would he go there?"

"If he couldn't catch up to Arlo, he probably wanted confirmation on whether Rowan had actually been sent to the afterworld or was being held captive. Hades is the only God who has access to that knowledge."

"A sensible decision on Hayden's part." Piper added, trying to sooth Liv. "He'll come back, Liv."

Liv nodded, still trying to wrap her head around the possibility of King Rowan no longer existing in this world. Liv sat down at the counter; it was a lot to take in. What would tonight mean for the Pure Gods if their leader were gone?

Suddenly, the doors burst open once more–this time with a blonde man standing in the corridor, head bowed, darkened by the hallway's light.

Liv stood up, recognizing Hayden immediately and ran over to him as he entered his loft, looking defeated. She wrapped her arms around him, holding him in an embrace and consoling him with all the strength she had–and he let her, bowing his head into her shoulder, exhaling as he tightened his grip around her.

And with that moment, Liv knew.

She took a deep breath, continuing to hold Hayden in her arms, so she could soothe the boy who had just lost his father but remain resilient enough to comfort the very powerful man that stood before her.

Because now, he was no longer just Hayden–he was Hayden, King of the Gods.

They stood there for an eternity, Hayden leaning on Liv, clinging to her as if she were his lifeline.

As a glimmer of sunlight appeared on the horizon, Daphne and Jocelyn decided it was time to leave; Rei and Peyton volunteered to see them safely back to the castle, and Piper left too, making Liv promise to summon her if they needed anything.

Liv nodded in agreement, unable to find the words. She looked over to Hayden, who returned to the couch after saying his silent goodbyes, and decided to make some coffee–if anything, to keep her distracted with a purpose for only a moment longer.

She had so many more questions, but knew today was not the time to ask them. Would Hayden continue classes at Puerdios University? Would his mother reign until he graduated or would he be crowned immediately?

And the war–how would that affect them now? They hadn't even completed their first task to secure a pillar's loyalty and so much turmoil had already occurred.

Liv poured herself a warm cup of coffee and turned back to join Hayden with the surprise of finding him already looking at her.

"Possible to bring another mug over here?" He asked quietly, detached from expressing any emotion.

Liv nodded eagerly, quickly pouring another glass and bringing it over to him.

"You don't have to tiptoe around, Ollie. I know you're here. I'm not damaged, or not completely. Anyway." He said bluntly, impassively taking a sip from his mug.

Liv blushed, sitting down next to him. "Sorry. I just feel like I'm going to say the wrong thing, or do something terribly unhelpful." Liv sighed in shock at what just came out of her mouth, adding judgmentally, "And now, talking about my insecurities is probably the wrong thing to even be saying…"

Hayden put his hand on her knee, eyes dimly sparkling. "You're here, and there's nothing better I could have or want more at this moment."

Liv blushed more, bowing her head, ashamed. "And now, you're the one consoling me."

"You're helping distract me." Hayden challenged in return.

Liv relaxed. Seeing Hayden act like a sliver of his normal self gave her hope.

"What happens next?" Liv asked, softly.

"Well, we'll have a passing on for my father. Then, shortly after, I suspect I will need to be crowned." He said dispassionately, inexpressive of any emotion. Hayden had returned to his unemotional state, a stale board.

"Will you stay at Puerdios?"

"Depends." Hayden eyed Liv, suspiciously. "You'll need to stay enrolled at Puerdios to learn as much as you can."

Liv panicked, "But if you're not…"

"Hold on." Hayden cut Liv off, with a slight smile. "Knowing that you would never agree to stay alone, and that I need proper schooling if I'm ever to gain full support, I will do my best to stay here as much as possible." Hayden sighed, "I'll admit, it will prove tricky–especially if we are to continue to visit and persuade each Pillar to side with us. I have a feeling that most will also ask to prove our worth, especially with Father gone now."

"How many pillars are left to visit?"

"Five more to visit. And I figure most will be structured with a task to prove our capabilities, like the Humanities Pillar, if they haven't already chosen a side."

"How do you suppose they lay out, now?" Liv was curious, and glad to hear Hayden speak with purpose again.

"Well, as you know, The Humanities Pillar is neutral–Arlo was quite persuasive when he visited them, hence the task at hand to prove their loyalty is just. We know that The Elements Pillar is Dark, and believe The Agriculture Pillar and Commerce Pillar have gone Dark, too–being able to control the humans would help profit in both their regards–but we should still visit. The Pillar of Life is neutral–they'll stay out at either cost, The Art Pillar is unconfirmed–but they've always favored the Dark Gods because of anger regarding mortals claiming their works, and with their successor Cleo going dark, that's not a good sign for us, so we'll need to prioritize visiting them, first. The Security Pillar, Candor Pillar and Government Pillar are Pure–thanks to Silas, mother and my position. Health Pillar should still remain Pure. Demetrius remains neutral, claiming the Solar System Pillar has nothing to do with humans, so refuses to claim a side. Centaurs came to fight Pure tonight, but the Cyclops are joining forces with the Dark Gods. Muses are unspoken for. Really, it couldn't hurt to visit them all, but prioritize the less confirmed ones first, and soon–while working on the tasks presented, simultaneously–if it comes to it."

"All while trying to maintain a collegiate degree, and…" Liv nodded to Hayden, "Ruling the deities and their pillars."

"The loyal ones, that is." Hayden nodded, not alluding to any of the stress or anxiety that Liv felt inside.

"And prepare for war." Liv nodded matter-of-factly, as if finalizing their list of to-dos made it seem just a fraction more achievable. She took another sip of coffee: the most attainable solve to begin with at the moment–she would definitely need more caffeine to help get her through the upcoming days.

"But we have help, Ollie." Hayden assured her, pulling her into his arms. "And we have each other."

"What I don't understand is how so many Pillars can be turning Dark, so quickly?" Liv wondered aloud.

"Similar to Puerdios University, our Gods have various beliefs. Most pillars may not be radicals like Arlo, but they may agree with his more subtle propositions. And don't think Arlo is acting as explosive around those he is trying to win over. Politics is what it is, really. We only revealed his truth from extensive spying, but we know he has not exposed his entire plan with all of the Pillar Elites, not yet."

Liv sighed, trying to wrap her head around the concept. She hoped, in time, it would become more comprehendible. She laid her head on Hayden's shoulder, thinking ahead to what may come. The riddle and painting they found in Elis simultaneously replaying in her mind. She closed her eyes as Hayden kissed her forehead, absorbing one last quiet moment with her love. For who knew what pain, challenges and adventure would lay ahead in this crazy, powerful world.

She instinctively looked out through the window, to the diminishing starry sky–relieved to spot Polaris, as she looked for a sense of direction or any reassuring hope.

But nothing came.

ACKNOWLEDGEMENTS

First and foremost, thank you to my husband, Jeremy, for supporting me and letting me explore this world on many countless evenings, nights, and weekends.

To my sister, Carrie, who encouraged me to pursue this dream when the book's concept was merely a Pinterest board, my best friend Yana for listening to my various ideas, and helping me troubleshoot through imaginary characters and navigate through their make-believe world. And finally, my longest BFF Rikki, whose passion for romance YA/NA novels proved encouraging when she first read my initial drafts and demanded that I write a sequel immediately (don't worry, I'm on it).

To my parents – who have always instilled the belief that I can do and achieve anything as along as I put my mind to it, and that true success is earned through hard work. They've been my champions since day one, and for that I am truly grateful.

And to Halsey, for without her song, "Young God," this book (and series) may never have come to fruition.

ABOUT THE AUTHOR

Andrea Blythe Liebman grew up in Sacramento, California, and although during adolescence she attempted various extra-curricular activities from soccer, tennis, and piano to diving–one thing remained constant in what she enjoyed as her pastime hobby: reading and writing.

Fast-forward twenty years–Andrea was able to transition her love of creative writing and fashion into a public relations career. As a creative at heart, her artistic side battled to resurface and after establishing herself in the PR industry, she realized it was time to switch up communicating brand initiatives with media and start telling her own imaginative stories once again.

Andrea graduated from the University of Oregon with a Bachelor of Arts in Journalism and Parsons The New School for Design with an Associate in Applied Science in Fashion Marketing.

Currently, Andrea lives with her husband and two Miniature Australian Shepherds in California.

Sneak Preview

Coming Soon

2019

ONE

One more shot.

Liv pointed her finger into the air, as if making a request instead of a demand.

"Are you sure?" Piper asked, consoling her friend, "You've had enough already today. It's not even 360 degrees SR…"

"First, it may be a drug, but it is the most socially acceptable kind. And second, I need all the caffeine I can get. I haven't slept in a week and you know I'm in much need of a picker upper…" Liv reached for the drink.

"Nope." Piper stretched her arm out and intercepted the miniature glass, taking it for herself instead. "It may only be an espresso, but you've had enough."

Liv's jaw clenched. Without thinking, she turned to her friend, aggressively grabbing Piper's wrist. "Never get between me and my coffee again."

After taking a breath and composing herself, Liv turned back to the barista, her pearly whites smiling.

"An Americano then. To go."

And with an irritated glance toward her overly protective friend, she added with a disingenuous smile, "Make it a double."

"It's strange going back to our regular class schedule. As if we weren't just battling for our lives a couple weeks ago, against our classmates." Piper commented, scowling at Cleo and her minions across the courtyard.

"Yeah, especially trying to attempt normalcy when the new normal is being stuck in a fishbowl." Liv subtly nodded toward the two security deities posted at the main hall entrance. She looked behind her shoulder, noting the additional ones stationed throughout the courtyard.

Security everywhere.

Liv could feel Piper's tension grow as she recognized the drastic changes her university had absorbed since the invasion. To lighten the mood, and still feeling a little guilty for her outbreak at breakfast, Liv turned around to Rei, who had become her personal shadow since the attack.

"You know, Rei. You *can* act like you know us." Liv winked at Piper.

"You're going to get the same response you got yesterday, and the day before that…"

Rei retorted back from behind.

The only time Rei deigned to give her a hint of space was this morning during his Warfare & Defense class.

"It's weird. We're friends." Liv countered, flipping her long blonde hair to the right side of her shoulder. "Come up here and participate in our conversations like a normal person."

Rei played along, chuckling. "I'm sure one of us would get sick of each other if we interacted the entire time I was on duty."

"Oh, come on Rei. I could never tire of you."

"Exactly my point."

Liv rolled her eyes. "Come on, Piper. Time for Meteorology class."

"Is Hayden still going to attend classes at Puerdios?" Piper inquired shyly, sitting in her designated front-row seat, even though as always, it was a room full of empty desks.

Liv paused, unsure how to respond. Instead, she set her books down and slid into the desk on Piper's left. Although Hayden had agreed to remain living at Puerdios and attend classes when he could, Liv had yet to see him yet during their first day back. She had barely even managed to see him throughout the past two weeks. She had no idea what was running through his mind anymore.

She turned to Rei, who was seated behind her, prompting him to respond on her behalf.

Rei only replied with a blank stare.

"Don't act all innocent, Rei. You're not returning to your normal schedule, obviously." She waved her hands around regarding his presence in their lame Meteorology class. "And you probably have a better idea of what Hayden's up to than I do."

As a Security Elite, Rei joined all royal-related meetings with his father, Silas. And, even when he couldn't attend because he was stuck babysitting Liv, she suspected that Silas still kept his son informed on any and all new details or developments regarding policies, the royal family and most importantly, the rebellious Dark God uprising.

"It's not my place to tell." Rei countered.

Liv glared into his glacier eyes, appearing almost silver in contrast to his creamy caramel skin.

Although Liv was Hayden's girlfriend and the rightful Elite heir to the Elements Pillar, she technically had no official title, nor rank to constitute anything of importance. She still didn't even consider herself a true deity half the time, having only uncovered her powers a couple months ago. So, Liv understood where Rei was coming from, even though it was annoying as hell. Rei reported to Hayden, the Prince of the Pure Gods, soon to be crowned king. His loyalties didn't reside with Liv.

"Hayden hasn't told you anything?" Piper whispered, her squeaky voice raising an octave with concern.

"I haven't really seen him." Liv shrugged, opening her book to their last studied chapter on moon phases, hoping to rekindle her memory and also close the conversation at present.

She understood why Hayden had been busy, distant. After the invasion at Puerdios University and consequently the death of his father, he had more than enough on his plate. Not only was he preparing for his coronation, but was constantly being pulled into all-day meetings with his mother and other Elites to discuss the state of the rebellion and other political affairs. If Hayden could even make it back to the loft late at night, he usually returned with Peyton or Silas at the door, and never spoke much about his day because 'after a full day of royal bullshit,' the last thing he wanted to do was 'waste his precious time with Liv' talking about it.

So instead, they discussed nothing of importance–like his plans for the future, *their* future, or any challenges he was experiencing with his new role. Nothing regarding any emotional family trauma from the loss of his father to the Underworld, and definitely nothing to give light as to what was actually running through Hayden's mind, when he tossed and turned throughout the night as nightmares attacked his dreams.

Even still, Liv hadn't seen Hayden since Thursday, and she thought weekends were supposed to promise some downtime. But alas, apparently there was no such concept for a soon-to-be-king.

When her best friend Piper wasn't sneaking around with Matthias, her Dark God boyfriend, the two typically spent the evenings studying or trying to find any more clues to help with the Humanities Pillar's request for loyalty to the Pure God cause: Find what humanity lost.

Had it really only been thirteen days since they travelled to Elis, found the painting with the accompanying phrase: *In 1871, the world's evil escaped. But what remained? Babrios witnessed*, and returned to Puerdios University in turmoil?

Liv shook her head; it had felt like an eternity since then and now. Zeus knows she had definitely read and absorbed enough information on Babrios to last an immortal lifetime. She could practically recite *Aesop's Fables*, since she *and* Piper both read all of his work *twice*.

Fortunately, Professor Deligne entered the class before Liv once again started organizing all she knew about the author in hopes that a new formation might spark an idea.

"Welcome back, class!" Professor Deligne clapped with excitement, always one to make a grand entrance. "Now, because of our unexpected little break, we have much to catch up on. So, who can tell me the 8 phases of the moon?"

Piper's hand shot into the air, as if she had been waiting for this moment to be called on all day.

After Professor Deligne called on Piper, Liv found Rei staring at disbelief as Piper began rambling on about the New Moon.

Liv leaned back in her chair, murmuring to Rei with a sarcastic smile, "Welcome to Meteorology."

After a first full day back of rigorous classes and each teacher wanting to double up on material to make up the past two week's curriculum, Piper and Liv both agreed it was better to take a night off from Babrios and rest. They expected the next day to be just as grueling, and their heads were already exhausted. Frankly, all Liv wanted to do was peel off her light blue, long-sleeved and intricately beaded gown. Had she actually gotten used to wearing heels and couture gowns at one point? At present, she just felt itchy and claustrophobic, and her feet were throbbing.

She saw Matthias approach as Piper said her goodbyes, giggly and excited as always to see her boyfriend. Liv kindly waved to Matthias as they departed, but couldn't help remember with a sad smile, the similar encounter she used to experience with Hayden after they completed their classes for the day.

She missed him.

Liv wished that easy, carefree lifetime could return–just two classmates falling in love in college-but she knew it would be forever lost to history.

Liv turned to Rei, shaking off the nostalgia. "Shall we head back to the loft?"

Rei smiled, kindly. As if he too, had been thinking similar thoughts.

Of course, Liv realized, if Rei was in charge of Liv, and consequently Peyton was Hayden's personal security guard now, and Liv rarely saw Hayden… when was the last time her two friends had time to spend alone?

"How's Peyton doing?" Liv asked.

"Sassy and demanding, as always." Rei replied.

"As she should be." Liv nodded with a grin, but turned to Rei after a moment, hoping he would further elaborate.

They walked down the main corridor in silence.

"Do you get to spend time with her? Since what happened to King Rowan?" Liv finally blurted out.

"We make it work." Rei calmly answered, no hint of emotion.

"If you ever wanted a night off, Rei, you know you can just ask, right?"

Rei's eyes sparkled with amusement at the offer. "Yes, Liv. I know. Thank you. But, I choose to be here. Hayden's my best friend. I would trust no one else with the responsibility of keeping you safe, except for Peyton, but alas, there's the Catch 22."

"Oh, the woes of being a powerful Security Elite." Liv cooed. "You know, we could always scheme a little. Get Hayden and Peyton here under false pretenses. Capture them for the night. I'd be safe with Hayden, you and Peyton would get the night off."

"You do realize kidnapping a member of the royal family is a criminal offense?"

"Ugh, you're no fun." Liv rolled her eyes, approaching the loft.

"I'm just next door if you need anything." Rei reminded Liv, terse and direct per usual, before saying good night.

"Good night, Rei." Liv waved. "Thanks for the stimulating conversation, as always." She'd break him down, eventually.

"Anytime." Rei smirked.

Liv rolled her eyes again as she entered Hayden's loft, which was now technically *their* loft. The echo from the door slamming shut emphasized the silence that brewed in the empty living space.

She was alone.

Liv thought she would have gotten used to the concept by now. Perhaps it was because Piper and Rei didn't fill up the space with personality and livelihood before leaving her, but tonight, the loft felt especially cold.

She heard a creak upstairs, and even though she had consoled herself repeatedly that it was just the old castle's growing pains, it still sent her heart racing as she jolted in the noise's direction for any additional clues to justify an intruder.

Liv *hated* the silence.

She immediately went over to the stereo system to play music and cancel out any additional opportunistic noises to freak her the fuck out.

Liv poured a glass of red wine, selecting what she called 'the deep stuff'–Merlot–which was specified as rightfully and deservingly needed for consumption after one endured a long and challenging day.

Or, the alternative: when one simply just wanted a glass of fucking wine.

She felt anxious, like she was in a dream and a nightmare was about to erupt.

Liv needed to find a way to block out the reoccurring dream she kept having at night. In the darkness, she continued to awake in frozen terror from formulating the same nightmare of being kidnapped by the Dark Gods from her bedroom window. It was starting to get to her, making her feel less secure in her home.

She wasn't entirely sure what brought her outside, possibly her second glass of the deep stuff, but for whatever reason, Liv found herself staring longingly at the stars above.

How did it get to this?

She felt lost.

Sure, she put on an act for Piper and Rei. She couldn't have Rei report to Hayden that Liv was losing her shit. He already had too much to worry about; she needed to be his strength during this time. But, she had only discovered that she was a deity with powers, *strong powers*, powers that were *still* growing, a month ago. She still hadn't processed what it would mean for her mom, her friends, her life. She could feel a change in her being: heightened senses, more nimble limbs, a luminescent glow, but had no idea what was to expect during the full transition.

Was the transition contributing to her feeling of urgency? Or were Arlo and Kai finally chipping away her soul?

She wished her father were still here. Someone who shared her blood and could guide her through this turbulent path, someone to share the knowledge of her pillar to claim, the history of her family and where she came from.

A clash of branches bristled in the wind, alerting Liv of a potential trespasser. She froze her movements into stone, not even letting the whisper of a breath give her location away.

Finally accepting it must have been a bird, or worse, her imagination, Liv released a breath and took another heavy sip of wine.

What the hell happened to this place where she used to feel so *secure*?

A place she once thought was magical, full of so many opportunities, now tarnished. The once beautiful iridescent lanterns now intensified the all too many shadows available for strangers to lurk behind in the dark. Reality had set in. Or maybe, now as a deity, and as one who recently lost a loved one to the Underworld, Liv had simple become above the magic of it all.

She looked up to the stars, trying to calm her mind and wondering if it would be possible to fly up there and sit on a star, Polaris - to become one with the galaxy and disappear amongst one of the billion rocks that shone so brightly.

"I could take you there, if you'd like."

Liv turned around, slowly. As if in a dream, she found Hayden's gaze upon her.

He looked beautiful, forever taking her breath away.

She snapped the image to lock into her memory vault: Hayden, radiant with his sun-kissed glow and golden locks, dapper in a loose white t-shirt, jeans and a grey wool lapel coat. Liv couldn't help wonder if moments like these were limited.

If it were so easy to send King Rowan to the Underworld, who would be next?

She turned back toward the sky, a chill catching her as she crossed her beaded arms tighter around her chest, and shivered.

Immediately, heat surrounded her, as Hayden wrapped her in his arms, a warm breath catching her neck and sending more chills–good chills–down her spine. She leaned into her boyfriend, feeling instantly at home.

"How did you know I needed this-needed you." She whispered with a sigh.

"Besides the fact that you avoided your constellation?" Hayden said with a grin, kissing the top of Liv's head.

"I know you're busy. I didn't want to bother you." Liv replied, meekly.

Hayden tensed. Then sighed, gently turning Liv around to face him, lifting her chin to look into his eyes. "You, are never a bother. You are my relief, my sanctuary." He kissed her lips before continuing, "I want to be here. I want to be here for you. Every moment I spend with you is a moment I cherish."

Liv smiled. She rested her head on Hayden's sturdy chest and nuzzled underneath his chin, tasting his scent of cedarwood and gray musk, before looking up again at the sky.

"How *did* you know I needed this? I didn't glimpse at Ollie."

She could feel Hayden smile.

"I'm not entirely sure how, or maybe I imagined it as an excuse to come visit you, but I've started to notice a feeling in my soul, similar to when you look at your constellation, but a little more subtle – I can sense you – sometimes, even what you're feeling."

"Really now?"

"It started faint. During the battle." Hayden closed his eyes as he paused, not wanting to remember. "I could feel your panic, strength, power."

Liv thought about how she sensed Hayden was in danger, when she found Hayden and Arlo…

"I only guessed at the sensations, but this morning when I was with my mother and she brought me coffee, the same sense came through my core–of being angry and aggravated. It made little sense since I was content with her gesture. I could only think it had to be somehow connected to you."

"Piper criticized me for my coffee consumption." Liv mumbled. "I may have flipped her the bird."

"As should anyone who gets denied his or her rightful coffee," Hayden chuckled.

"It may have been my fourth cup that morning," Liv admitted.

Hayden laughed and then sighed apologetically. "Ah, I'm sorry I haven't been here, Ollie."

Liv nestled closer into his neck, wanting to drink in all of him: his scent, warmth, how she so perfectly fit into his arms, absorbing his strength before she replied, "I understand. After the outbreak at Puerdios..." She took a deep breath, holding onto Hayden tighter.

He had been so close to capture, almost pulled into an eternity within the Underworld.

And almost without her.

A tear rolled down her eye. She held on tighter, not wanting to lose grasp of her only love, the only thing that made sense to her since the past months of whirlwinds and hurricanes. Liv wanted to soak it all in, so if it ever came to that, she could have enough memories to last, but shivered as she realized nothing could ever be enough without him.

"Hey, let's go inside." Hayden squeezed her, already understanding what was rolling through her mind. He gently kissed away her tear and then the top of her head before leading Liv back into the loft.

Liv let Hayden guide her inside, feeling a tug of urgency between the stillness of the apartment, understanding that she too, felt that connection, although faint–not necessarily her own–but there.

Hayden.

"I'm, sorry. I've become a wreck. And you have to go. I'm sure this isn't how you want to spend your free time with me anyway..." She sniffled, pulling away to grab a tissue. Giving her some time to pull it together.

Hayden had just lost *his* father, and here *she* was crying.

But before she could take a step away, Hayden pulled her back, not letting go of her hand.

"I'm not going anywhere, Liv. Not tonight. And I'll take any moment with you. Good or bad."

Liv smiled. Then frowned. "I thought I felt a sense of urgency from you. Our connection."

Hayden chuckled. "You did."

"What is it?" Liv asked as she tugged Hayden toward the couch. "I thought you had somewhere else to be."

Before she sat down, Hayden spun her in his arms, instead laying himself on top of her, pinning her down, still holding on to her hands. She could feel him against her, hard.

"Oh?" Liv raised her eyebrow, trying to sound calm as her heart began racing. *Did it ever stop? The wanting him?*

"You may need to get used to that feeling when I'm around you. You're quite breath-taking Ollie, there's never a second that goes by where I don't want you."

Liv rolled her eyes, but couldn't help smile at the flattery.

Hayden kissed her heavily in need before continuing. "Seriously, Ollie. Half the time I'm just plotting how I can get near you, alone. Annoyingly enough, it seems to delay my actual work and only motivates me more to figure out how to return back into your arms. To feel your skin, kiss your neck," he kissed her neck in response, gliding his hand softly down her arm, sending chills through her spine, "Any distance and time between us kills me slowly with hunger."

"Well, it's time to satiate that need, then." Liv giggled, lifting her head to his, wanting more. Tasting him as their lips finally met. "Awaken my soul, Hayden." She whispered in a breath, pleading as she looked back up to his eyes, mirroring the exact desire she felt.

Hayden leaned into her fully, letting her feel his hardness between them, intoxicating her with his touch as he kissed her lips. Then, he gently lifted himself off of her, holding out his hand to guide her to join him in a standing position.

"Challenging my restraint." Hayden explained to Liv's quizzical look. "However enticing it would be to take you in that seductive gown, I would hate to ruin yet again one of Piper's exquisite dresses." He spun her so Liv's back faced Hayden, and whispered into her ear, "Plus, half the fun is enjoying the process of you undressing."

Liv's inside stirred. She wanted to rip off her dress and appease her rapidly beating heart. Instead, she just breathed and let him take control.

Hayden gently glided her thick, blonde hair to the side of her neck, sending chills down her now revealed spine, and slowly unzipped the beaded garment, trailing the zipper with soft kisses down her back. Shortly after, the dress slipped to the ground, and Liv stepped out of it, once again facing Hayden.

"You must have known I was going to visit you if you decided to wear my favorite lingerie today." Hayden tried to sound calm, but Liv knew he was internally drooling over her selected undergarments. A navy and gold lace bra and panty set that accentuated all of her curves perfectly.

"Coincidence, perhaps. Or wishful thinking - the Gods were on my side today, apparently." Liv demurely replied, batting her eyelashes and slowly walking over to Hayden, before she grabbed the labels of his wool coat. "My turn."

Hayden gulped, but didn't move.

She tore off the jacket, revealing his toned arms, and grabbed his neck to bring him in for a long, demanding kiss. He might have been the rightful King of Gods, but she *ruled* him.

Her hands lazily drifted down his biceps, squeezing them once fabric turned to bare skin, pulling him closer—her mouth and tongue relentless in its grasp to his.

Fireworks were blasting between them as she finally unbuttoned his pants and prompted him to step out of his briefs before pulling his cotton tee over his head. Her heart stopped at the sight, but only long enough to take another snapshot of his impeccable body before colliding with him once more.

"Bedroom. Now." Liv panted, grabbing his neck.

In a swift movement, Hayden lifted Liv up, her legs wrapping around his waist, and carried her toward the staircase. He pushed her against the wall at the base, unstrapping her bra and tossing it aside during the pause. Liv couldn't wait any longer. He began massaging her breasts in desire.

"I want you in me, now." Liv demanded, lowering herself to his pelvis. She dragged him down, onto the staircase, wiggling out of her underwear, and pushed him into a seating position.

Hayden was breathing so heavily; Liv thought he was about to explode. She straddled on top of him, letting him grab her breasts, and then her back, as he placed her on top of him.

"Oh god, Ollie." Hayden exasperated, as she became filled by him, taken over by him.

She began moving up and down, needing to satiate the friction pulsating through her veins. The contact was too much; she craved more of him inside of her.

Hayden spun her around, spreading her legs wide as he plunged deeper into her. Holding her back upright so she didn't break against the staircase, he started moving faster and faster, so Liv couldn't breathe because the sensation was taking over her body, her soul.

"Hayden!" Liv screamed, moaning in pleasure.

He moved faster, deeper within her, until she shrieked gratification, hitting her climax at the base of the stair. She felt lightheaded and dizzy as he filled inside her and finished with a smile and satisfying murmur of her name.

After a moment of breathing, soaking up each other's scent, Liv finally commented with a grin, "So much for the bedroom."

"It was about time we christened the staircase." Hayden replied, grabbing Liv yet again and carrying her up the stairs.

Hayden let Liv get ready for bed while he cooked dinner for the both of them, deviously bringing it up to the room to enjoy while cozily laying beneath the blankets on their mattress.

"We'll let it slide this one time. It's late." Liv cooed, plopping a grape into her mouth.

Hayden had made a charcuterie board filled with cheese, prosciutto, fruits and nuts alongside a flatbread pizza Liv couldn't wait to try.

"Artichoke, caramelized onion, feta and garlic chicken." He nodded to his creation. Liv was drooling. "Yes, you're welcome for being perfect." He grinned.

Liv threw a grape at him in response, even more amused when he caught it in his mouth.

She grabbed her wine. "Cheers to you, my wonderful, always present boyfriend."

"Ouch." Hayden dramatically pretended to have been stabbed with a dagger.

Liv rolled her eyes. "You're lucky you're cute and can cook. I think I'll keep you." She bent over to kiss him on the lips before sitting down, and finally grabbed a slice the pizza.

"Even if I tell you I will be gone for the next week?"

"Ugh. You're the worst. How come?" Liv hoped her response didn't seem as anxious as she felt. A couple days without him was one thing, but one confirmed week…

"It's time to visit the Art Pillar. They've become rather difficult in meetings lately, and a true pain in my ass." Hayden growled.

Liv understood. Cleo's mother was the Art Elite and supporter of the Dark Gods, but if Cleo had taken after her mother in any way, that would be a meeting Liv would not want to take part in. But, The Art Elite was also the matron of Kai, The Element Elite, so she was powerful and influential, and therefore earning any loyalty, or neutrality agreement, would be crucial to their cause.

"How's everything else with the Elites?"

A frown hit Hayden's face, as she expected. "It's been… more challenging than I expected. I don't understand how my father put up with them for so long. Many refuse to state any loyal declaration until my coronation. Many won't even accept me in court until my position is official."

"That bad?" Liv took a bite of the flatbread, it was even better than she had imagined.

"They're all power hungry." Hayden sighed, following suit with another slice. "Every stipulation that could postpone my coronation many have requested in order to sway their vote. They're just playing games with infinity at this point."

"But you need their support?"

"You must have over 51% in agreement in order to be sworn in." Hayden shrugged. "Politics is already so fickle, I don't want to take any risks with losing votes if it can be avoided. So, I'll jump through their hoops, smile and schmooze at cocktail parties, bake them fucking lemon meringue pie if they asked for it."

Liv let out a laugh. "Actually, a fucking lemon meringue pie sounds great right now, any chance you can go whip one up for me?"

Hayden looked at her stunned before a huge grin spread across his face.

"If only you were the Element Elite, at least earning your loyalty could pose some rather interesting diversions." He playfully bit her ear.

Liv chuckled, gliding her hand through her long hair, before grabbing a piece of cheese. "You play a dangerous game Hayden, because in that case, I'm not sure I would ever fully pledge to you, only to keep the chase alive. Play with infinity. Receive unlimited lemon meringue pie."

"Ask, and you shall receive." Hayden snapped his fingers.

A slice of pie appeared before Liv.

Amused, he watched her scoop a forkful bite into her mouth. Her eyes closing as she hummed with joy.

"Now, about those hoops…" Liv smiled, mouth still full with dessert.

Hayden pounced on Liv, pinning her down on top of the bed. Plate of pie and fork gracefully saved as he held both in his right hand.

"Now who's playing the dangerous game Ollie? Kings don't like greedy courts."

Liv was quiet, softly breathing in anticipation. "I'm only greedy for you."

Hayden put the plate down, scooping pie onto his finger before tapping her nose and then kissing the pie remnants away.

The sweet gesture allowed Liv just enough time to wiggle out of his singular grasp, and grab Hayden's hand after the reaction, placing his finger in her mouth so she could suck off the remaining pie that lingered on his skin.

Hayden groaned in pleasure, before something clicked and he snapped back to the present and calmly commented, "Smart maneuver. Your defense classes must be working."

"Oh, don't remind me. I'm already dreading Wednesday." Liv sighed, remembering how brutal her training had been earlier that morning. She already felt the stiffness encompassing her sad muscles.

A week off from such brutal attack and strength training had made her morning class all the more painful, and Rei had given her no slack. Her muscles were already reaping from the exercises she completed, not to mention the additional workout she wasn't expecting to receive during the night.

"How did classes go today?"

"You should ask Rei." Liv snorted in return. "And consider releasing him from the torment of following me around. Forcing him to attend Meteorology on my behalf is just cruel."

Hayden laughed. "I'll consider it."

"Well, on second thought, wait a week. I could use a note taker since I'll probably be snoring tomorrow due to tonight's unexpected festivities."

Hayden bit Liv's ear in response, sending goose bumps down her neck as she smiled. She tried to remember her original point.

"You're abusing the system." Hayden joked indifferently, instead focusing more on leaving a trail of kisses from her neck to her chest before climbing on top of her and working his way further down.

"So much for getting a good night sleep like Piper and I had planned." Liv retorted, moaning softly as Hayden started massaging her sex with this tongue.

"Are you requesting I leave?"

"No," Liv breathed. "Not at least until you're finished," she added with a grin.

He flashed her a smile before continuing his devious maneuvers.

Oh, what Liv would give to have nights like this every day. She would sacrifice sleep, food, and her soul in exchange for any minute of this bliss. She started breathing heavily, watching Hayden move up and down, moaning in pleasure as her body naturally responded to his magical tongue and fingers. They moved meticulously, purposefully, hitting every desire she pleaded for.

Soon he was in her, driving his hardness into her growing need, as she cried his name until she climaxed. He followed immediately after her, ending with a final push where she could still feel him throbbing inside.

He finally rolled back to his side of the bed.

"I wasn't expecting a conversation about my classes to take such a sexy turn." Liv murmured, following suit as Hayden welcomed her into his arms. "Not that I'm complaining. I'm just not sure I'll ever be able to think about Meteorology the same way again."

"I promise I had a point to that conversation, but at the moment, I can't remember it, nor do I really care what it was." Hayden smirked, kissing Liv's head in satisfaction before relaxing his eyes. "I love you, Ollie."

"I love you, too. Hayden." Liv replied, smiling as she dozed off into a peaceful slumber.

Liv awoke to sunlight streaming into the room.

She *was* exhausted.

Hayden stirred. Liv instinctively turned in his direction, admiring the specimen she kept in her bed. Even with all of the meetings and royal responsibilities, Hayden was still trim and muscular as ever. A God of the

Gods perfectly described his statuesque body. Liv's toes curled, and she bit her lip, naturally arching her back in desire and ignoring the sore tissue as she stretched her muscles.

How he had this effect on her, even without being cognizant, was a question she did not care to answer, as long as it never stopped.

She leaned over to kiss his lips. Watching his smile grow as he came back to consciousness.

"Good morning." Liv murmured.

"Good morning." Hayden replied, his velvet voice setting off vibrations throughout Liv's entire body. "What time is it?"

Liv looked at the sunlight out the window. "A little after 7:30, er–I mean, 225 degrees."

Groaning, Hayden stretched before he finally stated, "I have to go."

Liv frowned as he promptly climbed to the edge of the bed.

Hayden chuckled, kissing her before fully leaving the cushioned safe haven.

"I do have a request before I leave."

"Stop being so god-damned perfect?" Liv jokingly suggested. "Sorry your royal high-ass, but no can do."

Hayden rolled his eyes, but Liv saw an inconceivable smile surface.

"I want you to start private training sessions with Rei in addition to your Security & Warfare class, but separate from your existing curriculum."

Liv's jaw dropped. She was barely surviving the week, and it was only *Tuesday.*

"Arlo is raising an army; we're most likely heading for war. I can't divulge much more, but it's in your best interest that you learn how to protect yourself as much as you can and as quickly as possible."

"Of course. Promise." Liv gulped, reality setting in. "A war, Hayden?"

To Liv's knowledge, the Pure Gods only had allies with the Government Pillar, Candor Pillar and Security Pillar. Arlo and the Dark Gods had support from the Elements Pillar, most likely the Arts Pillar-especially if Cleo was any representation–and suspected The Agriculture Pillar and Commerce Pillar were in alliance with the Dark Gods cause, as well. Both sides were aggressively pursuing The Humanities Pillar by playing their stupid riddle game–Hayden was right, if The Humanities Pillar served as any example of how the Elites liked to entertain politics–it would be a pain in the ass to maneuver through.

Three pillars against four, possibly *five* if they weren't able to even out the playing ground with the Humanities Pillar. Not even counting the mythological beasts: Cyclops had been reported Dark, Centaurs remained Pure. Sirens and Minotaurs were neutral.

With his visit approaching to the Arts Pillar, how could Hayden act so calm when he was venturing straight into the Lion's den as an un-coronated king amidst of so much uncertainty?

"What about allies? Demetrius… or…" Liv paused, absorbing the crazy idea that entered her mind. "What if all legends have some sort of truth to an extent?"

Hayden sighed, "I've told you that the mythology you've read is not a good example for our history."

"No, no, not that." Liv waved him off. "What about other the world's beliefs? Deities from China, Egypt, the Aztecs… there are thousands of stories and even more who believe in them. What if they exist in our world?"

Hayden contemplated the idea. "It's possible. Rei spent time with Norse Gods some time ago, but we haven't heard any whispers of them in a very long time; however, aside from that, there has been no records of other deity communities. So, either they don't exist anymore or the other Gods have separated their world from us very cleverly and purposefully, but I doubt that's a possibility. Any way, it would be a mad chase to try to find an alliance with those who may not even exist anymore. So, if we haven't encountered them in over a millennium, how would we be able to find them now?"

Liv admittedly agreed with his reasoning, although it disappointed her.

"Piper and I will continue working on the Humanities Pillar clue." Liv added, confirming aloud the actuality of what she could achieve within her internal wave of thinking. Any way she could help. She would do it.

As she got up to get ready for the day, Liv couldn't help flicker to the idea of her rightful claim to the Elements Pillar. If she could defeat Kai, it would change the circumstances greatly.

"Ollie, there will be a time and place to combat Kai. Now is not that time." Hayden grabbed a pair of navy slacks hanging from his closet with a crisp white button-down shirt, quickly getting dressed for his next task. "You've only had your powers for a month, I won't risk it."

"I'll talk to Rei about scheduling private combat classes." Liv promised, sneaking a kiss from Hayden as he walked past buttoning his shirt, carefully avoiding any agreement regarding Kai.

When the time came, she wanted to be ready and able to do to Kai as she pleased without betraying her word to Hayden. She wanted the opportunity to destroy him if the option presented itself.

"Already did. You start training tomorrow morning before classes." Hayden walked past Liv again, stealing another kiss from her this time, before going to the closet and grabbing the matching suit jacket.

"So, I'll have private combat and training, before my warfare and defense class?" Liv clarified, crossing her arms in the doorway. "Are you *trying* to send me to the Underworld?"

"No, just solely trying to torture my two favorite people by pinning them against each other before the coffee kicks in." Hayden flashed a grin.

Liv smirked, until she realized he was fully dressed and preparing to leave. Panic swept in at the sudden realization of goodbye.

"Hayden, how else can I help?"

Hayden held out his hand, pulling her into an embrace as she grabbed it. "Take security lessons with Rei. Continuing working with Piper on the Humanities puzzle for their support." He stepped back, his hands on her shoulders as he looked into her eyes. "Learn, as much as you can while you can. And, as soon as I know more, I'll let you know and we can figure out a game plan, together." He brought her in close; breathing in her scent, noticing Liv had switched her shampoo from coconut vanilla to a new pomegranate and citrus smell since he had last seen her.

"You have to go now, don't you," Liv mumbled in his arms.

She only felt the small vibration of a chuckle in the silence before he responded.

"How did you know?"

"I can just tell. Your tone changes and you start giving a lot of advice. Usually ends with a not-so-subtle inhalation of my fragrance before departure."

"Not-so-subtle?"

"It's flattering. And helps with the blow."

"Should I be concerned my girlfriend has started identifying patterns with my departure routine?"

"Possibly in that it's acknowledged when you're leaving her for long periods of time." Liv mumbled, half-heartedly joking, but not willing to look up at Hayden.

Hayden sighed, pulling her back into an embrace. "I know, I'm sorry. I'll figure out a way to fix this. I don't like being away from you, either."

Now she felt guilty again.

"No, Hayden… you already have so much to deal with, it would be selfish to ask you to be in two places at once. You have to be with your court in order to lead them, it's your responsibility. And I have to be at Puerdios to study. It's temporary. Please don't worry about me."

"I always worry about you." Hayden whispered back, kissing Liv's temple and getting one last whiff of her intoxicating scent.